THE HAVEN

Book 4
The first installment of
The Guard Trilogy Extended Series
The Guards of Haven

N. L. Westaway

Original Cover Photo by Nicholas Bartos
Cover designed by Beach House Press

This book is a work of fiction. Names, characters, places, and incidents either are products of the author's imagination or are used fictitiously. Any resemblance to actual persons, living or dead, events, or locales is entirely coincidental.

N. L. Westaway
Visit my website at www.NLWestaway.com
ISBN: 979-8-9850495-7-2
Printed in the United States of America

First Publication: December 2021 Beach House Press

The Haven

To the reader,

This novel, like the other books in succession, is not a standalone story. Book 4, *The Haven,* is the next in series and carries the reader forward from the original story in The Guard Trilogy, into The Guard Trilogy Extended Series, *The Guards of Haven.*

There are 2 more books in the series, with the expectation of at least 7 books total, although there is potential for more.

The Guard Trilogy
The Guard – Book 1
The Unseen – Book 2
The Believer – Book 3

The Guard Trilogy Extended Series/The Guards of Haven
The Haven – Book 4
Haven Lost – Book 5
Haven Found – Book 6
More to come...

This book is dedicated to all the fans who after reading the first three books of The Guard Trilogy, graciously yet fervently asked for *MORE*. This extended series was created for all of you because of your affection for the characters and for your devotion to Lynn's story.

"I've come to believe that in everyone's life, there's one undeniable moment of change, a set of circumstances that suddenly alters everything."
~ Nicholas Sparks, Safe Haven

Acknowledgements
This book would not have been possible without the constant encouragement, understanding, and support of my amazing husband.
Love you, Babe!
Thank you, Denise, for your steadfast friendship, enthusiasm, and reassurance, and for continually reminding me *not to give up*.
To Cathy and my wonderful Advanced Team of Beta Readers, I am grateful for all of you who have taken the time to read and push through the first drafts of my novels, and for continually providing helpful and valuable feedback. Special thanks to *Eagle-Eye* Jenna, who always manages to find those sneaky errors missed by the rest of us. And to my niece, Victoria, thank you for your assistance with the vital research needed for this story.

HAVEN - A place of refuge or rest; a sanctuary. A place where people or animals feel safe, secure, and happy. www.collinsdictionary.com

The following is a list of the main characters and their roles from the original trilogy, as a refresher should you need it.

Lynn Westlake – *MC, The Seer/Oracle, Halfling Daughter of Gabriel*
Redmond Credente – *Lynn's husband, The Believer, descendant of Azazel*

Vicki Quinn — *The Linguist, descendant of Michael*
Olivia White — *The Healer, descendent of Raphael*
Mackenzie (Mac) Miller – *The Sorceress, descendent of Uriel*
Alison Kiely – *The Scribe, descendent of Vretil*
Luc Marin — *The Theologian, descendent of Baraqel*
Derek (Shortcut) Jones — *The Cipher, descendent of Kokabiel*
Darius Stori — *The Guardian, descendent of Shamsiel*

The Archangels
Gabriel — *Lynn's birthfather*
Michael — *Celestial Warden of Vicki*
Raphael — *Celestial Warden of Olivia*
Uriel — *Celestial Warden of Mac*
Vretil — *Celestial Warden of Alison*

The Leaders of the 200 Fallen (There are 20 Leaders in total.)
Shamsiel – *the Celestial Warden of Mitra, Dunya, and Darius*
Zaqiel – *The Horseman Death, the Celestial Warden of Lynn's Birthmother, Mother, Aunt, and friend Louise*
Azazel — *The Horseman War, the Celestial Warden of Redmond*
Kokabiel–*The Horseman Conquest, the Celestial Warden of Derek*
Baraqel — *The Horseman Famine, and the Celestial Warden of Luc*

Prolog

From the *Epilog in The Believer, Book 3* of *The Guard Trilogy*

"I believe in love. I believe in hard times and love winning. I believe marriage is hard. I believe people make mistakes. I believe people can want two things at once. I believe people are selfish and generous at the same time. I believe very few people want to hurt others.
I believe that you can be surprised by life.
I believe in happy endings."
~ Isabel Gillies, Happens Every Day: An All-Too-True Story

I believe in love, family, and friendship….

Luc and Dunya moved in together. Who didn't see that one coming from a mile away?

Darius, along with Luc, were hired by Derek to do IT support for his company. Both work from home now, just like Derek.

Derek, as we all know, had the answers to the anagrams. He'd figured the rest of them out on the plane ride to Miami, figured out the whole thing, actually. *This gathering will keep the balance, and all shall know the…* bar the fifth = *Birthfather*. Faiths Fever = *Five fathers*, Heart News = *The answer*, and Guard the Glean = *Angel daughter*.

Vicki, she's now travelling the world for work. She'd met a nice guy on one of her trips who owns a private jet company, and I'm sure there will be a lot more travel in her future.

Mac stopped doing her jewelry business to focus on a new business with Olivia. They've opened a doula/holistic health business, where both can spend more time doing what they love, and while having more time with their families.

Alison and Ken had their bouncing baby boy, Kevin, on April 1st. He was originally due to arrive on the 7th, but Alison had had to go in early for an emergency C-section. *"Best April fool's joke ever,"* she'd told me. It was the *denouement,* as Alison had put it. That's French, it means they'd all reached *The End*... and they had happily survived.

And Me? Well, I moved on.... but, I still believe in coming together at Christmas.

Miami, December 20th, 2012

"What, Gabriel? I know you're here," I said, shaking my head.

Redmond was in the yard fetching more wood to place beside the hearth, but I knew I wasn't alone. I snuggled in deeper with my two best buds on the couch, Summer and Snow, the all-white Lab-Shepherd mixes, who each outweighed me now by at least 20 pounds. We'd rescued them from a local shelter last year as pups.

"Do you really think you can sneak in a visit without me knowing?" I laughed out, continuing to warm myself in front of the fireplace. I'd missed cozy nights like these—been forever since it'd been cold enough to use the fireplace and rare to have times like this in Miami.

"Lynn, you can't blame me for trying?" came Gabriel's voice just as he appeared before me. "Aren't you going to tell them what happened to you?"

"Tell who?" I said, moving my hands out towards the fire's warmth. There was something about warming yourself by the fire and sipping hot chocolate that made for a peaceful evening. "I'm excited the others would be here in time for Christmas day," I said. I knew the others were thrilled about what they'd referred to as *'warmer weather'*. But tonight, was just for Redmond and me… and Gabriel, apparently.

"Your believers—the ones who know the story now," Gabriel said.

I smirked and sipped my cocoa.

"This *is* nice," he said, settling into the big, oversized armchair next to the fireplace. He extended his hands like I had, as if warming them. *Then* he had those blue-grey eyes of his fixed on *my* big mug of cocoa.

"Get yer own." I grinned. "I like you and all, but I'm not sharing my hot chocolate—there's more in the kitchen."

He was gone and back, leaving only the sound of rattling cups in the kitchen upon his return. Comfortably back in the big chair, he happily coveted his own mug of goodness. He grinned back at me and took a sip.

"What would you have me tell them?" I asked, tucking my feet under a Christmas themed blanket, one that had once belonged to my mother.

Taking another loving sip of the hot brew, Gabriel eyeballed the small mound at my stomach, then grinned again. "Due in the spring I'm told," he said, proud as a peacock—a *grandfather* peacock.

"Yup," was all I gave him. He'd known before I had that I was pregnant. I'd had a *feeling*—but he knew. He hadn't said he'd known, only told me, "*You know, Babies smile in their sleep because they are listening to the whispering of angels.*" I was sure I'd read that quote somewhere before, but I'd gotten the gist of *his* meaning.

"Twins," he said, his grin widening still. He'd obviously learned more about the birth from the Amulet Angels—checking in with all 70 of them, I was sure. He could have simply asked me—his daughter.

"Uhmm yup," was my response. Redmond and I had found out about the duo ourselves only a few days ago.

"Twin girls," Gabriel added. He followed up with a big sip of cocoa and a wink.

I winked back and grinned.

And this is where I last left you all… so how about I fill you all in on what's happened to everyone since then.

Chapter 1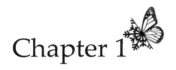

The South Island, December 16th, 2021, South Florida

"Someone better start explaining why I found—what I found in the garbage down here," I interrogated, staring each of them down, watching as the two glanced innocently back and forth from each other and then back to me. I shook the scrunched-up bag at them, then bent to look them in their faces one at a time, pausing to see if I could tell who had done it.

The larger of the two suspects shifted from gaping in shock at me to then scowling accusingly at who I assumed was her co-conspirator. "It wasn't me," she said, placing her hands on her hips as she glared at the other.

"It wasn't me either," the smaller of the two accomplices said, crossing her arms over her chest in further defense. She cut a glance at her accuser, then looked back at me. "Besides, I wouldn't have left the evidence around for you to find." She gave me a sarcastic grin, then turned her head and stuck out her tongue at her partner in crime, who was still scowling critically back at her.

"Both of you—back upstairs!" I demanded, pointing the way with the empty Oreo cookie bag.

"Mum," Ryley started, dropping her hands from her hips, a wayward, sun-kissed russet tendril coming loose from her braid. She tucked it behind her ear. She had red hair similar to but lighter than her father's.

"Don't mum me, young lady. I want both of you in your rooms — now." I pointed up the stairs again.

"But Mum," Hayley said, shoring up her crossed arms. The older of the twins by 9 minutes, yet the smaller of the two, frowned at me. Her pale blonde poker-straight hair was pulled back in a ponytail, and the accompanying bangs in need of a trim fell over one eye. With a swift uncross of her arms, she pushed her bangs to one side. Then she returned to crossing her arms, pushing her bottom lip out in defiance.

"I said both of you — now get, before I blow a fuse."

Hayley dropped her crossed arms and turned to head up the stairs to the main part of the house. Ryley followed her, but then paused to look back at me.

"Keep going," I said, pointing the way again with the empty cookie bag, the crumbs rattling as I shook it.

Neither said another word, but the sound of stomping feet tracked all the way up the stairway and further still overhead as they went off down the hall to their rooms, which was quickly followed up by the dual sound of slamming bedroom doors.

If I hadn't been doing my rounds in all the bathrooms and replacing the towels in the one on the lower level, I wouldn't have stumbled across the contraband in the garbage bin. It was Redmond's job to tidy the downstairs, that for the most part only he used, it being half music room, half workshop space, while I took care of the main part of the house. I wouldn't have even seen the evidence had I not been emptying bins for trash day. That too was normally on Redmond's chore list, but today he had been running late from work.

Glancing around the room, my gaze went from the line of guitars hanging on the far wall to the electronic drum kit in the far corner. Next to it was the vintage leather and teak chair that met up with a side table and then the matching teak leather sofa. Along the opposite wall were different size amps and other music gear that Redmond used for jamming. This was a *friend* jam space, not a work one. The space had two huge storage closets, one containing the guitar cases for all the guitars, the other had our seasonal stuff in it, like Christmas decorations along with emergency gear for hurricanes, etc. On the side of the room nearest to the exit was a large workbench flanked by two tall black metal cabinets full of tools and other handyman paraphernalia that had previously been held in the garages under Redmond's old apartment. And next to the door was a second fridge, that during the start of the pandemic had come in handy for storing and freezing extra food supplies. It also held the bags of freshly prepared food we fed the dogs. Other than that, right now, it mainly held the extra cases of flavored canned seltzer waters and beers. The space felt more like the basements we had up north, but unlike most basements, this space had a walkout to the outdoor space at the ground level of the house.

I took a deep breath to settle my nerves, then I opened the cookie bag and took a long inhale of the remaining cookie scent. That was about as close as I got to eating cookies these days, but those two little devils upstairs could almost push me to devouring a full bag myself some days.

This past May the twins turned 8 years old, and they are amazing—well, for the most part, twins can be a challenge. Every so often—like today, they pushed the boundaries and my buttons. And sending them to their rooms wasn't always a punishment for them. They had separate rooms now, we had set them up that way on purpose when we'd moved here, but on a previous room banishment, I'd caught them doing a puzzle together on the floor of the Jack & Jill bathroom that joined their two rooms. They were clever. But luckily for us, they are still at that age where they respect, fear—a little bit, and still think their parents are cool.

Redmond was amazing when the twins arrived—not to say we both didn't have our meltdowns, but we have a true partnership in our marriage, a trust and comfort I hadn't had before. He had this special dad awareness too when the girls were babies. A consciousness, like his ears would perk to noises in the night, tuned into the babies, sometimes even awake to their cries before me.

A lady from one of the *parents of twins* groups I had belonged to, suggested back when the twins were babies, that if we changed one diaper/feed/nap/whatever, that we should do both, treat it as one activity whenever possible. By doing this, it ended up you took less time, and it often created a sense of comfort for them in this routine. She had also recommended that we allow the girls to be individuals — not to focus on them being a pair.

An unusual thing we had learned about twins is that they sometimes have their own language, one that only they understand, and that was true with our girls. They had started a kind of gibberish speech early on when they had been learning to talk, that later transformed into an actual language that only they knew. I sourced a few of the words, only because I had heard a few repeated and had put two and two together to figure out what the topic of their conversation was at least. Redmond and I were envious of their secret conversations. They use a few of the words they had created when speaking to us or other people, like calling their father *Da*, that had stuck despite Redmond trying to get them to say Dad or Daddy. I had started with Mom or Mommy, but they had chosen to use *Mum*, and we were both good with the names. They had also created names for Redmond's parents as well, using Nana and Poppy in place of Grandma and Grandpa. Nana was their variation of her given name, Nainseadh, the Gaelic spelling of the more common use and pronunciation of *Nancy*. But Poppy, we figured resulted from hearing Redmond calling his father Enzo, *Pop*. And for everyone, the adopted names all felt so natural now.

They are fraternal twins and though they look similar, they are vastly different little people. Though each would die for the other, they would just as likely smack the other into tomorrow over a disagreement or the last piece of their father's homemade chocolate cake. Hayley, who was born first, but was — and still is, the smaller of the two, was born with light blond peach fuzz hair akin to what I'd had as a baby. Ryley, on the other hand — whose name I'd stolen from my first charges at the hospital, the twins Rylie and Finn, I had changed the spelling slightly to make the name unique to her, and I picked it not just because I loved the name, but because she too had red hair. It was like her father's though lighter. Redmond's hair, the dark russet colour, was a combination of his mother's true russet red hair and his father's deep brown. The twins both had the same eyes, the same shape as mine with a slight tilt up at the outer lashes, but the colour was neither like mine nor their father's, they were hazel, the outcome of my grey eyes mixed with Redmond's dark brown, though they had flecks of both grey and coffee brown throughout.

From watching our friends raise their now mostly grown kids, we'd become well aware that this *cool factor* we had as their parents right now would begin to fade over the next few years and as they headed into their teens. *Yeesh.* And with girls and their hormones, it would be a challenge, to say the least. But after the past year and a half of home-schooling due to the pandemic, we figured we might be able to manage just about anything going forward.

I pushed up the sleeves of my long-sleeved t-shirt, and grabbed up the garbage bag, then paused to listen for... well, *silence.* When I didn't hear any noise, I went on with the task of putting the garbage out.

Exiting the door on the lower level, I was struck by the fresh scent of the ocean air on a cool, seasonal breeze. Breathing in the clean air, I proceeded to the large rolling bins.

After tossing the bag in the green bin, I brushed my hands off on my jeans and did a slow spin, checking to see if there was any additional garbage in the carport space that needed to be thrown out.

It isn't exactly a carport; it's the under space of three-quarters of the upper level that is the main part of the beach house we now live in. The lower level of the house is under the other quarter of the house. Redmond's dream is to convert the lower outside part into an actual garage, but I like the openness and ocean breezes that waft through. I understood it would be safer and protect the cars from the salt spray. Plus, he could move all his workshop/garage stuff into a more usable space. It would be an enormous garage, as the area under the house currently contains Redmond's lifted 4-door white Ford Raptor pickup, his covered classic fully restored 1968 Mustang GT, and my new Fiat 500X crossover SUV. And that's just the vehicles. Around the back to the right, past the cars, is another open space under the house that has an outdoor shower that comes in handy after time at the beach. There is also access to another storage space that houses all the implements related to lawn maintenance, *and* all Redmond's beach toys.

Currently, he has one of those preformed kayaks, a paddle board that doubles as a windsurfer, and two surfboards, one is a longboard and the other is the freestyle kind, whatever that means. All I know is one is bigger than the other and with him being 6 foot 5, they are both way too long for me. Apparently, my New York City born music man husband has now become a beach bum.

A year after the gathering, Redmond and I moved in together, and then in the following year, 2011, a few days after Christmas, we were married. The August after that, I'd found out I was pregnant. I had been to see the doctor already, but it had been just before our 1st wedding anniversary that December, when Gabriel had felt the need to share that he knew all about the twins arriving in the spring. And as predicted and right on schedule, they were born that May, a week after my birthday.

It will be 10 years on the 27th of this month that we've been married, and lots of other changes have taken place over this period of time.

We had begun entertaining the idea of moving soon after the twins turned 3, realizing that despite how much fun Miami was, neither of us loved the idea of raising our daughters there. After both Darius and Luc had gone to work for Derek, Redmond, being the savvy businessman that he was, had offered to invest some of his money into Derek's growing high tech company. In fact, we had all put some money into it. And as fate would have it, that same year, Derek's company was bought by a giant of a company whose name rhymes with *frugal*. All of us who invested had made out like bandits after the sale.

Lily Shade, Redmond's assistant, had temporarily taken over his old apartment at that time, allowing her to be closer to the studio now that she was doing more and more of running the place. It had been she who had indirectly discovered the city we currently live in. She had been scouting out some of the local musical artists in the area when, on a whim, she'd turned down one of the streets in the newly revitalized downtown area and saw a building/property for purchase.

She had been on point with the find, as it turned out to be the perfect place for an expansion studio for the business. The place had a cool eclectic look and vibe, and the space was three times the size of the original studio. The cost to expand anywhere in the Grove in Miami, being what it was, the option to buy this building was far cheaper than it would ever be to expand and pay Miami taxes year after year. Plus, with the demand now for both Redmond and Lily's services, artists were willing to go anywhere to have them work on their music and marketing. The decision had been easy. Besides, who could turn down the opportunity for more space, less overhead, and a cool beach town community to be a part of?

So, I sold my home in Palmetto Bay. Redmond sold the building that housed his old studio to Nate, the friend of ours who owned the yoga place up the way. Nate had loved the idea of expanding his space—knowing that in order to get a bigger property along that same road in the Grove, he'd either have to pay through the nose or have to wait for someone to gift it to you through their last will and testament.

It's been 5 years this past September since we'd moved north. We'd sparked at the idea of a small town, a beach town for that matter, and it hadn't been long before we'd taken our own investment money from Derek's deal and purchased a house on the South Island situated between Jensen and Vero Beach. The island is connected to the city by beautiful four-lane bridges at the North and South ends. We had found the perfect stilted beach house literally right on the beach and set back away from the main road that ran the length of the island. And it was only a 10-minute drive to the new studio.

Done with my garbage collection chore, I strolled through the carport to the backyard. On the opposite side of the lawn is a line of fan palm trees that run the width of the yard. Behind them is a stretch of sea grape trees, and beyond that is the protective sea grass and small dunes that lead along a path to the private section of the beach we are on. Like most days, there were palm-size white butterflies that I had learned were called *Florida Whites*, flittering around the palm trees and through the leaves of the sea grape.

"Hi Mom," I said as one flew by my head.

It had been right around Mother's Day, at the old house, when just before the twins had turned 2 years of age, that they had both waved their tiny hands at a passing butterfly and had said, *"Hi Gamma."* I had shown the twins photos of my mother, and there were several of her on the shelves in the living room, so they knew who she was, but never had I told them about my saying *hi* to Mom. When I'd shot a look at Redmond, he'd said he had not prompted them to do it. Then when I had asked, *"Are you saying hi to Grandma?"* they had both nodded and waved again at the passing butterfly. We figured they must have overheard me saying *hi*, but they had taken it upon themselves to do the same with the greeting of *Gamma*, which later changed to *Gramma Sal* as they had gotten older. Then, when the twins were about 4 years old, I had told them about how their Grandma Sal had loved butterflies, to which they had responded with, *"We know"*, and again, Redmond had said he had never told them such either. I had let the mystery go, and in fact I liked it, frankly. It gave me the sense that Mom was truly around, watching the twins, watching them grow up, watching me as a mother, and watching Redmond and me parenting together. It was comforting.

I closed my eyes, letting the cool breeze caress my face as I manifested the memory of my mother's voice in my head. Just then the deep rumble of a motorcycle came into earshot, shifting the serene surroundings. As the roar got closer, I saw a large man riding a Harley Davidson pull on to our street. As he approached our house, I smiled, admiring how incredibly sexy he looked on that badass motorbike. He grinned back at me as he pulled into the driveway.

Redmond, my super sexy husband, had purchased the 2016 Harley Davidson Softail Deluxe shortly after we had moved here. The ad for the bike had described it as having a 'Vivid Black and chrome frame'. And since buying it, he has added removable Harley hard bags, low profile 'beach bar' handlebars and a custom 4 speaker stereo system. He had lowered the bike 2 inches with the adjustable suspension and had moved the foot controls 2 inches forward to accommodate his long legs. He had also swapped out the wheels for an 80 spoke 21-inch front wheel and matching 18 inch in the rear, with Avon white wall tires, along with a swap out of the standard seat to a custom La Pera Bare Bones solo seat that came with a removable passenger Pillion and backrest, and he'd added matching Harley Davidson passenger foot boards for me as well. *"No point in taking the truck the short drive off the island into the town square area to the studio,"* he had told me. And I had to agree with him. Unless it rained, he could use the bike most days. Plus, I loved being on the back of it for rides on and off the island. I often said—joked mostly, that I was going to get my own someday. Redmond loved the idea, but the girls normally just rolled their eyes at me and said, *"Sure, Mum."*

"Your daughters got into and finished off an entire bag of Oreo cookies," I said to him, when he pulled into the carport and shut off the engine. He was wearing dark blue jeans and a grey t-shirt that had a vintage motorbike on it with the words 'Treasure Coast Harley Davidson' below it.

"My daughters?" he questioned with a frown as he removed his bucket helmet. "Why are they always *my* daughters when they do something bad?" He pushed his sunglasses up to rest on the top of his head.

I hugged him then and went up on my toes to give him a big kiss. "Sawwy," I said, hugging him again, leading him into the house with an arm around his waist.

"I feel guilty now," he said, giving me a little squeeze before shutting the door behind us.

"Why?" I asked, looking up at his face and dropping my arm from around him.

"Well... the cookies. That was me," Redmond confessed, resting his helmet on one of the hooks near the door.

I shook my head, feeling guilty myself now for accusing the girls of the crime. Then with a sarcastic grin, I said, "What was that question again you asked me about *your* daughters?"

Chapter 2

Last night, over a delicious dinner of homemade pizza and Caesar salad that of course, Redmond had made, I had graciously apologized to the girls. Then I'd swiftly thrown their father under the bus when I had explained that it had been he who had eaten all the cookies. The girls had giggled when Redmond had shown no sign of remorse and then had proceeded to push out and rub his stomach at the boastful enjoyment of eating the cookies. When dinner was over, the twins had hugged and kissed us both before heading off to their rooms to pick out their school clothes for tomorrow.

Today is the last day of classes for the twins before the Christmas break, and they were both bouncing off the walls. They, along with their classmates, had started back to in-person school this past September, and they had gotten a new teacher which they adored. And right now, all they really needed to do in preparation for heading to school was pack their writing projects to turn in and wrap the Christmas gift I had graciously picked up for them a month ago, for their teacher Mr. McCray.

"Mum, I want to carry the gift to school," Ryley said as she approached me at the front door. She wore faded jeans and a navy-blue long-sleeved t-shirt with the arms pushed up to her elbows because it was a tad too small now, and her usual slip-on sneakers. She had her hair pulled back in a loose braid, that I'm assuming she had done herself based on the wavy strands that were already coming loose. And she was holding the wrapped Christmas present up over her head and evidently out of reach of her sister.

Hayley trailed behind her, wearing the same faded jeans, but her long-sleeved t-shirt was white and had a dancing unicorn with a rainbow mane on it, with the words 'Dance like no one is watching'. She had picked it out herself when we'd gone shopping for school clothes at the beginning of the semester. It was now only starting to fit her properly since she insisted on getting the same size as her sister. On her feet she wore matching rainbow flip-flops. Her hair was still damp, and she smelled like strawberry scented shampoo. She pushed at her sister's arm and jumped in an attempt to get the gift for herself. "Muuuum," she said, pleading for assistance.

I seized the Christmas gift from Ryley's outstretched hand. "Enough," I said. They both tried jumping up to get the gift from my hand, but I held it out of reach. It was nice to be taller than someone in this house. "If you break this—you won't have anything to give Mr. McCray. I had gotten the gift from one of my favorite local shops, the one the girls loved equally as much because of the seaside decor and knickknacks that were displayed there. Each year at Christmas, the owner does a special seasonal display throughout the shop of all things beachy-Christmas, and the twins had admired the beautiful hand-blown glass ornament. They had commented that their teacher would *love it*, mainly because it had a Santa riding a surfboard painted on it, and the words 'Life's a beach, find your wave' written just below the surfing Santa.

We had discovered through a parent-teacher meet and greet that Mr. McCray was not only an excellent teacher, but that he also wore Hawaiian shirts and flip-flops to class. He's got shoulder-length brown hair—normally pulled back in a ponytail, which gave him a bit of a beach bum vibe. Redmond had talked about surfing with him, and Gavin—Mr. McCray, had been the one who had shown my husband the surfing basics and further recommended the boards we currently owned. He had told us he travels to different surfing locations at least once a year, but unfortunately, there had been no travel for any of us for some time. The only surfing either of them had gotten to do of late had been minimal at best and had only been while the beaches were *not* part of the county lockdown. You wouldn't catch *me* in the water in December—too cold, but apparently it was the best time to catch some waves here.

"Do you have your writing projects?" I asked, handing each of them their lunch bags to put in their backpacks.

Hayley donned her backpack, then said, "Done." Then she adjusted the straps. The bag was a bit big for her, but we always got them the same size bookbags. It helped take the focus off the sometimes-sensitive topic of their difference in height. I often wondered if Hayley would eventually catch up in height. Redmond's parents were both tall, so her shorter stature was another thing she had unfortunately gotten from me. I believed she liked being the small one, but you would never get her to admit it.

"What about you, young lady?" I directed at her sister.

"Yup," Ryley said, zipping up her backpack, grabbing it up by the top handle. She didn't like wearing the thing on her back, and it was usually only over one shoulder. She had seen her dad do the same with his bag for his beach gear, and she had mimicked it ever since. She went ahead of me then, unlocking and opening the front door.

I wasn't a fan of knapsacks either, or purses, for that matter. I had readily used a tote bag instead in the past, since I could carry what I needed, including my laptop when traveling. When the twins had been born, I had moved to a much bigger carryall bag, for all that I needed when out and about with them. Once they were older, and now that they could carry their own stuff, I'd happily switched to a smaller cross-body bag style purse that allowed me to be hands free. And with twins, you needed to have two hands, so it was key to everyone's survival, not just mine.

Summer and Snow sat in their usual spots at the front door, waiting for their goodbye hugs from the girls. "I'll be back in a few," I said to my fur-babies, leaning down to kiss each of their heads. "Okay—let's go!" I snatched up my car keys from off the front side table. With the gift in my other hand, Hayley kindly offered to shut and lock the door behind us, and then we were on our way down the front steps.

When we got to my SUV, we found Gabriel already sitting buckled up in the front passenger side seat with a joyful grin on his face.

"Guuuup," the girls squealed in unison when I opened the back door for them. When my *birthfather* had begun calling himself Grandpa Gabriel, the name had morphed into *Gup*, the name created early on by the twins as a simplified version for them to us, and fortunately for us, it was easier to explain if it was ever overheard. The twins scooted into the back seat and quickly buckled themselves into their booster chairs for the ride. Until they hit a certain weight or height, they were required to use the safety seats. Ryley was almost there, but she would keep using hers until her sister was big enough for the regular seat too. She was sensitive to her sister's size difference, even if it was only a few inches.

"It's always nice to see you, but what are you doing here?" I asked, sliding into the driver's seat. I handed him my bag, and the wrapped gift, since he was sitting in the usual spot where I normally put stuff. Then I buckled myself in and started the car.

"I couldn't miss the last ride to school before Christmas break now, could I?" he said, clutching the items, shifting in his seat to turn back and smile at the girls.

"Noooo waaaaaay," the girls gave him in response.

"I like your outfit," I said as I backed out of the driveway.

"Thanks," he said with a grin, brushing a palm down the front of his shirt. He was wearing black jeans with dark loafers and a white button-down shirt with the top button open. After watching a ton of movies with the girls, he had decided to cut off his long hair, and went from looking like an older version of Brad Pitt's Tristan from Legends of the Fall, to that of Kevin from the more recent Ghostbusters movie with Chris Hemsworth. I guess you could say he went from Thor to Kevin with one haircut. He had begun wearing a more casual attire ever since the girls started to attend school, because he often rode along for the drop-offs *and* his typical white suit had attracted too much attention for my liking.

At the school, we moved along with the snail-paced procession of the parents in cars that led to the drop-off area just past the main front doors. When we came to a halt for our turn, Hayley pointed out the window and said, "There's the little boy that's like Mum."

"Like me?" I questioned, rolling down the passenger side window before Gabriel got out to help the girls. I caught a glimpse of the boy she had just pointed out, heading through the front entrance.

"Ya, but not like Da, or you, Gup," Hayley said, sliding down off her safety chair to the curb.

"What do you mean, *funny* like your mum?" Gabriel asked then. "I'm pretty funny too, you know," he added, giving his shoulders a quick shrug as he glanced my way.

"Nooo," Ryley laughed out. "Like Mum's vibration—not exactly, but sorta." She made a face like she was trying to think of a better word to use, then hefted her knapsack over her left shoulder.

"Like Da's guitars—the electric one is like Mum, the acoustic is like the little boy," Hayley cut in, before her sister could come up with a different word. She let Gabriel help her on with her backpack.

Gabriel and I exchanged looks through the open back door, glances that were full of questions and expletives. Then Gabriel bent down to give his little grand-cherubs each a big hug and then kisses on their cheeks. "Have a fantastic day," he said, straightening and shutting the back door.

"Bye, Mum," Hayley called through the open front window before turning to head for the entrance.

Ryley waved and blew me a kiss. Then she took up her sister's hand to walk with her over to the main doors. It made my heart glow to see her do that, care for her sister so, but that glow was short lived when I saw Ryley pull her then into a run that had Hayley struggling to keep up. I closed my eyes and gave my head a little shake.

Gabriel opened the passenger side door and got back in the car. Then he shut the door and glanced around as if checking to see if anyone was watching. He said nothing, only nodded, and then he disappeared.

I shook my head again, then put the car in drive and pulled away.

Gabriel had told me I was the only one who could sense all other celestials, well—other than the twins. The fact that the girls could sense them we had figured, was because of their unique genetic makeup.

They were hybrids of a sort, considering that my DNA and abilities comprised that of their seer grandmother—my birthmother, who was a descendant of one of The Fallen, a Leader and a Horseman, and their grandfather, who was an Archangel. Not to mention their father, who was also a descendant of a Fallen Leader—and Horseman, as well. Not what you would call a typical angel-human pairing—if you could even call something like that *typical*. With genetics as they were, who knew what traits/genes the twins had inherited. Chances are, with the fact that they weren't identical, the possibilities, the strength in their inherited genetics and abilities, were still yet to be determined.

In the first year after I had found out Gabriel was my birthfather, word had spread among the celestials, and since then I'd had more than a hundred face-to-face visits or visitations more accurately, to examine one such as I. I'd lost count of how many I had sensed in the vicinity, though only a minor few knew about the twins and what they could do, and we prefer to keep it that way. Life for them was weird enough without random angels popping in to see them. There had been a few visits in the first months after their birth, mainly the Amulet Angels, and that soon died off as our lives appeared to be that of typical humans. All the Archangels knew what they could do, the Leaders of the Fallen knew, and of course our friends knew, those who had been a part of this quest, the gathering, and its big reveal. But we'd had no idea the twins had been picking up on other angel castes as they came and went from the area, not until they had actually come out and mentioned it to their father and me.

When the twins were just babies, I had thought their sensing other celestials were like the babies in the hospital's nursery and how they calmed and quieted when an angel was present. But it wasn't. As babies and then as toddlers, they had reacted as though they could see them, not just sense the peace they brought. When the girls were older and could verbalize better, they had told us the sensing was like a soft sound or vibration they heard in their heads when celestials were near, and they could see them too when they were veiled. Each sound or vibration was different for each category of celestial. Like with Gabriel, his vibration differed from Shamsiel's, but was the same as the other Archangels. Shamsiel's, in turn, differed slightly from the Horsemen, but was the same as the other Fallen Leaders, and so on. There was even a difference between my girlfriends who were descendants of the Archangels to that of the guys and Redmond, who were descendants of the Leaders and Horsemen. And apparently, I had quite the unique signature vibration, something very distinct from the rest they had told us. But this little boy was *"like Mum,"* they had said, not quite the same but similar. I didn't know what that meant.

We had addressed the various types of angels they were sensing at different times. We had found ways of integrating the twins into the *knowing* as we had begun calling it, adding more and more details about angels as they had gotten older, but also making it very clear that if they told anyone, the first thing people outside the knowing would think, was that we were all crazy. Redmond and I, along with Gabriel, had gone as far as stating that there could be a threat of them being taken away from us—it was harsh we knew it, but it was what we had to do to keep them and the secret safe. None of us had wanted to scare them, but it was a possibility that if the human authorities got wind of—the level of detail, of what we told our children about angels, we feared they could potentially deem us unfit parents or worse. The twins had needed to understand the consequences of sharing this kind of information with those outside the knowing. The older they got, the better they understood the risks, and the less we had to push those realities home. In fact, they loved knowing they were different from the other children and it being our *special secret*.

I could sense other celestials if they were in a certain vicinity to my location, but my sensing differed from the twins. Plus, the girls could track each other, knew where the other was. Not *exactly* where the other was, but they could tell you if they were nearby to each other or not, and that radius had grown larger as they had gotten older. I couldn't do that with them. I could only tell if they were in the same vicinity as me, like with the other celestials, and consequently neither could Gabriel nor any of the other angels do it.

Our guess was it was a kind of twin *telepathy* of sorts. We were uncertain how far the reach had gotten; we had never really separated them further than the opposite ends of the county we lived in, during their separate activities, and not for any great length of time either. I was not interested in experimenting on my children, though to say I wasn't curious as to what they could do would be a lie. But right now, I just wanted them to have as normal a childhood as possible, and that meant having Redmond's parents—the twins' *human* grandparents, come down to visit for the holidays.

Chapter 3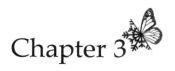

The Celaeno Building, December 17th, 2021, Ottawa, Canada

Thaddeus Smyth III sat waiting unenthusiastically in what had been labeled on the adjacent wall to the heavy walnut wooden soundproof door as *Boardroom A*. The secure meeting room was one of two such spaces on the topmost level of the Celaeno Building. The boardrooms had tinted windows, and he liked to keep all the rooms at a cool 70 degrees, even in winter. He was waiting on an exceptionally persistent man—whose name he had forgotten as soon as it had been said, and who had been relentless in hounding his personal assistant, for which he'd been informed had gone on for several months now, with the request to interview him. The man was with a prominent online magazine for which he was writing an article about inspiring entrepreneurs who were working to improve *health for all*, and he had wanted to converse with him about his work with childhood illnesses. Thaddeus had resisted at first, but then he had realized that the tedious task of sitting through an insipid series of questions was worth the positive exposure it would generate. And the more positive exposure he had, the better, as it shielded suspicious eyes from what he was truly dedicating his resources and energies on.

Thaddeus drew his Patek Philippe pocket watch from the inner breast pocket of his suit jacket. The watch he'd had since he first arrived in Ottawa, though it was an antique from 1845, when the company had first patented the keyless winding system. The suit, it was new. In fact, it was a Savile Row, Henry Poole tailored suit, made with the company's 170th Anniversary cloth, a luxurious black/blue spot super 100s worsted cloth which was the perfect weight to wear throughout the year. He'd had several made.

He had been to quite a few of the world's leading tailors of London's Savile Row, not to mention those in Rome, Milan, Naples, and Turin. But he had an established partnership at Henry Poole that one would believe was a somewhat intimate relationship, considering your tailor knows *which way you dress*, in every sense of the word. The exquisite result was what mattered to him, the exhaustive process to get them he wished he could do without. When you work with a tailor, they tend to take a hard look at you in a way that is not entirely comfortable. And the questions; when and where will you wear your suit? What time of year — winter-weight or breathable? What is the occasion — formal or casual? What type, what texture, pattern or colour. Single or double-breasted? What style of lapel? How many and what type of buttons, what type of lining? And so on. It is not a procedure for the indecisive.

He fancied a long slim single breasted suit jacket, like the one he wore today, and his trousers he preferred them made flat-fronted with a plain finish, medium width and a medium to high rise. He had even ordered matching pleated masks of the 170th anniversary cloth, which were made in breathable, cotton-based silica, which would not cause irritation to his skin or mouth area. Not that he needed to use them, but it had become customary to wear one on the exceptionally rare occasion in public, to give the impression he was making a socially conscious effort to protect himself and others. Though the masks needed to be washed at 30°C on a delicate cycle, he didn't care. He had all his clothing washed and dry-cleaned on the premises by one of his underlings. The only thing they didn't wash were his shoes, and today he was wearing his favorite style, a Gucci Horsebit loafer, of which he too had numerous pairs.

This man, the interviewer, reporter, article writer, whatever, was not actually late. In fact, he still had 30 minutes before he was scheduled to arrive. Thaddeus despised when people were late and he much preferred them to arrive early, though he also detested the eagerness that such early birds often came with. What he respected were those who came prepared, and that was his wish for this interview, since he predicted it might potentially be a deplorable waste of his precious time.

He was checking his pocket watch a second time when a woman came through the boardroom's open door. "Mr. Smith?" the unfamiliar, unremarkable dullard of a woman asked.

"It's Smyth, like *scythe*—but without the 'e'," he corrected the imbecile standing in the room now.

"Mr. Smyth, I'm Jordan Jefferies," she adjusted then.

Ah yes, the name I had forgotten, the JJ name for what I had believed was for a man. His assistant had not indicated a gender and had only referred to them as the *reporter*. He held back his disapproval with a forced smile. He had been accepting of the meeting when he had thought the person doing the interviewing would be a man, but now he searched for a justification to abandon the interview. "Miss Jefferies, is it?" Thaddeus began.

"It's Ms.," she cut in, adjusting the front of the dull grey blazer she wore. Her jacket and pants looked to be a suit, but she must have worn the pants more often because their grey colour had faded some, he observed.

Yes—of course it is. "Ms. Jefferies…," he stared again. *As if I care what your marital status is.*

She stepped up closer, eagerly extending her hand out in greeting. "I have been waiting to meet you for years," she said, cutting him off again and adjusting the grip on the large leather bag she carried in her other hand.

There's that eagerness I detest, beaming back and extended in request of a handshake. "Ms. Jefferies…," he began for a third time, the woman's fawning lessening his annoyance some. He had no interest in women— mainly because he had yet to find a female who could hold his attention, and not that she did. But he needed the good publicity, he reminded himself. She acted as though smitten, so he chose to use that to his advantage. "… please, have a seat," he finished, directing her to the lesser chair adjacent to his more prestigious one instead of shaking her hand. He knew he was handsome; he'd been told many times over the years. He had excellent posture emphasized by his 6-foot 4 height, and he had a long lean muscular build that he'd been informed was very appealing to *both* sexes. He kept his chestnut brown hair neat yet stylish, of course, and his eye colour and eyelashes were similar in shade to his hair. His jaw was square. His nose was narrow yet masculine, yet his lips were full, the bottom one a bit fuller, and he had been told time and again that his skin was perfect. He never went out in the sun—not if he could help it.

"Wonderful," she said, excitedly sliding into the leather seat of the boardroom chair. "I know your assistant had said, *'no photos'*, but do you mind if I video our interview?"

Thaddeus sucked in a breath, appalled by the woman's boldness, as she pulled out what Thaddeus now realized was a video recording device from the bag she had been carrying. "My publicist can get you a photo for your article," he said, staring down the video recorder like it was a feral cat that had him cornered. *What the hell?*

He had provided a few professionally done photos to his marketing and publicity firm in the past, for use with his organization and the publication of his research, but he had never, ever provided video.

"We need something fresh for our readers," she said, adjusting and lengthening the legs on the tripod attachment. "Video is the way to go."

He said nothing. He was paralyzed by the idea. *Was this drab woman in the dull suit trying to tell me about being 'fresh'?*

"You seem nervous—that's normal," she said when he continued to stare at the video camera. "Let me guide you through this."

Guide me? I don't need any guidance—especially not from the likes of you. I can do this. I could—I'm Thaddeus Smyth III, after all. At least that's who he claimed he was—what he told to the world. "Okay, Mizz Jefferies—let's do this," he said, straightening his high-priced necktie and crossing his legs.

"That's a lovely suit you're wearing," she said, flipping open a notepad that exposed a list of questions on it. "Did you have it tailormade?"

"Bespoke—or bespoken for," he said, the pounding of his heart changing to a calmer rhythm. "It comes from a time when words like *luxury* had a hallowed ring to them. It is not just tailormade, it means it is made to the client's precise specification—made to measure, as it were." *I wouldn't be caught dead in an off the rack suit. My specifications are always that of flawlessness, as are my measurements.*

"It's stunning, really—and you're stunning in it." She moved the camera a tad to the right. "It will be captured beautifully on video," she added, crossing her legs. Her flattery fostered more ease in him, all the while feeding his ego.

You might be smarter than you appear. But I know how amazing I look—no need to tell me. "Let us begin," he said, turning slightly to show his better side. *Who am I kidding, both my sides are perfect.*

She flipped the recording switch to *on*. "Let's talk about your father," she started. "Similar to those of your father, photos of *you* are hard to find."

"Is that a question?" *Of course, they're hard to find. I avoid being photographed as much as possible.*

"I wasn't actually able to find any of your father, but I found a photo of your grandfather, and the two of you look remarkably similar."

That was not a question either. I thought this was an interview about me. "What photo have you seen?" Thaddeus asked, though he knew of only one in existence. He had been in the background with several others who had been present when the scientists had made this breakthrough. He had witnessed the others working on the stabilization and mass production of penicillin, and the search for more productive strains.

"It's a photo of him with the contributors who had discovered and developed penicillin. Ernst Chain, Howard Florey, Norman Heatley and Edward Abraham along with the 1945 Nobel Prize winners in Physiology and Medicine," she said.

Again, that is not a question? "Alexander Fleming, along with Florey and Chain, shared the award," he said. *I know them all—had met them all and many more scientists in this field.*

"Dorothy Hodgkin received the *1964* Nobel Prize in Chemistry for determining the structures of vital biochemical substances including penicillin," she said, adjusting her ill-fitting suit jacket.

"Yes," he concurred. *Go ahead fluff up women in history—it is of no significance to me.* "But do you know what followed the discovery of penicillin? About the reports of penicillin resistance in many bacteria?" *I was there for all of it, sweetheart.*

"Of course, it's the research—that continues today, whose aim it is to circumvent and recognize the mechanisms of antibiotic resistance," she said, uncrossing her legs then, planting both feet on the floor.

Well-well, not such a dumb bunny after all. Touché. "Correct, Ms. Jefferies. Right you are." He gifted her a smile. "As I'm sure you know, many ancient cultures such as Egypt, Greece, and India discovered useful properties of plants and fungi in treating infections. The fact being, these treatments frequently worked mainly because many organisms, including some species of mold, spontaneously produced antibiotic substances. The struggle back then was that these ancient practitioners couldn't precisely isolate or identify the active components in these organisms. More trial and error. Error that often ended in death," he said, as though it were a matter of fact. *Now how about a question?*

"I didn't know that, actually," she said. "But thank you for informing our viewers." She gave him a small smile, but the rest of her face remained passive.

Right, I almost forgot I was being recorded. He fought the urge to roll his eyes.

"Now about your father," she said, circling back. "The photo."

"The photo?" he tossed back to her, adding a shrug.

"You look so amazingly alike—you could be twins." She looked him straight in the eye, deadpan. "I know that's impossible—the twin things, even so, you have to admit the likeness is astonishing."

What is with you, woman? Aren't you supposed to be asking questions about me or at the very least my work? "You would not have seen any, but from what I remember from seeing the few photos that did exist, my father looked a lot like *his* father, and I am my father's son. So, the family genes are robust, it seems," he said as a statement. *You have a suspicious nature. You couldn't know the truth—could you? No.*

"Tell me about your grandfather. He seemed to live a solitary life, much like you—a recluse." She leaned in as if she were waiting for some great admission.

To hell with this inquisition and your 'guiding me'. I'm leading this interview now. "Let's see. My grandfather pioneered the science behind what I do today," Thaddeus said. "My father brought it to the public, and I'm using it to help mankind—child-kind, more accurately." He smiled again, displaying confidence.

She pursed her lips, then glanced briefly at her notepad, then back at him. "I have it here that your grandfather was born in 1911 in the UK."

"Ireland." He gave her a nod. *I hated Ireland, too much green.*

"Then he came here to Canada in 1946." She glanced back down at her pad of paper again.

"That was just before my father was born." More declarations. *No actual questions about me. I'm getting bored.*

"Your grandmother. I have here that she died in childbirth," she said, giving him an accusatory look.

It's not like I had anything to do with her death. "That is correct. I don't recall ever knowing her name though. She was back in the UK somewhere, I believe. Ireland maybe—I don't know." *She didn't die— she didn't actually exist, for that matter.*

"Did you like your grandfather?" she asked.

A question finally, and sort of about me. "I never met him."

"When and how did your grandfather die?" She raised her eyebrows.

Oh look, two more questions, and still neither about me. "In 1950, my father would have only been 4 years old, when my grandfather passed away from malaria—hence the not meeting him." *I am growing impatient with this line of questioning.*

"I thought malaria was considered eliminated in the US by 1951?" She frowned then.

"It was, but he had been in the Philippines, taking part in research alongside the United States Public Health Services when he contracted the disease." *That should stifle these grandfather questions of yours.*

"What about your parents?" she asked then.

"Turn off the camera!" Thaddeus ran a thumb over the small burn scar on the back of his right hand. *Hello—I'm the topic of this interview.*

"Why, is something wrong?" Her expression changed from serious to that of naivety.

Don't give me that innocent look. "My personal assistant informed me you were interested in coming here to interview me about my work." *This is too much probing into my personal life—and I only have so much false history prepared.*

She appeared a bit uneasy then. "I am," she said, fiddling with the legs of the tripod. "I'm just getting some backstory for the article. I'll be editing the video once I'm done, to reflect the information about the work you're doing."

Thaddeus squinted at her with suspicion. "Okay, then. What about my parents?" *Parents—what a joke that is.*

"Well, I can't find any record of your mother, or a marriage license connected to your father." She flipped back a few pages in her notepad.

Thaddeus took a deep breath and then began reciting the story he had concocted so many years ago. "My father was never married. The woman—my birthmother, apparently had not been in a position to care for a baby, so she left me out on the front step of what had been my father's home here in Ottawa at the time. She had affixed a note—of all things, informing my father that the baby in the carrier was his son." He put up a hand when she tried to cut in. *Patience, lady reporter.* "Testing had been done comparing our blood types, of course, and when DNA testing came out in the late 80s, results then showed that I was indeed his biological son. Not having seen the person who had left me on the step, my father had shared that he vaguely recalled a woman he'd taken to his bed the year prior but could not remember her name." He twisted his chair right and left, self-satisfaction oozing from his pores. *You're feeling all sympathetic now, aren't you, lady reporter?*

"Did he try locating the woman?" She scribbled something down on her notepad.

"No." *There is no woman you fool.* "My father—though he had money, he was also unprepared to take care of the baby, and I was sent to Europe to be raised by a woman referred to as an aunt—but more like a nanny, as she is not a relation. I attended boarding school and university in Europe. All prestigious schools—as you can imagine, but I don't feel the need to advertise for them—they have enough accolades." He gave a quick tilt of his head to one side, in homage of his own accolades. *Drink it all in.*

"What did you study at university?" She flipped to a new page in the pad.

"I majored in biochemistry, a minor in zoology, and I have a master's in microbiology." *That's my story—but I could teach circles around any professor at any university on these subjects.*

"That's quite the combination of studies. Interest in science is another thing that runs in your family tree too—I see," she said, clearly impressed.

"Yes," Was all he gave her. *I spent several millennia overseeing the Earth's microorganisms, in fact.*

"How did the interest in science morph into a thriving business?" she asked, her interest now piqued.

It didn't morph—I made it happen. He fought an eye-roll. "My grandfather set up a business, Celaeno—hence the name on this building. He was a scientist but also a clever businessman. He was fortunate enough to have been present for several medical achievements. Antibiotics, tissue cultures, the risks of smoking, just to name a few. Though he was never recognized as a participant. What he did was invest in these medical breakthroughs. My father, he too invested in medical breakthroughs, but his interests were in research and advancements in the technology related to medicine. Like the CT scanner, artificial heart, laparoscopic surgery, and several others," he ended, giving her a big, beautiful grin.

"Clever investor." She nodded as if appreciating the endeavor.

"Yes, he was," Thaddeus agreed. *I am very impressive, I know. You are going to love this next part—everyone does.* "And now I am taking my family's resources and investing it in people—children primarily, and research into childhood diseases. Some of the rarest are on our research agenda. I have innovation grants and research facilities in seven countries now."

"Where are these research centers, exactly?" Her eyebrows pinched together in question.

Obviously, you didn't find the answers in your search for dirt about my family. The Sterope center is in Bergen, Norway. Merope is in the U.S., New York City. Electra is in Rome. Maia is in Tokyo, Japan. Taygeta is in Manau City, Brazil, and the Alcyone center is in the Netherlands— Amsterdam. In case you were wondering about the names—I named the centers after seven stars in the Pleiades star cluster—one of the nearest star clusters to Earth. They are also more commonly known as the 'Seven Sisters'. *I hate that reference—but you would like it, I'm sure.*

"Why did you choose to name them after stars?" She drew a star on the top of the page in her notepad.

I'll make you wait a couple heartbeats for this one. He steepled his hands then with his index fingers touching his chin. "I was told that my grandfather loved astronomy—and that was where he got the original name for the business." He gave her his best pensive expression. *You will eat this part up—the weaker sex always do.* "I guess you could say I'm a bit of a stargazer myself—just a hobby, really. And well, Pleiades is the cluster most noticeable to the naked eye in the night sky. It felt right to use the names of the other stars. It felt like kismet, almost dreamy in a way—romantic even. Do you like my choice in names?" He lowered his hands back to his lap and leant forward leisurely. Then he licked his lips, letting an intentionally slow smile pull at the corner of his mouth.

She was clearly blushing now. "Yes... you're very dreamy... I mean it's dreamy... excellent choice... really." Her mouth gaped as though she were in a trance.

"Oh—and this one here in Ottawa, Celaeno, is the largest," he added, leaning back into his chair. *So easy, this is too easy—you are too easy.*

She blinked rapidly then as if abruptly been pulled from that trance. "Why Ottawa?" she asked, shaking her head, and gathering herself.

You like me—you really like me. He almost burst into laughter. "It was the last center my father established before he died. The Canadians are wonderfully friendly people and hardworking, and they were kind to me when I was here after my father's death in 2001. They have an amazing children's hospital here as well." *The hospital helps with my cover, it's the cherry on top.*

"How did he die?" she asked, focused once again.

You caught that little morsel I tossed out—very good. "Anaphylaxis. He hadn't realized he was allergic to one of the agents they were testing, *Sulfur.* He was accidentally exposed to it while touring the facility in New York." Thaddeus rubbed his burn scar again. *It's a mistake I won't make again—though it did reveal a surprising vulnerability I currently exploit in my experiments.*

Her glance went to his hands. "I noticed you have a scar on your hand. How did that happen?" She glanced back up to his face.

Thaddeus covered the back of his right hand with his left. "Yes, well, it seems I too have a sensitivity to the same element. It's nothing as serious as my father's." He glanced over at the pad of paper on her lap then, and she seemed to pick up the message, his body language that said, *let it go.*

She shifted in her seat, then continued for the next almost hour with running through the remaining questions on her list, the ones about his work with children, and all the while maintaining her admiration for all things *Thaddeus.* In the end, he had found the experience curiously exhilarating.

Chapter 4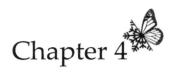

Menopause is a bitch, ask any woman in their 50s. But nothing compared to the challenges and worries I'd had with being pregnant so late in the game. We, meaning my girlfriends and I, worried not only because I was considered high risk, being that I was in my 40s at the time of my pregnancy, but also because I had been at additional risk due to my carrying twins. My delivery had gone better than expected, thankfully, and it hadn't hurt being surrounded by the neonatal nurses from my job at the hospital. I had a brilliant OB who specialized in multiple births, and Olivia had insisted on coming down for the delivery despite me already being in good hands. Mac, Vicki, and Allison had all come down as well but after the birth. They had staggered their visits overlapping weeks by arriving a day before the other was scheduled to leave, making their visits to help us with the twins even more enjoyable.

Unfortunately, a not-so-fun fact that sucked, was that I had put on 50 pounds during my pregnancy, part of it being the twins' combined weight of 11 pounds, Hayley chasing 5 pounds and Ryley being over 6 pounds at their birth, although the rest of it had been all me. But the part that really sucked, the part I hadn't considered with having babies in my 40s, was that I no longer had *youth* on my side when it came to getting back into shape. I eventually lost most of the pregnancy weight I'd gained and had conceded to settling into my *new* body shape. Though, I have to say, it takes a *real* man to support their wife getting back into shape, getting healthy again, and him not criticizing the extra weight. And I must admit, it takes an even more special man, like Redmond, who always knew how to make me feel beautiful in the ways that he had, no matter what I looked like or was struggling with.

Besides Redmond's support, the other thing that had helped me deal with the weight gain and the emotional and mental fatigue that came with having two babies, had been my new habit of going for long walks. I had taken the twins with me, using one of those running strollers that fits two babies. And though I never ran, I had kept a brisk pace that had aided in burning off the unwanted weight. The stroller walks had had a definite positive impact on the twins too as part of a routine of settling them into the day ahead. I had found that if I missed a day due to weather or other circumstances, the girls became restless and harder to manage, especially as they had gotten bigger and had started walking.

Four years ago, when we had moved up here and when I'd first started dropping the girls off at junior kindergarten, I had begun the ritual again of walking every morning. This time, I did it on my own and on the section of the private beach we live on. And today I was pushing to get my 5km walk in on my own, before the girls would be home on Christmas break and wanting to walk in the mornings again with me. They had started doing it with me before homeschooling had started for the day, but since they were back to in-person school again, I had been enjoying the alone time these past 4 months and doing the walk again on my own. Winter was the best time for walks with the cooler breeze and temperatures, and it had become more than just exercise for me. It was more like meditation, listening to the waves and smelling the ocean air. It was all good, especially for my hormones.

On my walks I usually did a lot of thinking, and today I found myself in disbelief at how quickly the past 12 years had gone by since the gathering. It has been 13 years since Mom passed away, though the time passing since her death, had felt like the blink of an eye.

Redmond and I had both aged some, but we joked it was the twins that had aged us, not the time. *"Having kids keeps you young in a way — but it also beats you up at the same time,"* Redmond had kidded. Though aging wasn't the same for men, was it? They tended to look more distinguished when the grey started to creep into their hair, but for women there always seems to be the need to cover the grey, cover the age, cover the years. And like several of my girlfriends, I too had some grey finding its way into my hair. Mine had begun weaving in and around the now sun-kissed highlights of my hair, mostly around my face, appearing as platinum highlights. When I'd lived up north in Canada, highlights like these only showed up late into summer, then faded away once you were into fall. Now they remained all year because of the amount of time we spend outside with the girls, the beach giving us all the excuses we needed to be out enjoying the sun.

Having a home on the beach with its deck facing the ocean gives us the chance to enjoy the beach at night as well, sitting out and gazing at the stars. We especially like it at this time of year in winter on chilly nights. Redmond had gotten us a small propane-tank driven firepit for on the deck to warm ourselves when sitting out in the evenings, and it has become one of our favorite things to do. The girls especially liked it when we brought out the quilted blankets, the ones I had found at a local secondhand store. We long for the cold nights to cuddle around the fire with the girls. It is a favorite when family and friends visit as well, with all of us gathering on the deck and chatting over drinks. Often it is at least 10 degrees cooler here than off island in town, even during the day. Who wouldn't love that?

I knew our dogs did. Summer and Snow, our two female all-white Lab-Shepherd mix rescues, were each upwards of 150 pounds now. We suspected that there was a much larger breed in the mix because they were more like small polar bears than dogs, and they were now in their 10th year with us. And like their owners, they were also beginning to slow down a bit. They were great with the twins and had been ever since we had brought the girls home from the hospital. They had acted like the girls' protectors in a way, sleeping in their rooms, always at their sides, playing with them and following them everywhere they went. They still slept in their rooms and played with them, however the following and keeping up had gotten harder for them this past year. With the girls being home so much with their remote schooling, they had started taking care of the dogs more, walking them, feeding them, and brushing them, etc., which was nice for all of them. And the girls' increased involvement with their care had helped to balance out the dogs' declining vitality.

Ending my walk, I cut through the sea grape trees to the backyard, where I saw Redmond outside with the dogs. He had left early this morning before the girls had gotten up, to head off the island to the studio and get work done with Lily before the weekend. His plan was to have the rest of the day and weekend off since his parents were arriving today.

"How was your beach therapy?" he asked when I got closer.

"Good—great actually. The girls are gonna want to go with me starting tomorrow, so I really wanted to get this last solo mission in," I said, joking but not really. I'd started my walk wearing shorts and a sweatshirt, knowing that even with the cooler temperatures I'd be stripping off and tying around my waist my top layer before the halfway mark of my walk.

"I'm heading to get Mom and Pop at the airport. Did you want to come with me?" Redmond asked.

"I need to clean myself up, and I still have a few things I need to get done before you guys get back. Plus, these pups need to be bathed too."

Summer and Snow both "Chuffed," in acknowledgement, at hearing me saying the word *bathed*.

"You look beautiful all sweaty and suntanned, but okay," he said, stepping up, brushing a strand of hair behind my ear that had come loose from my long ponytail. "Are you still thinking about what Hayley had said about the little boy?"

I smiled, but I guess my preoccupation was showing. I had given him the details over the phone when I'd got back to the house. "Aren't you curious?" I asked, heading for the shade of the carport.

"I guess—but it's not like it has anything to do with us," he said, following me. "It's been ages since we've had anything *strange* to deal with, and other than our regular life stuff like having babies and moving—and your occasional premonitions, life has been relatively normal."

"I know," I said, tipping my head back to look up at him.

"But?" he asked, placing his hands on my shoulders.

"But…," I started, then hesitated. My thoughts were scrambled.

"You haven't had a job — a project, something that's been just *yours* since the twins were born," he said, blowing the words out in a breath, and dropping his hands.

"Don't get me wrong — I love our life. Taking care of the girls and you and our home brings me joy… but you're right in a way." My throat felt dry suddenly. "Now that the girls are getting older, I'm starting to get sort of… restless. And that comment about the boy, and the concern in Gabriel's face — and his rushing off, reminded me of what it felt like back then."

"How did it feel — other than frustrating, overwhelming, and confusing?" he questioned, his eyebrows pinching together.

It had felt like an amazing adventure. "Like I had… *purpose*," I said, leaving out the adventure part. "Even working at the hospital had given me a sense of purpose. I don't know." I shook my head and glanced down at my bare feet.

"Maybe you should look into another gig here — at the hospital. You'd get glowing recommendations — you know that."

"Ya — maybe," I said, glancing back up at him.

"Let's talk more about it later — we'll brainstorm ideas. In the meantime, let Gabriel and the others deal with this situation with the boy." He jingled his keys.

"Okay, but don't you think it's weird he hasn't come back to tell me what's up? I mean he usually comes if I call." I followed Redmond as he started towards his truck.

"Lynn…," he said, not needing to complete the sentence.

"I know — I know, dog with a bone." He knew me too well.

He shook his head and grinned, then opened the driver's side door. "I'll be back soon," he said leaning down for a kiss before he climbed in. "Oh, I left you some cold water just inside the door."

"My hero." I wiped the side of my sweaty face against the shoulder of my t-shirt. "Drive safe," I called out, as he backed out of the carport.

As the truck pulled away, I turned back to the house to retrieve the waiting water. "Suuummerrr… Snooow," I called after the dogs, opening the door, and snatching up the water bottle.

But they didn't come.

Then I *felt* it.

Something, or someone—whatever, their presence was creating a tingling sensation all over the surface of my skin—the feeling like how pop-rocks feel on your tongue and the roof of your mouth, prickly but kind of invigorating. The sensation had me darting to the backyard, only to stop short when I saw the dogs… and a heavily muscled titan of a woman playing squeak-ball with them.

This gladiator—and when I say *gladiator*, I literally mean a gladiator, because she wore battle gear like you'd see worn by a Roman warrior. Her body armor was made of what looked like white leather and metal pieces fashioned around her arms, legs, and torso, but what really stood out was the headpiece she wore, and it was something from out of this world. The helmet was nothing like anything I had ever seen, not even on the sci-fi channel or in urban fantasy style movies. Her head-covering appeared to be made of a shiny metal like silver, and it had long tusk and horn-like protrusions as thick and long as my forearms, arching out from the front, top, sides, and back of the headpiece. These jutting horns shone as though made of white opal, the rainbow flecks gleaming in the sunlight. Descending from the underside of the helmet, in stark contrast to the rich colour of her dark skin, was a thick white braid of hair, which reached to her belt. If I didn't know any better and if it wasn't for the fact that we lived in a somewhat reclusive area away from the main part of town, I might have thought there was a Comicon event, or a movie being filmed nearby. But that wasn't it. And she was something… *else*.

I watched as the squeaking of the toys ceased and the female gladiator bent down to shake a paw with each of her playmates. Then she turned her head to gaze my way. Her eyes were… *otherworldly*. She smiled at me then, her striking eyes glowing as if backlit and in shades of fragmented blue like that of an iceberg. They were so stunning, they left me… well, *stunned*. She straightened and turned fully my way then, and that's when I saw she was holding some kind of weapon. It was reminiscent of something I'd seen in a 90s science fiction movie. The actor from the film had called it a Khopesh, stating it was like an Egyptian spear with its sickle-shaped sword, that had apparently evolved from a battle axe. Unlike the one in the film, this one was twice as long, and she held it out in front of her like a staff.

She smiled again and then bowed in my direction. "Daughter of Gabriel, I have little time," she said, straightening, expressing the words more like it was a title. "I have come to warn you." She took several brisk strides forward, coming to stand directly in front of me. Her size was intimidating, but she was not frightening, in fact she was magnificent.

"Warn *me*?" I asked, holding my ground, despite having to tilt my head back to look up at her face. She must have been at least 7 feet tall, because she stood loftier than even Redmond with his stature.

"Yes—I am sorry, I'm not allowed to share such things with the others... I mean, neither my brethren nor my sistren can't know that I am still traveling down to Earth. Though it has not been stated by any, that I am not permitted to share this information with *you*.

"What information—who are you? What are you?" It was my assumption that I had met all factions of celestials.

"I am Purah, Steward of Celaeno, the 7th Star of the Pleiades, also known by your people as the Seven Sisters." She bowed again, deeper this time. "It is my feeling—my belief, that I must share this—to make up for what had transpired... in that moment... of my absence."

"I'm not following—sorry." I shook my head, then placed the cold water bottle against the back of my neck. The tiny hairs on my neck bristled.

She bowed only her head this time and closed her eyes. "The tragic events that had ensued because of my ignorance. A betrayal by those whom I had presumed to be loyal and righteous." She lifted her head and looked down at me, then she thumped her spear on the ground.

"What? You've lost me here." I rolled the cold water bottle around the front of my neck, trying to further cool myself, hoping for some clarity.

"He knows," the statuesque female said then.

"He who? The big He," I asked, pointing to the sky. Thinking she might be referring to the big guy, the creator of the Heavens, whatever you want to call him.

"A collaborator—one of the Earthbound. He has told him of what he saw."

"Who he? Are there two hes? Earthbound?" Was I suffering heat exhaustion or was she not making any sense? "Who—who told who—what?" I questioned further, not actually helping myself.

"Of your gifts, your *abilities*. That you can sense the others, the celestials—not just the Archangels and The Fallen, as was once believed. You were seen... in that noisy city where the towers fell... you were seen speaking to a Watcher.

Okay, this was not getting any clearer. "In the noisy city? Do you mean New York?" I lifted an arm and wiped my cheek against the sleeve of my shirt.

"Yes, the city of *New* York." She nodded several times as if I had solved the riddle.

"That was two years ago," I said, remembering. It was before the pandemic.

"They had been watching you—before, I mean."

"Before what? Who's been watching me?" I didn't like the idea of someone watching me. It was bad enough that Gabriel and some of the others popped in unannounced occasionally.

"Since the gathering. It is your gift they seek. Their belief is that you can find the others." She glanced over her shoulder. "But you are in danger now." She cut a glance to the densely packed sea grape trees, then back to me. "*He* is the danger."

"Him? He who?" Oh-my-gawd, I was starting to sound like a freaking owl.

"*Thaddeus*," she whispered. "But I am not permitted to interfere—I am not even permitted to come here to Earth—not anymore, not since he was sent down," she said speedily. She cut a glance left and right this time, focusing on the side hedges. "I had ventured to Earth prior, and I had seen what had been occurring—what he had been doing. I had told the others back then. And at their command, my fellow Stewards and I cast him down. But he has not stopped—and now I cannot tell the others, I cannot risk them knowing I have continued to venture to Earth, against their authority. I risk my existence on Celaeno, by being here now. But you need to know what I have seen—what I have overheard, how I have heard them talking about you." She thumped the staff again. "I have seen the testing he does. He records everything—all of it, written in a language, a scribing I cannot understand, one I have never witnessed before. You must find it."

"Find what, where?" I was pretty sure my head was about to implode from the confusion I was suffering.

"The writings," she said.

"Let me call for Gabriel—he'll better understand what you are trying to tell me."

"No—please. *You* must tell the Archangels—explain to them of my risk to be here—to protect you, and that I beg for their forgiveness. I must go."

"No wait," I said, stepping in closer. But she shot a glance back over her shoulder and then vanished.

Standing there I stared at the now empty space where she had just stood. Then I cracked open the lid of the water bottle and took a long pull of the cold liquid. I leaned my head back and gazed up at the sky, taking in a deep breath. Then using the breath, I called out at the top of my lungs. "GABRIEL!"

Chapter 5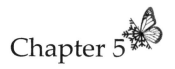

The Summer Pavilion, December 17ᵗʰ, Ottawa, Canada

Gabriel stood on the back deck of the ornate gazebo, overlooking the Ottawa River, with his back to the entrance and the snow-covered steps that led the way into the Summer Pavilion. The late morning sun glistened off the encrusted wind-driven snowdrifts that cast blue shadows in the spaces between them. Even though the cold never bothered him, he had worn a long tan wool coat over the casual outfit he'd worn for the ride to school with Lynn and his granddaughters. As always with his visit to this location, he read the plaque once again, the one that depicted the building's history. The original ornamental summer house was built in 1877, but in 1956, the building was demolished because of its poor condition. This replica was rebuilt in 1993, and forms part of the monument dedicated in 1994 as a memorial to Canadian police and peace officers. It had been a gift to the people of Canada from the Canadian police officers in memory of their fallen comrades. Gabriel had always loved the structure with its copper roof and its matching yet paler green painted wood construction and white trim. Like many of the historic buildings in Ottawa with similar roofs, this one had taken on the green verdigris colouring that resulted from 25-year-old oxidized copper.

"You cut your hair off," Michael said, approaching from behind him and coming to stand at his right. He still wore his long dark wavy hair to his waist, and like today, it was often tied back with a thin leather strapping.

Gabriel said nothing and continued to look out over the landscape covered in snow.

"I like it," Raphael said, upon his arrival to where the two others now stood, positioning himself at Michael's right. "I like shorter hair," he added, brushing a hand over his fiery red brush-cut hair, gazing out at the snowy scenery before him.

"Gabriel, did you bring us here to talk about hairstyles?" Vretil said, coming up to stand next to Raphael, continuing the theme on the right. Vretil kept his hair short, not in a tight cut like his red-haired brethren, maintaining his brown and golden waves at a tidy length above his collar.

Again, Gabriel gave no response.

Uriel appeared then, flanking Gabriel on his left. "Why are we here?" he said, turning to face Gabriel and the line of Archangels. A cool winter breeze blew his shoulder-length auburn hair forward into his face, and he brushed it aside.

"It seems..." Gabriel began then, "... that we have a new *issue* in regard to our Charges." He had summoned his fellow Archangels to this beautiful location behind the Library of Parliament, hoping the surrounding beauty would aid in padding the unsettling information he had to share with the others.

"Don't tell me that," Michael said, punching his hands into the pockets of his dark green bomber jacket. Like all of them, he too was not bothered by the cold, but he had found the switching up of his wardrobe these past few years enjoyable.

"Everyone has been doing so well, what kind of problem could they have now?" Vretil asked, shifting to stand at the left next to Uriel. They looked a bit like a matching set, both in navy-blue peacoats and navy dress pants.

Gabriel took two steps back from the railing to take in the view of his brethren as they turned to face him. "It's the Earthbound," he said then, panning their faces.

"Are we here at this location because it's a fitting tribute, like for the police and peace officers killed in the line of duty?" Uriel questioned, worry spreading across his face.

"Nobody has died, Uriel," Gabriel said, firmly. "Not yet anyway. And the original structure was intended to be used as a summer retreat for the speaker of the House of Commons and his family, if you must know."

"What—so now you're the speaker of the house?" Vretil asked, a hint of sarcasm escaping in his tone.

"What about the Earthbound?" Michael asked, interrupting the banter, and brushing away the snow from the railing to lean against it.

"Well, it's about what they have been up to," Gabriel said, shaking his head back and forth several times.

"Weren't the Guards keeping an eye out for Thaddeus?" Raphael asked.

"They are, but Thaddeus is not the problem I brought you here to discuss," Gabriel redirected. "There's a boy. A Nephilim boy."

There was a collective *gasp*, and then Uriel asked, "Whose offspring, is he?"

"Even if I knew that, it's not as though I can find the birth parents. You know we can't locate them—sense them." Gabriel knocked snow off the front of one of his loafers.

"Then how did you find out about this boy?" Uriel asked, stepping closer to Gabriel, examining him as though he were art on the wall of a gallery.

"Lynn." Gabriel glanced down and tapped snow off his other loafer.

"She found the boy?" Michael asked, standing up from leaning against the railing.

"No, the twins did actually." Gabriel put his hands in the pockets of his coat.

"What do you mean—the twins did?" Raphael asked, taking his turn to lean against the rail this time, crossing his arms over his chest.

Gabriel pursed his lips and then said, "I was with them—Lynn and the girls, at their school. They pointed him out, said he was '*like Mum*', like Lynn, though they expressed that he was not quite the same but similar."

"What does that mean—how do you know they meant he was a Nephilim?" Uriel asked.

"Because they said it was his *vibration* that was like their Mum's," Gabriel responded, pulling his hands free of his coat pockets, waving them in the air in frustration. "And you know how they sense others, through sound or vibration they hear in their heads when celestials are near," he reminded.

"Was Lynn able to sense the boy?" Michael asked then.

"No, I don't think so—but I'm not sure." Gabriel shook his head again.

"We need to assess if she can," Vretil suggested.

Gabriel sighed. "It's too late, the boy and his family have already relocated north to New York."

"How is it you know this?" Michael stepped up closer to Gabriel, his patience wearing thin.

"I spoke to their teacher. I'm on the safe list—the school believes I'm Lynn's cousin. Anyway, I found out that the boy was being raised by his grandparents and he has some serious health issues. The mother died in childbirth—a difficult pregnancy apparently, and the father is unknown. They had brought the boy here at the end of summer, thinking that the small beach community would be good for him—for his health. Unfortunately, they found getting the proper therapeutic attention for his condition quite problematic. They realized that having nearby, more sophisticated medical help, was required, and they all left back up to New York as soon as school broke for the holidays."

"Were you able to get their names?" Vretil asked.

"No, I wasn't able to get more details," Gabriel said. "I was beginning to feel that my inquest was odd enough—I'd made it appear the interest had come as an inquiry made from the twins. Further questioning would have come off as intrusive and inappropriate." Gabriel unbuttoned his coat and returned his hands to the pockets.

"There have been no Nephilim since The Fallen 200, other than Lynn—no unidentified celestials—none that we have been aware of, I should say," Vretil said.

"All descendants have been accounted for," Uriel said. "And their offspring would not be considered as Nephilim and would be classified much like our Charges and the descendants of The Fallen Leaders and Horsemen."

"Finding Nephilim has always been a challenge, even for us," Raphael stated, leaning still on the railing.

"We struggled to figure out who and what Lynn was, though her line was much more complex than any other celestial-human offspring," Michael added.

"Why is it we can sense and find each other—can recognize the Archangel essence in us, sense all other angels, but we cannot find the Nephilim?" Raphael asked then, crossing his feet at the ankles.

"Seraphim can sense and find each other too, but it seems that the Earthbound ones lost that ability when they lost their immortality. We can't sense them even if their location is unknown to us," Gabriel said. "With Lynn, you could only sense that something was divine in nature within her, not what she was exactly—nor her lineage," Gabriel added. "Your Charges don't have the ability to sense other celestials—no one other than Lynn possesses that ability, well—other than the twins, as you know."

"How do we know this boy is not the offspring of any of these others?" Uriel asked, though Gabriel was confident Uriel knew the answer already.

"You believe this boy is the offspring of one of the Earthbound?" Vretil asked, more as a statement.

"None would risk the punishment; it must be one of the Earthbound," Michael said with confidence.

"I knew this would happen," Uriel said, the angel's worry raising its ugly head.

"Knew what?" Gabriel asked, placing a hand on Uriel's shoulder.

Uriel crossed an arm over his chest to place his hand atop Gabriel's. "That things were going along too well—that our Charges would have to deal with something else beyond their day-to-day lives."

"There is no threat to our Charges," Raphael said, moving off the rail to come stand next to Uriel and the others. "What about Lynn?" he asked then, turning his glance to Gabriel. "Maybe she can sense these other celestial—the Earthbound, even if we can't."

"It wasn't like she was a secret among our kind. Numerous angels have visited her over the years since the gathering, all 70 of the Amulet Angels visited after the birth of the twins," Raphael said.

"Does Thaddeus know about her? Michael asked.

"I hope not." Gabriel cut a glance at Michael. "But I'm going to go talk to one of the Guards," Gabriel added.

"They've had enough trouble keeping track of these Earthbound and their whereabouts, let alone knowing what Thaddeus does or doesn't know," Vretil noted.

"They have never had any interest in our Charges before," Uriel said, a tiny spark of hope showing itself.

"Let's hope it stays that way," Gabriel said. But they were all well aware of Thaddeus's past behavior and of the likelihood that this Earthbound bastard could have other sinister plans in play.

Chapter 6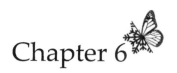

Redmond was on his way to get his parents at the airport, which would take him almost an hour and a half, though this latest celestial visitation was not something I could call and talk to him about, especially not with his parents in the truck with him. To keep my mind occupied while waiting for Gabriel, I fulfilled my chores of bathing both dogs, and then I moved on to the kitchen to tidy the breakfast dishes. Downstairs, I double-checked that there were clean towels and plenty of tissue and toilet paper in the bathroom, and then I vacuumed the entry rug up of the sand that the dogs had brought in with them. There weren't any more tasks that needed doing and I was grateful we'd prepared earlier in the week for expectant guests. Redmond had already cleared a spacious area in the lower level and set up the surprisingly comfortable portable queen bed for his parents. They would have privacy down there and would also have their own bathroom to use.

Done with my tidying, I retreated to the upper floor again, to shower and change. Wanting to sit out on the deck out back to enjoy the cooler December weather, I dressed in my comfy grey yoga pants and a matching grey t-shirt, topped with a zippered light blue hoodie.

Exiting the master bedroom, I crossed the open concept living area to the wall of sliding glass doors that stretched from the living room to the kitchen. I had left the dogs out on the deck to dry off, and when I cracked the sliding door, they didn't even rouse from their reclined positions. Though, Summer did lift her head a little as I passed by them to sit on the deck couch.

The visit from this latest celestial, Purah, should have had me frazzled, and though what she had told me did have my brain racing, it was my age related hormones that were seriously out of whack and causing me to be more exhausted than anything. I still had 30 minutes before Redmond and my in-laws would be back. So, while the dogs continued to dry off from their baths by laying on the side of the deck with the warm day's sun, I stretched out on the couch in the shade opposite them and gave myself over to the fatigue, granting myself permission to shut my eyes for just a few moments.

I'm standing in a small hallway. A nurse in scrubs pushes a gurney carrying a small boy, and I notice he has dark circles around his closed eyes. As they pass by me, they head through sliding doors on the opposite side of the hall, and I follow them through and into what looks like an oversized hospital room.

The room appears to be a testing area of a sort, with four beds on the side furthest from the doors. Near the entrance is a tall male doctor holding a clipboard and exchanging words with a female nurse. I notice then that the beds nearest me have clipboards hanging off the ends of each of them.

I move forward and see that the first bed now contains the child I saw in the hallway. An IV bag hangs on a pole next to his bed. Beside it is a cart with various medical implements atop a large tray. The same nurse hovers over him now, making notes on a tablet. He lets out a tiny cry and then moans as the nurse continues to examine him.

The bed next to them has another child in it, with the same IV setup and medical cart, but this patient is a little girl hooked up to a ventilation system. Questionable food smells hang in the air from the remnants of a nearby meal tray along with the stench of urine. I quickly cover my nose with my hand.

Pushing further into the room, past the child on the ventilator, I see that the third bed in the row is empty. A male staffer is in the process of pulling up the stained sheets, and the smell of vomit and blood wafts from the bedding my way. I gag, covering my nose and mouth this time, and move past the sight towards the fourth bed. It too is empty but in contrast to the last, this one is pristine, and the sharp smell of bleach and cleaners, along with antiseptic, blankets the areas around it. I turn away then and glance towards the area past the beds.

At the end of the room are two folding style privacy partitions that are extended out from the side walls meeting in the middle of the room to block the back section. As I approach the barriers and peer through the narrow opening between them the metallic tang of stainless-steel hit my tastebuds. I step up and slide a hand through the opening and grab the side of the right barrier, pushing it aside, trundling it outward on its affixed wheels. I blow out a breath as a gruesome sight comes into view.

The tiny body of a child lay face down on what I recognize as a metal autopsy table. The child's back is covered in bruises, and the torn flesh near the shoulder blades exposes two openings that resemble circular boreholes into the underlying tissue. A guttural bellowing roar pulls my attention from the child on the table to an open door on the far wall. I turn, heading towards the open door, and then trip on something. There, plugged into the wall next to the last bed, is a grouping of black cords that lead along the floor into the open door. I step over the cables, following them further in through the doorway.

Standing in the opening, I see to the right of the room two medical staff positioned next to monitoring equipment and a portable patient X-ray, and they are speaking in low voices. The stench of something foul pulls my attention to the left and I turn, only to let out an audible gasp at the sight before me.

In front of me is a massive man. His back is turned, and it is then that I realize he is suspended several inches off the ground by straps around his shoulders and waist. Looking up, I see the straps are attached to chains hanging down from a hoist mechanism fixed to the ceiling. His upper body is bare, and his legs are covered by hospital scrubs, the waist of which is stained with both dried and fresh blood. On his bare back there are opened gashes, similar to that of the child in the postmortem area. He has the same boreholes only bigger, though these hollows seep with blood and what looks like pus. The smell of both along with the pungent scent of sweat emanates from his skin. I cross an arm over my lower face, pressing my nose and mouth into my elbow to block the stench. Next to him in a tray on a small rolling table, are what looks like pieces of severed bone, their thickness comparable to that of a femur bone though the man's legs appear to be intact. I circle around to the front of the man's body. Glancing up, I stare into his bruised and sweat-covered face.

I stood fixated at the sight in front of me. The magnificence of his features, I could still see through the bloodstains on his cheeks. A grunt then a hiss of pain suddenly escape his swollen lips and his eyes flutter open. He is still alive. Barking noises sound then….

"What the fuuuuuu…," I began, my eyes shooting open as I sat up. I turned my head to see Summer and Snow were barking at the local Coastguard helicopter as it passed overhead doing its survey of the beaches. "Wowsers," I said resting back into my prone position. My fragmented dream memories churned, and my brain fog began to clear as the barking of the dogs and whirring of the helicopter dissipated. The dogs returned to their relaxing place in the sun, but I was left still with my brain and ears humming from both the disturbing dream and the manner in which I had been woken.

I'd had dreams about people in hospital settings before, but this one was much different, it was so vivid and palpable as though I was there, walking through the lab. The horrid smells from the dream lingered with me still.

The other dreams, the ones I had experienced earlier on in the year, those I figured had been mainly due to all the imagery I had seen of people sick and dying from the coronavirus, which had been shown daily on the news and online on every social media outlet. We were only just now starting to see a light at the end of an exceptionally dark almost two-year tunnel.

In the year prior to the vaccine distribution which had started earlier in this year, it had been an all-angels-on-deck kind of thing in regard to families and loved ones who were unable to be with the people suffering and dying. Our Archangel designates and The Fallen Leaders, had explained to us in the *knowing*, that most celestials had taken it upon themselves to be present, focusing on being with patients and the medical staff, when one of their patients passed. The dying would not be alone, and a feeling of peace—conscious or not, was given to them by any Angel who could provide it. There wasn't much else they could do. So many were sick and dying around the world. And when time permitted it, Angels did their best to provide comfort to the medical staff who had to witness the losses all day, every day. The human brain can only handle so much loss, fear, and helplessness alone. Anger had become prevalent among the medical staff, outrage at the constant need to be separated from their own families while dealing with what they had to face on a daily basis, all the while watching as too many of their fellow humans ignored the warnings and conducted their lives as if nothing devastating were occurring across the world, let alone across in their own cities.

Vicki's mother and father had been living in a seniors' living facility when the virus hit, and when it had made its way into their seniors' home, they'd both been hit by the virus. And as Jeanette's symptoms had gotten worse, she'd had to be separated from her husband. When the facility went into lockdown, Vicki hadn't been able to visit her parents. It had been an overwhelming time for everyone involved, especially for Vicki and her siblings not being able to see either of their parents. Only staff could be there to comfort her father while he waited to see if his wife would get better or not. Tragically, we lost Jeanette, as she had not been able to fight the virus and had passed away before she could even get to the hospital for further medical help. The most heart wrenching thing had been that neither Vicki and her siblings nor her father were permitted to be with Jeanette during her final moments. To aid in giving some comfort, Archangel Michael had told Vicki that the Horseman, Zaqiel, had been at her mother's bedside, hidden from the staff, yet unveiled for Jeanette in the image of her loving husband. Michael had further shared these images with Vicki's father through a dream. Vicki's father had later told her about a dream, sharing how *'it had helped, and it had felt as though I had been with her'* he had said. Now that they are all up to date with their vaccines, Vicki and her siblings visit their father regularly. Though there are still a few precautions in place as you can never be too cautious with these types of things.

Last Christmas, due to the pandemic, we had not been able to see Redmond's parents, but they were happily on their way here now to celebrate Christmas with us this year. It's going on 3 years now since I have seen my brother, and I am way overdue to see my girlfriends as well. We all video chat of course, like most of the world has done, but we all agree it is no replacement for in-person contact. Everyone was missing everyone, the girls needed to spend more time with their grandparents, and Redmond and I were especially in need of some time with friends and the jovial comradery that came with it.

We'd been considering going up to Canada to see everyone between Christmas and New Year's, and if we went, this time it would be without the twins. The plan would be to be back for New Year's here with the girls and their grandparents, but it all still needed a bit of coordinating. Vicki's boyfriend Eric had generously offered to use his plane to come get us and fly us back, so we could celebrate our 10th anniversary together with the whole crew. And since we had all been looking for something, a reason to celebrate, and since we wouldn't all be together for Christmas, our anniversary seemed an excellent excuse to head north.

We'd all been up to Canada together several times over the years prior to the pandemic, but the last time we had *all* been together, meaning all of us from the gathering including Dunya and Mitra, plus the spouses and any extras in the *knowing*, had been at our wedding.

It had been a perfect day, a perfect wedding, though not in the way of having all the bells and whistles that typically accompanied a wedding. It was more in the fact we had chosen the perfect place and that we had our perfectly imperfect friends and family there with us.

We'd chosen to have it at the Fairchild Gardens, which I hadn't known prior to the gathering, that they even did that kind of event. It had been Redmond's suggestion; he'd looked into it around the same time he had proposed. The Cycad Vista Lawn option shown in the brochure had been the most appropriate choice of the available selection since the location culminated at the stunning Bailey Palm Glade which was closest to where the final events of the gathering had taken place. Redmond had especially liked the melodic description that had read, '*Listen as the Southeasterly winds rustle through the adjoining Rainforest's canopy to create the epitome of a tropical sound scape.*' I on the other hand, had liked the part about our journey as a couple commencing among the cycads '*whose beauty and other-worldliness represented billions of years of botanical wonder*'. It being the *other worldliness* part that had caught my attention, to be honest. Redmond's parents had generously offered to pay for everything since they had such a large family, and most had attended. His parents had asked that we add the *Evening Event Exclusivity*, which was a pricy upgrade. This addition gave you exclusive use of the garden, making sure we didn't have to share the day with any other wedding or event.

Redmond's family consisted of his mother's five siblings which comprised his mother's twin brother, two younger brothers who were a year apart, and the youngest two sisters, who were also twins, along with all their spouses, their children and their spouses, and any grandchildren. The lot of them took up one side of the aisle.

My friends and my brother James, plus our mutual friends, were on the other aisle, the bride's side. Some of Redmond's family helped to fill in the open spots on the bride's side and kept the seating from being one-side heavy.

Mac had helped pick the dress of course, and it was perfect too, being that it was simple yet elegant, and not overly girly. We'd opted for no bridesmaids or groomsmen, with the goal of not torturing any of our family or friends with wearing matching wedding party attire that they'd never wear again. I had chosen to go down the aisle on my own, though Luc had trained Raven to bring the rings up the aisle to us when instructed. And Nate, who we had found out during the planning of the wedding, was a licensed justice of the peace, and he had kindly offered to officiate our vows. He had ended the ceremony with a Native Indian Blessing,

> Listen to the wind, it talks.
> Listen to the silence, it speaks.
> Listen to your heart, it knows.

… which had made it feel even more official. We had danced and partied until the wee hours, the whole wedding and reception feeling like a dream then too. The memories of that day revisit me often, though that day had been the absolute opposite style of *dream* feeling, to the nightmare state I had just been woken from, and these the type of memories were not what I wanted lingering or revisiting me.

Pushing away the haunting imagery, I took a deep breath, savoring the fresh ocean air, reminding myself where I was. I turned my head to see the dogs resting calmly in what remained of the sun still on the deck. I checked my watch to find that 20 minutes had passed while I'd been sleeping. Redmond would be back with his parents anytime now I realized, and *still* I hadn't heard from Gabriel.

I knew I hadn't needed to yell for Gabriel earlier for him to hear me, since somehow it seemed he always knew when I needed him. I was envious of that ability and often wished I could do the same with my own daughters. But then again, he wasn't just my birthfather, was he? He was an Archangel who could disappear in a flash and travel upon the ether of the universe.

I sat up then on the couch planting my feet on the deck and took in another cleansing breath. *"Please tell me you have the answers,"* I breathed out, whispering to the universe.

Chapter 7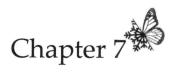

This time of the year is one of my favorites, and I especially love Christmas Eve the most, though on this night before Christmas, I was beyond furious at the fact that I still had not heard from nor had there been one single stirring from Gabriel.

On that same day as the encounter with Purah, when Redmond had arrived back with his parents, I'd brought him up to speed about my not-so-little visitor, but without any contact from Gabriel I'd been at a dead end for more details. I had wanted to tell the gang about what had happened, but Redmond convinced me not to say anything just yet, and that they didn't need this sort of news at Christmas, especially without more context. By the middle of the week, I had thought to call out for another, thinking perhaps Shamsiel might help, but then quickly realized that too would have been selfish of me to interrupt his time. It wasn't like I had much; a boy that was like me, and a giant that had said I was in danger—no biggy right? I didn't like not having the answers and Redmond knew it, but he had reminded me that there really wasn't anything I could do about it until Gabriel returned. Then with any luck, we would have the answers to all my questions, like who's kid is this little boy, what are these Earthbound, and who the hell is this, Thaddeus?

In the meantime, we'd spent the agonizing span of time waiting and filling the days with a combination of Christmas prep and family time out on the beach, so frankly, it wasn't exactly all bad. And as I had predicted, the girls had wanted to revisit doing the walks with me on the beach again. So, I took advantage of the time with them, knowing that all too soon it would be a struggle to get them to do much of anything with me.

When we'd first moved to the beach, I'd been nervous about the girls near the water. Our section of the beach has some very rough-wave months, though Redmond had enjoyed it because he'd been entertaining the idea of learning to surf. But watching and chasing after the girls as they ran headstrong into the water and in the path of crashing waves had frazzled my nerves and raised my stress meter to the limit. We'd gotten them swimming lessons early on, so they were proficient at that, but the girls were fearless. If their dad went in the water, they were going to go in too, no ifs-ands-or-buts about it. Redmond had said to me at that point, *"Let them go in. Let them get knocked down by the waves—I'll be right there."* I just about had a conniption at the idea, but then he'd added, *"They need to learn and respect the power of the water."* That's when I'd decided that my fear of water would not keep me on the beach. I had gone in with them, staying by Redmond while the twins learned these lessons. Wave after wave they got knocked down, then they scrambled up and away, but after each recovery they went at it again, battling the waves. It hadn't taken them long to get stronger, to handle themselves, and become more self-sufficient in the water. Redmond, who had been learning about surfing, had shown them how to dive into the wave's belly, lessening the impact. Redmond's parents were both experienced swimmers, so that too had added to my confidence with the girls in the water. And as the twins had gotten more skilled, I had become less afraid, and I had even started venturing out into the waves with them. If they could do this, then I could get over my fears. And I did. Though I much preferred just bobbing in the water amongst the waves, over taking the waves on like it was a game. I'd left that to Redmond and the girls—it was their thing.

This past week, with the roughness and the cold-water temperatures, it had only been Redmond who had ventured into the waves, and that was with the comfort of a wetsuit. The rest of us had hung out on the beach chatting and watching Redmond, along with Gavin—the girls' teacher, surf some *righteous* waves.

The girls continued to spend quality time with their grandparents, playing board games and watching movies in the evenings, while during the day they built sandcastles and collected shells on the beach. We'd spent one night out on the deck around the firepit, with Enzo and Nainseadh telling stories about Christmas when they were young. It had been a pleasant change of pace for Redmond's parents, relaxing at the beach house and taking in the serenity of the beach and the calmness of our small town versus the usual hustle and bustle of the big city of New York. Near the middle of the week, they'd helped the girls with wrapping gifts and the trimming of the tree.

We put the tree up a few weeks before, but we always wait to decorate it during the lead-up to Christmas. This year Redmond and I left it to his parents and the girls to work out the theme and design for the tree. They'd chosen to make this year's tree all about silver, blue, and *starfish*, as we'd snagged a slew of starfish ornaments at a yearly event held by the same shop, we'd gotten the ornament for the girls' teacher. Once the girls had been old enough to have an opinion on the theme of the tree, we'd made a point to change it each year, with their help. But the one thing that always remained the same was the angel that went on the very top. It was a craft style homemade looking representation of an angel, having its base structure composed of a cardboard cone for the body, a Styrofoam ball head, and white pipe cleaners shaped for the wings. The whole structure was covered in a straw-coloured soft hemp thread and was trimmed around the bottom of the cone and wings with a thicker gold coloured, slightly metallic looking string. It had a very earthy natural look and feel, and I loved it. I don't remember where it came from, but it had been Mom's and it was one of the few ornaments that I still had of hers. I was always open to the themes, it didn't really matter to me as long as the girls enjoyed doing it, but this angel was the one thing I insisted I got to place on the tree once the rest was done.

Last night we'd ventured out to the beach with beach chairs and cozy blankets, along with the fixings to make s'mores by the bonfire. Redmond and his dad had set up the portable firepit earlier in the day, and we considered this more a winter tradition than a Christmas one, since we partook in s'more making several times during the colder months. We found that this type of activity allowed us more family time and got the girls away from the TV that was often a time sucker in the evenings.

Christmas Eve for our little family was always Christmas movie time, and when we all got to eat dinner in the living room using TV-tables. It was something I had always loved as a kid myself as it had felt like a treat to eat in front of the TV. For Christmas Eve dinner, we'd adopted for my mother's tradition of having homemade French onion soup, plus it was something that Redmond and I always made *together*. I'd shared the tradition with him on our 2nd Christmas together and it had become part of our own tradition ever since. Of course, being the skilled cook that Redmond is, he had changed up my lazy method of using packaged soup for the base, to doing the full prep and cooking with the onions and other ingredients to make the soup. We still used the freshly grated extra old cheese and toasted baguette rounds for the topping, but I had to admit his recipe for the soup part, really was the tastier way to go.

Prior to dinner, we had all exchanged our regular clothing for our holiday season themed pajamas, including Nana and Poppy. Then before digging in, and as they had done over the past several years, the girls got on Redmond's laptop to video chat with their Uncle James. Their enjoyment came from seeing him and telling him they were having their traditional *Gramma Sal's* soup and they always asked him if he was having it too. It was the sweetest thing to hear and watch them banter back and forth together with their Uncle James. Redmond and I make a point to chat with him every couple of weeks and have done so since the girls were born. Redmond and he always talk about two subjects: classic music and house repairs. My dialog with him was usually about the goings on where he lived, now that we were both living in small towns.

"Merry Christmas," we all said to James, a jumbled union of voices of the six of us crowded in view of the laptop's camera.

"Merry Christmas," James said back. "Love you guys."

"Love you too," we all tossed back, along with the girls blowing him kisses.

"Enjoy your soup," he added, lifting his soupspoon up in view of his camera.

"You too," I said, "I'll check in on the weekend." Then we ended our call and returned to our places in front of the TV to eat.

It had been a very full week for all of us, and even the dogs were exhausted. The two of them were sprawled out on the floor next to the couch where the girls sat. With everyone finished their meals, the girls were now cuddled together with their grandparents under blankets and were watching their second Christmas movie of the evening.

Redmond and I were in the kitchen tidying up the dishes when I heard the front door open. I already knew who it was without looking, plus anyone else would have had the dogs up and barking.

"It's a wonderful life—great movie. That Clarence—what a character he is," I heard Gabriel's familiar voice say then. He knew the code for the keyless entry on all the doors into the house, and he also knew to use it when making an entrance when those *not* in the knowing were present. We hadn't brought Redmond's parents in on things, what with them being up in New York City most of the time. And as for Gabriel being in our lives, well, explaining him had actually been easier than I'd anticipated, though we'd had to lie a bit.

We'd had to explain his presence when the girls had started mentioning him. I'd explained to Nainseadh and Enzo that with me being adopted and now having my own children, that I had wanted to learn more about my heritage. And in doing so, I had taken a DNA test as part of one of those ancestry history tracking websites. The story we had come up with was that I'd gotten a fairly quick response regarding the results, and that it had shown a close match, a birth relative on my birthfather's side. There was no way of explaining who Gabriel really was, especially with his youngish appearance, so instead we had gone with the consideration that we were cousins at best, because there were no other details available, and that whatever the biological connect, we were each thrilled to have a birth relative in our lives. This had helped to explain the striking resemblance between us as well, though as part of Gabriel's story, he had indicated that he too had been adopted, and that like me, he knew basically nothing about his birth family. This lack of direction and details had luckily kept any further questioning about our birth family at bay.

Nainseadh and Enzo had accepted the tale, and since then they have become quite fond of Gabriel. They are always happy to see him and now consider him part of their family as well. They also appreciated how well he got on with the twins.

"Guuuup!" the girls squealed, leaping up from their spots on the couch and racing to greet him in the front hallway.

"Nainseadh, Enzo—so wonderful to see you both," Gabriel said, sending out his salutations through hugs with the girls. "Lynn, Redmond—Merry Christmas, all," he added when Redmond and I rounded the corner from the kitchen. He nodded at me then, quickly hiding the guilty expression that had briefly marred his handsome features.

"Merry Christmas—to you," Redmond said, leaning past the girls to give Gabriel a quick embrace and pat on the back. Redmond went and took up residence on the adjacent couch, as Gabriel guided the girls back to their spots on the couch. Then he went and placed several gift bags next to the Christmas tree. "What have you watched so far tonight," Gabriel asked, directing his inquiry at the girls.

I stood at the perimeter of the living room, watching as Gabriel sat down on the couch then, leaving an open space between him and Redmond.

"Elf," Redmond said, answering the question for them.

I love that movie, Redmond not so much. His favorite has always been *A Christmas Story*, which for whatever reason plays 24 hours around the clock at this time of year. It's an okay movie, but I can only watch a kid stick his tongue to a metal pole so many times. When I was a kid growing up in Canada, it was a common occurrence around the school yard in winter. Guaranteed, each year there would be one gullible kid bullied into doing it.

Redmond patted the seat beside him indicating for me to come join the movie watching, but I remained where I was watching them, pretending to dry my hands with the dishtowel I'd grabbed from off the counter.

"Where have you been?" I asked Gabriel, stepping forward to where he sat on the couch. I eyed his festive outfit that consisted of red flannel pajama bottoms that had candy canes all over them, and a matching red thermal long-sleeved shirt that had one big candy cane in the center.

He grinned up at me from where he sat. "You like?" he asked, pointing both his thumbs at his shirt.

I could feel my anger rising. "I've been calling you all week. *Calling out for you,*" I added, under my breath.

"Oh, you know—work has been crazy, but I wanted to drop off a few Christmas gifts for my—the family, before I had to get back at it."

"How goes the work with the foundation?" Enzo asked then. Along with the DNA storyline, we had given Gabriel a career cover story, one where he worked with a privately funded organization that assisted children in need of special care, those that couldn't afford the expense.

"I'm working on a difficult project, actually," Gabriel said, "and as a matter of fact, I wanted to tap Lynn's brain for help regarding a few details on a new case. She has all that insight from her old job with working at the hospital. And I have a few computer-related challenges I need her assistance with." He gave me an innocent grin.

"We can talk privately on the deck," I said in response, turning back towards the kitchen. I tossed the dishtowel on the kitchen counter on the way to the sliding glass door that led out to the back deck.

"Don't goooowaaa," Ryley and Hayley protested, when Gabriel got up off the couch to head my way.

"You'll stay and watch the movies with us after—won't you Gabriel," their Nana added, beaming up at him.

"I would love to," he said, flashing his radiant smile back at her. "I'll be right back," Gabriel assured the twins, giving each a little tug and tickle of their earlobes as he passed by.

I gave Redmond a nod, before grabbing up one of the quilts from the blanket box near the door, then I proceeded out to the deck behind Gabriel.

Once we were both out on the deck and behind the cone of silence that was the hurricane rated glass sliding doors, I wrapped myself up in the quilt. Then I asked Gabriel again where he had been, though this time I'd used a few curse words to emphasize my upset. "I can't believe you left me hanging for a week—do you have any idea what happened while you were out doing your investigating?" I blew out an irritated breath.

Gabriel gave me a shocked expression and just shook his head in return at my outburst.

"I had a visitor while you were gone—and why couldn't you at least pop in for two minutes after I called for you?" I said, continuing my rant.

He shook his head again, and then said, "I was with the others—discussing the child." He glanced over his shoulder as if checking to see that all eyes and ears were busy with the movie. "What do you mean you had a visitor—who?"

"First tell me what you found out about the little boy," I said, blowing out another breath. I crossed my arms and the ends of the blanket over my chest, waiting for his response.

Gabriel blew out his own breath of frustration. "Well, I spoke to the twins' teacher," he started to say.

"What—why?" I cut in, tightening my crossed arms.

"Don't worry—I made it sound as though the girls had been asking about him."

"Sorry," I said, relaxing my arms a bit, realizing I was spoiling the whole Christmas Eve vibe with my impatience.

"No—I'm sorry I didn't come sooner, but I was trying to get clear answers before sharing what I found." Gabriel slid into one of the two high-top Adirondack chairs that faced out to the beach. "I went first to speak to Michael and the others—to inform them of what had occurred at the school with the girls."

"Do they know whose kid he is?" I asked, fully expecting to hear that some angel had risked putting their soul on the line.

He shook his head *no*.

"Then where did this kid come from? Were you able to get any intel on his parents?" A new frustration was beginning to set in. With the quilt still wrapped around me, I slid into the high-top chair next to him.

"The teacher told me that the mother died in childbirth—father is unknown. His grandparents have been taking care of him since. Apparently, he is unwell. They've taken him back up to New York for treatment—they won't be coming back." He rested an elbow on the arm of the chair, then leaned his chin against the knuckles of his balled up hand.

"Any chance his mother was a descendant—or one of his grandparents for that matter?"

"All descendants have been accounted for and there have been no Nephilim born since the 200 Fallen, other than you. We hadn't considered there were any unidentified descendants of celestials out there."

"What do you mean?" I asked, rubbing the corner of the blanket against my cold nose.

"Do you remember me telling you about the Seraphim?"

"Yes—they monitor the earth and its environment," I said, shifting in my chair to look at him.

"I spoke to one of them… about the boy," he said, glancing my way before turning his attention back to the moonlit ocean.

"And?"

"He was able to trace the boy's history and bloodline."

"And what—the boy is the offspring of one of the Seraphim?"

"Not exactly… but we believe his father is one of the Earthbound," Gabriel said.

There was that word again, *earthbound*. "Speaking of unidentified celestials," I said. "What kind of being wears battle armor?"

"A Steward was here—in the yard?" Gabriel's eyes bulged out of their sockets. "Did they see you?"

"Well—ya, I spoke with her," I said. Gabriel fidgeted in his seat as I went on to explain the extremely puzzling visitation that I'd had the week prior.

"Had she spoken with anyone else prior—who else knows she was here?" he asked, blowing a breath upwards so hard it rustled his bangs.

I shook my head. "Not that I know of—why? And why is she not supposed to come down to Earth?" She had been so nervous about being there and her message had been awfully cryptic. Now Gabriel was showing signs of alarm. "Should I be worried—am I really in danger? And who is Thaddeus?" I asked, leaning forward, feeling my nerve endings tingle.

Gabriel drew in a long breath, then let it out in an equally long exhale. "He's one of the Earthbound from Pleiades—the Seraphim who were cast down."

"Why—I don't understand," I said, moving my hands outside the blanket to rest on my lap. He hadn't given me any great details prior about these particular angels.

Gabriel reached over and patted one of my hands. "It was an unfortunate set of circumstances," he began. Then he went on to explain how some Pleiades had grown impatient with tending to Earth. How a small few wanted Earth for themselves and wanted to make humans serve them. Not all were content with the way things were organized on the stars, and a small faction of them had chosen to rebel against the traditions. "It had been Thaddeus who had led the rebellion, but when it was discovered that he and his followers were up to no good, Purah and the other six Stewards sent the rebels down to Earth—for good."

"Why didn't you tell me this before?" I sighed and leaned back into my chair.

"We've known about Thaddeus and the others—for some time, but we hadn't worried about them, because there were others on Earth assigned to watch them. Leo, the one I spoke with, has been watching him for the last 6 years—since they found he had set up shop in Ottawa."

"Yer telling me this Thaddeus—Seraph—angel—whatever, is in Ottawa—and you didn't think it was something I should know about?" I turned to look directly at him, squinting as if it would make what he had said clearer.

"We didn't think it was something you needed to be concerned about. And, yes, it's one of the locations he has been seen at."

"But now you think I should be concerned? How many more offspring are there?"

"It is unknown. Like you, they are hard to detect," he said, glancing my way again. "I'll look into this further—but I'm sure there is nothing to be concerned about," he added, patting my hand again.

But I wasn't buying it. "Wait—let me get this straight," I said, turning my upper body to look at him again as if it would help. "This Thaddeus is one of these Earthbound. And that means what, exactly—that he's an angel who can't leave Earth?"

"There is more to it than that—but essentially, yes," Gabriel said, nodding.

"What does he do now that he's on Earth—in Ottawa? Just pop around, back and forth to these other locations?" I asked, though not really sure how the information would help me.

"It seems he had done considerable planning prior to his casting down," Gabriel said. "To the humans of this world he appears to be the third-generation owner of an organization, with facilities in six other locations around the world. He has humans believing his organization helps sick kids, that they do research and testing in order to find cures for childhood diseases. But what he is really doing—no one knows, though you can be assured it's not helping anyone but himself."

Memories suddenly flashed across my brain like images on a movie screen.

"What is it?" Gabriel asked, catching the expression of conjecture that must have crossed my face.

"My dream," I said, remembering the images of the testing lab, from my dream when I'd dozed off on the deck. "I need to call my friends—there's definitely more going on here."

Chapter 8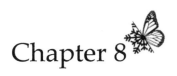

It had been ridiculous of me to think I could coordinate a video call I realized; it was Christmas Eve after all.

So, while Gabriel returned to the happy movie watching, I brought Redmond with me to our bedroom, faking that we had a few more Christmas presents to wrap—which we did, but used the opportunity to apprise him of what Gabriel had shared with me. When I'd finished, Redmond admitted that he too had been eager to get answers from Gabriel, but he had not wanted to feed my impatience with his own. We were both feeling a bit better having more information from Gabriel, but Redmond knew that this vivid dream of mine coupled with the now tingling sensation that was circling my neck and poking at the base of my cervical spine, was more than just a little unease. Like me, he knew the others needed to hear this information, and he suggested we send off a quick email to everyone.

I composed an email stating that we had some interesting *angel* news to share, and could we organize a video chat in the next few days. Then for the rest of the evening, I did my best to keep my brain from buzzing and allowed myself to enjoy this time with my family.

After the fourth movie of the night ended, it was now bedtime for the girls. They had requested to sleep in the same bed for just tonight, so we tucked the two of them in bed in Ryley's room, where Gabriel read them the traditional *Night Before Christmas* story. And then after, "… and too all a goodnight" and several "goodbyes" to Gabriel, it was off to bed for the rest of us.

* * *

It was now Christmas morning, and the responses to my email had started to come in shortly after we had finished opening presents.

Luc's response was first, and he'd emailed saying that he was doing Christmas dinner over at his sister's place, and that he would circle back around on Boxing Day for the scoop.

Darius too had sent a message explaining he couldn't do a video chat, but only because he was going to be in Miami at his mom's house for the night. We all knew how much he loved his mom, though she hated anything technical and didn't even have internet. And we also knew for an IT guy, that the real thorn in his side wasn't the lack of internet, it was more about her not wanting him to be on any of his *gadgets* while he was there visiting her.

Following coffee and breakfast, I received another response, this one from Mac, stating that she wouldn't be available either, as they were having the whole crew over for dinner. With Mac's three older siblings and their spouses, plus all the nieces and nephews, and the fact that her two boys were now 16 and 14 years old, they had quickly outgrown their starter home. And with their homelife being all about family and gatherings, they had moved into a newer larger one, two blocks over from where Olivia and her family lived. I could only imagine what a great treat it would be for Mac to have them all together and especially after the past year of separation they had been under.

While the girls and Nainseadh worked on one of the puzzles Gabriel had gotten the family, and while Redmond and his father worked on our Christmas dinner, I proceeded with cleaning up the boxes, ribbons, and wrapping paper from the day's gift-exchanging and unwrapping.

Following our fabulous dinner, and as the girls along with their Nana and Poppy all with full bellies, rested in front of the TV watching, yes—*A Christmas Story*, Redmond and I took the opportunity then to take the recycling and garbage downstairs and out to the bins in the carport. Frankly, I would do this any day over having to watch that movie again—but you wouldn't catch me telling anyone that.

We stood under the dim carport lighting and in the reflection of the coloured Christmas lights that ran up the rails of the outside staircase, taking in the night air. Redmond wrapped his arms around me for warmth and pulled me in close as we listened to the *almost* quiet evening. The neighbor across the way had a life-size animatronic Santa whose arms moved up and down, that he set out on his upper balcony during the week between Christmas and New Year's, and it played several familiar Christmas songs that ran on repeat. I heard then the jolly sound of Santa's voice as he said the "Ho, Ho, Ho, Merry Christmas," that always ended the loop of songs. The girls loved it, and they always got excited when the neighbor put it out each year. At first, I had thought it was kind of creepy with it looking so much like a real person, but now I kind of enjoyed it.

"Ho, Ho, Ho," I said, tilting my head back and grinning up at my wonderful husband.

To which he responded, "Merry Christmas, my love." Then he gave me one of those kisses that you don't do in front of family.

"Someone's phone was making chiming noises," Enzo said, when we came back up through the door from the lower level.

"Must be yours," Redmond said, patting the phone in his back pocket.

"Thank you," I said to Enzo, snatching up my phone from the kitchen island. It had been *four* chimes I noted checking my email. The others, Vicki, Olivia, Alison, and Derek had all written back confirming that they would be available early evening following Christmas dinners with their families. Apparently, they had conferred with each other earlier on a time and had picked 8 p.m. to get online. Which waaasss… 10 minutes from now.

After our exchange of season's greetings with the others, and as Redmond sat side-by-side with me in view of the camera, I gave our captive video-chat audience a recap of what had happened; with the girls at school, the gladiator-like female who had visited me, and the follow-up that Gabriel had shared. "And this *Seraph* — Thaddeus — whatever, he and his followers, who were cast down permanently to Earth, I'm pretty sure this organization of his is nowhere near aboveboard," I said, ending my summary of the angel update on a skeptical note.

"I've got it all down, Lynn," Alison said jotting down the last of the details in her latest notebook. She had been keeping a record of everything that had happened from and since the gathering, angel related mainly. The original codex, the *Book of Balance*, she had placed in a security box at her bank and the safest place we could come up with. She kept the notebooks until each was full, further transcribing her writing onto a computer, and then saved to a heavily fortified drive that Derek had devised for her. Each of her notebooks was then shredded and burned once her notes were protected.

"Are you really in danger?" Olivia asked, displaying her worried-mom face. Once a mother—always a mother, and I was quite familiar with that sentiment now.

"Where are the girls," I asked, instead of answering her question. Her daughters are both in their 20s now—and it kills me to even think of them as being all grown up. Her youngest, Rachel is 24 and a registered practical nurse at the same hospital where Olivia works. They have both been in the thick of it since the virus hit. Olivia's oldest, Katherine—Kate, is 26 and works currently as an analyst for the training and development team at the University of Ottawa and has only recently returned to working back in the office.

"Rachel had to work—poor thing. Kate is still over, she's watching a movie with her dad," Olivia said. The girls had both been living at home with their parents until recently, but mainly because of the virus situation, like many families had done with the college-age kids doing their studies remotely. Kate had just bought a small garden home in one of the housing divisions a block over from her parents, and Rachel was planning to rent a house next month, one close to work and with two other nurses. "I told Mike I'd give him the details after the movie." She gave us a wink. Her daughters were not in the *knowing*, though they did suspect that something was different about their mom. They had assumed it was just newfound confidence—and it was, but since the mothers-and-daughters balance thing was no longer an issue, Olivia had thought it best to keep the details about her new skills at a need-to-know level. Right now, they both had a lot on their grownup plates, and she felt they did *not* need to know.

"All quiet on the home front then, eh? Wonderful, blissful," Vicki said in response to Olivia. "I love my family—but too many people in one room gets rough on the nerves—oh and the noise." She massaged the edges of her ears. She had attended a big family dinner at her brother's home across town. Like Mac, Vicki had three siblings, but all younger than her, and they all had spouses and several children, some of whom were now grown and had boyfriends and girlfriends, which again like Mac, made for a sizeable gathering.

"Oh Redmond, Lynn—I'm so thrilled the twins' grandparents were able to come down for Christmas," Alison said, her cheeks bunching into a smile. Despite her smile I knew Alison was feeling the loss of her parents during the holidays again this year. She'd lost her father only 4 years ago, and I'm guessing because of the bond her son had had with him, he'd also be feeling the loss similarly. Alison's husband, Ken, came into view then. He was wearing a grey t-shirt with Santa and his sleigh on it, but instead of traditional reindeer pulling it, the sleigh was tethered to a rocket ship. He gave us a gentle smile and a silent wave back.

I smiled, and I gave him the peace sign, then attempting to circle back around to Olivia's question, and said, "Well, as for the danger, Liv…." I chewed the corner of my lower lip. "… it was the Steward who suggested as much—but Gabriel is not sure why she would say that or why she felt the need to come to me directly." I rubbed my forehead. "Until we get more facts—I'm gonna try not to think about it," I added, running the charms of my necklace back and forth along its chain. The necklace had been a gift from Redmond on our first Christmas together, and it was one of my favorite things that he'd ever given me—next to the twins of course. I adored the sentiment of the tiny butterfly charm in honor of my mom, coupled with the XO kiss and hug symbol which signified good friendship. But the running it back and forth, that had become a nervous tell of mine, and Redmond knew it.

"Hey, check out my Christmas gift from the twins," Redmond said then, lightening the mood, stretching out the bottom of the latest vintage t-shirt he had gotten. It was a pale blue one with a surfer and the 'Hang Ten' footprint logo on it.

"Nice!" Derek tossed out, "I love a good vintage style tee." He too was an aficionado of t-shirts that displayed old-school and pop culture references. He had been especially appreciative of Redmond's Mr. Bubble t-shirt, and he often wore t-shirts along similar lines, though today he wore a simple navy button-down shirt, and most likely because he'd just had Christmas dinner over at his parents' place.

"I should work on a few designs like that," Ken said. After the payout from their investment in Derek's company, Ken had dropped his IT gig as a Senior Network Analyst and was now doing his dream job as a 3D Animator. He was quite the innovative artist, so he appreciated a quality graphic t-shirt as well.

"Yes—just what he needs, another t-shirt," I said, rolling my eyes. But I liked them too, and I had helped the girls pick this one out for their dad.

Vicki laughed. "What's the count now?" she asked.

"I've lost count," Redmond said, smoothing out his shirt and leaning over to kiss me on my cheek.

"I can't count that high." I chuckled, shaking my head, though it had been well timed comical relief on Redmond's part.

"Well, I have nothing in response to that," Vicki said, fighting another laugh. "But what I *can* tell you, is that I'm happy to be home where it's quiet." She still travelled some for her job, but since the pandemic she had been doing most of her work remotely, plus the need for translation services has died down due to the impact on the international economy. Over the past 10 years she's honed her translation skills by learning to speak several languages. She has a new beau too, Eric Weber. They met that first year after the gathering at an event Vicki had been attending for work. He's multilingual like she is, and he speaks German, English, French, some Russian and Polish. When Alison had found out about him speaking that many languages, she had beamed at the opportunity to use one of her newfound words, naming them the *hyperpolyglot* couple, meaning that they had both mastered six or more different languages.

"Here, here," Alison said, in response to Vicki's need for peace and quiet. With all the time she had spent in Ottawa that year leading up to the gathering, and then following the death of her father in 2017, she had found herself homesick again. Thus, in 2018, after 23 years of her living out west, she and Ken sold their home, packed up their belongings, and moved to Ottawa. And with Alison having the need to be closer to the ladies, they had found a great home in Barrhaven.

"I second that," Ken said, following his wife's sentiment. He still had a big extended family in Calgary that they had traveled to and from to see over the past few years, though despite the pandemic limitations this year, they had actually enjoyed a quiet Christmas at home with just the three of them.

"So, Gabriel believes this little guy might be the offspring of one of these star angels?" Alison asked then.

I glanced over to the wall of framed photos of our family and friends, focusing specifically on the one of Alison holding baby Kevin. He had almost never been born—being that he was born as a result of their *last* try at fertility treatments. He turned 10 this past April and from the get-go he's been a fast learner, one of his first spoken words was *"zipper"* of all things, and he has been doing French immersion schooling. For a kid his age, he has a fascinating take on life too. He had only been 6 years old at the time of his grandfather passing, and never having met his grandmother, he had said to his mother, *"Now he can take care of Bubby again,"* in reflect of his grandparents being reunited. It had given Alison a simple gift of peace with his perceptive words. Time passes fast and even faster when you're watching your kids grow, and those extraordinary circumstances regarding him are two I will never forget.

"Are they even permitted to do that?" Ken asked, pulling my attention back to the conversation on offspring.

I drew in a breath. "I'm not sure what the deal is on that," I said, letting my breath out in a *sigh*.

"Gabriel had been given special dispensation when it came to you, Lynn," Derek stated. "He'd had to ask for permission, and his request had been given certain stipulations."

"Who would risk the punishment, if it wasn't allowed?" Olivia asked, her steadfast concern for others shining through.

"Are the Seraphim like those Sanctuary Angels?" Vicki asked.

"Those are The Watchers, the ones who currently reside in the realm known as Sanctuary, and they are the advocates of The Fallen Watchers—those like Shamsiel, the other leaders, and the rest of the 200 Fallen," Alison said, refreshing the details for us. "They're a select group of angels, aided by Archangel Zadkiel." She grinned proudly at her recollection of the few details we had on this select group of angels.

We had discovered that as part of Alison's gifts as Vretil's descendant, she could not only remember details from memory after only seeing something once, but she also had an eidetic recall of high precision on things she hadn't been present for, and with things we'd only told her about. She could recite the details, as if she could see it in her head.

"I can sense these Sanctuary angels—and they can sense and find each other," I said. "I met one of them once, remember? He's the same Watcher that the Purah had referred to." It had been two years ago, Christmas 2019, when we'd taken the girls to see their grandparents in New York City for the holidays. The twins and I had sensed him. Though, once he revealed himself to Redmond, I had sent Redmond and the girls to go look at the Macy's shop windows again, so I could speak with him privately. His interest had been about the fact that the girls and I *could* sense and see him while he'd been veiled. I had asked Gabriel about him afterwards, and he had shared more details about their existence, about a war fought in support of The Fallen 200, about the gift they had been granted by Archangel Zadkiel, and the fact that they had been given the capability to have offspring, though they all resided in Sanctuary I'd been told. "During my brief conversation with this angel, I'm assuming that one of these Earthbound must have somehow spotted me speaking to him. I don't recall sensing another, but then I was caught up in my dialog with this Watcher," I said, chewing the corner of my lip again.

Gabriel and the other Archangels, along with Shamsiel and The Horseman, had given us all a thorough education on the history and hierarchy of their mostly unseen world. We had learned about the different castes of angels, the distinct roles, and the realms they functioned in, as well as what this cast of characters were up to in these modern days. The human documentation had it wrong it seemed. People had an interesting way of doing that with human history as well. For example, there were no baby angels like cherubs, only those that resembled grown humans, albeit extraordinarily beautiful male and female likenesses of human beings. The more practiced religions had had things fairly well defined, but none knew the real deal, the true details. Although, anytime one of us broached the subject of the afterlife, was there a god, or how any of us or the angels were created, those questions had swiftly been thwarted, and we'd been told that this knowledge was strictly prohibited for humans to know. We couldn't even get them to nod or shake their heads to questions on the topics.

Gabriel had made mention of other angels here and there, and some of the roles they played, like those of the Amulet Angels who I knew watched over childbirth. Among the grouping of angels there were the *Archangels,* the *Seraphim* from Pleiades—we'd just learned more about, and *The Watchers,* which comprised two subgroups, the original Fallen 200 and the Sanctuary Angels. All others fell into that of *common* Angels. And there was no chain of command. It was more like titles and responsibilities, the only hierarchy being that of the Archangels being above the rest. All the others were grouped based on their roles. The Archangels we were all reasonably familiar with, for obvious reasons, though we'd found out that there were actually *ten* Archangels in total, not seven as we'd found in our earlier research. We had also become quite familiar with The Fallen Leaders, Shamsiel and The Horsemen: Zaqiel, Baraqel, Azazel, and Kokabiel, more specifically.

"Why can't the Archangels find these Earthbound?" Derek asked.

I shook my head and shrugged. "Gabriel and the others can sense and find each other—can recognize their essences, so to speak," I said.

"Like with Lynn, they knew something was divine in nature there," Redmond shared. "They can also sense all the other angels including the Seraphim."

"Gabriel said that Seraphim can sense and find each other, but those who were cast down—they can't, for some reason," I added.

"The Fallen 200 can sense and find each other," Vicki said.

"Yes—but they were not cast down permanently to Earth, like these others," I reminded. "Maybe that has something to do with it." I pursed my lips and rubbed my jaw.

"For the most part, it seems that these groups tend to govern themselves—with the occasional Archangels playing a role in granting assistance. Most are watching over humans, some are actively aiding the Earth, but none are really dishing out punishment to their own kind or to humans that we know of," Derek said, his eyebrows rising up.

I was confident we didn't know all there was to know about them. Who could know a millennium of angel lore, well, other than the keepers of the knowledge? We had asked lots of questions in the beginning, and we'd been given answers. Some of it we didn't quite grasp, but mostly the information given had been enough to satisfy nearly all our little brains. Derek on the other hand, his big brain had needed more, and he had spent a great deal of time with Kokabiel, his Horseman ancestor, grilling the angel hard.

"So, *Star of God*—what did Santa bring you for Christmas?" I asked Derek, teasing, using the associated meaning to the name of his Horseman designate. Derek had let his hair grow even longer, past his shoulders, after selling his company. And to get his brain out of work mode and into fun again, he had set up a home studio to play and record music. He, Luc, and Redmond had all bonded over music in the years following the gathering. Derek had also bought himself a beautiful traditional Southern style home on the water in South Carolina, just outside of town to stay close to his folks who still lived in the area. He was still a bachelor, but I had hope for him now that he wasn't spending 150% of his time working. He'd started traveling the world, coming to visit us more, and Luc and his clan. He had even taken a couple trips up to visit with the ladies in Ottawa a few times before the pandemic had hit and forced all of us to stay close to home.

"If you must ask," Derek said, wriggling in his seat like an excited child. "I got the coolest guitar accessory as a Christmas gift from myself.

"Oh man—*whadyouget?*" Redmond asked, practically salivating at the possibilities.

"Wait for it," Derek said, reaching to the side of his desk. "May I present to you the tool that emulates all kinds of the history's greatest—rarest, and most used amps and effects all in one easy-to-use box...," he brought a small rectangular button-filled board up to his face, "... the *Kemper Profiler Stage*," he announced, doing a Vanna White movement along the bottom of the unit with his free hand.

"Yes!" Redmond shot out. "It works great live and for recording." Redmond rubbed his palms together several times. "You can build rigs just like Hendrix or Jimmy Page to get their classic tone or build your own rig and perfect your own new tone."

"A *rig*—being a setup of the amp, speaker cabinet and effects boxes to achieve a desired set of guitar tones...," Derek began to explain, for all of us none instrument players.

"I know what a *rig* is, Derek. Married to a musician—remember," I said, poking Redmond in the side.

"But Lynn, you don't understand," Derek continued, "the tones range from clean sounds to heavy distortion—and all the special effects like reverbs and delays. With this unit—all the world's gear is available in one package for the user to mix and match...."

"Okay, I get it—I get it," I interrupted again.

Redmond tightened his lips, as if trying not to laugh.

Derek gave a grin and chin tilt directed at Redmond.

And Redmond nodded his silent agreement to talk music gear later.

"Hrrrmm—sorry, uhhh—back to the Pleiades," Derek grumbled then. He cleared his throat. "The brightest stars of the Pleiades are named for the Seven Sisters of Greek mythology: Sterope, Merope, Electra, Maia, Taygeta, Celaeno, and Alcyone."

"They live on the stars?" Olivia asked, fiddling with one of her dangly earrings.

"Gabriel explained it like this," I said. "Their world is composed of seven Havens, the seven stars closest to Earth—the names Derek just mentioned. The host of angels is composed of those somewhat like The Watchers, but the role of these angels, is to manage Earth—its ecosystem, not watch over its people." I nodded when no one interrupted, and then I went on. "There is a Steward for each star, and on each star, 200 Seraphim reside. The space they inhabit is mostly made up of light and energy, and they basically just rest until needed. They function in pairs with specialized responsibilities for aiding the Earth, its element, minerals and compounds, as well as its non-human inhabitants from the smallest microorganism all the way up to the largest animal."

"Okay," Olivia said, blinking a few times, though I'm not sure she was quite sure of the info.

"Pairs—Got it—Check," Alison said, finishing her latest note.

"But what about the ones who were cast down," Vicki asked, her expression in contrast to her normal skepticism and more like that of a child who was being read a story.

It made me grin.

"What?" Vicki asked, catching me smiling.

"Nothing—I just love your interest," I said, smiling again at my once upon a time, skeptic's curiosity. "Gabriel said there was discourse among the Seraphim, and that the leader of this rebellion along with thirteen of his followers, had started visiting Earth on a regular basis. And apparently prior to that even, the leader had established some kind of organization—the one he claims is a research center for sick kids. Though Gabriel was told that this leader had been working on some plan for much longer than that it seems.

"Told by who," Alison asked, looking up from her notetaking.

"That's the other thing—Gabriel said that there are Seraphim on Earth watching them. One of them, Leo—he said his name was, has been keeping an eye on the leader in Ottawa for the past 6 years.

"Do you know if you can sense these Earthbound or the Pleiades angels—whatever?" Derek asked.

"You need to meet with one of them," Ken suggested. "Couldn't this Leo come see you there?"

"I'd rather go up to Ottawa and meet him, see that building—this research center." The anticipation of it made my heart pound faster in my chest.

"I know you guys were considering coming up here and all—for your anniversary, and heaven knows we could use something more to celebrate, but do you think that's wise, to go where he is—where they are, I mean?" Olivia asked, her hands fidgeting with both her earrings now.

"He has other locations, so this isn't the only place he could be. Besides, no one would dare come near me with my big strong husband at my side," I said, rubbing my hand over Redmond's shoulder. "And Gabriel will hopefully be around."

"Besides—it's already decided. We're coming," Redmond announced. We had discussed the possibility with Redmond's parents days prior to their coming down, and we'd confirmed with them last night after the girls had fallen asleep.

"Great!" Vicki hollered. "I'll let Eric know when he gets back. He's off making a last-minute Christmas meal delivery to the children's hospital for the staff that have to work the holiday." She made a quick check of her phone. "He'll be so excited to come down to get you guys."

"Did I just hear my name," Eric's voice sounded then, though he was out of sight of the camera. "Are we firming up your pickup time and return," Erik asked, his face coming into view over Vicki's shoulder. Eric currently owns and runs what we'd deemed as an ad-hoc air taxi service; people basically hire him and his private jet for various excursions. Where they lived was close enough to the airport for his business but far enough that the planes didn't get on your nerves. Eric's private jet business had not been impacted the same as the commercial airlines, mainly because of the limited number of people per flight allowed on these planes. Important and wealthy people still needed to get places it seemed, although the demand was still slower than in past years. And we had been granted an open invitation to get picked up and brought to Ottawa anytime.

"Hey, taxi any famous rockers lately?" Redmond asked. Eric had started his career in the German air force where he learned to fly. Then he'd left that career to be a private pilot for a famous German rock band. He had been married to his high school sweetheart when he was a pilot, but they never had kids, and surprise-surprise the marriage hadn't survived the rock star entourage days.

"Not lately, no. Just some jolly old fella in a red suit with a long white beard—who needed a lift," he joked, wiggling his eyebrows up and down.

We all laughed at that, though I'd been sure I had met a similar looking fellow once upon a time ago at Christmas.

"Okay, crew. I'll update Luc and Darius tomorrow," Derek said, flashing his new music toy once again across the screen in front of his face.

"I want one," Redmond said with a whine.

"Shortcut—out," Derek added with a wave.

"Later, Derek," I said, tossing him a peace sign as he logged off. "Alison—Ken, you guys good?" I asked then.

"Rodger—Spookeralla," Alison said, giving me the thumbs up.

"Yup," Ken added, giving us his own thumbs up before logging them off.

"And I'll get with Mac—get her up to speed *and* get her to help me look into this kids' research center place," Olivia said. "I think I know the one." She gave a wink and then signed off.

"You guys work out the logistics for your trip up here," Vicki said, "I need to get organized and get your room ready. We'll talk more face-to-face when you get here." Vicki waved and then she was out of view of the camera, leaving us with Eric's cheerful face grinning back at us.

Chapter 9

The Celaeno Building, Midnight, December 25th, Ottawa, Canada

"Call from Marcus," a soft-spoken male voice announced through a hidden overhead speaker, followed by a chiming sound indicating a phone call was coming in.

Thaddeus paused his video game. "*Attendant*, answer call," he said to the personal assistant connected to his phone app. "Marcus."

"The old couple are back with the kid," said his former second in command—now Head of *Merope*, the New York City facility.

"And?" Thaddeus asked, staring at the paused game on the TV screen.

"They say they are willing to let us test him and try our treatments," Marcus said, followed by the sound of papers rustling. "They understand that he has to be admitted."

The older couple had sought out help from them before but hadn't liked the idea of leaving the child alone at the facility, not without knowing more about the testing and treatments. It seemed that now they were desperate, and Thaddeus thought to take advantage of this. The pandemic had not gone as he had expected, and he'd not been able to find another like this case for over a year now. He had hoped it might flush out more of his fallen brethren or their offspring, giving him more opportunities to test his theories, but it had not. He had begun to think that he might have to create his own progeny, but the idea had disgusted him. Plus having his own would be too much to explain or hide. There would also be too long a wait for them to be born. The others that he had sought, had not made it to term since the mothers often died in labour.

Thaddeus dropped the game controller on his bed and stood up. "Excellent news," he said, traversing the room and heading for his closet. Three quarters of the open space of his personal abode had a large king size bed, with expensive soft grey linens, which he preferred to sleep in with only one pillow. On the opposite wall was a massive flatscreen TV that he mostly used for playing video games, and for watching the occasional movie, mainly horrors. He did not drink alcohol, nor did he use drugs, though for the amount of time he spent using his game console, one could say his drug of choice was gaming. And he relished video games, the more violent the better. "I'll make arrangements for coverage here—then I'll be there in the morning."

"See you soon," Marcus responded, before ending the call.

Thaddeus didn't need to pack for the trip, he'd be traveling light. Besides, he kept duplicates of most of his favorite suits and other clothing at each of his facilities' locations. Though the other private residences were not as luxuriously set up as this one and readily only housed his basic needs. However, he did need to get dressed, as he had been resting on his bed in nothing but his underwear, his preferred attire while playing his video games.

"Hello, Brutus," Thaddeus said to his companion as he entered and crossed the expanse of his closet. His *companion* was a 3-inch long, dark purple Rosetail Siamese fighting fish. "How is your Friday night going?" He put his forefinger against the glass in greeting, and the fish bumped his head against the clear wall of the tank. With the way Thaddeus traveled, he wasn't able to bring Brutus with him, so he didn't like to be away for too long. He dreaded leaving him here with anyone else, because despite leaving explicit instructions on his diet and music preferences, he still worried they would not care for him as he did.

Thaddeus had been drawn to this creature for two reasons; one, they are carnivores, and two, they mirrored his own nature, being that the male bettas are solitary and often aggressive towards one another. Brutus's pigment was the rarest solid colour, and he was a variation with so much finnage that it overlapped and looked like a rose. And Thaddeus had had him created through selective breeding, since only the best would do. There were very few things Thaddeus cared about on this planet, and Brutus was one of them. He always made sure the ideal water temperature was kept around 24–28 °C, and despite this species frequently being displayed and sold in tiny containers in the pet trade, Thaddeus had him put him in a larger aquarium. The breeder had informed him that they are much happier, healthier, and longer-lived in a larger tank of no less than 9 liters. Thaddeus kept the ornate glass tank, which was 12 by 6 inches and only 8 inches tall, on a small platform next to the floor-to-ceiling window within his massive walk-in closet, so that Brutus could see outside. And he'd customized the height of stand to be at eye level, making it easier for Thaddeus to talk to Brutus directly.

The expansive closet was Thaddeus's favorite part of the residence, the space alone taking up more than half the condo, and he had designed it that way because of his passion for clothing. He did not particularly like to be seen by the staff who worked in the building, nor did he like them to know of his comings and goings, unless of course he'd informed them officially. And because of this need, he had also designed the building to have a private elevator that took him to and from this penthouse floor to the lowest-level and the underground lab.

"Brutus, I know I've told you this before, but one of the most crucial elements of dressing oneself, is to make sure the clothing that you own and wear, fits you perfectly," Thaddeus said, as he began realigning his shirts that hung in the space closest to the window. "There is nothing worse or more off-putting than a person wearing ill-fitted clothing."

He turned to see Brutus watching him from the tank. "I know I'm a bit obsessed with my clothing—so don't give me any grief." He turned back and began straightening the trousers that hung below his shirts. Then he removed a pair of dark blue denim pants from their spot in the lineup. Checking over his shoulder, he saw Brutus was still very attentive. He smiled at him and then stepped into the jeans.

"When I first started out on my style journey and was constructing my attire," he said to his observant friend, "I focused my attention on the building blocks like crew-neck T-shirts and sweatshirts, a selection of Oxford button-down shirts—a wardrobe staple, along with dress shirts, dark slim-leg jeans and chinos. I have several good sets of shirts at my disposal, and with them being the most worn pieces in my wardrobe, I replace them once they start to lose their luster or shape." He moved on to the next section of clothing.

"As staples, I own several fitted navy or charcoal lounge suits, a few durable overcoats, and lightweight jackets; leather, bomber, Harrington, field, denim and a few others." He removed a navy blue coloured bomber jacket from the hanger, placing it on a single hook on the section divider.

The next section in the closet had an array of assorted colours and shades of shirts. "They say the classics never die, but this world would be a dull place if no one ever strayed away from the basic navy suit, Oxford shirt or plain white tee. The plain white T-shirt does set the foundation of any stylish person's wardrobe. It can be integrated within a plethora of looks or stand out by its simplicity. But the real secret is to know when to experiment—and you know how I love to experiment," he laughed out, removing one of several white t-shirts that hung from hangers. "Even classics are ultimately a result of a trend you know." He pulled on the shirt and then turned again to look Brutus's way, noting that he was still facing him. He had not been distracted by the nighttime lights of the surrounding buildings that could be seen from the window.

"I know what works for me and what to stick with. I alternate colours, throw in the odd accessory or switch up my outerwear. I recall one of the fashion designers to the queen once said, *'a man should look as if he bought his clothes with intelligence, put them on with care—then forgot all about them'* or something along those lines." He waved his hands in the air once, then moved to the next section.

"As you know, I take particular pride in my footwear," he stated, running a hand over a brown leather pair of shoes on the middle shelf before seizing them as his selection. "I adore a Gucci Horsebit loafer. They are not the most expensive shoe—far from it, but they are pricey, and the quality and comfort are what I require most." He shook an informative finger in Brutus's direction. "Some of the most expensive shoes are just that—expensive. I like fine things, but I'm not stupid when it comes to my footwear. And of course, I store mine with shoe trees in order to retain their shape and draw out any excess moisture. My service staff take care of any regular protection spraying or shining, mind you. If I find any wear or damage to them, I promptly replace them with a new pair. That goes for both my formal and casual shoes."

The last section, next to his tower of accessories, housed a column of drawers that ended at chest height. Thaddeus bent down and pulled out the bottom drawer. "My real obsession is with the variety of undergarments available—and they've definitely come a long way over the centuries. All but this drawer in the dresser are dedicated to my array of underwear." With his free hand, he retrieved a pair of brown designer socks from their confines and then pushed the drawer back in. Going to the next drawer, he pulled it out, peering into marvel at its contents. He continued upward with each drawer until all the contents had been likewise admired. He took in a deep breath and then turned to stroll back over to Brutus's pedestal. But Brutus had turned away as if he were uninterested in the undergarments. That's when Thaddeus saw what had gotten his little friend's attention.

Outside the window it had begun snowing.

Thaddeus understood the beauty that was snow—snowflakes in particular, but he hated when it snowed. It made his clothing damp and sometimes the bottoms of his pants became damaged from the salt that was put out on the street when the weather shifted like this.

"Washing clothing is very important—you know," Thaddeus said, redirecting things. "So, I have laundry staff to take care of that. They can read the labels and address the needs of my clothing. All my suits are stored in individual suit covers." He pointed to his suits. "My knitwear is folded and stored on shelves and in drawers rather than hung on hangers to reduce any warp or stretching." He waved a hand in the direction of the shelves and other drawers. "Of the items that are hung, they are put on quality wooden hangers." He slid a light blue long-sleeved thermal pullover from the closest hanger.

Donning the second layer, Thaddeus then noticed that Brutus had returned to the side of the tank that faced inward to the closet. Thaddeus having his attention again, he said, "Grooming—something else you don't have to worry about—because you're so gorgeous, is a daily regime." It had not been until Thaddeus had been trapped on this godforsaken planet that he had realized that maintaining his perfect skin would take genuine effort. "Skincare and general upkeep of your complexion is one of the first things people notice—you know, good or bad." He'd had to figure out what his skin type was, then try different products to see which worked for him best. Lavish or lower-priced, they needed to be tailored to your skin type. He stroked his chin with the tips of his fingers. "I have a strict routine with cleansing every day, and twice a week with an exfoliating scrub to get rid of any dirt or oil build up." He stroked his cheek. "Shaving—who knew that would be such a brutal pain in the ass," he said, but facial hair—he wasn't having it.

His hairstyle had changed over the years to keep up with the fashion of the time, and he currently had a stylist come twice a month to tidy his hair up. Standing in front of the floor-length mirror, he adjusted the neck of the thermal shirt to reveal the white band of his first layer t-shirt. Then ran his fingers through his hair to fix it back into place. He took care of the daily maintenance himself, so he liked to keep his hair easy yet stylish.

"How would you like a little snack," he asked Brutus then. He could use a little midnight snack himself he thought, placing a hand on his stomach. "I'll be right back with a treat for both of us," he said, leaving the closet area in search of nourishment for the two of them.

The remaining part of his personal space contained a small kitchen-like area on the left against the wall, which had only a fridge and microwave with a small counter, and it took up just a quarter of the open room. Mind you, the fridge was huge, like one you would see in a restaurant that does catering, the width of two regular fridges with one side divided into a lower freezer drawer, the upper door having a water filter with numerous dispensing options for ice. Other than a few cupboards with a basic set of plain white dishes and cups, and drawers with cutlery, there wasn't much else he required. He had a personal chef who prepared and cooked all his meals for him. The used dishes from those meals he placed in a special cart that he left outside his condo entrance when he was done. The chef took care of those as well, plus he maintained the fridge stocked with all of Thaddeus's favorite foods and drinks, should he require sustenance in the chef's absence. Thaddeus had deemed this location his 'home base' and other than the two boardrooms and an actual professional kitchen, his personal residence was the only other chamber on the topmost floor of the Celaeno building.

When Marcus had transferred to head up the New York City facility, he'd sent another capable follower to return in his stead.

"*Attendant,* call Amahle," Thaddeus said, needing to notify his next in command.

"Yes, Sir," came a strong yet exotic female voice, a moment later.

"I'm heading to Merope in a few hours," he said. It was closing in on 2 a.m. he realized. "I need you to take care of Brutus. He'll be on your desk when you get to your office, with the food and the music he likes." He opened the left side of the fridge and retrieved a package of the brine shrimp set aside for Brutus's meals. "I don't know how long I'll be gone—so take good care of him." He grabbed a second package of the food just in case. "If anything happens to him—there will be hell to pay."

"He will be safe with me, Sir," she said. "Safe trip," she added, before hanging up.

He quite enjoyed taking care of Brutus, but watching over the Earth, watching humans destroy their world, that he had loathed. Although, their indulgences, their sexual perversions, those such observations of them, Thaddeus had found these quite fascinating, and he appreciated the creativity shown by some. He was especially fond of watching those causing pain, those in agony, especially the children. They were the weaker of these creatures, and he understood why the humans sometimes abandoned them as most were more trouble than they were worth. This new specimen, this halfling boy that he was heading to see, could very well be what was needed. However, if these next experiments did not result in the desired outcome this time, and though it would be enormously problematic, he would then have to set his sights on discovering the whereabouts of the other. This grown halfling, the Archangel's abomination, the one he'd been told of having the ability to sense other celestials, this one could be the solution he required, the key element, the catalyst as it were that he needed for confirming his theories.

Chapter 10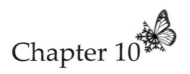

Home of Olivia White, December 26th, Ottawa, Canada

Olivia had known it would be a longshot reaching anyone on Boxing Day, but she had tried calling the number from the website for that research facility first thing this morning. She had heard mention of the organization prior to Lynn telling them about it. It had been when she'd worked with the director of the NICU at the children's hospital, so she had a general idea of what kind of work they did there. She had made a second and then a third call, and what do you know? Someone at the facility other than an answering service, had actually picked up.

Olivia had told them who she was, mentioned where she worked and which specific program she was essentially running now, and had explained that her interest was in getting a tour of the facility for her and a colleague, Mac. Unfortunately, the woman on the other end had informed her that only she, security, and a small crew monitoring experiments would be the only staff present. Though she did say that she would check with the person in charge to see if he would grant approval to provide a private tour.

Less than an hour later, Olivia's cell phone rang. It was the woman from the research facility, calling to say, *"I've got the go-ahead to give you and your colleague the tour you requested. Does 11 a.m. work for you."*

Olivia guessed that telling the woman that she ran the Childbirth Program at the Queensway Carleton Hospital had facilitated the decision further in getting them in today for a tour. Olivia's new opportunity with the program had been a big change, but it didn't feel like work to her. It was nothing like the grueling years she had spent taking care of the doctors and their appointments and meetings, etc. in her previous jobs. She felt like she was really helping, making an impact finally. Good relationships with local health programs were valuable, and Olivia knew that. And the time the woman had suggested worked perfectly for her, as it gave her the time she needed to shower and dress. Plus, she was able to give Mac enough notice to get ready, before heading over there to pick her up.

"I'm heading out now — over to get Mac," Olivia called out to Mike from the front hall. She had dressed in black dress pants, a teal sweater and a camel-coloured wool car coat with similar coloured ankle boots, and she chose a tiny cross-body bag that was basically a wallet that fit only her cell phone and keys. To give her a more official air for today's tour and little adventure, she'd grabbed a hospital notepad from her briefcase to bring with her.

"Drive safe — say *hi* to Mac for me," came Mike's voice from the TV room.

"Will do," she called out again, before shutting the front door.

Like the rest of the gang, Mike and Olivia had invested in Derek's company, and after the sale they'd had paid off their mortgage, paid for their girls' college tuitions, and put aside an excellent nest egg for their retirement. Mike had basically retired, neither *needed* to work now, and he was content with being the happy house husband while Olivia excitedly went off to work each day. Especially with knowing that she was helping women, all the while using her newfound gifts and working side by side with Mac.

Olivia pulled her car into Mac's driveway and honked the horn.

Mac had moved to an area near Olivia in a newer part of Barrhaven that had been only an open field that Christmas before the gathering. Now that open field contained a new neighborhood with both starter and full family homes. They had purchased a new 4-bedroom home, with 3.5 bathrooms, a huge garage, and a finished basement. The first floor had a spacious family room open-concept kitchen, dining room, and home office, and plenty of room for guests and gatherings. The second level had all the bedrooms, the laundry room, and a lounge space for watching television or just hanging out.

Olivia gave a second honk, and within minutes the front door opened and out came Mac.

She was wearing fitted black pants tucked into tall black leather boots. She had on a black turtleneck sweater that hung past her bum. Covering most of her upper body, she had on a long black wool wraparound shall, the one end tossed over her left shoulder. She did still look like a fashion plate, though she had stopped doing her jewelry business to redirect her focus on this current venture with Olivia. They had originally started out with a holistic health business, with Olivia functioning as a doula, where both of them could spend more time doing what they loved while having more time with their families. Then, with Olivia having such solid connections at the children's hospital, several of the doctors there had recommended her for the position of managing the childbirth program. When Olivia had told Mac that she could bring her onboard too, Mac had jumped at the idea to be part of something bigger.

"Got everything?" Olivia asked, when Mac climbed into the SUV.

"When do I not?" Mac questioned back, followed by a hearty laugh as she buckled herself in. In contrast to Olivia's tiny purse, Mac had a large hobo style bag swung over her left shoulder, that was big enough to store and safely carry her essential witchy toolkit everywhere she went.

The years following the gathering, Mac had continued with learning the ways of contemporary witchcraft. Like those into Wicca, she worshipped the Goddess, honored nature, and performed ceremonial magic, though she invoked the aid of angels verses that of the deities. She practiced with her abilities and nature worship regularly, but unlike most in the Wiccan tradition, she had rejected it as a religion. And like the parallel movement of Neo-Paganism, she had incorporated the emotional involvement and ritual practices into her beliefs as *practicing magic* rather than being part of the Wiccan religion. Reflecting both Wiccans and Neo-Pagans, Mac had strong ecological and environmental concerns and she celebrated the change of seasons with elaborate rituals.

"Okay—we're off then," Olivia said, backing out of the driveway.

On the drive downtown towards the facility, Mac went over what she had brought today in that huge bag of hers. As part of her practice, Mac had learned that casting jar spells were one of the most important things any self-respecting witch can do. After all, this form of spellcasting allows you to help yourself, your loved ones, or even set specific intentions on actual places, like the spell she'd created for this building they were headed to. Today, with them venturing into unknown territory and without Lynn at their side, Mac had chosen to use a small mason jar and had filled it with chamomile, lavender, and mugwort. "Chamomile is famous for its soothing effects with promoting sleep and relaxation, and for reducing inflammation and pain," Mac said out loud as Olivia took the ramp on to the highway. "Needless to say, it's ideal for anxiety and stress-relieving spells. Lavender too is used to attract serenity and is generally considered to be an anxiety-relieving plant." When Olivia turned her worried face her way, Mac just grinned at her. Then she went on with, "Plus, it was good for enhancing clairvoyant abilities for sensing anything we might find we need to well, *find*."

Olivia nodded, keeping her eyes on the road ahead.

"In folk magic practices, people might put mugwort leaves in their shoes before embarking on a long journey, but I just put it in the jar with the other two." She pulled the jar from her bag. "It also gives the caster psychic properties that work well with Lunar magic—and the moon is in excellent alignment for us today." She shook the glass jar, the dried contents making scratching noises.

"Is that all we need?" Olivia asked, cutting a quick glance in Mac's direction.

"We'd be fine with just those, but I've added a crap load of other elements to be on the safe side," Mac shared.

"Like what?" Olivia asked, clicking the car signal to move into the lane closest to the exit to get off the highway, as indicated on the GPS map.

Mac shook the jar again. "Well, I've got rock salt for grounding and absorbing — or deflecting negative energy." Olivia shot her another worried glance. "Sugar for attracting the objects of your desire — which is just getting answers for now. Sage, rosemary, and thyme for protection and strength." She tilted the jar. "Rice for luck. Dried rose petals for attracting good feelings. Black pepper and chili powder for warding off negativity and evil," she said, then patted Olivia's arm. Olivia had grown some lady-balls along with a truckload of confidence in her abilities over the past few years, but Mac knew she still got nervous venturing out to do things like this, and that she hated fibbing even if it was for a good reason. "Positive intent," Mac reminded. Olivia had lied to the woman about the real reason they were meeting, but they both knew her intentions had been in the right place.

"What about a sigil," Olivia asked, quickly checking the GPS map. The display screen on the dash of her car showed they were approaching the entrance to their destination.

"Done," Mac said. "Sigil making isn't difficult, but it isn't something I normally do in a crowded room — like with Don and the boys making a ruckus." You needed to be able to focus your intent and if you are distracted, it wouldn't be as powerful as possible, and you could be too late if the ingredients were fast activating. Sigils were generally something made in a peaceful environment. "Not to mention, last-minute sigils are rarely effective as they don't have time to manifest one's desires." Mac held the jar on her lap and opened the lid.

"Okay good," Olivia said, pulling up in front of the building.

The building was situated next to one of the newer edifices associated to the University of Ottawa, and despite there being no official signage at the entrance, they were both confident that they had arrived at the right place. Over the massive steel front doors of the building, displayed in a relief style font on a large solid slab of dark wood, was the name and lone word *Celaeno*.

Neither uttered a word, as they circled past the front entrance towards the available parking. Then when Olivia pulled into a spot and shut off the car, Mac turned in her seat to look at her.

"Let's charge it up," Mac said, holding the open jar out and over the center console between them. A small piece of paper with a sigil drawing of their initials poked free of the jar. "Clear you mind," she said, resting the jar's lid in her lap, and digging in her bag again. "Focus your intent." Then, freeing her hand from the bag, Mac lifted a wooden match to the paper. "I set this match on fire," she said, the matchstick igniting. Mac lit the corner of the paper, then blew out the match. Tossing the match in the jar, she replaced the jar's lid, screwing it tight.

Knowing what to do, Olivia placed one hand on top of the jar, and with her other hand she cupped the bottom.

Mac placed her free hand over Olivia's on the top of the jar and then said, "Let the Universe do its thing." They watched as the sigil burned using up what air remained in the jar. When the fire went out, Olivia removed her hands. Mac shook the jar one last time and then placed it back in her bag. "Ready?" she asked, staring across at Olivia.

Ready or not, they exited the car and strolled over to the building's main entrance. Though, at the entrance they were met with locked doors, and there didn't seem to be an intercom or ringer. There must have been cameras, because seconds later a buzzing noise sounded, and then the heavy steel doors slowly swung open, revealing a statuesque woman in the front lobby.

Standing before them was a woman with an athletic build that brought to mind that of Serena Williams, though this woman was even taller, and not because she was wearing 4-inch black patent leather *Jimmy Choo* pumps, it was obvious that without the heels, she still stood nearly 6 feet tall. "Welcome. I am Amahle," she said then, turning to the side and extending an arm, directing for them to enter the building.

The woman's midnight black hair was pulled back tight against her scalp into a long ponytail that hung to her waist in an equally tight braid. Her lush dark skin was only a shade lighter than her hair and it was flawless. Though she did not appear to be wearing makeup other than lipstick and perhaps mascara because her lashes were full lengthy shadows over large amber-coloured eyes. *Contacts*, Mac assumed based on the rest of the woman's colouring. As they continued towards the front desk, Mac couldn't help but notice how exquisitely dressed the woman was. Her high-end clothing was elegant and fit her in a way that made you feel like you'd shown up to a fashion show in your bathrobe and slippers. She wore a pair of black flowy silk pants, and a silk blouse in a deep plum, that crisscrossed in the front and tied in a soft knot with long ends at one hip, and it was in the same shade as her lip colour.

Mac and Olivia moved leisurely forward past the woman and further into the open atrium. "You'll need to sign in and leave your cell phones at the security desk," she said, pulling Mac's attention back to the woman's stunning face.

"Not a problem," Mac said with a toothy grin. She submerged her hand into her purse and pulled free her phone.

"Which of you is Olivia White?" Amahle asked them.

Olivia raised her hand as if she were in grade school. Saying nothing, she smiled and handed her cell phone over to the nearest of the two gentlemen behind the large reception desk. When the woman pointed to the sign-in blotter, Olivia took the pen and signed them both in.

"Follow me, please," Amahle directed, strolling ahead of them towards the far entry.

Mac took a last look around before moving forward with Olivia. Near the entrance they had just walked through were luxurious brown leather chairs, two on each wall, facing towards the front desk. The flooring was a beautiful marble tile with gold veining running through it. The walls were covered in a pale birch woodgrain paneling that looked so real it made you want to reach out and touch it to see if it was. There was soft lighting overhead and music playing through speakers she couldn't see, and it gave the space a spa-like feel Mac hoped set the tone for the rest of the building's space.

At the door past the security desk, Amahle removed the translucent plastic coiled cording from around her wrist and then selected a white rectangular plastic card from an array of coloured cards attached to it. Then she swiped the card through the card reader on the right next to the door. There were no handles, but when a green light lit up on the card scanner, the door made a sound as if releasing a suction, and then with a soft hiss it glided open.

Chapter 11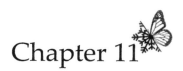

Even from the master bedroom, I could hear the thunderous knocking on the front door. Following it came Redmond's muffled voice mixed with that of the girls shrieking and running up the hall from their bedrooms towards the front entrance. "Lyyyyynn," Redmond called out to me. As I left the bedroom, two figures, one large and one small, were entering through the main doorway and into the front foyer of our house.

"Merry Boxing Day Christmas," Darius said, bending down to scoop up the girls, each wrapped in one of his enormous arms.

"We come bearing gifts," Lily said, giving me a quick wave and smile, as I ventured from the bedroom to meet them in the front hall.

Lily had loved the area here so much that she had happily moved into the nicer one of the two apartments above the new studio and had promptly made it her own. She'd done all the setup for the new studio, the recording rooms, and the offices and common areas. The second apartment was a two bedroom, and since time in the studio was precious, she had furnished that one for visiting bands, musicians, or singers to use. We had also had to bring her in on the 'knowing' and she handled it as I had expected. In fact, she had told me she'd had a sense about me from the beginning, and had said, *"I always suspected there was something mystical about you."* She liked spooky stuff and was a big believer of all things unseen, and it was another reason she and Redmond had gotten on so well. We'd given her most of the basic details, but Darius had taken it upon himself to fill her in on the additional bits. He'd been the last to know about things back before the gathering, so he had liked the idea of being the one sharing all he knew this time.

"Merry Christmas—Boxing Day," I said, as I went in for a hug.

"Happy Boxing Day Christmas to you," she said back, as I released my hold on her.

"I know you guys are leaving tomorrow to head up to Ottawa," Lily said, "So we wanted to come see you all—and give you these before you left." She held up several decorative gift bags.

Neither Darius nor Lily had ever been particularly good in the kitchen, so as our gift to both of them, Redmond and I had made it a tradition to order and deliver for them an annual Christmas Eve dinner. Normally with other celebrations they just came over for meals. Darius was always appreciative of food and Lily was grateful she didn't have to create another disaster in her attempt at making the holiday meal. Plus, for us, it made it easy not having to figure out gifts for them each year. So, it was a win-win-win.

"Did you close the gym early," Redmond directed at Darius. Redmond always closed the studio between Christmas and New Year's, so we knew Lily hadn't needed to work today.

Tipping the girls to one side and then the other, Darius said, "Actually, I put a notice on the doors Christmas eve. *Closed Christmas Day and Boxing Day*." He tipped the girls forward then pretending to lose his grip, and they squealed.

Darius too had made out well from his investment in Derek's company and he didn't *need* to work. Before moving up here, he had spent most of his time—when not in the gym, volunteering at the children's hospital in Miami, and when he'd come up to see our new place he had fallen in love with the area. The small downtown was going through a revitalization and there was potential for businesses of all kinds. To him, the one thing that was missing was a decent gym. It hadn't been long after that he had taken his investment money and opened one right downtown, and right down the street from Redmond's studio. Other than his mother, he had no other ties to

Miami. And he knew he could always volunteer at one of the hospitals in the area if he felt the desire to help again.

"You and your gym rats will survive another day without lifting dumbbells," Lily said, rubbing Darius's back as he lowered the girls back down to the floor.

We hadn't foreseen this relationship blossoming, nor did we see Darius as Lily's type, though neither did she. Originally, Lily had thought he was just a muscle-head like most of the roadies she worked with at the music gigs. She had soon realized that there was more to Darius than she had assumed.

Back when Darius had moved up here to our little town and opened his gym, we had been thrilled and more than happy to have him local again. Redmond had additionally appreciated the extra strong helping hands with moving and setting up music equipment at the local venues. Similar to Lily moving into the apartment above the new studio, Darius had moved into the one above the gym space he had established. And due to the proximity of the gym near the studio and our crisscrossing friendships, Lily had soon learned that Darius was actually a computer geek, a video gamer, and not the dumb bodybuilder she'd originally mistaken him for. She had never been into musicians, and since her taste in men ran something along the lines of hipster-geek, it had been Darius's geekier side that had ultimately gotten her attention. Plus, being that she was naturally slim, exercising hadn't been on her learn-how-to list. But because of her curiosity regarding the other parts of Darius's life, she'd enrolled in the beginner program at his gym. It was there that she found, despite her complete lack of knowledge of weight training and pretty much anything fitness related, that not only was Darius a smart, patient instructor, he was very kind and gentle, notably in contrast to his monstrous size. From there, they had developed a nice friendship that eventually grew into what is now a strong and loving relationship.

"What did you bring?" Ryley asked, taking Darius's big hand, leading him into the living room.

Lily passed the two gift bags to Darius's free hand as he was led away. Then she bent down and lifted a waiting Hayley up and into a side-hip hold-and-carry to follow behind the other two.

Neither Darius nor Lily had any interest in having kids, in fact, they relished having their own space and separate apartments. Nevertheless, the undeniable affection they had for our girls was that of a fierce love and protectiveness that made having both living nearby, even that much better.

Lily sat on the couch with Hayley cuddled in her arms next to Darius as he handed out the gifts they had brought with them. When Hayley was handed her present, she slid off Lily's lap to stand and open it. Once the items were out of the wrappings, Ryley and Hayley together lifted their gifts up to show us.

They both held out long-sleeved t-shirts, a blue one for Ryley with the phrase 'Do you even lift bro?' displayed on it, and a pink one for Hayley with the words 'Weights before dates' on hers. Both had the barbell logo from Darius's gym, but the part of the shirts that had clearly been Lily's creative idea, were the actual sleeves themselves that had tattoo images of 70s kids' cartoons on them.

"I want one," I whined, admiring the artwork I was confident Lily had done herself.

"I'll get you one—if yer good," Darius said. "I've got connections." He winked at me and then elbowed Lily.

"Okay—but do I really have to be good?" I asked. I laughed when the twins gave me wide-eyed looks. "Right—be good," I added, nodding my head, and holding in another laugh.

Next on the gift opening was Redmond and based on the size and shape of the wrapped present, it looked to be either a calendar or an album. "Yer gonna love this," Darius said, handing over the flat gift.

"It was his idea—believe it or not, but I had to source it," Lily added, giving a chin tilt in Redmond's direction. Then she slid a small wrapped yet obvious CD-shaped gift my way.

"*Thank you,*" I mouthed, giving her hand a little squeeze. She always made me a CD each Christmas with new music that she always knew somehow, I would like. The best part of her gifts though, were that she designed small album covers for the CD cases that accompanied each of them. They were autographed and one-of-a-kind pieces of beautiful artwork, and I kept them all on a long thin shelf in the dining room, displayed on individual tiny easels that I'd found at the framing shop in town. I used pieces of card stock in the CD cases numbered and with the songs and artists written on in replace of them for the music. I had told her she should make larger versions of the covers and sell them, but she'd blown off my enthusiasm, stating that she wanted to keep her personal artwork as something she did just for special friends and family. And I knew she considered us family, so it meant even more to me that she had made these for me.

"Let's see what you got," I said, feeling the joy and love in the room.

Without further hesitation, Redmond tore off the Christmas wrapping only to find the gift double-wrapped in brown paper. When he tore away just a corner of the next layer of wrapping, he gasped then glanced back and forth between Darius and Lily. "This. Is. Soooo. Cool. Thank—you! This is going in the office for sure."

"What?" I asked, leaning over to get a better look at the corner peeking out from the paper.

"What is it-what is it?" the girls asked in unison, moving to hover next to their dad on either side of him.

Redmond continued, slowly peeling away the last layer that hid the identity of the gift. When the last piece fell away, I saw that it was in fact an album, though not just any album. This particular one was titled, *A Question of Balance*. Redmond had told me about this album, and I'd heard several of the tracks and had liked most. It had been originally released in 1970 and was the sixth album recorded by The Moody Blues. Redmond had said that this album had been an attempt by the group to strip down their well-known opulent, psychedelic sound to be able to better perform the songs in concert. What made this copy of the album so special was that it was clearly an original pressing and based on its clean appearance it looked to be in pristine condition.

"Aw, man—yer welcome. I saw the cover awhile back," Darius said, "But it's the artwork and title that made me think how perfect it was—considering the journey that brought us all together. All of us— all of us," he added, meaning the gathering and everything that had taken place since.

"Do you know what makes this album cover so unique?" he asked the girls, turning it over to show them the artwork. When they shook their heads *no*, he opened it, and said, "They call this a *gatefold*, and that means it opens top to bottom instead of the standard left to right." The artist had painted the vivid pictures of this cover rich with symbolism and lots of detail. It displayed ordinary people on the shore for a day at the beach, oblivious to the storm on the horizon, and unaware of the brooding on-goings in the sky above them. Several of the images had caused some controversy, and apparently the one with the man holding the gun had been based on an actual person. The inner gatefold showed several pictures of The Moody Blues, and though the album cover as a whole was fascinating to look at, the theme and images depicting *Balance*, had not been missed by any of us.

"On the subject of balance, we should probably chat about *things*," I said, glancing at each of the adults.

Just then, Redmond's parents came through the sliding patio doors from their walk on the beach. "Darius, Lily," Nainseadh said, crossing the open space to greet them.

Darius stood up from his spot on the couch then turned and took one giant step towards them bridging the distance. "Nan," he said, catching her up in a hug. "Pop," he said then, releasing Redmond's mom, shifting to shake the outstretched hand of Redmond's father. "Happy holidays," Darius said to both. When Redmond's parents had first met Darius, they had graciously offered that he address them as such. Lily had been doing it for years, so it had made it feel even more comfortable for Darius to be doing so.

"Lily—love. Has this big brute been treating you well?" Redmond's mom asked.

Lily had gotten up to go get her own hug. Squeezing Nainseadh, she said, "He'd be a fool not to."

"I'm a fool for you—Lil," Darius said, reaching over and tickling her ribs. Then he leaned in for a kiss.

"Aw gross," Ryley said, she and her sister both making faces like they had smelled something bad.

"Come here you two," Enzo said, "Nana and I want to take you gals into town—to hear the swing band that's playing in the square. The island news flyer mentioned something about a Boxing Day band," he added, directing the last part at Redmond and me.

"Perfect," I responded, knowing the others and I had some secret business to discuss.

"Lily—are you and Darius staying for supper?" Enzo asked. "I'm making a special Italian Boxing Day meal." Enzo raised his eyebrows and then rocked back and forth on his heels.

At the mention of food, Darius turned to Lily with an expression much like that of a puppy awaiting a treat.

"There'll be plenty," Redmond added, grinning at Lily.

"We would love that," Lily said, knowing she along with Enzo, had just made Darius's day.

"Yes—thank you—that would be great," Darius added, hugging Lily, then followed up his appreciation with a hug for Enzo.

"It's settled then," Nainseadh said, grabbing up the girls' zip-up hoodies from the hooks near the door. "We'll see you back here in time to prep for dinner." She handed the girls their respective sweatshirts.

Before putting them on, the girls ran over to Darius and Lily. "Thank you. Thank you," they said, embracing each of them.

"I'm so glad you're staying," I heard Hayley whisper to Lily. The two had always had a special bond, and though the twins both knew good folks when they *sensed* them. I think that Hayley's unique connection to her was partially due to the fact that Lily was tiny too.

"Come along girls," Enzo said, waving the twins over. "We've got music to dance to," he added, shuffling them along and out the front door.

"Bye Muuum—bye Daaa," they said in chorus, heading down the steps hand-in-hand with their Nana and Poppy.

We all waved from the front deck as they pulled away. Then Redmond and I, along with Lily and Darius, re-situated ourselves back in the living room.

"I take it you spoke to Luc—brought him up to speed," I asked, more as a confirmation. I took my place on the couch, the one facing the wall of windows out to the deck and beach beyond. Redmond came and sat on the arm of the couch.

"Ya. We—Lily and I, video chatted with Derek, and Luc and Dunya late last night," Darius said, sitting down, leaning back against the couch opposite us. Lily scooted in next to him.

Luc and Dunya had moved in together and like everyone, they had basically gone on with their lives after the gathering. Redmond, Luc, and Derek had however spent a considerable amount of time conversing with their Horsemen designates, while exploring the world of angels a little more closely. My four girlfriends had continued to hone their crafts so to speak, though the guys did not have any otherworldly gifts to focus on. Well, except for Darius. The gift he had received from being a descendant of Shamsiel's wasn't exactly something he could hone, it was simply the instincts of a guardian, a protector of sorts, although his internal alarm system for danger had come in handy on several occasions.

"That's some f'd up shit, Lynn. Just hearing about it—gave the overprotective guardian in me some brutal warning tremors. I haven't felt anything like that since the twins were born," Darius said, his shoulder cracking as he stretched an arm out around Lily.

"That was more about the volume of angelic visitors coming to see them—not them being in danger, and more like being on high alert, really," Lily reminded. "But you were quite a mess—with those protective vibrations shaking your world." She nodded.

I nodded too, recalling those turbulent first three months after the girls had been born. Darius had been out in the waiting room when I had first gone into the hospital. Then for several weeks after, when his inner alarm bells continued to go off every time someone otherworldly came to visit the twins, he had basically camped out in the living room to avoid the additional angst of having to drive over each time. When his nervous system finally registered that all was safe, he'd been able to go back home, but there had always remained an underlying humming that he had said never seemed to go away.

"Did Derek tell you guys that we're going up to Ottawa, as well?" Redmond asked, moving from the arm to sit on the couch next to me.

"They threw us all the details—including your trip up to Canada," Darius confirmed, then frowned.

"Yeah, they were bummed like us—that they wouldn't be with you and the others for your big celebration," Lily said. "But I told them we'd do something together—maybe for New Year's, if they wanted to join us." Lily pushed out a pouty lip, then she switched it up then to give me a sweet smile.

I mirrored her pout. "It's been tough not having the option to get all of us together," I said, with a sigh.

"I for one, am grateful we're edging further past this pandemic though," Redmond said, "We'll have plenty more opportunities to get everyone in one place."

"True," Darius said. "But I hate us all being scattered around." He rubbed a big palm down one of his thick thighs as though suddenly nervous.

Darius had hated that we'd all moved north without him, and it was another reason he'd come to live in the same city as Redmond and me. In 2017, the same year we moved up here, Dunya and Luc had moved too. They had gone just north of us, about a half hour shy of Orlando. This move had allowed them to be closer to everyone, including to Luc's sister and her family, as well as being near Dunya's daughter, who currently worked in the office at the Disney World Resort headquarters. That had been quite the year, for both moving and for losses. Sadly, following the death of Alison's father in January, it was in February, a week after Valentine's day, that we had been hit with more heartbreak.

Dunya had thought her grandmother had just been sleeping soundly, but when she had shaken Mitra's shoulder to wake her, she had painfully understood that her grandmother had passed away. When Dunya had called out for Luc, it was then that she had realized that Raven, who had taken to sleeping in Mitra's bed next to her, had left them as well. When Luc and Raven had moved in with Dunya and her grandmother, Raven had begun following Mitra everywhere, never leaving her side. That same night, I'd had a dream about Shamsiel being on the front lawn, and Mitra and Raven out in our backyard with Zaqiel—*Death*. When I had awoken, I'd already known what had happened, and I'd sent Redmond over to check on Luc and Dunya. Shamsiel had shown himself to Dunya just as Redmond had knocked on her front door. Shamsiel explained to them that he had been present for Mitra's passing, and that knowledge had aided Dunya in accepting that her grandmother was now gone. It was Shamsiel too who had later taken Raven's body from the room, however, it had been Dunya who had suggested that Mitra's faithful companion be included with her cremation and ceremony. Moving up north closer to her daughter, had helped ease the sting of Dunya's loss, but the terrible truth is that a wound like that never does heal. Mitra had had a positive impact on everyone in our group, and her death had been a wound on us all.

"Luc will be coming down more now too," Redmond reassured Darius. "I'm getting more and more requests for studio musicians all the time."

Luc was the youngest of us and not yet in his 50s, having only just turned 46 this past June. He was even two months younger than Dunya. And his and Dunya's investment in Derek's company had allowed for Luc to pursue his dream job. Being that he plays both acoustic and electric, he comes down to Redmond's studio whenever needed, to play guitar for singers who didn't have bands to accompany them. Along with that, he currently heads up the youth band at the non-denominational Christian church he attends.

"True, again," Darius said, turning a quick glance at Lily.

Leaning forward in her seat, Lily said, "About your trip, you plan to meet this Leo guy, yes?" She had not been on the video call the other night, though I knew Darius would have shared the conversation details with her.

"Yes," I said, nodding, leaning forward to rest my elbows on my knees. "Mac and Olivia messaged that they were heading to the research facility today for some tour."

"Not sure what they expect to find," Redmond interjected. "But hopefully they'll get some clarity on what's been going on there."

"Mac's spell work has enhanced her sight—her psychic ability, for sensing and finding things hidden," Darius said. "And Olivia is now able to sense unusual disruptions in people's nervous systems. Like she did with me when your twins were born."

Lily caressed Darius's knee. "Maybe they won't know what they are looking for until they find it," Lily said, adding some optimism.

Nodding again, I took in a deep breath, then let it out as I checked my watch. "It's past noon already," I said, realizing I hadn't heard anything from our *psychic sensory* friends. I took in another breath, holding it as I pondered whether leaving here to travel up to Canada was the right thing to do.

"And don't worry, we'll watch over things while you're gone," Darius said, as if reading my mind, giving me a reassuring smile.

I blew out the breath and forced the corners of my mouth into a smile.

"On that note," Redmond said, pushing up from the couch. "How about a beer—anyone?"

"Got any snacks," Darius asked, heading in the direction of the kitchen behind Redmond.

At 2 p.m. Nana and Poppy along with our two giggling girls, came through the front door. We'd situated ourselves out on the deck, but I'd spotted them coming in, when I'd ventured to the kitchen to open a bottle of wine for Lily and me.

"How was it?" I asked the girls, reaching into the top drawer for the wine opener.

"Oh-my-gosh-it-was so-great!" Hayley said, as she headed over and cracked open the fridge door. "But I'm soooo thirsty—they only had bottled water."

"That's bad for the environment," Ryley said, poking her head into the fridge next to her sister.

"We use bottled water," I reminded them.

"Ya—we have to stop doing that," Hayley said, cracking the tab of lime-flavored bubbly water, tipping back a can to take a sip.

"There was an info booth about the environment at the farmer's market," Enzo said, grinning innocently at me.

"Okay—no more water bottles, only reusable drink bottles from now on. Good—deal? We'll keep the remaining water bottles in the downstairs fridge for emergencies." I looked to each of them for agreement.

"Deal," Hayley said, chugging back her cherry flavored seltzer as she headed off in the direction of their bedrooms followed by her sister.

"What deal," Redmond asked, as he came through the patio door with his empty beer bottle.

"I'll tell ya later," I said, popping the cork from the bottle of red wine. "Can I pour you some wine," I directed to my in-laws.

Beverages in hand, the four of us went back out to the deck to continue relaxing with Lily and Darius.

"Your father and I were talking it over with the girls," Nainseadh tossed out, even before her butt had a chance to hit the patio chair cushion. "And we were thinking that we'd like to go down to Fairchild Gardens in Miami, when you get back—for New Year's Eve."

"Since you won't be here for your anniversary," Enzo said then, as if steering the guilt train.

"That's one of my favorite places to visit," Lily said, before Redmond or I could respond.

"The girls asked if you and Darius could come too," Nainseadh added, giving us all a hopeful grin.

"Sounds like a terrific idea. They're having a special Night Garden New Year's event," Redmond said, winking at me, suspiciously as if he were all in-the-know.

"Yes of course we can," I said, finally able to get a word in. "Lily—Darius, you'll come, won't you?" It was one of my favorite places to go too… but they all knew that.

Chapter 12

The Celaeno Building, December 26th, Ottawa, Canada

Mac and Olivia followed their guide through the door and into what appeared to be a small antechamber of sorts with another door opposite, this one too had no handle. The area was tight, the ceiling scarcely 8 feet high with recessed lighting, and there was barely enough room for two, let alone three people to stand comfortably in the space. The door they had come through suddenly shut, sealing them all in.

Mac heard Olivia suck in a breath and knew that a sudden wave of claustrophobia had just hit her friend. When the bright overhead lighting unexpectedly went out, Olivia let out a gasp, and she grabbed for Mac's hand. The blackness was replaced then with bursts of colour, the flashing running through a series of varying intensities of magenta, cyan, teal green, then abruptly returned to basic white again. It was as though they were being sterilized or disinfected or something, Mac thought. She looked to Olivia who was still holding her hand and gave her a confused shrug. Olivia returned the shrug with a headshake, then swiftly let go of Mac's hand.

Neither said a word, as Amahle lifted a small white key fob this time to a sensor on the door in front of them. When the sensor displayed a green light, the door suctioned open like the first one had done.

Following Amahle through the open door, they stepped into a large open space similar in size to the high ceiling open area of the front lobby, though the floors and walls here were a stark white and not the soft warm woodgrain that had welcomed them. The air too was different, dryer and much colder. There were no windows, nor seating, and in place of where the large desk would have been, there were three sizeable elevator doors. These were the bigger kind of elevators you would see in hospitals, the ones used for transferring patients to gurneys.

"What does your program involve?" Amahle asked, continuing forward to the elevators, undaunted by the temperature change. She stopped at the one to the right and then from her spiral cord, she selected another plastic card, this time a royal blue one, and ran it through the swiper next to the doors.

"The program services include outpatient clinics for care before and after baby is born, the *Birth Unit*, a *Special Care Nursery*, and the *Mother and Baby Unit*. I help out in that unit," Mac said, stepping confidently up next to her.

Joining Mac at her left, Olivia said, "We have one of the largest hospital-based obstetrical services in Ontario." She pulled out a pen from her small purse and then forced a nervous smile. "We find our close partnership with The Children's Hospital of Eastern Ontario— CHEO, and The Ottawa Hospital, crucial in ensuring the best care for the patients."

"We welcome any new connections with maternity wards at the local hospitals," Amahle said. "And like your program here, we are already connected with the children's hospital." The door to the elevator opened then and Amahle extended an arm, allowing for the two of them to board ahead of her.

The elevator had another door on the opposite side and Mac was unsure which way to face, so she turned back towards their tour guide. "We've only been with the initiative a few years, but the program has been going since 1999, and we welcome close to 2,500 babies into the world each year," Mac added, smiling along with Olivia.

"What do you do, exactly?" Amahle asked Mac, filing in behind them.

Interesting question, Mac mused. The woman hadn't bothered to ask Mac's name but now she wanted to know what she brought to the table. "Olivia, has me partnered with one of the top OB-GYNs, and together we offer the women and their new babies complementary or holistic therapies that fall under the alternative medicine domain."

Clearly her response hadn't been the answer the woman had hoped for, because she gave her a simple nod, then turned to address Olivia. "Ms. White, at this location we specialize and treat a full range of child and infant respiratory symptoms and disorders." She paused as the door closed behind her, then used her key fob again on a sensor pad inside the elevator coupled with pressing the button for the second floor.

Mac expected to feel her stomach lurch, but the elevator was exceptionally smooth and other than a soft hum, she could barely feel the thing move.

"The symptoms range from chronic cough, wheezing, recurrent respiratory infections, and pneumonia. As well as asthma, respiratory failure, and ventilator dependency," Amahle continued, as the elevator took them to their first destination. "We have a team whose primary focus is lung diseases of premature infants, including bronchopulmonary dysplasia—one of the chronic lung diseases." She sucked in her cheeks, displaying a smug expression.

"We see babies with conditions like those too often, I'm afraid," Olivia said, just as the elevator stopped and the door behind them slid open.

Mac and Olivia turned in unison to face the open elevator door.

A waft of strong antiseptic slammed into the back of Mac's nostrils making her almost gag.

"The second floor is where we have and use our advanced diagnostic capabilities for patients," Amahle said, stepping past the two of them. "The diagnosis is the first step in establishing an effective treatment plan for the patient," she added, directing them left down a long white hallway.

As Olivia hurried along and flipped open her notepad, Mac too picked up the pace to follow along behind their tour guide.

Similar to the level they had boarded the elevator on, this space was also decorated floor to ceiling in a sterile stark white. Every closed door they passed was white, everything white, white, and white. Mac had expected to hear their footfalls echoing in such bare halls but when she didn't, she figured they must have installed some kind of noise-cancelling or deadening device, as she could barely hear the clicking of their tour guide's high heels. It reminded her of the sensation of clogged ears when you're in an airplane, but without the need to plug your nose and blow. Still, she wiggled an index finger in her ear canal, expecting some relief.

"We have an array of diagnostic services and a state-of-the-art pediatric pulmonary function laboratory where our team performs a thorough list of testing," Mac heard Amahle say, as they came to a stop halfway down the hall.

Using her key fob again, Amahle placed her right thumb on a scanner. When the door slid into the wall Star Trek style, she said, "Here we have methacholine challenge testing."

"That's for diagnosing asthma," Olivia said, turning to Mac.

"They do exhaled nitric oxide testing for measurement of airway inflammation, as well as skin allergy testing for common allergens that cause asthma," Amahle added, leading them into a three-sided glass enclosure with sliding doors opposite the solid one they'd entered through. When the door behind them slid shut, Amahle did not move to go through the glass doors, instead she stood to the side as if to let them see through to the mostly white space beyond.

Olivia smiled and continued to jot down notes, then she nodded as if ready for more.

Pointing to the far side of the patient testing space, Amahle said, "Over here we utilize flexible bronchoscopy to detect airway structural lesions, bronchoalveolar lavage to detect infection or aspiration, and high-resolution chest imaging protocols to reduce radiation exposure."

Mac grimaced; she couldn't help it. The thought of kids going through these kinds of tests made her feel sick to her stomach.

Amahle must have noticed her expression, because she said, "We often combine procedures to reduce anesthesia exposures." As if that made it any less horrid. Waving an arm to the next area, she added,

"We have a dedicated pediatric pathology team for ciliary and lung biopsy analysis. They also do nasal nitric oxide testing for diagnosis of primary ciliary dyskinesia."

Though Mac didn't know what *primary ciliary* whatever was, her throat constricted slightly, and she cringed again at the thought of any child going through these extensive tests.

"Do you see many CF kids?" Olivia asked, looking up from her notes. "Cystic fibrosis," she said, informing Mac.

Mac wasn't along for the tour to learn about tests and treatments, she was there to get her *witchy* ways on, potentially to find if anything non-copacetic was happening behind the do-gooder company's persona. She knew Lynn had suspicions there was more to this place than was being shown to the public.

"Yes," she said to Olivia. "And we do a lot of genetic testing for CF and interstitial lung diseases, along with sweat tests for diagnosis of cystic fibrosis. For early detection of CF lung disease and other disorders we do infant lung function testing as well." She turned in the direction of the door they'd come through. "Let me take you to our second floor," she said, using her key fob to swoosh open the door.

She moved remarkably fast for someone walking in 4-inch heels, Mac noted, watching as she traveled back down the hall towards the elevator.

On the third floor, they found it much the same as the second, though they were told that the medical staff on this level were dedicated to studying and testing cystic fibrosis and a condition called Primary Ciliary Dyskinesia. The symptoms of such often resembled those of other conditions like allergies and other chronic respiratory conditions.

"Accurate, definitive diagnosis of PCD is critical. It allows for optimal treatment," Olivia advised Mac.

When they stopped in front of a large observation window, Amahle said, "We have a team of pulmonologists, several of whom specialize in the diagnosis and treatment of this rare condition."

On the other side of the window appeared to be a highly sophisticated testing enclosure with three people dressed in those full facial masks and head-to-toe white sterilized jumpsuits. All three were sitting in front of high-tech microscopes, with trays of test tubes on the counters next to them.

"Only three lab technicians in today," Olivia said, stating the obvious, though Mac suspected that Olivia's chakras were sensing more staff than they could see.

Amahle's stoic expression shifted ever so slightly, Mac noticed. "Yes—holiday staff," she said to Olivia.

Olivia cut Mac a glance using only her eyes, then she tapped the side of her neck with two fingers, indicating a *racing pulse*, a covert signal the two had established to use when dealing with anxious mothers. Mac gave back a nod. Olivia sometimes used this gesture at work to let Mac know when she sensed if any of the new mothers were frightened or worried about treatments they had discussed, but now she was using it as a BS detector.

"The most important diagnostic tests are the nasal nitric oxide testing—as I mentioned earlier," Amahle continued, unaware, "is an incredibly sensitive way of diagnosing PCD, along with the use of the electron microscope, and the genetic testing that I pointed out in the lab on the second floor."

Geeze, was there going to be an exam at the end of this tour Mac wondered? "What is the treatment?" Mac asked, even though she wasn't sure she wanted to know.

"Treatment for PCD, requires patients to have daily breathing treatments and chest physiotherapy. As well, they often need antibiotics for infection," Amahle informed them.

"Can you cure it?" Mac asked, hopeful.

"No, there is no cure for PCD," she said, stomping Mac's optimism.

"But at our hospital, we have found that if we can stay on top of the disease with regular visits with doctors and lung function testing, we can help patients live more happy, active lives," Olivia countered, smiling at Mac.

"Unfortunately, with PCD being such a rare disease, there are very few hospitals—or facilities like ours, with the tools and experience necessary to diagnose and treat it," Amahle said, the condescension in praise of her company seeping out.

Talk about an egotistic killjoy, Mac thought, feeling a sudden need to slap the woman.

"More than 75 percent of people with CF are diagnosed by age 2, and more than half of the CF population is age 18 or older," Amahle continued. "But here we deal with those under the age of 18."

Ah, yes—more happy information, Mac mused. "What is cystic fibrosis?" she asked.

"It's a life-threatening, genetic disease that causes persistent lung infections and progressively limits a person's ability to breathe," Amahle responded, emotionless as if the particulars weren't about actual people—kids in fact.

"Anyone with CF has to follow the 6-foot rule all the time," Olivia added.

"Why?" Mac asked, wanting to kick herself now for asking.

"With the excess mucus in the lungs, bacteria can get trapped and cause infections. And that's super dangerous—even life-threatening to people with CF," Olivia told Mac. "The 6-foot rule applies to anyone who is sick and other CF people. They can get infections that the general population usually doesn't—and are more likely to pass those germs to others with the disease. Like with the coronavirus, experts chose the distance of 6 feet because it's how far germs can spread— when a person coughs, sneezes, or even speaks."

"You seem well versed in this disease," Amahle stated, as though questioning Olivia, and a little too over-curious for Mac's liking.

"Well, the *6-foot rule* is widely known—and I used to work at CHEO," Olivia said, her spine straightening with pride. "They have strict regulations about keeping CF patients away from each other."

"What's the deal?" Mac asked.

Before Olivia could offer Mac more clarity, their condescending tour guide said, "In people with CF, a defective gene causes a thick buildup of mucus in the lungs, the pancreas, and in other organs. In the lungs, the mucus clogs the airways and traps bacteria leading to infections, extensive lung damage, and eventually, respiratory failure." Like an emotionless robot, Amahle turned away from the observation window and headed back towards the elevator, continuing to speak as she went. "In the pancreas, the mucus prevents the release of digestive enzymes which impacts how the body breaks down food and absorbs the vital nutrients," she added, as though reading facts from a textbook.

Though Mac could have sworn she saw the woman grin as she relayed the details. "And I'm guessing there is no cure for CF either?" Mac asked, already presuming the answer as they followed their guide back to the elevator.

Olivia shook her head when Mac glanced her way, then said, "The disease generally gets worse over time. However, thanks to screening and new treatments, people with CF can live into their 40s and even longer now."

Mac nodded, but her heart felt heavy, and she couldn't bring herself to force a smile.

"Let me take you to the fourth floor, where we address Aerodigestive disorders," Amahle said, her tone joyful as if such illnesses like this thrilled her. She swiped the blue key card again to open the elevator door.

Mac looked to Olivia confused as they stepped onto the elevator.

Olivia shrugged and then asked, "Aerodigestive?"

"Yes, these are congenital abnormalities of airway and lung development. The team focuses on rare lung diseases including interstitial lung disease and bronchiolitis obliterans, such as tracheobronchomalacia."

"Now that was a mouthful," Mac said, making no attempt to repeat the 50-foot-long word.

With an irritated expression, Amahle turned to face Olivia. "Our AD program specializes in the treatment of complex breathing and swallowing disorders of the aerodigestive tract—nose, mouth, throat, lungs, esophagus and stomach. As well as upper airway disorders, craniofacial syndromes that cause breathing and feeding problems. Laryngeal cleft is common—which I'm sure you're familiar with," she directed at Olivia. "There is a lengthy list, but I won't bore you with the rest. That information is also available on our website," she said, before going on to list off all the symptoms for them.

Mac had had enough medical talk and tuned the woman out as they rode the elevator to the next floor. When the elevator stopped and the door opened again, Mac tuned back in to hear the woman say something about how their specialists use a wide array of state-of-the-art tools to make accurate diagnoses, blah, blah, blah. Returning then to tune out the details, Mac followed behind Olivia.

This floor had an open lab that displayed beyond glass walls that lined one side of the hall. When they stopped in the center, and as their guide went on with naming off the equipment and testing sections, Mac stretched out her witchy senses to see if she could pick up on anything hinky.

Stealthily, she reached into her purse and grasped hold of the jar. She took in a quick breath, then coughed it out to muffle any sound of her shaking the jar. But luckily even she couldn't hear it. She made a mental note then to ask Olivia later if she had experienced the same lack of sound issue she was having now. She drew in a slow steady breath, and held it, stretching out her senses. Not one single tingle or prickle Mac noted. "Nothing," she breathed out. Olivia and Amahle turned to stare at her. *Crap*, she'd said that aloud. She gave them a quick innocent grin.

Amahle huffed out a breath and then continued, "… our treatment is committed to supporting both the short and long-term medical needs of our patients." Amahle pointed to different sections laid out in view through the long window. The first part of the discussion Mac hadn't heard obviously, nor had she been paying attention to anything said about the different sectioned areas, though her ears perked up at Amahle's next words. "… they review available medical therapies first to determine if alternative medical treatment or modifications of the current treatment might be appropriate," she said.

"Alternative medical treatment?" Mac asked, clearly interrupting, and only because it was her and Olivia's area of expertise.

"Yes," she said, waving a dismissive hand at Mac as she moved then to venture further down the hall. "For patients whose conditions aren't well managed through medication alone, we offer a full range of procedural and surgical techniques to give the most up-to-date and effective options for resolving conditions."

That sounded more like a sales pitch, Mac thought, than the desire to help these kids.

"For rehabilitation and support—do you make sure to assist patients with specialized pediatric social work teams?" Olivia asked, jumping in. "We use child life therapists to help patients understand and cope with anxiety related to their condition and treatment." Olivia straightened her back again, then tossed Mac a quick smile full of satisfaction.

"Oh yes, of course. We also coordinate with audiology and speech-language pathology teams to provide integrated support for children with speech, language, and swallowing/feeding disorders," Amahle answered, giving them a little side head tilt and a haughty grin.

That was good to hear, but her delivery had still felt too sales pitchy for Mac's taste, and that smug grin, *yeesh*.

"You'll be happy to see this next floor. On the patient floor—when we have patients, we have pediatric pulmonary staff on site that care for the children," Amahle said, spinning around, heading swiftly back the way they'd come.

At the next floor, when the elevator doors opened this time, Mac's airplane pressure hearing was gone. She could hear the sharp clicking of Amahle's shoes now as she led them out and on to the floor.

On this level, the temperature was comfortably warm, and there were no halls this time, only a large open room with hospital beds sectioned off by curtained dividers, much like the day patient treatment area for her and Olivia's program section of the hospital. "Why did you think we would be happy to see this floor," Mac asked, scanning the room and its decorative walls. There were cartoon animals and superheroes adorning each of the white walls.

"We like it when there are *no* patients in for treatments, as you can imagine," she responded, smiling then, and showing us her perfect white teeth.

But Mac wasn't sold. Everything just looked too… well, *staged*. It didn't even smell like a hospital. In fact, it smelled like *tropical* flowers. And was that chirping Mac was hearing? "Do I hear birds?" Mac asked, figuring it was one of those tropical rainforest recordings being fed through speakers.

"On the sixth floor—yes. That's a special floor—quite unique," Amahle shared. She gave another smile, this one having a sinister edge, an edge Mac believed the woman thought she had concealed.

After a quick walkthrough of the patient floor, they were brought to the sixth floor, and it too was a comfortable temperature, though they were not permitted to go in without protective gear, Amahle informed them. There were several small 2 by 6-inch viewing slots in the walls between the only two doors into the aviary space. "Why the small, slotted openings?" Mac asked, leaning in to look through one. She couldn't actually see much, other than a few wire cages with nothing in them, but she could definitely hear the different bird sounds.

"Birds and windows," Amahle said, "not a good mix."

"Oh-my-gosh," Olivia said, bringing a hand to her mouth, realizing the possible implications.

"For research purposes, we have found that examining birds and their lungs very insightful," Amahle said, dismissing Olivia's alarm. "Respiratory diseases are among the most common problems seen in all species of domesticated birds. And since they can have a variety of causes for lung and airway disorders, early diagnosis and proper treatment is also necessary to prevent severe illness. It is *alternative* research, as is our greenhouse. I'll show you that last."

Back in the elevator, this time instead of choosing the button for the next floor up, the seventh, Amahle pressed the 'L' for the first floor, but neither Mac nor Olivia said anything. Though Mac shot Olivia a quick inquisitive glance before the door shut.

"Are you familiar with greenhouses?" Amahle asked, addressing no one in particular,

Olivia said, "I've walked through some—but that's it."

Mac shook her head, speculating that the woman's question was most likely asked just to fill in the dead air as they rode the elevator down. When the elevator door opened on the same side it had for the other floors, and not the original door they'd entered from the lobby floor, Mac was pleasantly surprised to find this side's hallway had pleasing décor, not white on white, but similar to that of the main entry lobby.

In front of them was a wall of floor to ceiling windows with humidity evident on them and the two doors that showed patches of greenery through their foggy wet windows. To the right of the glass wall was a windowless alarm warning emergency exit. To the left there was a solid door with no handles, that looked much like the doors to the elevator though this one was a more standard size and was done in a black matt metal finish.

"You are permitted to go inside—but do not touch the plant life," Amahle said, sharply. She used a green swipe card this time to open things up.

"Feels... *tropical*," Olivia said, stepping inside only a few feet past the doors.

Following in behind, Mac patted her mouth with the corner of her shawl, her upper lip unexpectedly beading with moisture. A second later the bottom of Mac's feet began tingling.

"Yes, these plants are mainly from the rainforest," Amahle shared.

Witchy senses firing, Mac said, "Is there a level below us?" The tingling and heat on the bottoms of her feet continued, building to a point of near discomfort.

"Below us—no," Amahle said, tightening her lips.

"Where does that go?" Mac asked, pointing to another door, this one on the far side of the greenhouse.

Her question was followed by a long, very uneasy pause, then Amahle said, "That's uhm... the stairwell to the additional... uhm—water system, drainage—you know, for the greenhouse." She wrung her hands. "It was added when this structure was built—to accommodate the additional watering needs." She waved both her hands around as if gesturing to the plant requirements.

"It's very warm in here," Olivia said, her face dewy with perspiration.

"Okay then—let's get you back to the front lobby," their tour guide said hurriedly, waving an arm and ushering them out into the hall again.

"*That was fast,*" Mac said, under her breath. She pressed the back of her thumb to her mouth, chewing the corner of her lower lip. Whatever this lady was selling, Mac wasn't buying it. That's when she noticed that the unmarked elevator door had a key fob sensor and one of those finger scanning devices next to it. "Private elevator?" Mac asked, swapping out her thumb for a quick lick of her tongue. She stared toward the black door.

"That…," Amahle began, then hesitated. "… that goes to and from this floor up to the seventh floor—directly, to where we have our boardrooms and my boss's private office." She turned away to tap her key fob on the elevator's security sensor.

"Your boss? Mac asked, the nerve endings on the bottoms of her feet still firing uncomfortably.

"Thaddeus Smyth III," she said, as the elevator door opened. "But he's out of the building at the moment. He had a special child to visit in another location." That *name*, Mac recognized, noticing also that when Amahle had spoken the word *special* she had done so as though she needed to cushion the fact that her boss was unavailable.

"*Thaddeus,*" Mac heard Olivia whisper, recognizing too the same name Lynn had mentioned on their video call.

"Yes," Amahle said, evidently hearing Olivia speak the name. "He's in New York City—meeting a new patient, as I mentioned." Her eyes narrowed as if in suspicion of Olivia.

"Right—gotcha," Mac said, heading towards the elevator, pulling on the arm of a still bewildered Olivia.

They were through the elevator door to the now open one on the far side and then into the cold white hall before anyone could say another word. The silence stretched as they continued the route back through the low ceiling airlock chamber and into the main lobby. At the security desk, Amahle instructed the two security guards to return their phones.

"Thank you for accommodating us today—on the holiday," Olivia said graciously, breaking the non-dialogue that had occurred.

"My boss will be satisfied to know we have made a new connection," Amahle said, all diplomatic like.

Then when Olivia reached out a hand and went to step forward, Amahle took a step back and placed both of her hands behind her back, as if subtly indicating she was not open to any potential handshake.

Olivia shrugged and said, "Okay—thank you again."

Mac turned away from their frosty tour guide and Olivia followed, the two of them moving hurriedly through the large steel currently wide-open main front door and hustling it off to the car.

"What the...?" Olivia started to say, as she got into her car.

"I-don't-know," Mac shot out, heart pounding, settling in on the passenger side. "But something is seriously *off* with that chick—and this place."

Chapter 13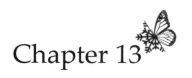

Monday morning, early, there was a knock-knock-knocking on our bedroom door.

"Come in," Redmond called, sleepily, giving my shoulder a nudge, as if I hadn't heard the rapping on the door.

"Here we go," I whispered, grinning at him as I sat up in bed.

The bedroom door swung open then, letting loose an onslaught of giggling small humans and barking dogs. Following them were Redmond's parents carrying what appeared to be breakfast trays.

"Happy Anniversary," they all chimed, crossing the threshold into the bedroom.

Fluffing his pillows behind him to sit up properly, Redmond said, "What a wonderful surprise."

"You guys didn't need to do this—but I'm glad you did," I said, when the girls crawled up at the foot of our bed.

Enzo set the tray he was carrying on Redmond's lap and then sat down on the corner at the end of the bed. "I did the toast," he said, grinning.

At closer inspection they were indeed the portable trays we'd been given as a wedding gift, though the meals that were presented on them were clearly a combination of adult and *child* preparation.

"We did the eggs," Ryley said, shifting to her knees and leaning her weight against her grandfather.

Hayley crossed her arms over her chest and frowned, pushing her bottom lip out in a sulk.

"What's wrong?" I asked her, adjusting the cover to make a level surface.

Hayley huffed, then said, "They were supposed to be over-easy — but Ryley messed them up." She gave her sister the side eye.

"I did not," Ryley shot back at her sister.

"Giiiirls," their Nana said, shutting things down and handing me the other tray that she'd been carrying.

The toast looked edible and had smears of crunchy peanut butter on them. The eggs on the other hand, based on the scattering of burnt pieces, *scrambled* had been an afterthought in their preparation. There were no telltale signs of shells, but after past experiences with the girls' cooking techniques, I'd be sure to chew carefully the yellow and brown mishmash. When I glanced at the cup of hot coffee on my tray, Nainseadh said, "I made that." And then she winked at me knowingly.

"Thank you," I mouthed, before picking up my steamy cup wake-up brew.

"Everything looks fantastic," Redmond added, taking a small forkful of the eggs to taste. "Mmmm," he said, turning to look at me, his eyes wide in a clear message that they were *not* edible.

Normally I would have been starving for breakfast, but after the big Boxing Day meal from last night, and the flow of red wine with our guests during the meal *and* after we had put the girls to bed, the only thing I was interested in doing was coveting and sipping this wonderful cup of coffee.

"Where is your gift, girls?" Enzo asked, glancing back at the open bedroom door.

"Forgot," Hayley said, scooting off the bed, followed by her sister.

The two returned in less than a minute, climbing back up on the bed again, each with one of their hands gripped to the sides of the oblong shaped wrapped gift.

"We both wrapped it," Hayley said, beaming with pride.

"I did the tape part," Ryley added, as they both handed over their creatively packaged gift to us.

Redmond and I mirrored their actions, each taking one side as the gift was presented. Together we gently unwrapped our respective sides, to reveal the back side of what I assumed was a picture frame. Redmond released his side of the frame, and I flipped it over.

Based on the scattered arrangement of seashells, it was obvious the frame had been hand decorated by the girls, using the shells they and their grandparents had gathered from their walks on the beach this past week. Within the frame was one of my most favorite pictures, a selfie Redmond had taken of the four of us at the beach from this past summer. It didn't get any better than this, I thought, glancing up from the photo to look around at the loving faces of our little family. "It's… perfect," I said, barely holding back tears of gratitude.

"The frame is beautifully done," Redmond said, taking it from me and examining it closer. "An excellent photo-frame combination." He smiled big and nodded his approval.

"I really love it—and thank you all for preparing this special breakfast for us too," I said, grinning hard, fighting back the waterworks.

"Okay—you two, let's go clean up the kitchen," Enzo said, grinning again.

"You two enjoy your breakfast," Nainseadh said then, rolling her eyes. "Trust me—you don't want to see the kitchen right now." She patted my shoulder.

"Thanks, Mom," Redmond said, shifting off the bed to give his mother a kiss before she left the room.

She nodded and winked at me again before heading off to what I was sure was a disaster in the kitchen.

I set the frame on the night table next to my side of the bed and then picked up my coffee again, savoring the aroma.

Last night, after Lily and Darius had left, and since his parents had done all the meal prep and cooking, Redmond and I had made sure the task of cleaning up the kitchen and the dishes was ours alone. So, whatever had taken place and was left over from this morning's breakfast creation, I was in no hurry to witness. And I was quite content to stay in bed a little longer to enjoy my coffee.

Redmond and I had tucked the girls into their beds last night just shy of their normal bedtimes, and with the dogs next to them on the floor. All were evidently exhausted from the week's festivities. Outside the girls' rooms, Gabriel had appeared in the hall just as we had closed their bedroom doors. Before rejoining the others out on the deck, he had explained that Zaqiel would be here in his stead, watching over the girls while he was up in Ottawa with us. I had already sensed the Horseman, but obviously with the in-laws here, he had been keeping his presence at a stealthy distance. I was comfortable leaving the girls in the capable hands of their grandparents, and I would take the extra surveillance anytime, but we still needed to make sure the twins knew about the arrangement as well.

"Girls!" Redmond called out, as though reading my mind.

When the twins came scampering back into the bedroom, Redmond closed the door to give us a bit of privacy.

"You probably already know it—sense it—him, but Zaqiel will be around watching over you guys while your Mum and I are up in Ottawa," Redmond said to them, sitting down on the edge of the bed.

"Ya—he's here," Ryley said, climbing back up on the bed.

Hayley nodded, following her sister onto the bed.

"If you see him—don't say anything around your grandparents—don't forget," I informed them. This would be the first time since they were born that we could not be under the same roof at night, and the first time traveling without them.

"We know, Mum," Hayley said, with a little grin.

"In the knowing only," Ryley added, placing the index finger of her left hand against her lips.

Hayley copied her, doing the same but using her right.

"We knew we could count on you two," Redmond said, getting up off the bed and opening the door again.

"We love you guys," I said, stretching my arms wide for a double hug.

"Love you too," they said in harmony, crawling across the bed towards me. They each gave me a hug and a kiss before hoping off the bed and then did the same with their father. "Love you, Da," they said, on their departure from the room.

I checked my phone then and realized I had missed a text from Olivia that she had sent last night. Her text stated she had lots to tell us regarding their mission to the research center, and that she had a video she wanted us to see as well, but also stated that it could wait until we got there, and better that they explain it all in person. Before getting out of bed, I texted her back saying that we couldn't wait to see everyone and to hear how things went with her and Mac on their tour.

Redmond's phone chimed then, indicating he'd gotten a text.

"It's from Eric," he said, checking the message. "His plan is to land here by noon—to pick us up."

I checked the time on my phone. "Plenty of time to get packed and cleaned up," I said, leaving the bed and padding off to our en suite bathroom.

"I'll let him know we'll be ready and good to go," I heard Redmond say before I turned on the shower.

An hour later, we were both showered, dressed, and packed for our trip up north. It was easy this time to dress for this trip since it was cooler today like it had been the past few weeks, and both of us had chosen jeans and long-sleeved tops to wear. I'd picked a three-button pale blue thermal worn over the same colour t-shirt. Redmond had decided on a dark green round-neck thermal shirt—which I loved because it complemented his russet hair so nicely. And I had put on my Doc Martins while Redmond had opted to wear his black and white Converse high-tops.

Then after going over a few household and dog care tasks with Redmond's parents that needed to be done in our absence, we chose to dedicate the last hour before having to leave, to cuddling with the girls out on the back deck. The sun was bright, but the air was cool, so we snuggled under quilts and sipped on the delicious hot chocolate their grandmother had made for all of us.

"I better do a trip to the bathroom before we have to leave," I said, shifting out from under the cozy blankets.

Just then the patio door slid open.

"Do you need me to take the two of you to the airport?" Enzo asked, leaning out from the open patio door.

"Do you have to go already?" Hayley asked, scooching to get off the couch.

Ryley gathered up the blankets and began dragging them off to the open patio door. "Can we come with you to the airport?" she asked, almost tripping on the blankets as she stepped through the opening.

"A taxi is easier—less driving for you," Redmond said to his father, getting up from his spot on the patio couch. "You guys have to keep Nana and Poppy company," he said to the girls, as he followed us all in.

Back in our bedroom, Redmond and I gathered up the last of the items we needed to take with us. For me that included my phone charger I remembered, that was currently plugged in next to my side of the bed. When I straightened and turned from pulling out the charger cord to put in the side pouch of my carry-on, Redmond was standing next to me holding up the necklace he had given me on our first Christmas. I touched a hand to my neck at the realization I hadn't put it back on after my shower. "Oh, thank you," I said, turning my back to him and lifting my hair off my shoulders. Redmond lifted the chain up and over in front of me, but instead of placing it around my neck, he let it hang in front of my face.

There, dangling next to the butterfly and XO charms, was a third charm, its design I recognized right away. It was the atomic symbol for the number 50, that looked like a fancy number 4, which was also the symbol for *tin,* and the traditional gift for a 10th anniversary.

"Happy Anniversary," Redmond said, breathing the words against my ear. He lowered the chain and fastened it around my neck, then slid his arms around my waist, leaning me back into an embrace.

"I love it—how perfect," I said, folding my arms over his, resting back against his body. When Redmond had turned 50 a few years back, he'd had the same symbol tattooed on his inner left wrist in about the size of a dime and next to the scrollwork names of our daughters that he'd had done when they were born. "Time to go—I guess?" I sighed out.

"Ya," Redmond said, pressing a soft kiss to the side of my neck. "Taxi should be here any minute." He released his hold on me and then he grabbed up his luggage from off the bed.

I sighed and finished stuffing the phone cord into the pouch of my bag, then zipped it up and proceeded to follow Redmond, rolling my bag with me.

Then after several rounds of hugs, kisses and *I love yous* from the girls and their grandparents on the driveway, Redmond and I got in the cab and were on our way.

The small local airport we would be flying out of was one that catered mostly to private planes, and it was not the one that Redmond's parents had flown into south of us. This airport had a tiny building set up for passenger and luggage screening, and there was no walkway taking you to board any of the planes. You basically went in one door, did your screening, and then went out the door on the other side, straight on to the tarmac.

Upon exiting the door, I spotted Eric over on the left and next to his Cessna Citation Bravo flying taxi. He was a big man, similar in height to Redmond, but he was built more like that of a retired linebacker. He had an easygoing disposition and was quick with a smile and I appreciated that about him. He wasn't much older than Redmond though he did have a full head of mostly *salt* and pepper hair. We had seen photos of Eric's plane; however, this was the first time we'd be flying in it. I had flown in a small plane before, *once*, back when Santa—I mean, Nicolaas Bakker—St. Nick, as his friends called him, had offered me a ride back to Miami in his two-seater plane that Christmas so long ago. Eric's plane thankfully, was larger and could hold up to seven passengers comfortably, and in a little over 3 hours, we would be setting down in my hometown of Ottawa in good old Canada.

Redmond and I took turns exchanging hugs with our pilot, and then Eric took our luggage up into the plane and stored it somewhere out of sight.

"Here," Eric said, when I climbed in and took one of the two first seats in the row. He handed me a bag of what I recognized as Vicki's healthy taste-like-they're-bad-for-you cookies. "She figured you guys might be hungry." Then when Redmond sat down, Eric handed both of us cellophane wrapped stuffed-to-the-brim submarine sandwiches, and a cooler, which on further examination, contained two waters and four cold beers in it.

"You run a fancy enterprise," Redmond said appreciatively, grinning big and patting Eric on the shoulder.

"Only the best—for my guests," Eric said, before closing and securing the door of the airplane.

I opened the bag of cookies and sniffed. "How do I love thee—let me count the cookies," I said, before grabbing one and biting into it. I had not eaten the breakfast the girls had prepared and had only consumed the coffee and the hot chocolate before we'd left, so I was more than thankful that Eric-the-saint and Vicki-the-food-goddess, had thought to supply snacks for our trip.

"Vicki made the sandwiches too. She's an excellent cook, my Vick," he added, rubbing his barely-there belly. Then he turned and headed to the pilot's section of the plane.

"Thank you-thank you," I said shoving another cookie into my mouth. Then I sent off a quick group text to ladies up north.

Chapter 14

Half Moon Bay Park in Barrhaven, December 27th, Ottawa, Canada

As dusk crept into the day, Gabriel stood gazing up at the 13-foot-high cast aluminum sculpture of the Fallen Star, created by artist Don Maynard in 2013. The star itself is balanced on one of its 5 points in representation of a star falling to the earth. The sculpture has thousands of tiny holes which emulate a twinkling starry sky whenever a light source shines through it. Around the star, small footprints in the snow and sled tracks covered the space near it giving evidence that tobogganers had been there recently, and down the slight hill at the far side of the park, the playground was trampled with more footprints, suggesting that the joyous merriment of children playing had taken place. But right now, all Gabriel could hear was the soft crunch of snow as one of his brethren approached.

"Gabriel," Michael's voice sounded as he came to a stop behind him.

"It's good to see them all together, isn't it?" Gabriel stated, his back still to Michael.

The sound of crunching stopped. "The others are always together these days," Michael said.

"Except for Lynn." Gabriel tilted his head back to look up at the sky.

"That was only because of the pandemic." Michael sighed.

"Still." Gabriel reached out to touch the aluminum star.

"The others have chosen to live in close proximity—Lynn chose to stay where she was."

"Her life is South now—you know that," Gabriel responded, running his hand over the textured metal. "She is grateful to get up here finally to see them again though. She and Redmond will be staying with *your* Charge on this trip. I quite like Vicki's mate—and the new dwelling they share together," Gabriel added.

"Nice that they chose to live in Barrhaven too—so close to the others," Michael said.

"Like I said—it's nice to see them all together." Gabriel huffed out a breath into the cold late afternoon air.

"Yes—it is. But that's not what you brought me here to talk about—is it?" Michael stated.

Gabriel knew Michael was correct in his assumption. He hadn't asked him here to talk about Lynn being with her friends. In fact, he dreaded being the bearer of bad tiding, but he also wasn't about to keep things from him and the others again. Gabriel turned to face his fellow Archangel. "Lynn had a visitor the other day."

"Don't tell me—one of the Horsemen?"

"No—but Zaqiel is watching the twins while I'm—while we're away," Gabriel said, sliding his hands into the pocket of his coat.

"Who then?" Michael asked, tilting his head, and frowning, his patience obviously beginning to wear thin.

"A Seraphim from Pleiades." Gabriel glanced up at the sky again.

"A Seraphim—that's a first. None have visited her before. From which star?" Michael glanced up then too.

"Celaeno," Gabriel said, dropping his head to stare down at his feet.

"Gabriel…," Michael began, "… there is only *one* Seraphim left on that star." The snow squeaked under Michael's feet as he shifted his weight. "Why would the Steward of Celaeno be visiting Lynn?"

Gabriel brought his head up to look Michael in the face. "She came to warn her—and now Lynn knows."

"Everything?" Michael questioned, taking a step forward then back as if there was no place for him to go.

"No." Gabriel ran a hand through his short hair. For months after the gathering, he and his fellow Archangels had spent a considerable amount of time answering questions that their Charges had presented them with, but there were still some things they had held back. Like any details that pertained to heaven, what happened to humans when they died, and who exactly had created the celestials. Luckily, none had pushed for answers when they'd been told which subjects had been off limits. And since no one had asked them to explain the specifics on the genetic makeup or the biological structure and functions pertaining to Angels, they had not had to elaborate on the biological differences of each Angel caste.

"Just spill it Gabriel—I'm tired of this cryptic dialog." Michael threw his hands in the air. "What does Lynn know?"

Gabriel drew in a frigid breath. "That Thaddeus knows about her—her abilities, that she can sense other celestials," he breathed out.

"How does he know?" Michael asked, his voice rising.

"One of the others saw her—talking to a Watcher," Gabriel said. "They put two-and-two together—now they know she can sense more than us and The Fallen." Gabriel passed the palm of his left hand across his jaw.

"What else did she tell Lynn?" Michael crossed his arms over his broad chest.

"That Lynn could be in danger." Gabriel tightened his lips.

"Does Lynn know what Thaddeus did?"

"Not fully—just that he and his followers were up to no good, and that they were cast down," Gabriel said, turning his face to the star sculpture and then back to Michael. He had confirmed Lynn's idea about Thaddeus being an Angel stuck on Earth, though he'd not expanded on what that meant exactly, nor had he shared with her what Seraphim could and couldn't do—Earthbound or not.

"Well—it seems that my and Raphael's Charges—are involved now," Uriel tossed out, appearing next to Michael. "Olivia and Mac went on a little reconnaissance mission for Lynn to Thaddeus's building it seems."

"What?" Michael barked out. "Did you know about this, Gabriel?"

Gabriel scowled. "They are not babies!" he bellowed. "Have you forgotten what they accomplished together?" Of course, he knew they were going to go, but what he hadn't known was what they might encounter or find on that little excursion.

"Why has your Charge involved ours?" came Raphael's inquiry as he appeared between Michael and Uriel.

"She simply shared what she knew—Mac and Olivia took it upon themselves to go to the building." Gabriel returned his hands to the pockets of his coat. "And the two were smart about it," Gabriel added.

"They are all involved now," Vretil's voice boomed, followed by the sound of his footfalls crunching in the snow as he came to stand next to Uriel. "They all know about Purah visiting Lynn and the boy identified as being a Nephelium. The Theologian, The Guardian—everyone's mates, and don't forget The Cipher," he added, as though exasperated.

"The others pushed Lynn out last time—when they actually needed her. And you all know—they'd never let something like that happen again." Gabriel blew out an infuriated breath, frosted air streaming from his nostrils. "I've arranged for Lynn and Redmond to meet Leo tomorrow morning."

"Leo—are you sure about this?" Uriel asked, his brows furrowing.

"And of course, they'll be sharing whatever they learn from him as well—I presume," Vretil said, angrily.

"Why not?" Gabriel asked. "This is their friendship—unwavering, unbreakable."

"I bet you fifty bucks, they uncover more—than we ever could," Michael said, as if onboard now with their Charges' involvement.

"Are you a betting Angel now, Michael," Vretil asked then, with a smirk, his anger dulling.

"You don't have fifty *cents*—let along fifty dollars," Raphael said. "But I'd bet on our Charges too—in a heartbeat." He gave Michael a pat on the back.

Gabriel smiled back at Raphael and Michael, then turned his sights on Vretil and Uriel. "What say you?" he asked the pair.

Vretil turned to look at Uriel. "It's not like we can stop them, anyway," he said. "Better to be by their side, rather than on the sidelines—don't you think?"

Chapter 15

Ottawa International Airport, December 27th, Ottawa, Canada

The flight had been so smooth that I had fallen asleep in my chair, although I'm sure part of my sleepiness had been a combination of the previous late night and the delicious inflight homemade food and cold beers. As we taxied in, I sent a quick text to the girls and Redmond sent one to his parents, to let everyone know we had landed safely.

A private plane was a truly luxurious way to fly, and other than having to walk across the tarmac in December in Ottawa to get into the airport, the only other painful part of the journey was having to snake through the long line for immigration with the multitude of passengers from the commercial flights that had arrived ahead of us.

Once through the last set of doors and out to our freedom into the meet-and-greet part of the airport, we were immediately welcomed by the smiling faces of Mac, Olivia, Vicki, and Alison, two of whom were holding up a huge *Happy 10th Anniversary* sign. Next to them were the grinning faces of the guys, Don, Mike, and Ken, who held out in front of them their own sign, this one resembling a giant *Get Out of Jail Free* card from the Monopoly game.

"You guys are such characters," I said, addressing the men.

Stepping forward, Mac held out two winter coats for us. She always kept our winter-wear and boots at her place to make our packing easier when we visited during the colder months. Ottawa was having a mild winter, so there was no need for winter footwear at the moment. "Welcome, peeps," Mac said, handing off the coats.

Redmond took his coat, and then he gave Mac a noisy squeak of a kiss on her cheek.

When I slipped into my coat, Mac grabbed me for a hug and said, "Feels like it's been a hundred years since I've seen you."

"Two hundred," I said, squeezing her tighter. Then the embrace got even tighter as Olivia and Alison encircled the two of us in their arms.

"Yer coming with us," Vicki directed at Redmond and me before hugging her pilot boyfriend. "Meet you back at our house," she instructed the rest of the gang.

Since Vicki and her new boyfriend had recently bought a new house, we were staying with them on this trip. They had been living together for a few years now, so I guess he wasn't exactly *new*, but he was 5 years younger than she was—so go Vicki! Neither had small nor grown kids living with them, therefore they had plenty of room for us to make their house our home base. Vicki's son, Jeffrey, is in his 30s now and has been out of the house for some time. Like his mother, he had caught the travel bug early in life, and prior to the pandemic he had been traveling the world learning to cook the local cuisines at each stop, all the while building his photography portfolio and business.

It was Monday after the Christmas holiday, so there wasn't a ton of traffic between the airport and Barrhaven where my four girlfriends and their families currently resided, and Vicki made great work of getting us to the new neighborhood she and Eric lived in. I had forgotten how early it started to get dark here in December, and being just after 4 p.m., the twilight was already beginning to settle in.

"Here we are," Vicki announced, as we pulled into the driveway of their new two storey, two-car garage home. They'd had this house built in a neighborhood close to Olivia in a newer part of Barrhaven called Half Moon Bay, and they had chosen a model called the—no joke, *Westlynn*. Seriously, I'd needed to see the plans for myself, and it was real. I couldn't make that stuff up. And of course, I had to tease her about it, how she missed me so much that she had to pick a house that was practically named after me.

"Gorgeous, Vicki—and more beautiful than in the photos you sent us," I said, exiting the SUV. The other cars pulled in behind and next to us in the driveway. "Thank you, again," I said to Eric as he yanked our suitcases from the back of the vehicle. As I moved towards the front door, I spotted a small black pickup truck roll to a stop along the snowy front lawn of the house. "Heeey," I called out when James circled around from the driver's side of his truck.

"What a great surprise," Redmond said, traversing the stretch of the driveway to meet up with my brother for a hug.

"I'm here for the BBQ—what are you guys doing here?" he joked, strolling up the driveway with Redmond.

"Vicki—Eric, thanks for the invite," James said. He and I took our turn at a hug, then together we followed the rest of the crew into the house.

Inside after dropping the suitcases in our room, Redmond came through to the kitchen, and said, "Mom texted back saying the girls were good—all was well, and that they were playing the Clue Junior game they'd gotten the twins for Christmas." Then he donned his coat again. "Going outside to the back patio with the guys," he added, zipping up his coat.

"To consume some beers while Eric cooks the kabobs on the barbeque—I'm guessing," I tossed out, just before he slid the patio door shut. The girls were the only ones in the kitchen working on the other parts of the meal, thus I could only assume the guys were outside swapping barbeque techniques. "Where are your boys?" I asked Mac as she mixed up something that resembled potato salad.

"Out with friends," Mac said. "They aren't home much now that things have opened up—and they can see their friends more. But don't worry—I've still got locator spells on them," she added with a wink, handing me a spoonful of the mixture for me to taste.

I took the spoon offered and devoured what I already knew would be delectable. "Mmmmm," I swooned, trying at a smile with my full mouth.

"Our girls are out with friends, too," Olivia said, smirking and shaking her head at me.

"Remember when they wanted to be with us all the time?" I reminded Olivia, licking the back of the spoon.

Olivia blew out a "*pffft*" rolling her eyes and then said, "Not aaanymooore."

"My son is hanging out with his friend next door to us," Alison said. "They're both into this new video game we got him for Christmas." She poured the spiral pasta from a pot of water she'd had on the stove into a colander resting in the sink. "He couldn't care less about time with his dad and me."

"Can you blame them?" Mac asked. "I'd be sick of us too." She gave a hearty laugh.

"No kidding," I said, laughing along with her. Any of us as kids would have been dying to get away from our families after such a prolonged isolated timeframe. "I have to admit though—I've enjoyed my walks alone in the morning." I reached for one of the warm buns Mac had put out in a basket, but she tapped my hand away just as the back patio door slid open.

In came Eric, carrying a large tray filled with hot sizzling skewers. "We have prepared the meat for our women," he announced with a chuckle, as he passed through to the kitchen. The rest of the cavemen followed in behind through the patio door.

When Eric set the tray down on the kitchen island, my stomach gave a loud, audible growl. "What—did you expect anything different from me?" I asked when all eyes turned my way. More laughing and more headshaking followed my comment, along with a one-arm squeeze and a kiss from my husband.

Once dinner was done and tummies were full, including mine, we all retreated to the large living room space to converse and digest our meals.

I took up residence next to Redmond on the loveseat next to the stone hearth. I've always loved a wood-burning fireplace. "The doorbell is going to ring," I said, grinning over at Olivia.

Then the doorbell rang.

It always freaked her out when I did that or told her the phone was going to ring. She shook her head at me again, then gave a nervous giggle.

"That must be my parents," Mac said, rushing off to the front door. "I told them we'd all be over here."

"Happy Anniversary!" came the booming voice of Mac's dad, as Redmond and I met up with Mac and her parents in the front hall.

Fred had turned 85 this past February, and Mac's mom, Monica, who was currently carrying one of those Tupperware cake/dessert containers in her little hands, had turned 83 in May. "We can't stay," Monica announced, handing her daughter the container. "These old bones tire easily now—but we wanted to bring you a little something for your celebration." She shuffled past her daughter then and into my waiting open arms. I squeezed her tight, although not *too* tight. She was the last Mom after all, and she was a delicate treasure to us daughters. *"Happy Anniversary. Your mother would be so happy for you,"* she whispered into my ear, holding me just a little firmer.

She felt so small and fragile in my arms, and my words caught in my throat as I tried to respond, the realization of her mortality hitting me like a tidal wave. *"Thank you,"* I managed to get out, refocusing my blurry eyes over her shoulder on Redmond embracing Mac's father. With a quick sniffle, I released my hold on her, as the others gathered in the hall to say their *hellos* and *goodbyes*.

"Let's go, Monica," Mac's dad barked, waving one hand at us and the other in the direction of the front door.

"Okay-Okay. Don't rush me," Monica said, reaching out and touching the hands of my girlfriends and their mates, as if transferring some of her magic to each of them as she passed by.

"Bye, Lynn, Redmond," she said with a wave before turning to go out the front door.

"Byyyye," Redmond and I called out, before the door shut.

"That was quick," I said to Mac, with a shrug.

"Ya, they are all about the quick visits these days," Mac said, giving me a nod as she headed for the kitchen with the not so *little something* from her mom.

"I hate to eat-and-run," James said then, "but I have to get back and take care of the dogs. Two-hour drive'n all."

"Another quick visit," I said, wrapping my arms around my brother.

"Thanks for making the drive," Redmond added, leaning in to give him a hug.

Goodbyes all around, and then James too was out the door.

As we stood in the doorway waving, James honked the horn as he drove off. And it reminded me of Mom and how she had always done that before driving away. I missed her every day, and seeing Mac's mom today reminded me of how precious life was and of how fast the time passes.

"Speaking of doggies," Mac said, pulling my attention back as I closed the front door. Redmond, Don, and I followed Mac back to the kitchen. The others returned to the living room. "Don got us a special little Christmas gift." She held up her phone to reveal a photo of a not so *little* puppy. "This is Fergus. Don got him from the bull mastiff rescue," she informed us. And based on the size of his paws he was going to be a big'un.

Don, like the other husbands, was no longer at his previous lackluster job and was now doing his dream job. *Fishing.* What he did specifically was book charters and fishing excursions for other people, while acting as a sort of guide for newbies in the fishing realm. He booked tours in advance during the winter months and then did the actual trips in the warmer ones. It was not a bad gig if you could get it—and he had it. "Someone had surrendered the mother—pregnant," Don added. "And now the mom and pups are all adopted." He smiled at me knowing I would think that was the best part of the story.

They had lost their dog, Cooper, in 2010, and Mac had deemed it the worst year of her life. He had stopped using his back right leg and after some x-rays, it was determined that Cooper had a mass in his chest. They had chosen to have him put to rest in their home, and Mac had told me it had been the most painful yet at the same time the most beautiful thing that she had ever witnessed. Losing a beloved family pet comes with a unique type of grief, so I was grateful to see that they were ready to bring a new pup into their fold.

"He's going to be a big boy," Redmond said, flipping through the other photos of him on Mac's phone.

"We love big dogs, obviously," I added. Our two doggies were way above standard size for their combined breeds.

"Obviously," Mac said, chuckling, setting out small plates and forks on the kitchen counter, before she headed back to the living room.

I shot a glance at the dessert container. From the shadow showing through the fogged yellow container, the 'little something' appeared to be a dark circular shaped item that I was hoping was chocolate cake. Redmond took my hand then, stealing me away from sweet musings.

"You have some interesting stuff to tell us—I take it?" Redmond asked, redirecting the conversation, and sending his inquiry to Mac and Olivia as we reclaimed our seats.

"Gifts first," Alison said, getting up to retrieve two gift bags from near the front foyer. Before sitting again, she handed Redmond and me the bags. "The red one is from Vicki and Eric, and Ken and me."

"The silver one is from Mac and Don, and me and Mike," Olivia followed up.

"I'll open the red one first," Redmond said, since he was holding that one.

I peeked into the bag when he removed the matching red tissue, but I wasn't sure what the gift was.

"Ah, nostalgia," Redmond said, removing the items from the bag.

"It's a grown-up version of one of childhood's greatest gadgets," Ken said like an announcer of a gameshow.

"A View-master?" I questioned. I loved them as a kid, but I wasn't grasping the relevancy here.

Obviously seeing my confused expression, Vicki said, "The company that makes it, lets you pick your favorite photo memories to create made-to-order reels. Take a look—check it out."

Redmond put the viewer up to his eyes. "Oh—cool!" he said, clicking the lever to move the reel images through the viewer.

"We got you a set of seven reels—custom picked," Alison said excitedly.

"Let me see—let me see," I said, playfully tugging on Redmond's arm.

"Yer gonna love this, Lynn," he said, clicking through the last image on the current reel. Then he smiled and handed me the viewer.

I put the viewer up to my face, and as the first image came into focus, I saw it was a photo of Redmond and me from our wedding. As I clicked through the reel, I was shown a series of my favorite moments from that day. "Oh-my-gawd-you-guys," I sobbed out, tears blurring my view of the images.

"The other reels have images from when the twins were born, their 1st birthday, your new beach house, and other special moments from your lives together," Eric said. "I'd seen one of my clients with one — and thought it was a clever idea."

"It's the coolest," I said, clicking through the reel again. "Thank you so much, guys." I lowered the viewer, grinning, wiping my eyes with the edge of my sleeve.

"Ours next," Mac said, bouncing a little in her seat.

Their present too was in a bag, though there was no tissue, though the contents itself was wrapped in silver paper that matched the silver bag. I removed the rectangular shaped package and set the bag aside. Then prompted Redmond to share in the unwrapping, and together we tore away the shining paper.

Beneath the paper was an 8 x 10 silver framed rendering of a stylized white tree with leaves on top and roots on the bottom. At the base of the tree were my and Redmond's initials, and in the tree on a branch were two red lovebirds. And there, beneath the roots, was the stamped date of our wedding day.

"It's tin," Olivia said. "And the image is pressed into the metal."

"Tin is for the 10th year of marriage," Mac added, but I knew that already. I touched the charms on my necklace.

"We wanted to get you a bigger version — but with traveling and all," Mike stated.

"No — it's perfect," Redmond said, encircling my shoulders with one of his big arms.

"Perfect — both gifts are utterly... *perfect*," I breathed out, fighting back another wash of tears.

"You can go ahead now and tell them," Alison said, referring to the details of the latest venture Mac and Olivia had been on.

"Can we do a quick video call with the girls first," I asked, checking my watch. "They'll want to say goodnight to you all—it's almost their bedtime."

"Of course," Olivia said. "Everyone else knows the scoop anyway, and they've seen the video I mentioned already too."

"Did you already bring Derek, Luc and Darius up to speed—send them the video?" Redmond asked.

"Yes—earlier in the day," Mac said, "You two are the last—so, it can wait."

"You can use my office—my laptop, to show them the video, after the call," Vicki added.

Redmond retrieved his phone and dialed his father's number for the video call. When Enzo answered, he gave a quick *"hello"* and then handed the phone to the girls.

As Redmond passed his phone around, I could hear how excited the girls were to see and speak to everyone. Then, after Redmond had said his *I love yous* and *goodnights* to the girls, he passed the phone to me. I took the phone and got up off the couch, then went off down the hall to sit in Vicki's office.

On the screen I could see that the girls were in Hayley's room, sitting on her bed, but I couldn't see either of Redmond's parents. "Hey—are Nana and Poppy behaving?" I asked, trying to keep a calm expression. Redmond's parents were more than capable of taking care of the twins, they were retired medical doctors after all, and we did have that added layer of celestial security, so I wasn't nervous, not really.

"I think Poppy cheats in cards," Hayley said, scrunching up her face.

"What?" I asked. She giggled then when I saw her grandfather lean in and tickle her ribs. "Yer such a kidder," I said, pleased to see they were somewhat supervised.

"Can Summer and Snow sleep in our beds tonight?" Ryley asked, her face popping in and out of view, most likely bending to pet one of the dogs.

"Are you feeling a bit nervous without us there?" I asked, feeling a tad anxious myself.

"Noooo," Ryley said, settling in view of the screen.

"But I think they are," Hayley added, her head bobbing out of view, taking a turn to pet the dogs.

The dogs always slept in their rooms on the floor, and the girls had only ever asked to have them in their beds once before, and that had been during hurricane Dorian, back in September 2019. In fact, we had all slept in our big bed during that time, even the dogs. "Okay — I think the dogs would like that," I said, remembering how it had been equally beneficial for both the girls and the dogs. Though I doubted the dogs needed comforting this time.

"Mum said yeeeeessss," Hayley called out.

"We heard her," came their Nana's voice in the distance through the phone. "Okay — say good night now."

"Alright girls — off to bed," I said, adding to their Nana's request. "Love you — sweet dreams."

"Love you, Mum," they each said, blowing kisses at the phone.

"Goodnight, dear," Enzo said, smiling into the phone.

"Goodnight," I returned before ending the call.

Redmond came into the office then, followed by Olivia and Mac, and finally Vicki, who proceeded to lean around me and log into her laptop.

"It's all yours," Vicki said before exiting the room again.

"Okay — give us the scoop," Redmond said, resting a hip against the desk.

"Well, we saw a shitload of medical testing equipment but not many people," Olivia said, before rambling out words such as methacholine, bronchoscopy, dyskinesia, and referring to their diagnosing of PCD and CF, and swallowing disorders of the aerodigestive tract, and tracheobronchomalacia — something, a crazy ten-foot-long word that sounded made up.

"Let me tell you about the woman who gave us the tour," Mac said, leading into a detailed description of the woman, her behavior as they went through the tour, as well as her clothing. After the gathering when we'd had a long list of questions for the Archangels, Mac, being the fashionista, had asked a lot about their wardrobes. We had been informed that what they wore typically mirrored the standard attire of humans and had evolved as fashions evolved. And the whole white clothes and black clothes to represent good or evil, had the propensity to be more of a stereotype and what colours they wore was a more personal choice. Most preferred dressing in whatever floated their boats, much like with Gabriel picking his recent wardrobe based on the movies he had watched.

"Speaking of well dressed," Olivia said, as she brought up the video recording, she had been wanting to show us. "I knew I recognized the building's name from somewhere." The video buffered. "I looked up the name and found this video. I'd seen it before—it's an interview from an online health magazine I subscribe to," Olivia added as the footage finally started.

"Arrogant much?" Redmond asked more as a statement, as we watched *Thaddeus Smyth III* being interviewed.

"Could this be the guy—Gabriel mentioned?" Olivia queried as the video ended.

"Did you get to meet him," I asked, restarting the interview, this time with the sound muted.

"No—Miss Tall-Dark'n-Frosty said he was in New York City seeing a *special* patient," Mac said, rolling her eyes and crossing her arms over her chest.

"Didn't Gabriel say this guy was based in Ottawa now?" Redmond reminded.

"That's what his contact, Leo, told him," I confirmed. "But evidently he has other locations too he said." I paused the video to take in the appearance and characteristics of what I had deemed a potential new foe.

"When are you supposed to meet up with this Leo guy?" Mac asked.

"Gabriel was going to arrange the meeting for us," Redmond said.

I'd been so caught up with finally getting to see everyone that I'd not wanted to get into the Angel business right away. "Not sure—waiting on Gabriel—like Redmond said," I stated. Though based on the eager expressions on my friends' faces, I was guessing it was time to work out more of the details of this meeting. "Kitchen?" I suggested getting up from the office chair. I headed out of the office and the others followed without uttering a word.

"Hey," Alison said in greeting, waving at us with a big spoon as we entered the kitchen. "What's shakin'?"

"Angel conjuring time—sorta," Mac said, leaning against the side counter.

I glanced around at my husband and my girlfriends, then did what everyone was now waiting for. "Gabriel," I called then, sending his name out to the universe. A familiar tingle ran across my skin, indicating that he was nearby.

"I love macaroni salad," Gabriel announced, showing himself and appearing next to where Alison and Vicki, who were packaging up leftovers on the kitchen island.

"Whoa!" Vicki shouted, almost dropping the barbeque tongs.

"Holy crap!" Alison hollered, startled by Vicki's shout and Gabriel's arrival, spilling some of her famous pasta salad on the counter. She had been in the process of transferring the remnants into one of the square containers set out on the island. "Sorry about that. I'll never get used to the popping in—you guys do."

"Can we fix you a plate?" Vicki asked, composed now, clicking the barbeque tongs.

Chapter 16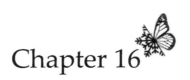

Following Gabriel's comment last night on his love of pasta salad, the second thing out of his mouth had been, *"The others are in agreement with the plan for you to meet with Leo."* Meaning that all the Archangel designates, and Gabriel, had discussed and approved the plans we had already agreed upon doing. It was nice to know they had everyone's back, but Redmond and I would have gone forward with this Monday morning meeting either way.

Gabriel had assured us that today's initial meeting would be a simple visit with his contact to learn what we could about Thaddeus and the potential threat he may pose. He had arranged for us to meet at Leo's home, and had given the address to Redmond, instructing us to meet there for 9 a.m. sharp. My clever husband had gotten on the phone right away to have the rental service drop off a car for us first thing this morning, saving us the hassle of going there in the morning such that we could arrive at the given location at the proper time. And after a quick morning call with the twins, we set out into the chilly winter morning in pursuit of knowledge.

The rental car's GPS showed 8:50 a.m. as we pulled in out front of a building that we had been told was Leo's private residence. From the front it looked to be a reclaimed two-storey motel now converted into multi-unit, two-level apartments. The upper level now only windows, had been relieved of the old walkway and doors, having the individual entrances just on the first level. Though there seemed to be a main entrance at the left-hand corner of the building that, before its conversion, had probably been the office section of the earlier motel. We went to that door instead of dealing with the confusion of having to choose one of the seven other doors available.

At the double doors we found there were no knobs or handles, but we did find it had a doorbell and intercom system. Above it, in the overhang covering the entrance and the front stairs, were what Redmond explained to me were fisheye camera lenses and were more than likely hooked up to a security system.

Redmond hit the button for the doorbell. A second later a man's voice came through the intercom. "Hello. We'll be right with you," the deep clear voice said. In equal time, there was a buzzing sound and then the right side of the double doors opened wide.

In the doorway stood a smiling, well-dressed man with light brown hair, a kind face and slight build who appeared to be in his early 50s. I had pictured Leo to be of a similar age as the other angels, between 30 and 40, based on their appearances, and certainly not close in age to Redmond and me. "Greetings—I'm Max, please come in," he said then, blowing up my assumptions. "Leo is expecting you—he'll be along any moment." Max extended an arm showing the way in.

Redmond went in first, and as I followed, I noticed we were entering into what I realized was not the office space I had imagined based on the outside but was in fact that of a beautifully decorated front foyer that led further into an open concept floor plan of a high-end home.

"Your home is…," I started to say as I glanced around.

"A surprise," Max finished for me, grinning.

"Yes—exactly—and gorgeous," I said, in agreement. And though the décor was completely different, I had felt the same wonderment as when I'd entered the Vizcaya Mansion in Miami that first time. "And so not what I expected," I added. It was a grand space, with the kitchen and eat-at island to the left. To the right was a long living room with two sofas/sitting areas, a billiards space with both a pool table and snooker table, a bar setup near it, and probably the biggest TV and largest multi-seat sectional I'd ever seen.

"We've heard that before," came the joyful voice of a second man, also nicely dressed, and who had a head of long luscious silvery grey hair tied loosely back behind his shoulders. He was similar in build to Max, though a few inches shorter. "Hi, I'm Julian," he said, extending a hand to Redmond. His bright blue eyes sparkled when he smiled.

"Redmond," my husband said back, shaking the man's hand.

"Welcome," he said, addressing me and extending his hand my way. "May I take your coats?"

I shook his hand. "I'm Lynn—thank you. Beautiful place you have here." I shrugged out of my coat and handed it to him.

Redmond removed his coat and handed it off to Julian, who stowed them away in a small closet set into the wall near the front entry. No handles on its door either. Julian simply pressed his hand to a spot on the side of the door and it opened as if spring-loaded, then pressed the door shut after he'd hung our coats inside.

"How many…," Redmond started, "… of you live here?" Redmond turned to the right, waving a hand toward the long stretch of wall and the numerous dark wood doors within it.

From where we stood in this open floor plan, the one, two—*seven* doors, showed to be equally spaced and aligned with the entrances we'd seen upon our arrival, the entries to which I'd assumed were to individual units. My guess was that my husband—like I did, presumed that along with Leo, these two males were part of the 'others' Gabriel had told us about, those assigned to monitoring the Earthbound, Thaddeus in particular.

"Our personal space is in the back," Max said, pointing to the opening of a hallway I couldn't quite see down. "We take care of the compound for Leo and the others—but we'll let Leo explain all that to you," he added.

"So, you're not…," Redmond began again, "… like Leo?"

Max laughed. "No. We are not one of The Guards. But I'll take the compliment—thank you."

"We are human like you," Julian said. "Well—not like you." He directed at me. "We are like your husband—if you know what I mean." Julian glanced at Max. "No gifts," he clarified.

"You are certainly gifted in the kitchen—my love," Max directed at Julian, ending with a little air-kiss.

"Charmer." Julian winked at his partner, waving a dismissive hand.

"Lynn—Redmond, please have a seat," Max said, leading us to a small seating area that was just left of the entrance and right of the open kitchen. The only other seating near this space were the stools set up in front of the large kitchen island.

Redmond and I sat in two pale blue, denim-like fabric covered chairs. The space felt more like a part of the home than a designated waiting space. A wave of relief blanketed me, and I wasn't sure if it was the space, these lovely gentlemen, or something else. I couldn't quite put my finger on it, but it felt to me like comfort.

"How do you know Leo?" I asked, before I could stop myself. "Sorry, that's none of my business." I felt my face flush.

"No-no," Max said, "that's perfectly okay." He pulled out one of the stools and sat.

Julian went around to the other side of the island and continued to work on whatever our arrival had caught him in the middle of preparing.

"It's just that I've—we've, never known anyone other than our crew who were in the knowing," I said, removing my bag from over my shoulder and resting it in my lap.

"*In the knowing*—that's what we call it, when someone is part of the inner circle," Redmond said, giving our hosts a kind grin.

"The *knowing*—I like that," Max said, nodding.

"I used to work for Leo at his architecture firm—back in the day, designing industrial kitchens," Julian said, glancing up from his chopping. "That's how I met Max. He was the project manager overseeing the build-out for several exclusive posh restaurants across the globe." He smiled at his mate.

"I'm sorry—Leo runs an architecture firm?" I questioned, shaking my head, thrown off by the casualness of what they were sharing. I had never known of any celestials who had *jobs*, let alone ran businesses. Well, other than this Thaddeus character who currently played at being human. "I thought it was Leo's job to watch over the Earthbound?"

"The architecture firm is one of several companies Leo has owned over the years. I had originally gone to work for him straight out of university," Julian stated. "But he sold that firm shortly after we came to work for him here."

"Trust is a process—as I'm sure you both know," Max said. "We've both been with Leo for almost 25 years. We basically just take care of Leo and the others now though. And our daughter grew up here," he added.

"Daughter? Adopted?" I asked boldly, mainly because of my adopted status. Although their relaxed attitudes made it feel as though I could ask them anything.

"Yes. Her name's Lane. And no—we had a surrogate," Max said, grinning. "Don't ask me how, but she has my colouring and Julian's gorgeous hair."

"She lives here too—though she's rarely home. Young people," Julian said, rolling his eyes. "She's doing her master's degree in environmental engineering at Ottawa U." He beamed then.

"She's a smarty-pants," I said, smiling and nodding at the two proud papas.

"We like to think so," Max said, smiling even bigger.

"Does she know…?" Redmond asked, trying at another question.

"About Leo and the others—yes. She refers to him as *Uncle Leo*."

"You keep referring to the *others*," I said. "Those like Leo who help to watch out for Thaddeus and his followers—they all live here?" Before either could answer, a prickly yet exhilarating sensation akin to what I'd felt upon Purah's arrival, pop-rocked it across the surface of my skin. "He's here—Leo—I feel him… his presence."

Max and Julian shot each other surprised glances. "You can *feel* him?" Julian asked, wiping his hands off on a dishtowel. "We've met very few people in the *knowing*—as you can imagine, but never anyone like you, one with preternatural abilities."

"Hello—sorry to keep you waiting," the Seraph Leo said, entering through the first of the doors along the wall. And he too was not what I was expecting. Note to self—*stop expecting*.

Redmond was big and tall, Gabriel was similar in height and marginally bigger than Redmond—but not by much, however this guy—this celestial, he was... well, he was basically the male equivalent in body type to that of the Steward Purah, in that he had that extra-large gladiator build. And though most celestials tended to be tall and fit looking, this kind of muscular development they most certainly did not have, none that I'd seen that is. His thick muscles could be seen generously distributed even through his tailored shirt and loose-fitting casual khakis, and his body had a muscular symmetry and perfection that matched his towering height.

"You must be Lynn," he said as he approached. His movements were fluid, unlike that of the average bodybuilder with one speed carrying heavy muscle. "I'm Leonardo—but everyone calls me Leo."

"Leo—Yes—hi," I said back. "This is my husband, Redmond." He shook my hand, but it was more like mine had disappeared into his baseball-glove size of a hand.

"Lynn. Redmond—it's a pleasure to meet you both finally," Leo said, courteously. I stared up at him as he shook Redmond's hand.

He had dark blond hair, darkest near the sides and nape of his neck, and cut short on the back and sides and long on top similar to Redmond's with the messy bangs, though his bangs were pushed back with the aid of some kind of hair product. And the only attributes he seemed to have in common with the other celestials were his flawless skin, straight white teeth, and impeccable bone structure. I'd gotten used to the magnificent appearances of the Archangels, The Fallen, and all other angels I'd encountered, although until I had met Purah, I'd never seen any that looked like these Seraphim. They appeared as though they could physically and quite literally fight a full-grown dragon. Impressive was an understatement.

"Greetings," Gabriel said, appearing next to my chair.

I had not felt his arrival, probably because I'd been too distracted by the casually dressed warrior in front of me. "Perfect timing," I said, turning away from Leo to look up at Gabriel.

"Let me show you around The Haven—we can talk as we go," Leo said, extending his big arm in the direction of the wall of doors. "Gabriel—we'll be back in a bit. I think Julian has your favorite homemade cookies in the kitchen."

Gabriel's eyes widened. "Delightful—see you all in a few," he said, rushing off to where Julian and Max were fussing in the kitchen.

Getting up from my chair, I narrowed my eyes on Gabriel as he hurried off. How could I have not noticed it before, I pondered? My being highly food motivated must be another one of those traits that I had inherited from him. I grinned at the idea, and the thought of homemade cookies.

"Max and Julian mentioned that you have had several businesses," Redmond said to Leo, as he got up.

Refocusing my attention, I followed my husband and our host as we set off out on our tour.

"We have found it easier to do our jobs, if we blend in, pretend to be human. And it helps since our targets can't sense us. We don't want them to suspect we are Seraphim. So, the more human we appear—the better we can interact with those around the Earthbound."

Superhuman, *maybe*, I considered.

As we walked, Leo explained further about the structure of this home he'd termed *The Haven*, and it had originally been, as I had suspected, a motel. This one, having been abandoned, had made it easy to purchase the land and convert it into what the outside world thought were two-story condos. And they kind of were. The individual entrances to each on the outside went through to a small private main floor living space with a set of stairs to a second-floor bedchamber, all set up for each of their individual needs and tastes. The back doors we saw from within the home worked as a pass-through into the open concept living space, we had originally started in.

In total, there were ten separate private living spaces with a bedroom as part of each. Leo and the other *Guards* occupied the front seven, while Max and Julian, along with Lane, occupied the two of the three on the far side of the compound. The extra living space had yet to be used, although Leo had designed it as a potential visitor's space. As part of the open common area, the large kitchen with its massive prep island, was long enough to accommodate eight stools on the opposite side. They had not one but two TV watching areas, the one in the main area we'd seen when we'd first arrived, and another enclosed room set up like a mini theater. I was all for that, I loved movies. There was no formal dining room, which made sense to me since it wasn't as though they would hold dinner parties here, not that I imagined anyway. The home was amazing and exquisitely decorated, and very well maintained. Max and Julian were masters at making the space feel elegant yet still giving it the impression of a comfy home. The kicker though, had been the hyper-secured basement level.

On the lower level, Leo showed us his office where he had a super-geek's setup of monitoring for safety and security. The spacious room next to it was a full facility gym and training area, with a tactical room loaded with all kinds of weapons. But the most fascinating area had been the last room, which was filled with a multitude of elements used for *disguises*. Everything from tailored suits to maintenance staff coveralls, wigs, facial hair, eyewear, hats, and more. They had a table set up for creating any kind of fake identification badges or logos, and signs and plates for vehicles, which were all part of the blending in Leo said they needed to do. And despite the fact that Seraphim from Pleiades were already focused on taking care of the Earth, Leo had utilized his business connections to incorporate a plethora of environmentally friendly features in his design and restoration of the complete structure. "The building incorporates a wide range of sustainable design features which reduces energy consumption, use of natural resources, and impact on the Earth's environment, all while improving our health and comfort," Leo informed us.

Returning through to the main open living space again, I noticed Gabriel was seated at one of the stools at the island in the kitchen alone, happily eating cookies with a large glass of milk. I had expected to find him still with Max and Julian. I gave him a wave, then shook my head.

"The water saving in landscape design and plumbing, and control of storm water run-off, it's fascinating—all of it," Redmond said, his handyman side crushing on the amazing structure Leo had created.

"Don't forget the rooftop garden with the small trees and shrubs, to reduce the heat impact on the roof," Leo added, before coming to a stop in the living room area.

Turning my gaze to the kitchen area again, I rolled my eyes. I was happy to hear about the earth friendly stuff, but it was Redmond who was genuinely fascinated by the individual features that had been incorporated. "It's amazing what you've set up here. Truly," I said, and I meant it. But we were here to talk about his *real* job and this Thaddeus character. "Can you tell me more about what you are doing here?" I asked, straight and to the point.

Gabriel turned on his stool at my words, still chewing a cookie.

"Yes... of course," Leo said, clearing his throat as if suddenly uncomfortable and remembering the true reason we were here. "Please—let's sit." He turned and directed us to a large, plush, dark grey sectional near the TV and billiards area.

"Gabriel told me that each Seraph has individual specialties—so to speak, for taking care of Earth," I said, sinking into the oh-my-gawd comfy couch next to Redmond. "What did you do before this—what was your specialty?"

"Nothing," Leo said, plainly, resting down in a large light grey cushy chair opposite us. "There was nothing before this for me."

"What about the others from the stars—these Guards," Redmond asked.

"To them, there was nothing before what they do as well now. This is all they know; all we have known," Leo said, resting an elbow on the padded arm of the chair.

Cryptic much, I mused? "Why are you here watching over the Earthbound—this Thaddeus?"

Leo drew in a breath. "The bio research and testing that he tells the world he does, it's a front for his own research and testing." Leo lowered his gaze and sighed. There was a long pause, and then he glanced up, and said, "For 20 years, Thaddeus and his followers have been searching out the offspring of our kind. Pretending to do genetic testing for childhood diseases—for cures, but in reality... he has been testing *on* them—not for them."

"What is he testing them for?" I asked, a tad queasy suddenly. I hadn't wanted to believe what I had suspected—felt, but I had known when Gabriel had first shared the information there was more going on with this Thaddeus and his facility.

"He's been trying—with no success mind you, to create offspring amongst his followers. His desire is to create a domination of powerful offspring—and not to help Earth's inhabitants, but to rule over them."

"Why the hell is he able to get away with things like this?" I barked out, despite the stomach acids creeping up my esophagus.

"Thaddeus has had plans on dominating Earth for a very long time—before being cast down, but he'd given our sistren and brethren the idea he'd only been following along with the human innovators within the field of microbiology. All the while he had been setting things in motion to serve his own agenda."

"How many followers does he have?" Redmond asked.

"One other from his star, and two from each of the other stars. Fourteen in total."

My lungs felt tight. "Why did Purah and the other Stewards cast them down to Earth?" I asked, taking in a steady breath in hopes of calming my unease.

"Thaddeus's plotting involved setting up several early research labs around the globe, but he had been telling Purah, the Steward from his star, that he was helping with research on human illnesses," Leo explained. He went on to tell us how Purah had been charmed by what she'd thought were Thaddeus's *selfless* initiatives. During which time, she had shared with him the process of how the Stewards guided the others to their requested destinations. Thaddeus's talk of choices had also swayed her, how they would make an excellent pairing, and that she could use her knowledge of the world map to help him make the Earth a better place. He had shown her the latest lab he'd set up here in Ottawa, and he had instructed her to tell no one of his ideas or of their visits to Earth Leo added. "She is never supposed to leave without informing another Steward. She later admitted she had gone down to Earth several times after the initial one with Thaddeus, but those other times were just to see what he'd been working on."

"What was Thaddeus's specialty—before he was cast down," Redmond asked, interrupting before Leo could go on.

"It had been his role to manage the microorganisms or microbes—microscopic organisms that exist as unicellular, multicellular, or cell clusters," Leo stated.

"That was his job?" I asked, perplexed.

"Microorganisms are widespread in nature and are beneficial to life, but some can cause serious harm. There are six major types; bacteria, archaea, fungi, protozoa, algae, and *viruses*."

My breath caught. "Holy shit," I said, realizing the implication and swallowing back a hint of bile that tickled the back of my throat.

"Purah thought Thaddeus was using his skills to help, but she soon understood that some experiments he was conducting were to create a super-spreader environment. It was 10 years ago when she realized Thaddeus had been involved with an earlier spread, the H1N1 virus. And she believes he may have been involved with this latest pandemic. She'd overheard him talking about it, and he'd said, '*I did not create the virus — man did, but let's just say I paved the way for it to travel — and travel it will*'."

"So — you can't send him back to Pleiades — but he's allowed to remain and wreak havoc on Earth?" Redmond asked, leaning forward resting his forearms on his knees.

"Unfortunately, yes," Leo said. "And we haven't established a way in which to apprehend him. And notifying the authorities would only bring unwanted attention to all of us." He gave a heavy, defeated sigh.

"Have you been in the Celaeno building?" I asked, shifting gears.

"Yes, at the time of its initial construction. Why do you ask?" His eyebrows pinched together.

I glanced at Redmond, then said, "Well... two of my friends recently did a tour of the facility."

"A tour?" He arched an eyebrow.

"It was more a hunt and find task — I guess you could say." I pressed my lips together. "The testing they do there is mainly on lung and airway disorders and diseases in children it seems. Oh, and they have a floor dedicated to testing for lung issues in birds. A floor with actual birds flying around. But other than that weirdness, they didn't really uncover anything, nor did they see Thaddeus. Although they were pretty confident more was going on there. Olivia told us, that when Mac asked about a lower level, the heart rate of the woman giving them the tour had doubled *and* she was suddenly uncomfortable and eager to get them out. She was polite about it, but the questions had definitely rattled her." I crossed my arms over my chest.

"How did she know the woman's heart rate had sped up?" He tilted his head slightly to one side, the movement suggestive of a golden retriever.

"It's one of Olivia's gifts—she's tuned in to the systems of the body and the chakras." I pointed to a few chakra spots on my body.

"And this Mac—what gift does he possess?"

"*She.* Mackenzie—Mac for short. Magic. She is our witch. She's connected to the Earth, you could say."

"I see," he said, raising both his eyebrows and nodding. "I would like to meet these friends of yours."

"I'll let them know. But you'll probably want to meet Vicki and Alison too. And I'm sure Luc and Derek would appreciate a chance to talk with you as well." I uncrossed my arms, relaxing my hands down to my lap.

"Darius would love that training and gym area," Redmond said with a chuckle.

"I would like to hear more about them. Are there others?" Leo queried.

"Are you familiar with the gathering?" Redmond asked.

"I have knowledge of it—yes. Gabriel has filled us in on some—though mainly about you, Lynn." He glanced over to Gabriel in the kitchen.

"There are eight of us—descendants. Not including Lynn," Redmond said. "Though their spouses are part of our inner circle as well."

"Kind of like Max and Julian," I said, giving Leo an appreciative smile.

"Right. I welcome the opportunity to dialog with them all." Leo nodded again, offering a sincere smile.

"How does it work—how were they cast down?" I asked, more demanding than I had meant to. "We've been told very little about your kind."

"When Seraphim leave their star, they are provided a kind of tracker—you could call it, that they wear around their wrist, the elements of it come from the star. Stewards use their staff to open a pathway of sorts, to send and then locate those who have gone down to Earth," Leo shared, attempting to explain. "In this event, Purah travelled to the other stars to inform her fellow Stewards of what she had discovered about Thaddeus. She had also asked for their forgiveness for her travelling to Earth unreported and as well as for her ignorance."

"How were seven Stewards able to overpower Thaddeus and the others," Redmond asked, before glancing my way.

Leo shifted his gaze from Redmond then and on to me. "You see, Stewards were *made* to guide the others to their destination, but they were also created to protect each star—even battle, but it had never been needed until this event." He paused briefly, then said, "She and the other Stewards assembled at the dispatching and receiving area on Thaddeus's star, and when he and his fellow rebels returned, they were caught off guard. The Stewards surrounded them, forcibly removed their bracelets, then immediately sent them back through to the location from where they'd just come from, Ottawa, casting them down for good. Where they went from there, we weren't sure, but luckily— we have the locations of the seven labs Thaddeus had set up."

"Wouldn't they all be together?" I asked.

"Together—no." Leo shook his head. "It seems that not all Thaddeus's followers stuck by him after. And we believe it's these unintended pregnancies—the births of the halflings, that Thaddeus continues to search for." He blew out a huffed breath. "Once they were cast down without the tracking bands, the Stewards lost the ability to locate them. Though the Earthbound are also at a disadvantage, as they cannot sense each other, nor other Seraphim now either."

"This is so confusing, all this who-can-sense-who crap. And this BS of not being able to go to the police makes me feel helpless," I said, and what I guessed was the same overwhelming frustration that Leo and The Guards must deal with on a regular basis.

"Are the offspring strictly Seraph and human?" I didn't want to make any more assumptions at this point.

"Yes," Leo said.

"Let me see if I understand this correctly," I said. "These Earthbound have been creating offspring, and Thaddeus has been tracking them down and testing on them, along with testing on human children as well, you're saying?"

"Yes," he said, again with the one-word answer.

"How many halflings could there possibly be? And where are they?" I questioned. There were only fourteen of them, and it had only been 10 years, and not all had left Thaddeus's group.

"We don't know how many, nor do we know where any of them are—not precisely."

"What about this boy?" Redmond asked. "Gabriel said you could trace his bloodline. Do you know where he is?"

"Only that he is in the New York City area." He brushed a hand across his jaw. "We try to get access to documents related to any offspring we encounter. Then we make our own records. But like I mentioned—we are unsure how many currently exist. One thing we know for sure, is that pregnancies resulting from human and Seraph couplings are exceptionally dangerous," Leo said. "Therefore, the number of halflings would predictably be quite small."

"Why dangerous?" I asked, although I wasn't sure I really wanted to know. My heart knocked in my chest.

"Well, Angels in general don't produce offspring—not together that is, just with humans—as you know." He gave me a quick grin. "I'm not exactly sure what happens—genetically, when offspring are conceived, but depending on who the female is—human or angel, there are often complications with either the delivery or with the infant itself. It's part of why we suspect Thaddeus's attitude towards them is so callous, and that he believes he is testing on what he deems are abominations. His goal it seems is to discern how to use these halflings and these human patients of his, to solve the mystery of why angels don't—or can't, reproduce amongst their own kind."

"Is there any way to tell if a child is a halfling—other than tracing their lineage? Is there anything different about them from a regular child?" Redmond, my ever-clever husband asked. I hadn't even thought of that, I was too caught up in the *testing on children* part of things to have considered it.

"We have found that they readily have markings… on their backs… pale almost white marks near the shoulder blades. You would call them birthmarks, I suppose. Pleiadeans all have these markings, but they are much more prominent, being dark grey or black."

"It must be part of the DNA combination—something dominant from the celestial parent's side—showing itself," I said, speculating. I glanced over to Gabriel who was still watching us from his seat in the kitchen.

"That was our conclusion too," Leo said, drawing my attention back.

"Okay, I think I have a better understanding of what's going on, but I'm still not clear on why Purah felt I was in danger."

"You were able to sense Purah, true?" Leo asked then.

"Yes. And you as well." I nodded. "Though the signature sensation differed from hers."

"How so?" Leo leaned forward in his chair, steepling his fingers and resting his elbows on his thick thighs.

"It's hard to put into words. It was subtle—the difference." I wriggled my fingers searching for a way to explain the distinction in *feelings*.

"Like the difference between a tangerine and a regular orange," Redmond said then, cutting a glance my way and smirking. "Know what I mean?" he asked, turning back to Leo.

I grinned. The twins had used that comparison when trying to explain how things felt to them when distinguishing between each of the Archangels and had suggested they were all like different types of oranges.

"I think so," Leo said, glancing back at me. "Could you discern between the two—identify who was who if needed?"

"Sure. I can distinguish between all celestials," I said. "Like with The Fallen, I can differentiate the regular 200 from the Leaders, and even the Horsemen."

"That could be helpful to us, since we are at a disadvantage in this area." He seemed hopeful, but then his eyebrows furrowed. "Purah believes Thaddeus knows about you. And if he finds out where you are, who knows what he'll do."

"At this point, I would think most—if not all, Angels would know about me. And that I can sense Archangels and The Fallen," I said, the sick feeling in my stomach lessening now as I leaned back against the soft couch cushion. "She told me that one of his followers saw me *talking* to a Watcher—but that doesn't mean he knows I can sense them—all Angels."

"Either way—you're going to need protection," Leo said, straightening in his seat, conviction set in his expression.

"Yer not expecting me to change how I conduct my life—just because some grounded Seraph *might* know about my abilities—are you?" I questioned, scanning the faces of both he and then Gabriel who had come now to stand next to Leo's chair.

Leo glanced up at Gabriel, then shot a glance at Redmond. Then taking in a noticeable breath, he turned those piercing blue eyes back on me. "Yes," he breathed out.

Chapter 17

There was no doubt that the expression I'd thrown back at Leo was that of a stubborn child who was in no-way-no-how going to cooperate with what the *adults* had decided for me. However, having been on the receiving end of such an expression—too many times to count, I sat up straight in my spot on the couch, took in a deep breath, and then said, "What did you have in mind."

Unfortunately for them, after listening to a short list of warden-style options, the only thing I was willing to agree to at this juncture, was with my stomach and the fact that it was time for lunch. "I really need to get something in my stomach—it's been feeling wonky all morning," I said, hoping to halt the domineering dialog still going on between the males in my life. "There will be plenty of time to talk more about my *safety* later." I actually did finger air quotes for the word safety, before pushing myself up off the couch.

Like a gentleman, Leo stood when I did. "Yes—we have time," he said, though I wasn't sure he believed his own words.

Admittedly, I respected these guys for their perseverance in wanting to keep me safe, but this was something we would have to work out together. I wouldn't be told what to do. However, I would listen to their ideas. Just not now when my stomach was disagreeing with me.

Redmond, being the smart man that he was, knew that a *hangry* Lynn would not be a cooperative Lynn, and he got up from the couch as well, then said, "We promised Vicki and the others that we would be back for lunch." He rubbed a warm hand across the middle of my back.

I turned my head to look up at Redmond, and then Gabriel. Refocusing on Leo, I took in a cleansing breath, and said, "Thank you, for making time to speak with us—to inform us, of what's been going on. I understand your concern regarding my safety, and I promise you I will be back in touch to discuss further on how we can...." I breathed out as the nausea all but faded away. "... come to an agreement—create a plan, on how to keep the Earthbound from discovering more about me—and my skills." I cut a glance to Gabriel, then turned my attention back to Leo. "We'll get back to you later—okay?"

"Of course," Leo said, graciously. "This must be a lot to take in, and I understand your resistance to changing how you conduct your life. But please know that we only have your best interest in mind." He gave me a heartfelt smile, one that reached his eyes, then he turned toward the main entrance.

As Redmond and I moved to the double doors, I glanced around realizing that Gabriel had vanished. Max and Julian reappeared then, entering from down the hall. Max stepped up and opened the panel door to the closet and retrieved our coats.

Claiming mine, I said, "Thank you so much. It was lovely to meet you both. You have a spectacular home here." I knew the residence belonged to Leo and the others, but it was these two gentlemen who had made it feel like a home.

"We like it," Max said, waving his hands as though brushing off the praise.

"But we hope to see you again," Julian said, raising his grey eyebrows in question.

"I'd love that," I said, grinning, feeling much better now, although I was still hungry. "I'd love to meet Lane sometime too," I added, before taking another step towards the door.

"Thanks again," Redmond said, donning his jacket. When the main door opened on its own, Redmond turned to look over his shoulder at Leo. "We'll be in touch—don't worry."

I turned to look at Leo too and gave him a reassuring smile and nod. Then without a word, I turned back and went out the open door.

Back at Vicki's place, we found her and Eric in the kitchen doing an assembly line of sandwiches for what I guessed were for Redmond and me, along with the rest of the crew who I could see from the open kitchen, were in the living room, sitting and chatting around the fireplace.

"Come and get'em," Eric called out to the others, as Vicki moved the mountain of sandwiches to the dining table. She had put out bowls of pita chips and hummus as well, and both homemade no doubt.

My girlfriends had a long list of notable qualities, a common one of which was how amazing they all were in the kitchen. They have always fed me well. I can cook, but lucky for me, I have Redmond to do most of it. He loves to cook, and I love to eat. We're a perfect match.

"Eric and I have to grab ours to go," Redmond said, snatching up a few sandwiches and wrapping them in a paper towel. "We're heading over to your place, Mac. Going to go check out Don's new garage setup." He gave me a big grin. "I put the rental car keys on a hook near the front door, it case Mac needs to get her car out—and you need to move it."

"We're meeting Mike and Ken there too," Eric said, taking a bite of a sandwich and securing another in the same manner in which Redmond had done.

"I'm sure you can bring them all up to speed," Redmond said, shrugging back into his jacket. "I'll let the guys know what we found out." He kissed my cheek and then headed for the front door after Eric.

"Spill," Vicki said, when the front door shut. She took a bite off the corner of her sandwich.

Alison's chair squeaked. "Wait, let me grab my notepad," she said, getting up from the table. A split second later she was back with her favorite fine-tipped rollerball pen, specifically in light blue, along with one of the much larger notepads she'd opted to use these days. She currently works with a division of Children's Services, not full time, just on a case-by-case basis, though before moving to Calgary, she'd worked with several group homes, The Children's Help Line, and the Children's Wish Foundation. Prior to her moving back to Ottawa, in

Calgary she had spent 20 years working with services dedicated to that of seniors' housing, so when she'd gotten the offer to help with kids again, she welcomed the new opportunity. It was her ability to accurately record what people shared with her that made her an ideal candidate to help interview children, especially those who had been in abusive circumstances. Sometimes it was her role to aid in getting them out of these abusive environments and with placing them in the right foster homes. Often it was to assist them with sharing the facts, their testimony, in court against their abuser. Alison had a real knack with these kids and for getting them to disclose what had happened to them, and she did so side by side with the assigned psychologist on each case. "I'm ready," she said, waving her pen in the air. A length of her long caramel-coloured hair fell across her writing arm.

Like most of us, Alison had let her hair grow out longer than she'd worn it in the past. Even Vicki's hair was way past her shoulders now, though she'd had hers recently cut in a shag style with fringes around her face to give her longer thin hair more body. With Mac's, her hair had been quite long before, and it was still a lengthy thick brunette curtain when she wore it down. Similar to me though, she tended to put it up in a top knot to keep it out of the way. Getting proper haircuts during the pandemic had been a big no-no, and all of us, excluding Olivia, had let our hair grow. Olivia, the minute she could, had gone out and got her blond hair cut short and tight into her usual pixie style.

"We should see if Derek, Luc and Darius are available for a video chat," Vicki suggested.

"I'll have it recorded in my notes, but it would save us having to repeat it all for them later," Alison said, tracing the tiny blue heart she had just drawn in the corner of the page.

"I'll send them a text," Vicki said, getting up and grabbing her phone off the kitchen counter. "Let me get my laptop," she added.

I began gathering up the plates from lunch as Vicki ran off to the back office. By the time she returned to the dining room with her laptop, we had cleared a space on the table for it. She had already received responses from all the guys too, and she stated that only Luc and Derek were available, and that Darius was with a client.

We scooted our chairs to one end of the table when Vicki set down the laptop, making it easier for the video chat. Getting comfortable in her chair again, Vicki fired up her computer. Using the video chat software, she opened a private meeting for the guys from her contacts list, and then the two additional display squares opened in view next to ours. I was sitting in the middle of our display, with Alison to my right and Vicki to my left. Olivia and Mac were off screen on the periphery to Vicki and Alison, but they could still see the display.

When the faces of Derek and Luc appeared on screen, I started off the chat by getting straight to the details and telling everyone about The Haven and what happened when Leo arrived. "I could sense Leo before he came through the door," I said. "These Seraphim seem to cause distinct sensations for me when they are around, and the feeling when Leo arrived, was similar to Purah, yet still distinctly unique—like with The Fallen.

"I did some research with Derek on the Seraphim," Luc said, his focus switching to the right as though he were opening up something else on his computer screen. "I pulled together whatever elements we found applicable and put them in a separate document. Some of it you probably already know—but I can send it to you."

"It's not much," Derek cut in. "Most of the references were heavily religious and not the sort of details we would consider relevant."

"Send it," I said, "but can you read out the highlights?"

"Sure... let me seeee," Luc said, searching his notes. "Okay—here. A seraph—plural seraphim, are often referred to as 'the burning one'. They are a type of celestial or heavenly being, originating in Ancient Judaism." Luc looked away from reading his spreadsheet, to look directly at us. "We saw that the same term plays a role in subsequent Judaism, Christianity, and Islam religious documentation. Spiritual traditions place them in the highest rank in Christian angelology, but we found they are placed in the fifth rank out of ten, in the Jewish angelic hierarchy. In the Book of Isaiah, the term is used to describe beings with six wings that fly around the Throne of God." Luc paused, glancing at his notes, then he added, "Seraphim are mentioned as celestial beings in the Book of Enoch and the Hellenistic Book of Revelation as well."

"We found even earlier mention of images used to display seraphs in Hyksos-era Canaan—that means when Egypt was ruled by foreign rulers," Derek said, "and that they came from Egyptian uraeus iconography—like with the cobra on the crowns. You've probably seen it before—it's depicted a lot in movies."

"Ya—I've seen it," I said. "Keep going."

"There was one Hebrew scholar who claimed that in the Hebrew Bible, Seraphim didn't have the status of angels, and it was only in later sources like Summa Theologies that they were considered as a branch of the celestial messengers," Luc added next. Then his eyebrows pinched together.

"What?" I asked.

"I know we were told there really aren't any ranks or levels—other than Archangels being sort of at the top, but the religious doctrine show them to be part of different ranks," Luc said. "Like in Judaism—there's another reference that puts them as the higher angels of the World of Beriah—the first created realm. Medieval Christian theology places them in the highest choir of the angelic hierarchy. They are said to be the caretakers of God's throne and viewed as helping him maintain perfect order. Though they rarely appear in Islam," he added.

"I always find it interesting how angels are documented in most if not all religions," Alison said, looking up from her notetaking.

"It's like the flood story—how it was told in variations across the ancient world," Derek said, reminding us of his much earlier research findings.

"In other research, we found that there were two classes of celestial beings mentioned alongside the Seraphim," Luc said, "known as the phoenixes and the chalkydri, the 'hydra' and 'water-serpent'. Both are described as 'flying elements of the sun'. They reside in either the 4th or 6th heaven, and these guys have twelve wings and burst into song at sunrise."

"If I had twelve wings and could fly, I'd probably burst into song too," I laughed out.

"Ha—me too," Luc said, chuckling. "Check this. There's an ancient Judean seal from the 8th century BCE that depicts them as flying asps, having human traits. That's the only reference we found where they talk about them having a human appearance."

"They are part of the angelarchy of modern Orthodox Judaism," Derek said. "Although a literal belief in angels is not universal among devotees—they generally take images of angels as symbolic. In non-biblical sources they are sometimes called the 'serpents' or 'dragons', and an alternate term for Hell." Derek's pale eyebrows rose with that last detail.

Luc glanced back towards his notes. "The last part I have here, states they are known for being 'exuberant in their intense, perpetual, tireless activities and by the unquenchable, radiant, and enlightening power of dispelling and destroying the shadows of darkness'. Christian theology developed an idea of them as 'beings of pure light' and who have direct contact with God," Luc said, concluding the last of his research.

"We obviously found nothing in the human records about them residing on Pleiades or about them tending to the Earth," Derek said. "Interestingly enough though, the term *Seraph* applies to the mysterious 'Beings of Light' in various Battlestar Galactica comics and in numerous video games and TV shows," he added, amused.

"Well, I don't know about all that religious stuff," I said, "but in a nutshell, we learned that this Thaddeus was basically found to be up to some nasty shit. And he engaged others who were also angry with their roles, to be on the takeover-the-Earth team. They were found out—fortunately, and the Stewards—these gladiator guide angels, stripped them of their tickets back to the stars, and stranded them here on Earth."

"How many?" Derek asked.

"Including Thaddeus, there's fourteen total," I said.

"All males?" Mac asked, leaning over to wave at the guys.

"Not sure—didn't ask."

"Are they all in Ottawa?" Alison inquired then.

"It seemed as though Leo didn't know where all the Earthbound were exactly. I'm thinking they're scattered around at each of these lab locations—but that's just a guess." I scratched my head, wondering where else the others could be.

"We should get the location of the other labs," Mac suggested.

"I agree," I said. "But along with keeping tabs on them, Leo's other focus is on locating these halflings before Thaddeus does."

"How many are there?" Mac asked again, apparently curious about the numbers.

"They don't know." I shook my head.

"Do they know where any of them are?" Alison asked, offering another question about the whereabouts.

"Nope—they can't sense them. Though that little boy—the twins pointed out, he's supposedly in New York," I shared.

"How do they know if somebody is a halfling or not?" Olivia asked, tossing out her first inquiry, leaning over to smile at the guys on screen.

"Leo said they have birthmarks on their backs—pale almost white at the shoulder blades. All Pleiadeans have markings like them he said, but theirs are dark grey or black. Leo said they keep records of the ones they encounter."

"What's with the markings?" Luc asked, passing his palm over his opposite arm and forearm tattoos in view of the camera.

"I don't know." I thought I had gotten lots of information from Leo, but apparently not according to the questions being tossed at me.

"What did he mean by *if the female is*—*human or angel*? Does that mean there are females among the Earthbound?" Vicki asked. She had been silent up until now.

"I don't recall if he said anything about that." I had not written anything down. "Jeez, I should have asked more questions—but I'd gotten so worked up over the whole *change my life*—protection thing, that it kind of clouded my line of questioning. Not every day you get introduced to a new cast of Angels—not recently, anyway. Plus, I was starving by then," I explained, patting my stomach.

"I've got it all down," Alison said. "You've pretty much covered what Leo told you, Lynn. I can see it all." She gave me a sympathetic smile.

"Did you tell Leo about our trip to Celaeno?" Mac asked.

"Yup. What you saw—and how that woman had acted. He's been in the building before too he said."

"I've already recorded those details too, Mac," Alison said, "I'll just add his being there before to those notes."

"Ya—about your tour," I said, making it my turn with questions. "Why all the focus on lung conditions—and what was with the testing on birds? If he's trying to create offspring, wouldn't his focus be on fertility?"

"True," Olivia said, a puzzled expression crossing her face. "What issues could these offspring have I wonder?"

"I don't know—it's all pretty convoluted." I frowned.

"It's all pretty twisted if you ask me," Mac said, making an *ick* face.

"Did you meet any of the others—these Guards?" Derek asked.

"It's interesting how we were referred to as *The Guards* too in the Book of Balance," Alison said, turning to Vicki. Her cheeks bunched as she grinned.

"They are *actual* guards, our reference was just an anagram," Vicki reminded.

"I know it's *daughter*—but still, we're the guards—they're the guards. Bizarre right?" Alison said, pointing out the obvious, glancing around as if for some kind of recognition.

"I didn't meet the others," I said, answering Derek's question. "Leo said that he and the others—six others, based on their housing setup, were *made* to watch over the Earthbound—it's like their job. Though Leo talked about having actual human jobs, and businesses that he owned, as part of the blending in thing. You guys need to see his place too—it's amazing. Remind me to tell you about the secured basement with the weapons and the disguise areas," I said. "Leo expressed he wanted to meet you all," I added. "We did meet the two guys who take care of the compound—the home. Max and Julian— their daughter lives there too, apparently."

"Must have been weird to meet people who are in the knowing— ones outside our circle," Olivia said, shrugging a shoulder.

"So, they all know—Max, Julian, and their daughter, I mean?" Mac asked.

"Ya—Max and Julian have been with Leo for almost 25 years. They've been in the knowing longer than any of us, come to think about it."

"It's interesting to think that The Guards have been here all this time—25 years at least," Olivia noted.

"Wait—back up here," Derek interjected. "Didn't Leo say it was 10 years ago that Thaddeus and his followers were sent to Earth?"

"Ya. But Thaddeus had been planning and plotting long before that. Something like 20 years of searching for offspring."

"Thaddeus was looking for offspring before he was cast down?" Olivia questioned, following a similar vein as Derek, her eyebrows furrowing.

"Both Gabriel and Leo told you he's been watching over the Earthbound for 6 years—so how could these two guys have known Leo that long then?" Derek asked, adding to the growing quandary on the facts.

"Why would he need a *Haven* as he called it, and humans to take care of it?" Luc asked, further extending the list of discrepancies.

"Why all the weapons, and what about the disguises? If you recall, Armaros used angel magic to veil himself in Gabriel's form," Mac reminded.

"Why would they all need places to sleep for that matter? Angels don't sleep—do they?" Vicki questioned, shifting a glance to each of us.

"Lynn, there's more to this than what Gabriel or Leo told you," Derek said, summing up what I'd already been debating in my own head.

Chapter 18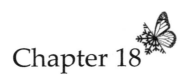

After we closed out the video chat, I had Alison make me a list of all the questions that had come up, because I was going back over there—to The Haven, to get some answers.

"Do you think you should talk to Gabriel first?" Alison asked, as I got my coat from the front hall closet.

"Nope," I said, grabbing the rental car keys off the hook near the front door.

"We'll text you if we think of more questions," Vicki said.

I checked the battery life on my phone. It showed it at 89%. "I'll be back soon." I slipped my phone back into my cross-shoulder bag. "Wish me luck," I said, opening the front door.

"Luuuck," I heard them call out, before shutting the door behind me.

It was a tad warmer now that the sun was trying to peek out from behind the cloud cover, but I still let the car heat up a bit. The thing about warming weather in winter is that it makes for the ideal temperature for it to snow. And just as I pulled out of the driveway—what do you know, it began to snow.

As I drove out of Vicki's neighborhood and on to the main road, the hints of sunlight made the tiny snowflakes coming down look like sparkling diamonds. I loved the magical appearance the falling snow made, though driving in it, I didn't love. I did, however, miss having it at Christmas time when down south.

We had spent Christmas at our new home that first year. The following year, when the girls were 4 years old, we had gone up to Ottawa for the holidays and we'd taken them skiing. They'd taken to it like pros as if they'd been born with skis on their feet. Their father and I had promised them we'd do it again, but the following year we'd stayed home for the holidays, and then in 2019 we'd gone up to visit Redmond's parents in New York City for Christmas. Since then, we'd not had the chance to take them skiing. Covid hit in 2020 and we have been major homebodies for almost two years. Next year, we would take them skiing again, Redmond and I had promised each other when we'd made the decision to come up to Ottawa alone. But right now, the only thing I could promise was to get all our questions answered by Leo.

I pulled into the same spot out front of The Haven, that Redmond had used earlier today. Even before I reached the property, I'd felt that now familiar prickling as I stretched out my senses to check if Leo was around. And now getting out of the car and walking to the main doors, the sensation only heightened, indicating with clarity that he was in fact at home.

"Hi, Lynn," came a voice through the intercom, even before I could hit the buzzer. It was Julian.

"Hi—sorry to come unannounced, but I need to speak with Leo," I said, looking up and around to whatever cameras were on me. My heart was pounding a little in my chest.

I heard the door crack open, and then Julian and his cheerful smile greeted me as the door swung wide. "Come in-come in," he said, before peeking his head out as though checking…. the weather maybe? Or if I had been followed, whatever, I wasn't sure. The windows near the front entrance were long narrow rectangles high up on the wall, allowing the light in, but you couldn't see in or out of them without a ladder.

"Thank you," I said, stepping into the beautiful front foyer again.

"Leo will be right with you. May I take your coat?"

"Uhm, sure," I said, undoing the zipper and removing my coat. "I'm not sure how long I'll be staying though."

Julian waved a hand as if the length of time didn't matter, then he hung up my coat.

My skin prickled again as though my clothes were full of static cling.

"Lynn," Leo said, grabbing my attention as he entered the room from the far hall. I knew now that the hallway led to the entry to the top-secret basement. "What brings you back over so soon?" He was smiling. Evidently, he hadn't guessed that there was an onslaught of questions coming his way.

"I'm sorry—I would have called first but, well—I don't have a way to contact you," I said, bluntly, stepping forward.

He lifted his hands and clapped them once together. "Yes—how silly of me," he said. "I guess I thought Gabriel would be the one communicating with me. I'll give you my cell number. I should never have assumed—my apologies." He reached into his back pocket and pulled out a wallet. An actual wallet that from what I could see had several credit card or debit cards in slots, along with a driver's license that showed a photo of his likeness through the plastic picture window. He retrieved a small card from one of the slots. "This is my business card," he said, handing it to me. "My cell number is on there." He tapped the card with his index finger.

Stunned, I said, "Your business card? You have a cell phone?"

He stared back at me as if even more shocked than I was. "Of course. Who can function without a cell phone these days?"

That was the point wasn't it? The reason I was back here in the first place. Not who, but *what*... what are you, my brain questioned?

"Are you alright?" Leo asked, his expression growing grim.

"Yes—sorry," I said, "I—we just had some questions for you." I took in a deep breath, letting the air out slowly.

"Shall we sit," he said, extending his arm to the seating area we had previously sat in.

I nodded, and he led the way.

He resumed the original seat he had used for our conversation from earlier in the day, then said, "What can I assist you with?"

I took in another deep breath, but this time I blew it out, sitting across from him, in the spot where Redmond had previously sat. "Answers," I said, "that's what we need your assistance with."

"I'll do my best." He smiled, but it seemed forced.

Heart still pounding, I retrieved the list of questions Alison had made for me. Then I set my bag on the floor next to my feet. Unfolding the paper, I said, "I discussed what we talked about earlier with my friends—the people in the knowing we told you about."

"I understood that you would be speaking with them. Did something happen?" He leaned forward in his chair, resting his elbows on his thighs like he had earlier. Concern spread across his handsome features.

"Nothing has happened—no, but we have some questions as I said and.... I'm not sure how you are going to feel about them." I bit the side of my lip, blowing out a breath through my nose.

"Well, let's start and I'll let you know how I... *feel*." The smile he gave me was a sincere one now.

Feeling more at ease, I said, "Okay." Then I glanced down at my list of questions. "Regarding the halflings. You mentioned there were difficulties with the births—that the severity depended on *if* the mother was Angel or human." I glanced up.

"Yes," he said, his eyebrows knitting together.

"Then I take it that the Earthbound are not all males?" I pressed my lips together. This was the first in a long line of what I had a feeling would come off as an interrogation and not just simple curiosity.

"Yes. There are two females, but we only know the whereabouts of one of them." He wrung his hands once.

I nodded and then read the next question. "Thaddeus has been bound to Earth for 10 years now, yes?"

"Correct."

"How long have you been monitoring him in Ottawa?" I asked, keeping my eyes on my paper.

"6 years." He rocked forward in his seat as if in anticipation of the next easy question.

"Why not 10 years?" I glanced up.

"We had only been able to locate him 6 years ago."

"What were you doing before that?" I asked. Then I reached for my purse and slid out a small notepad Alison had loaned me to take notes this time.

His eyes went to the notepad as I flipped it open and took the pen from its tucked place in the notepad's coil.

"I was surveilling the other lab locations," he said, his eyes raising back up to me.

"How is it that Max and Julian have known you for 25 years—I mean—since you have only needed to *blend in* while keeping an eye on Thaddeus and his crew—for 10 years," I queried, my words rushing out, knowing this question was a doozie.

A muscle twitched in Leo's jaw.

When he didn't respond, I asked, "Why is it that you even need this place—these human helpers?" I took a quick look around the open space.

He said nothing again.

"You all have bedrooms—do you sleep?" I tilted my head slightly to one side, then squinted.

Leo leaned back in his chair, though he remained silent.

"Why the disguises? Can't you just change your appearance like other angels can—veiling yourself in another identity, or completely?" I questioned, my voice raising a little in annoyance at not getting more answers from him.

Leo opened his mouth as if to speak, then closed it. He swallowed hard enough that I could see his Adam's apple rise and fall.

Pushing again, I asked, "And why was Thaddeus looking for offspring long before he was even cast down? Whose offspring was he looking for?" I tapped my pen on the notepad.

Gabriel appeared next to Leo then.

"I know there is more going on here," I said, glaring up at Gabriel. "How do you even know Thaddeus has been doing these experiments—if you can't sense or find him?"

"We have a contact," Leo said, speaking finally.

"A Pleiadean?" I waggled the pen between my fingers.

"An Earthbound," Leo countered, staring up at Gabriel.

I said nothing this time.

Looking back at me, Leo said, "Her area of expertise is with the conservation of rainforests. She is currently involved with the largest one in Brazil, the Amazon Rainforest, and she notified us that Thaddeus had been there, searching for *healing* elements—plants."

I scribbled down everything he was saying. "That explains the greenhouse, Olivia and Mac saw at the Celaeno building. What about the halflings?" I asked, feeling no need to explain the question further.

"The offspring aren't from Thaddeus's followers," Gabriel said then, answering for Leo.

"You said they were conceived by the Earthbound." I tapped my pen on the page of my notepad again.

"They are," Leo answered, "just not those Earthbound."

I stopped tapping. "There are others?"

"Yes." Leo's chin dropped to his chest, and he closed his eyes.

"Tell me," I said, glancing back and forth from him to Gabriel.

Leo lifted his head to look up at Gabriel once more. "Let me explain Pleiades and its inhabitants first," Leo said, before settling his gaze back on me.

"Sterope, Merope, Electra, Maia, Taygeta, Alcyone, and Celaeno make up the stars of Pleiades," Leo began. "They are also the names Thaddeus chose to use for his seven facilities around the world."

I nodded to let him know I understood what he was saying. Derek had told us about these star names already. I gave him a concerned smile to let him know I grasped the weight of what he was about to share with me.

When I didn't say anything back, Gabriel came over and sat down next to me on the couch. "Go on," Gabriel said to Leo.

Leo drew a long breath in through his nose. Letting it slowly out, he said, "Seraphim draw their energies—their powers, from the stars themselves, though the stars are basically just balls of light with mass. Seraphim have never existed anywhere else. What the cosmogeny of the universe is—well, I can't tell you that. But what I *can* tell you, is what Pleiadean venerate most, *purpose*."

"Watching over the Earth must be an exhausting challenge," I said.

Leo nodded several times. "For most it has been all they care about, watching over the Earth. It's like a cooperative science experiment/echo system to them. They have had to learn as they went, as well. Helping the basic organisms evolve."

"Hence the creation and evolution discussion that humans often have," Gabriel added, clarify things for me.

"It is both in a way," Leo said. "All things in the solar system were formed by the creator, but they are maintained by the Seraphim." Leo glanced at Gabriel as though thinking of what to say next. Then changing direction, he said, "The 200 Watchers—now Fallen, were sent down to do just that, *watch*... but that didn't work out as planned. They were cast down as an example to all of us, restricting the Seraphim's involvement. Some found loopholes as you discovered, while the rest chose not to risk whatever other punishments could be put upon them."

"Yes, I'm well aware of the loopholes—but what does this have to do with Thaddeus?" I asked. I didn't need a refresher on the 200 Fallen and what their actions had caused.

"Thaddeus is convinced he's the good guy," Leo said. "He even displays likeable qualities. He's clever and accomplished enough that others lend him begrudging respect. But you can't let that mislead you. He is deceitful, even vengeful, and he will stop at nothing to get what he wants." He sighed. "And he's no fool."

"He's the *big-bad* guy—I get it," I said, realizing that he must be a seriously nasty piece of work if this huge angel was unnerved by him.

"It has been 120 years since the first of my brethren and sistren were cast down. But it has only been 20 years since Thaddeus had begun grooming the Steward, Purah," Leo said, leaning forward in his chair again.

"What did he groom her for," I asked, reluctantly. It felt as though he was about to tell me the worst true-crime story ever.

"He can be very persuasive, but he is a jealous being—especially of his own kind," Leo stated. "As part of his planning, he had been setting up these testing facilities in key locations around the world, and he made a point to include Purah in the knowledge of what he was doing. He even asked for her review, her approval of the last facility in Ottawa. She was flattered by this, of course, but he then asked that she let him try his hand at sending and bringing her back from Earth. She hadn't wanted him to think she didn't trust him, so she allowed him to use her staff. While she was on Earth, it was then that Thaddeus gathered his rebels from the other stars. Once they were assembled, he informed the other Seraphim from his star that he wanted to share some amazing discoveries that he had found regarding the work he had been doing. He told them that Purah was on Earth waiting for them, and that she would personally guide them through what he explained was something he was immensely proud of and had been working on for a long time. He assured them it wouldn't take long, and that they all needed to go together—for their collective approval. They had seemed unsure about what Thaddeus had been asking them to do, so to encourage them, he said they would have much to celebrate once they saw what he had created."

"How was he going to send them down without Purah? I get that he was able to send her down, but that's a lot of angels. Wouldn't that take some—I don't know, extra training?" I questioned. It wasn't like I had any idea how the whole thing worked. Gabriel and the others basically just came and went at will.

"Purah had previously shown him how to prepare their fellow Seraphim for travel," Leo stated, wrapping the fingers of his left hand around his opposite wrist. "How to adorn them with bracelets on their wrists. But what they hadn't known, was that Thaddeus had swapped out the star fragments with fake elements, rendering the bracelets useless in their purpose." He twisted his wrist within his fingers. "When Thaddeus finally returned Purah to the star, he told her that when the others had seen him with her staff, that they demanded he send them to the destination they wished—and they could not wait for her to return. He lied again when telling her they had informed him that they had their bracelets, but after when he'd checked the place where she kept them—all 200 were still there." Leo shook his head as if in disbelief. "She asked where her fellow Seraphim had gone, but he'd told her he didn't know, that all they had said to him was that they were ready. And that he had simply opened the path they had chosen in their minds. Purah was left confused as was the rest of the Seraphim from the other stars. There had never been such an event before."

Stunned by the story, I'd let my mouth hang open. I shut it, then asked, "What did the others do?" I brushed my mouth with the back of my hand.

"It caused unrest of course. And at the same time, it gave Thaddeus the opportunity to roll out his plan. Thaddeus later told the others that it was his belief they had chosen to leave them. That they could be anywhere—and that they must not want any of us to know where they went or for us to find them."

"And they believed him?" I questioned, raising my eyebrows.

"Why would they not? He had never given any of them any reason to doubt his words," Gabriel said.

"How many remain on that star?"

"Thaddeus and one other—plus Purah, were the only ones left on Celaeno. And with the others cast down, Thaddeus and his followers chose to no longer participate in aiding the Earth. They all remained on the seventh star and did whatever they wanted, coming and going to Earth for nefarious means. For the next 100 years they furthered their plans, while awaiting the 70 generation hold that had been put on all angels."

I nodded again my understanding and sighed out a breath. "I have to tell you this is not what I had anticipated hearing from you." I didn't know what I had thought his answer would be—but it hadn't been about the casting down of more angels.

"I hadn't expected to be telling you any of this either," Leo said, coolly. "However, I feel now it can only help us if you know more." He glanced at Gabriel.

"I agree—I've always hated you not having the information you needed. Having to stand back and watch all of you struggle to figure things out—find the answers. It was excruciating," Gabriel said, turning in his seat to look at me. "I'm sorry you had to go through that." He brushed a gentle hand up and down my upper arm.

"It's okay," I said, and I meant it. I patted his hand. We hadn't grasped the magnitude of the journey we had been on until we'd actually completed it. The tasks we had been challenged with, we only understood later once we'd had a chance to ask questions and had gotten clarity on the 'what ifs' we'd been up against. We knew what we'd accomplished, and we had every right to be prideful, but it had humbled us instead. All of us had felt extremely grounded after and grateful for how the events had ultimately brought us all together.

"In the year 2001, Thaddeus executed his plan with the creation of a front to his true deception, using the labs across the world. Prior to this, the remaining Seraphim from the other stars had been unable to help their lost brethren and sistren, due to the 70-generation hold, not without impacting humans or further risking the possible devastating corruption of humankind."

"Why weren't they scouring the Earth for them? I get that Thaddeus had convinced them they wanted to be left alone—but still?"

"Seraphim can't travel like Gabriel and the other angels," Leo said. "Never could."

"What?" I massaged my forehead. "I don't understand."

"Seraphim were created this way. They are only ever sent and retrieved from a destination when needed," Leo explained further. Though I wasn't sure I completely understood. "These first Earthbound, had to learn to live among humans. And they needed to protect themselves now that they were more vulnerable than before."

"I take it—you eventually found out where they'd been sent down to?" I jotted down a note about Seraphim not having the same method of travel as other angels.

"Yes. Once the 70-generation hold was up, they were able to track down and communicate with the scattered few that now reside on Earth—it hadn't been easy, mind you. And it's how we knew where they had been sent."

"Where?"

"To an area near the North Pole in the vicinity of what is known as Nunavut now. Two still remain there in fact, while the others spread out in the world."

"Why stay? Why not stick together?" I shrugged, baffled at the idea of them splitting off.

"The two remained in case more were sent down. They hadn't wanted others to suffer as they had. Eventually, with the help of the Inuit people from the area, they created a safe haven for themselves. They have become a kind of legend among the people there, and their existence and the exact location of their dwelling, remains a secret among them to this day."

"Who are the two who remained?"

"Anael and Thanael, who were paired at the time of their casting down," he said. "Her skills had been associated with meteorology, climatology, atmospheric physics, and atmospheric chemistry, the sub-disciplines of the atmospheric sciences. And Thanael oversaw the seven layers of the atmosphere, making them perfectly matched. They have been paired for several decades—one of the longest pairings since that of the essential land and water pairing before any living organisms were created."

There was a pressure and a rushing sound building in my ears. I blinked, wondering if my brain had just exploded. "Wow," I managed to say.

"There were several pairings at the time of the takeover, and although some of the others eventually paired off for companionship and survival, the original pairs remained together," Leo said. He rested his elbows on the arms of the chair, clasping his fingers together in front of him. His mouth turned up then in a tight grin as though feeling some relief in telling me the story. "As travel across the sea became commonplace, the Earthbound eventually scattered further across the globe," he added, before sharing the rest as it led into the present day. "Most of the Earthbound went out among humans to learn languages and skills not previously required for life on the stars, such as cooking, reading, and writing. And as man evolved, they learned to drive cars and the ways of the economy. They found ways to be near the humans, some choosing to stay hidden, while others chose to live among humans." He sighed, then said, "And they are no longer immortal."

"Wait—what?" I asked, taken aback, the pressure in my ears a ringing now.

He sighed again. "They can be killed like humans although they have exceptional healing abilities. They cannot grow back limbs or anything like that, but they can heal at miraculous speeds. They have their weaknesses, although they are not susceptible to human diseases. And they live longer than humans, no illnesses—none that we know of so far that is," Leo said, spreading his fingers wide, palms forward.

"Unfortunately, being so long on Earth, they had started to feel the effects, changes in appearance—aging, the hunger and thirst, and a host of other human defined weaknesses." He grimaced as if these things injured him personally. "As time went on, those who did not stay in hiding, found human companions. Though this choice proved to be heartbreaking for both, as Earthbound now age at a rate of 1 year for every 10 human years. Plus, they had to continue to cover up this fact."

"I can't even imagine what that would be like," I said, my heart squeezing, the weight of their challenged existence seeping deep into my soul. I remembered seeing something like that in the *Highlander* movie, the burden of hiding and reinventing oneself in order to continue to exist in the human world. There was a lot more to it, but it ends with the good guy battling it out with the bad guy, and the good guy wins. I'm always open to a win, but right now my overactive imagination was begging the universe not to do a real-life version of that story.

"Free will was also part of their evolution on Earth," Gabriel said then, pulling my brain back from its musings. "Corruption is not always visible to the innocent or the not-so innocent." Gabriel blew out an exhaustive breath and shook his head. "Some took advantage of the slow aging process to obtain power and wealth, and there are those who participated in destruction of both humans and Seraph alike."

Leo gave a slow nod, and then said, "The Earthbound—not all but some, those who craved knowledge of a different kind, began to indulge themselves, in drinking, drugs and sex. None were immune, all felt the pull, the need, the curiosity. Some participated and reveled in their findings, while others quickly returned to their original observer ways. And a small few found their way to Thaddeus." Leo wrung a hand around his wrist again like this part of the story anguished him. "The Earth's population was out of control and the abuse of the Earth had increased. Humans and other species on Earth have evolved. Unfortunately, many species have become extinct because of man's abuse of the Earth, *and* the imbalance from the stars of Pleiades."

"The human race was becoming a fast-paced reality and keeping up had become challenging for many and often stimulating to both the mind and body," Gabriel acknowledged.

"What about these new Nephilim—when did they start being born this time?"

"During the years since his casting of his brethren and sistren, Thaddeus discovered that there had been Seraph and human couplings—that have produced these halflings, and in his disturbed mind, it was a muddying of our kind. He'd originally thought to kill them off but instead he chose to experiment on them. He wanted to see how they were conceived or even existed, since our kind had not been granted this ability."

"It is our belief that he has also been conducting very invasive tests on some of the Earthbound," Gabriel interjected. "For 10 years, before the 70 generations were up, Thaddeus had been preparing for his existence on Earth, however, not in the manner of losing his immortality. It was Purah who had told Anael and Thanael about the locations of the testing facilities. And Thanael has been the one who continued to maintain contact with some of the other Earthbound. Once we figured out where Thaddeus was, Leo was sent here to monitor him. The other Guards—they sometimes come and go from here, but mainly keep an eye on the other locations."

Neither said another word as I shifted my glance back and forth between the two angels. "That's everything?" I asked, uncertain.

"Beyond the issue of Thaddeus, our immediate concern is with Anael—well not her specifically," Gabriel said, adding to my uncertainty.

"Long-story-short, when she heard about Thaddeus trying to find the halflings and testing on them, it was then that she revealed to Thanael… that 20 years ago… she had given birth to a baby… and that she'd given the infant up for adoption."

"Yup—my brain just exploded," I said, shaking my head like its contents needed to be rattled.

"Were you able to sense the child—the boy at your daughters' school?" Leo asked.

I shook my head again. "I'm not sure—I was kind of distracted at the time."

"We both were," Gabriel said.

"I would be curious, Lynn—to know if you can sense the offspring," Leo said, his eyes narrowing as if speculating. "In any case, like I said, I think you need protection. You would be too valuable a prize for Thaddeus since you can sense Seraphim and those like him.

"Who is to say what halflings might bring to the table—but finding them is not easy," Gabriel added.

"How did he find the ones he has tested on?" I asked, my stomach doing a little flip at the thought.

"Thaddeus cannot sense his kind, and obviously none of the offspring, but once other Earthbound were located, they kept record of any Seraph-human relationships like we did, then they watched to see if any pregnancies developed."

I scribbled that last bit in with my notes, then shut the notepad. "Now what?" I asked, sliding the pad and pen back into my bag. I should have been furious they kept all this from me, but I was too blown away by this latest information, to be angry over their holding back now.

Gabriel turned in his seat to face me. "None of us can sense the Earthbound," he said, before shooting a look Leo's way.

"I know that," I said. Why was he restating the fact?

Leo cleared his throat, then shifted in his seat to sit forward on the edge of the chair as though what he had to say next required him to lean in closer. "Lynn. None but *you* can sense them—sense *us*."

Chapter 19

My brain exploded for a third time, and this time it was messy.

He'd said, *us.* Not him and me—but he and the other Earthbound. The Guards were part of the original Seraphim who had been sent down by Thaddeus so long ago. I couldn't understand, after everything that I and my friends had been through, why Leo and Gabriel felt they needed to feed this information to me in chunks. But Leo and the others being part of the original Earthbound, did explain why they needed a place like The Haven to live in. Hell, it explained a lot of things that had been boggling my brain.

"Why all the secrets—why not just tell me from the beginning?" I asked, calmer than I was actually feeling. I was letting my mind settle in with these latest tidbits of wisdom.

Leo sat back in his chair and blew out a breath as if relieved I hadn't freaked out. "We are so used to keeping a low profile that we have become protective of what others know. So, few know of our existence outside the celestial realm." He blew out another heavy breath.

I glanced at Gabriel examining his stoic expression. "I could say the same—but I have been completely forthcoming." I turned back to Leo.

"Please forgive me," Leo said, "my worry was more about your vulnerabilities and not of exposing our own."

"I'm going to leave the two of you to talk," Gabriel said, standing. He cut a sharp glance at Leo that gave me the impression they were exchanging unspoken words between them.

"What?" I asked, narrowing my eyes, and shifting my questioning gaze back and forth between the two of them.

"Nothing—I'm sure Leo is fully capable of informing you of the answers that you seek." Gabriel gave me an innocent grin, then kissed the top of my head like a parent would do. Then he disappeared.

I stared back at Leo for a long moment, and then said, "You mentioned you'd only been watching Thaddeus for 6 years." I breathed in. "Was that a lie?" I breathed out.

"Not exactly. I have been watching him for 6 years, but I've been here in Ottawa almost since the beginning—since the first Seraphim became the Earthbound, and in the position as an architect since the movement of modern architecture in 1901." He leaned forward, crossing his legs, right ankle resting over his left knee, relaxing both his hands over his calf.

"Why an architect?" I asked, lifting my bag from the floor, and setting it next to me where Gabriel had sat.

"I guess you could say I have an affinity for it—for the construct of structures." He smiled as if pleased by the simple question, then he went on. "I was part of several builds here in Ottawa, starting with the original Ottawa Public Library building—I worked with E. L. Horwood on the design back in 1903. In 1906 it was the Booth House. In 1909 it was the Murphy-Gamble department store. My favorites were the Château Laurier Hotel and Canadian Museum of Nature a few years after."

"The hotel and museum are favorites of mine," I said, nodding with appreciation. What I was also appreciative of was the fact my ears had stopped ringing.

"You may have heard about this before—but the Centre Block of the Parliament buildings was destroyed by fire in 1916, and a new Center Block was completed in 1922, and I had the privilege to work on that and the Victoria Tower."

"The Peace Tower," I said, in acknowledgement. "That's a great one." Canadian money wasn't something I used that often these days, but I remembered the tower was on the Canadian twenty-dollar bill, and the clock tower always serves as a Canadian icon.

"Correct." He nodded. "In 1920, it was The Capital Cinema with its 2,530 seats."

"I don't think I've been there," I said, tilting my head and trying to remember.

"Well, it was the largest movie theatre ever built in Ottawa—they called them movie palaces back then, and it was regarded as one of the best cinemas designed by T. W. Lamb—if I do say so myself." He grinned knowingly at me. "It was demolished in 1970—and probably why you've never been there." He shrugged.

"Ya," I said, followed by a laugh. "I would have only been 2 years old."

He brought an index finger to his mouth, tapping it in the center of his lips. He stopped then, and said, "Hmmm, in 1953 I worked on the Montfort Hospital. In 1964 we completed the Diefenbunker. We opened the Library and Archives Canada in 1967." One corner of his mouth tilted up in an almost smile. "In the 1960s and 1970s, the building boom transformed Ottawa's skyline. Ottawa became one of Canada's largest high-tech cities—nicknamed Silicon Valley North."

"Have you done major buildings recently?" I asked, fascinated by all he'd been a part of and witness to, plus I got the impression he was enjoying the telling of this history.

"The Ottawa Courthouse, 1986," he said, proudly.

"And the Celaeno building—did you do that one? You said you'd been in it. When?"

"Oh gosh, yes—I've worked on several conventional buildings around Ottawa over the years—including that building, 20 years ago." He leaned back in his chair and uncrossed his legs. "It's near one of the newer University buildings," he said, passing a hand over his jaw. "But going back to the beginning…." He paused glancing down as though remembering something. Then he said, "There was a fire in 1903 that destroyed the main building of the University." He paused again.

"Lots of fires in Ottawa in 1903," I said, cutting in.

He nodded, still gazing down, and rubbing the side of his jaw. "After the fire, the university hired a New York architect, a guy named

A. O. Von Herbulis. This was another of the earlier buildings I'd worked on, and I'd assisted in the design of its replacement, Tabaret Hall. It's one of the first Canadian structures to be completely fireproof—built with reinforced concrete."

"Sounds like a smart direction to go. Mac and Olivia were told that Thaddeus is in New York City—or was at the time of their tour," I said then, switching directions.

He glanced up, dropping his hand from his face. "Yes," he said. "We've confirmed that he's there—at the Merope facility. The building is near Broadway and West 70th. Though Kris says he has only seen him once so far on this visit.

"Kris?"

"Kristopher, actually," Leo said, resting an elbow on the arm of the chair. "He's Earthbound—one of The Guards like me, and similarly, he readily goes by the shortened version of his given name.

"Gotcha," I said. "But how would he know Thaddeus was there?"

"Kris owns a business in the vicinity, and he's seen him on other occasions. He said the bastard has a weakness for the mini icebox cakes from Magnolia Bakery on the Upper West Side—typically goes there every morning. Kris's location works well for keeping an eye out for the comings and goings at that facility."

"Right—okay." My stomach rumbled at the mention of cakes. "Sooo, Kris doesn't stay here then?" I glanced over my shoulder to the row of doors along the side wall.

"Like the rest of us, he has his own dedicated space here," Leo said, though he didn't expand any further.

Changing directions again, I asked, "The offspring Thaddeus has been looking for—are they those of the first Earthbound?"

"Yes," he said, his bright expression going grim.

"Have you met any of the halflings?" I asked, prompting for more.

A muscle in his jaw flexed, causing me to wonder if he was going to hold something back. I wanted to trust him, but he needed to prove to me he was trustworthy.

His lips tightened, and then he said, "Do you remember us telling you about the contact we have—the one working in the rainforest?"

"The one who said she'd seen Thaddeus," I recalled.

"Correct," he said. "Her name is Julianna—Jules, she... well, she has a son.

"Is she one of The Guards? Does she normally live here with you?"

"No... and no," he said. "They are both in Brazil."

I wasn't sure what question to ask next, the list was too long.

And before I could choose one, Leo said, "He's grown—19 years old I believe."

"And is he okay—did he suffer any issues at birth? Julianna is fine I imagine—if she's still doing her conservation job."

"She is, yes—no complications. And her son, all things considered, I'd say he's fine. Though he doesn't speak, he had issues with his airway as a child. Some kind of vocal cord disorder.

"Aerooodigestive?" I asked, drawing out the name I recalled for those disorders Olivia had mentioned.

Leo looked at me shocked.

"Not sure I pronounced that right, but it's one of the conditions Olivia and Mac were told about on their tour." The only reason I had remembered it was that it had made me think of the Arrowroot and Digestives cookies I'd had as a child.

"Yes, that is correct." He rubbed his jaw again. "He'd had a congenital abnormality during the development of his airway. Jules said he'd had HP...." He paused. "... hypersensitivity pneumonitis— it's a rare immune system disorder that affects the lungs. His condition had been compared to something called BFL—Bird fancier's lung. It's triggered by exposure to avian proteins found in the dry dust of bird droppings and sometimes in the feathers of a variety of birds." He ran the palm of his hand down along his throat.

"Huh. Maybe that's why Thaddeus has that floor in the building dedicated to bird lung studies," I said, retrieving my notepad and pen from my bag. Leo was quiet as I flipped open my notepad and wrote out the HP immune disorder stuff to share with the others later. "Do you know what kinds of birds he was exposed to?"

He frowned. "Parrots... macaws maybe." He shook his head. "But I'm told the offspring often have issues with their lung development and the structures related, like with their ribcages. And sometimes with their limb growth—but it's rarer."

"But other than not being able to talk, her son is good—healthy, right?"

He nodded.

"I still don't understand why Thaddeus's focus isn't on fertility—considering he's trying to figure out how to make... well—an angel," I stated. "Did Anael have any problems with childbirth? Did her baby suffer any issues?"

"None that I have been informed of," he said.

"How could Thanael not know—about her pregnancy, I mean?

Leo drew in a long deep breath, then huffed it out. "There was a time...," he began, then paused, "... when Anael had grown restless in her safe haven... and so she had chosen to go out into the world. She made her way to the big booming city of New York, where she met a man. We have very little information on him—just that he was in his late 40s and that he had been visiting the city like she had been. She stayed away for the duration of the pregnancy, only returning after the adoption. She'd said nothing to Thanael, though she had longed to share her experience with him—about the birth of her child, her daughter. She just hadn't expected she would have to share it under these circumstances."

"And she's afraid Thaddeus might find her—the daughter?

"Yes—we all are." The muscles in his jaw tightened.

"So now what?" I asked, feeling as though my head was starting to spin from all these additional shared elements.

"The other Guards and I will be heading to see Anael up North—to get more information," he said. "We are hopeful that speaking with her and the additional information she has for us will help us narrow down the search."

"How can I—we help?" I slid the notebook back into my bag.

Leo leaned forward, placing his elbows on his thighs, letting his hands hang loose. "It would help us if we could establish if you can sense the halflings or not. But like I said, we will have more information in a few days."

My phone buzzed then, and I slid it from the pocket in my bag.

"It's Redmond," I said, glancing up briefly from my phone.

Redmond had written,

Are you still at Leo's?

I wrote back,

Yes.

He replied quickly with,

You shouldn't have gone alone.

To ease his mind, I wrote.

Gabriel was with me.

To which he responded,

Good.

To further assure him I added,

I'll be back soon.

His reply was a single blue heart emoji, that for us meant *I love you but I'm worried.*

I sent him back a green heart, which signified *I love you and I'm okay.*

"I need to head back—bring everyone up to speed," I said, returning my phone to the inner pocket of my bag.

"Of course," Leo said, standing. "Again—I'm sorry for the secrecy."

I stood too. "Hey—I get it," I said, draping my bag crosswise over my chest. "But no more secrets going forward—especially if you want us to help. Agreed?" I put my hand out to shake on it.

"Agreed," Leo said, grinning down at me as he shook my hand.

Chapter 20

As it often does, time passes quickly in the presence of angels, even with the Earthbound ones, and despite it beginning to darken outside, I hadn't grasped how much time had passed until I pulled up to Vicki and Eric's place. There were several cars parked out front, showing that the others were back over again for dinner, and I didn't bother to knock before heading inside.

"Hey—did ya miss me?" I said in greeting, when I found Vicki, Mac and Alison in their favorite place, the kitchen.

"Always," Alison said, giving me a quick squeeze before she sashayed over to the fridge.

"How is it you always arrive just in time for food," Mac asked.

"I have impeccable timing—it's a gift," I tossed back at her with a wink.

She laughed, then shook her head like she always did with my comical responses to my relationship with food.

"I made your favorite," Vicki said. "Healthy mac'n cheese. Just preparing some garlic bread to go with it."

"The bread for it is homemade too—Vicki made it," Alison said, handing Vicki the butter she'd retrieved from the fridge.

"Of course, she did," I said, smiling big with appreciation. I glanced past them to the living room. "Where's Olivia?" I asked.

Redmond came through to the kitchen then from down the hall. "She's checking on a lead," he said, obviously overhearing my question.

"Wow, detective Olivia is on the case," I said, impressed. Though I needed to speak to all of them about how deeply they wanted to be involved, if at all.

"Hi Babe," Redmond said, wrapping a big arm around my waist. *"I'm not very happy with you,"* he whispered into my ear.

I turned in his hold to face him, placing my hands up on his shoulders. Gazing up at him I said, "But you still love me." Then I tippy-toed up to give him a kiss. My kiss was well received, so I knew he couldn't be that pissed with me.

"That I do," he replied, kissing me on the forehead and releasing his hold on me, before heading off to the living room.

"You probably shouldn't have gone alone," Mac said, setting out dinner bowls on the kitchen island. She set forks and napkins next to them for buffet style usage.

"I've done worse alone," I reminded.

"We know," Alison said, putting her hands on her hips for emphasis.

Vicki's phone that was charging on the counter, let out a chime. Grabbing it up, she said, "It's Olivia. She says to go ahead and eat when it's ready—but to save her some, and that she'll be back over as soon as she can."

"I've got more info—answers to our questions, and yer not going to believe it," I said, hoping to shift their disapproval of my venturing out on my own. "But you don't have to be involved," I'd added, the comment tossed out more as a joke, sort of.

"Ya that's not going to happen," Mac said, gliding the tray of garlic bread into the oven to broil. She set the oven's timer for 10 minutes.

"Esprit de corps," Alison added, handing Vicki the big serving spoon for the ooey-gooey—goodness.

"It means, we have a common interest—responsibilities, as a closely knit group," Vicki said, translating for me.

But I knew what it meant, and I knew what it meant for us to do this together. I leaned over the huge casserole dish and took in a healthy sniff. "Okay. But I'll go over the new stuff after we eat."

Olivia arrived minutes after everyone had hungrily cleaned their bowls of the delicious meal. "Hi all," she said, entering the kitchen.

Then she waved a hand to rest in the living room when she realized I was the only one in the kitchen.

"Yours is on the counter—ready to reheat," I said, as I wedged the last of the dinner dishes into Vicki's dishwasher.

Olivia let out a *squeal* of excitement as she promptly placed the dish in the microwave. "I guess I'm lucky you didn't eat my serving," she said, poking me in the ribs.

"There's half a casserole dish left over in the fridge." I gave her a toothy grin and patted my stomach.

She laughed and then dug into the cutlery drawer for a fork.

"We should get the others on video," Redmond called from the living room.

"Can Vicki cast the video call up on the TV," I responded back, hoping we didn't all have to gather around the laptop this time.

"I'm on it," Vicki said, getting up from her place on the loveseat.

When the microwave binged, I handed Olivia a tea towel. "Here use this—it'll be hot. Bring the dish with you."

The two of us met up with everyone else in the living room as Vicki set up her laptop on the coffee table. A few clicks and her laptop screen was showing on the TV.

"I texted Darius," Redmond said, "And he contacted Derek and Luc—so they're all ready."

Redmond had taken the chair furthest from the TV and I'd settled in on the floor in front of him facing the laptop with my notepad in hand. "Whenever you're ready, Vicki," I prompted. When Vicki glanced my way, I nodded. And then she hit dial.

The smiling faces of our friends Derek, Darius, and then Luc, swiftly appeared on screen.

"We have you up on the TV," I said, "You can't see all of us, but we're all here—and we can all see you. Say hi everyone." I opened my notepad and glanced at Alison. She had her notepad too. Then following the round of greetings, I dove into answering the list of questions Alison had recorded for me. "So, the Earthbound—the ones that were cast down with Thaddeus, are not all males. Two are female but they only know where one of them is. And since we know there are more Earthbound now—The Guards included, we got our answer as to if Leo and the others actually sleep—the answer being, *yes*."

"How long has it been since the first were cast down?" Alison asked.

"I'm told it's been 120 years since Thaddeus cast them down and though he'd been working on his plan since before then—he'd only started cultivating his relationship with Purah 20 years ago. Prior to that he'd been bound by the 70-generation hold like the other angels. It was after that he'd executed his full plan, creating this cover—this organization and the labs."

"That's pretty diabolical," Derek said. "I know Leo is in Ottawa now, but where were they sent down originally?"

"The Seraphim found out where they had been sent, and it was near the North Pole. Nunavut, Leo said."

"Talk about your desolate location—especially back in 1901," Vicki said.

"Ya, they're kind of a legend among the Inuit in the area and they had helped keep them hidden. How cool is that? There's still two of them there—the rest spread out across the globe."

"Why stay?" Mac asked, like I had done when I'd asked the same question.

"Anael and Thanael—the two that stayed, did so just in case more were sent down. The Seraphim can't come and go like the other angels—Earthbound or not, and the ones still on the stars, need Stewards like Purah to aid in their travel."

"You said, Purah is the one who told them about the other locations," Redmond stated.

"Yup, once they knew where Thaddeus was—Leo and the other 6 Guards began watching him at all the locations," I said, taking a quick glance up at Redmond. "Purah is the only Seraph left on Celaeno now. Derek, you told us about the different star names. Well, they are also the names Thaddeus used for the other facilities. Celaeno, we know was used for Ottawa."

"How original," Luc said with blowing out a loud breath.

"Oh, I also found out that Leo has a contact—another of the first Earthbound, who saw Thaddeus sourcing plants for their healing ingredients."

"Healing—my ass, probably for poison," Mac said. "Explains the greenhouse though."

"That's my feeling too," I said. "Leo told me that Thaddeus believes he's the good guy, and that he's clever. But mostly he's deceitful, and vengeful, and apparently, he will stop at nothing to get what he wants. His weakness is jealousy—especially of his own kind."

"Leo told you that most of the Earthbound went out among humans to learn stuff, and to survive basically. Did Leo and The Guards have to do that?" Vicki asked.

"Yes… some found ways to be near the humans, others hid, and some—like The Guards, live with humans… because, they're not immortal anymore," I shared.

"What does it mean that they aren't immortal anymore?" Luc asked. He was probably questioning like I had, how it was possible that an angel could lose their immortality.

"That explains the reason for the disguises," Redmond said.

"These angels not being on Pleiades—the Celaeno star specially, explains a lot of things happening with the Earth," I said. "Them not being able to use their skills—the ones for maintaining eco-balance, has impacted the Earth." I sighed out a breath.

"Global warming for example," Mac cut in, "humans continue to abuse the planet and if the others are missing skills to balance things— the Earth will continue to be a mess."

Everyone nodded at that.

"And the last thing on my notes, are these new Nephilim. They are the offspring of the originally Seraphim sent down—and not from Thaddeus's group," I said. "When Thaddeus discovered the couplings, he had initially wanted to kill them off—but went with experimenting on them instead. He wanted to see how they were able to do it, since his kind together, can't make babies. Leo believes he's testing on the Earthbound as well too." I closed my notepad.

"So, when Anael heard about the testing, that's when she decided to come clean about her own pregnancy and the child she'd given up for adoption?" Alison asked. She'd had her own challenges with conceiving, so this was a tender topic for her.

"That's what he told me," I said. "But he also said they were going to get more information in a few days—to hopefully help locate the daughter."

"How have they survived all this time?" Olivia asked, tossing out the question I'm sure all of us were pondering.

"I'm sure Leo can provide us with the details, share how they've done it," I said. I hadn't asked that level of detail. I flipped open my notepad again and jotted down a note to myself to ask more details on their survival.

"I think it would be a terrible fate to be immortal or practically immortal," Darius stated. "The boredom... the torture of emotional anguish of watching anyone you love, die. Anyone you got close to would eventually die." He ran a hand over his strawberry blonde brush cut hair.

"You'd more than likely have to keep moving from place to place every few years—before people, neighbors got suspicious," Luc said.

"I've read studies about this kind of thing," Derek said. "The research implies that as you get older—that you feel time pass more quickly. When you were 5 years old, half an hour seemed like forever—because it was relative to how long you'd been alive. Yet that same half hour would pass in a blink, when you are thousands of years old."

"Even if you were with others of your kind, you'd run out of things to do, places to see—it would become repetitive," Redmond said, "and your memories... you'd welcome senility, so you didn't have to remember that you'd done something a million times."

"Boredom," Vicki said then, echoing Darius's original sentiment. "How much of trying everything could you take before you needed to witness something new?"

"Near immortality means they have great healing you said, right?" Olivia stated. "Because if you don't, you may be at the mercy of slow healing to go with your slow aging."

"Do Leo and the others have perfect health?" Mac asked.

"Do they have immunity to human diseases?" Olivia asked, tossing out another good question, that I didn't have the answer to.

I sighed in frustration. "Leo explained they can be killed—but have exceptional healing capabilities. They are not vulnerable to human diseases, but they have their weaknesses he said." I sighed again. "Don't ask me what they are—he didn't say. But they do age at a rate of 1 year for every 10 of ours."

"Do they have to worry about eating and drinking? Good thing they sleep—if they didn't, the boredom would be even worse. You'd have to be good at finding hobbies," Derek said, adding to the ever-growing list of new questions.

"You could learn new skills but how many?" Olivia asked.

"Would you remember all of them?" Mac asked then. "How to do everything?"

I shrugged and shook my head, then leaned to look up at Redmond.

"Loneliness," Olivia said, forcing a smile.

"Arrogance," Redmond said, glancing around the room. "Eventually you could come to believe that anyone younger than you is just plain ignorant—of basically everything."

"What about mental degradation of so much time?" Alison added. She'd continued taking notes as I'd gone over the stuff I'd learned.

"What about the risk of someone finding out about you?" I stated, adding my own question, a more obvious one. Clearly, I'd have another list of questions for Leo, but he had to know there would be more.

"There are hosts of government, military, intelligence agencies, private organizations and criminal ones that have their hands on advanced technology," Redmond noted. "What do you think, Derek?"

We all knew Derek was basically our very own technology savant.

Derek nodded slowly. "Going undetected would become harder as technology advances. Facial recognition. Voice recognition," he said. "You'd have to be skilled in disguises, even aging yourself, to extend how long you could stay in one place. You'd have to fake your death—have an in at the morgue even." Derek typed something on his keyboard. "Fingerprints—don't get me started on the reasons for that. Even worse, is your DNA," he added. "And even if someone isn't actually looking for you, the problem is how all these things are becoming automated, databases being merged. You'd be considered an anomaly if there were two incidents of you—and they were several decades apart." He nodded at his own comment.

"If you didn't keep yourself off the grid, you would need to develop freakishly excellent skills at identity forgery," Darius interjected.

"You'd constantly need to keep ahead of new technology," Derek continued. "Compare the difficulty of faking a passport from the 50s, to that of the current day. Driver's licenses and other ID cards use chips and hologram and other security you don't see. Algorithms are used to flag and look for patterns and instances that *break* those patterns."

"Superpowers would be helpful—something that let you change your DNA, your appearance," I said, cutting into the overwhelm and dilemma of the topic of longevity.

"Your record keeping would have to be your superpower, where you've been, lived etc." Vicki said, panning the faces of the group.

"You would have to accumulate immense wealth," Luc said.

"Some did take advantage of the slow aging process, obtaining power and money—Leo told me," I responded. "And some found their way to Thaddeus."

"Well, from what we were shown in that home of Leo's—he had money," Redmond stated.

"I agree," I said, my memory running back over the luxury of the place and that which was hidden from the world. "Evidently, we have a new list of questions, but those answers are not really the concern of the moment." I glanced around and then back to the other on the TV. "If we are going to help them locate these halflings—locate Anael's daughter, I'm going to need to test my gifts on one—don't you think?" I glanced around again. "See if I can sense them like I do all the others."

Olivia's fork clinked in her dish and all eyes turned her way, even those on the TV screen. She grinned. Swallowing the last bite of her meal, she said, "I may have a lead on one."

After Mac, Alison and Olivia took off back to their homes, Vicki went to her office to work on her latest assignment. And Redmond and I went into our bedroom to video chat and catch up with the girls and

Redmond's parents, though my brain still hummed from the news Olivia had shared with us.

When I clicked the video chat dial button, within seconds, four grinning faces appeared on screen. From what I could see they were set up on the big couch in the living room, the tablet positioned on the coffee table.

"Hiiiii Muuum. Hiiii Daaaaaaa," Ryley bellowed, shoving her sister slightly out of view.

Hayley shoved back, then smiled again into the camera. "Hiiii," she said, waving. "I have a loose tooth," she added, trying to show us, pinching a tooth on the lower left side between her fingers and wiggling it.

"It's not that loose," Nainseadh said, reassuring us. "How is your visit going?"

"So far so good," Redmond said. "Great to see everyone after so long."

"Hayley, Ryley, are you two being good for your grandparents?" I interrogated, my brows furrowing.

"We want them to come visit us again soon—so don't wear them out," Redmond added.

Redmond's words were followed by the shared commentary of Ryley and Hayley as they relayed for us the last 24 hours of their time with their grandparents. I always loved hearing the different versions of the same events as told by each of them. Hayley was always very precise in descriptions, while Ryley conveyed things in a mostly animated way.

"How are you guys faring," I asked then, directing that question at the adults.

"Tired—but good," Enzo said, shifting to rub his wife's shoulder.

Nainseadh gave Enso a quick smile. "We're keeping up, but I forgot how much energy small humans have." She wrapped an arm around Ryley, pressing a kiss to her cheek and making a squeaky noise against it.

"Zerbert," Ryley said, giggling, referring to the squeaky-style kiss.

Nainseadh did the same to Hayley on her opposite cheek. "We are all having a blast—really."

Redmond and I always did that squeak kiss on them too. He must have learned it from his mother I figured. My mom used to do the same to me when I was a kid and it always made me laugh.

"We are having fun," Hayley said, "But we miss you—wish you were here with us having fun." She pushed out a pouty bottom lip.

Ryley followed suit, placing her elbows on her knees, then rested a pouty face in the palms of her hands.

"I know—I know," Redmond said, "we'll be back soon. Had to check in on the gang up North, spend some time with them after so long—you know that."

"They all miss you guys," I said. "Would you like them to come visit?" I asked, raising my eyebrows in question, hoping to derail the pouting.

"Yaaaaaaa," Ryley said, sitting up straight then.

"When-when—can they come back with you?" Hayley asked, full of anticipation.

"We'll work something out in the new year—maybe in a few months," Redmond said.

The two slumped where they sat, their enthusiasm quashed. "Oh *kaaay*," they said in unison, voices petering to a whisper.

"But we'll be home soon," I tossed out hoping for a return of their bright eagerness.

"In time for New Years?" Ryley asked, her eyes lighting up again.

"Yes—Friday," Redmond said. "Isn't it time for bed?" Redmond tilted his head in question.

Hayley let out a heavy sigh. "Ya," she said in a soft voice.

"I love you, Hayley." I paused. "I love you, Ryley," I said, purposely addressing them one at a time. "You guys take good care of your grandparents and we'll be home before you know it."

The corner of Hayley's mouth turned up in a half smile. "Love you too, Mum."

Ryley glanced over her shoulder at her grandparents. "*I don't think they need us to take care of them*," she whispered, as if they couldn't hear her. "But we got this," she added. "Love you, Mum."

"Okay girls—time for bed," Redmond said, "Love you with all my heart. Sweet dreams." He blew them each a kiss.

"Love you too Da," Ryley said, kissing her fingertips then placing them on the screen.

Hayley blew a kiss from her palm." Love you, Da," she said, before hopping down from the couch and followed by her sister.

"Niiiight," I heard them both call as though down the hall.

Enzo and Nainseadh both let out exhausted breaths. "They're a handful," Enzo said. "But we are both thrilled to have this time with them—thank you."

"No—thank you," I said. "We really appreciate your coming down for the holidays, to be with us—them, watching them while we are up here."

"Anytime," Nainseadh said. "They will be grown before you can say *teenager*, and not interested in hanging out with their old Nana and Poppy."

"They will grow tired of *us*—before they ever do with you guys," Redmond said, laughing. "They are already starting to show signs that we are no longer cool." He laughed again.

"Speak for yourself," I said, "I'll always be cool." I chuckled. "Ya right," I added.

"You guys have everything you need there?" Redmond asked. "Darius and Lily are just a phone call away if you need anything."

"They've been over already," Enzo said. "They helped wear the girls out today." He blew out another exhaustive breath.

"They stopped by this afternoon," Nainseadh said. "Guess they figured we needed a reprieve—and they were right." She let out a soft laugh. "Wonderful friends you both have here." She gave us a smile then that made her eyes sparkle with emotion.

I nodded. "We are so grateful for our amazing family and friends." I smiled back, feeling the distance.

"Okay—the twins aren't the only ones who need to get to bed. Early night for us—we have a full day tomorrow," Enzo said, groaning as he stood. "Need to be up early and ready for pancake making." He rubbed his stomach. "Love you."

Nainseadh rolled her eyes then laughed. "Enjoy your visit, you two—don't worry about us. Love you."

"Night," I said, "Wish I was going to be there for your famous pancakes," I said with a wink.

"Night, Mom—Night, Pop," Redmond said. "Love you."

"Love you both," I added before the video call ended.

"You, okay?" Redmond asked, shifting to get up off the bed.

"I guess," I said, still staring at the blank screen.

He came around and sat next to me on my side of the bed. "What?"

I let out a breath full of mixed emotions. "I miss my friends so much—but I feel guilty for leaving the girls behind. And I hate that we are missing out on time with them and your parents too." There had been so much loss over the past few years, and so much time lost with friends and family. "I hope you're right—about being able to arrange for the Ottawa peeps to come down to visit." Travel between the US and Canada had been up and down, and we never knew what restrictions might be put in place for crossing the border. The pandemic had changed so much.

"We'll make it work. They'll make it work—they always do," he said, rubbing my leg. "We still have a few more days with them—and you ladies have a new quest." He grinned at me. "Didn't you say you wanted to have that feeling again?"

"What feeling?" I asked.

"Of purpose," he said, kissing my forehead before getting up off the bed. He went in and shut the door to the en suite bathroom before I could reply.

But he was right. I had wanted to feel that *purpose* again, that feeling of being part of something bigger than myself. What I didn't want was all the secrecy again on the part of the angel team, and the fact that what we were looking into involved experimenting on children. I'd gotten a pretty good grip on the fact that angels existed, that I was genetically related to a few, and that I and my daughters had the ability to sense them, though I never expected to hear that there were a whole group of them stuck on Earth. We'd been told about the many wars amongst angels, but those battles had been long before my time, close to the beginning of Earth's existence in fact. But knowing that conflict as recent as 120 years ago had occurred was distressing to say the least.

I'd learned about the wars that humans fought, those before my time. I'd watched other wars unfold and be reported on the news, and I'd seen the results, the aftermath with the victims, the soldiers, and civilians alike. Humans continue to war still, and I understood that I had no influence over how those events unfolded. I am merely a witness, a bystander viewing the destruction through my TV. And I also had no influence on what happened between angels in their past, nor do I have influence on their potential rivalries either. Although, I do feel strongly that my friends and I could potentially help those angels in need here on Earth, to find others, their brethren and sistren, and best case, find and protect these halflings.

My need to help was presenting more like a compulsion, like the ones I used to get when given the choice of doing or not doing something, where the not doing often made me nauseous if I resisted. I'd felt that queasiness today at Leo's place, when I'd attempted to wrap myself in denial over what he had been telling Redmond and me. Once I'd let the truth in, listened to the details of what had previously been hidden from me, the nausea had subsided. I'd allowed the acceptance that my direction on these new facts, was to believe, to listen and move forward in aiding wherever I could.

Redmond had supported the idea of us learning more, and he supported my need to assist these Earthbound. I never want Redmond to think he wasn't enough, or that my life wasn't fulfilling. It was more than I could have ever imagined for myself. I loved my life, and I would never take for granted this wonderful rollercoaster love-filled existence I had with him, with our girls. Nonetheless, that feeling that overwhelms me, the one that resonated as though my reason for being here, for being born, really meant something, that maybe I could help, make a difference, that I might be the one who could change things for these Earthbound… it was a sensation I couldn't truly put into words. And I knew it was more than purpose, it was… destiny, *maybe*?

Chapter 21

Surprisingly, I'd had a goodnight's sleep absent of dreams, none that I remembered anyway. I had expected a menagerie of images to invade my sleep, especially after all that Leo had told me, plus what Olivia had shared last night about a potential halfling she may have located. I was grateful I'd slept right through the night, and it was a good thing I did too, because I was going to need to be on my *seer* game today.

Olivia's lead was a colleague that she'd reached out to, a woman whose job it was at the hospital, to place any baby born that had been orphaned and become a Crown Ward into foster care. I wasn't familiar with the term Crown Ward, but she explained it was a status used in Canada to mean a ward of the state which I had heard of in the US. Olivia had asked her colleague if she could recall any babies she'd placed, that had been born with any lung issues. When the woman had checked her records, she'd come up with only one. The mother had died in childbirth, and the baby had been placed into what she had thought to be an ideal foster situation, the foster parent having resources and the means to care for the baby's special physical needs. The child's needs originally were that he was born with an enlarged ribcage and vocal cord damage, along with missing part of his legs from the mid-thigh down. The details on the foster parent had been kept confidential, even from the caseworker, but after 5 years in that foster care, the child had been returned to Children's Services because of a new diagnosis, that of autism. The foster parent had gone on record saying that this type of special need was not something they were equipped to handle. Now the child resides in a privately funded group home that specializes in this level of special care. When the woman had spoken about the baby's condition, Olivia remembered having been there at the birthing center for the birth. She'd witnessed several babies born with disfigurements, and at the time, she'd let the detail fade into her mind's databank with the others. It wasn't until I shared what Leo had said about the halflings and the markings on their backs that the memory had resurfaced. She had recalled the deformities when mentioned by her colleague, but what had made this child stand out further in Olivia's memory had been the fact the baby had been born with unusual birthmarks on their shoulder blades.

Alison had added that she often works on cases where the Crown Ward is more often a foster *child*, who cannot be reunited with their natural family, though she's yet to work with anyone younger than three years old. Although, she did say, with her credentials, she could help get us in to meet with those in charge of the group home, and potentially even meet this child, if Olivia was able to get the contact information for the place. As luck would have it, when Olivia mentioned Alison's name to her colleague, it was the combination of Olivia's work at the hospital and Alison's reputation that had made handing over the contact details a cinch for the woman. And sweet-talking Alison had set up a meeting this morning for the three of us to go and meet with the group home's coordinator.

After Redmond and I had a quick morning video chat with the girls over breakfast, I'd cleaned myself up and donned the nicest clothes I'd brought with me, black pants, and a grey knit sweater, in hopes of making a professional impression as the tag-along to Olivia and Alison. I sent Leo a quick text to let him know we were checking out a lead on a potential halfling at a group home.

"You'll be careful, right?" Redmond asked me, though it was more like he was telling me than asking. "Be the follower—not the leader on this outing." He fiddled with and then smoothed the strap of my cross-shoulder bag as if he were nervous about letting me leave without him at my side.

"Don't worry—I'll be following their lead," I said, taking hold of his hand. "This is not my area of expertise. I've dealt with babies in the NICU, but group homes are not something I'm even remotely familiar with." Especially not those dedicated to special needs kids. Alison, on the other hand, had been dealing with kids with a diversity of needs, and mostly those in need of loving, caring people in their lives. That part I could relate to. "What are you going to do today?" I redirected.

"I'm heading back over to Mac and Don's place—to help Don work on his latest project car." He grinned then cracked his knuckles as if showing he had a big serious job ahead of him.

"Big boys and their big fast cars, eh?" I squeezed his hand.

"Sharing my other talents," he said, rolling his shoulders like a big show off.

I went up on my tiptoes and kissed him. "You are so generous," I said, just as a double honk sounded from the driveway. "That's Olivia and Alison.

"I am generous," he said, smacking me on the butt. "Now get!" He turned me around and gave me a little shove towards the front door, followed by another smack on my butt.

"Trying to get rid of me now—are you?" I darted for the front door and out of his reach this time. "Bye—I love you," I said, turning and giving him a big smile before shutting the door behind me.

The group home was located East and across town and would take a bit of time to get there since it was just the start of rush-hour, now that most people were headed back to work today after the holiday.

On the drive, Alison explained that there were dozens of group homes around Ottawa, many of them set up for those with neurological disorders. "I contacted The Children's Residential Services, and they put me in touch with the person who runs this particular group home," Alison said, glancing over her shoulder to look at me in the backseat. "This organization serves some of the most vulnerable and dependent populations in our society, and they've done so since 1996. And we should be able to meet the child." She grinned at me, then turned forward again.

"How did you arrange for us to visit with the kid?" I asked.

"I just contacted the home directly," Alison said.

"Are kids at this place grouped by age or disability or both?" I leaned, looking between the front seats, watching the road ahead.

"The facility we are going to is all about the disabilities, but the age range goes up to 18," Alison said, glancing back between the seats at me.

I saw Olivia peek at me via the rearview mirror. "Visits have to be approved by a social worker. Alison isn't a social worker, but she qualifies for approval, and they'll document our visits for paperwork purposes," Olivia stated.

"Gotcha," I said. I had nothing else to ask at the moment and I zoned out, watching the sights go by as we travelled across the city. Every time I visited Ottawa, there was always something that had changed since the last time I visited, be it the landscape or storefronts, or even the visibility of scenery from the highway that was now often disrupted by high-rises and office building that had sprouted up along the way. I was glad I wasn't driving this time. I'm not sure I'd recognize how to get myself back to the West end, to where my friends all lived now. I'd never really been familiar with the East end of Ottawa when I did live here, but now I couldn't even find what had been easy landmarks for me when I had traversed the main highway in the past. Thank goodness for the highway signs and GPS.

At the entrance to the group home, which was a repurposed old mansion, we were met by the facility program coordinator. He was short and stout, with short cropped dark hair, mid-30's, and he had a pudgy face that seemed to redden when he smiled. "Hello, Ladies— Welcome," he said in greeting, leading us into the front vestibule of the home. He's said his name, but I didn't register it, I was too busy checking out the facade of the manor-style home.

Based on the outer part of the grand home, I had expected to find opulent furnishing to mirror the luxurious appearance of the outside, but what I found inside was more minimalist in furnishing and décor, and a tad clinical. There were several chairs placed in an arc around what would have been a rather large living room, and next to each were small desks that displayed one or two children's toys, the kinds that encourage more learning than fun, several of which were no doubt used for working on skills like coordination and communication. At the desk furthest from the entrance I saw there was a young woman, whom I assumed was an aide, tending to a small child in a walker. The chairs I had assumed would have been for the children, but I realized now they were for the aids, and that more than likely most of the kids here would be using walkers or wheelchairs and the open space opposite from each desk was for that need.

The man glanced down at the ID credentials Alison had pinned to her coat. "Please sign in your coworkers—won't you," he directed at Alison.

"Yes—of course," Alison said, picking up the pen on the desk near the entrance. She proceeded to fill out one of the forms provided.

"This looks like a wonderful facility," Olivia said, glancing around the large room.

"The residential services provide us this building," the man said, "But we provide a loving and nurturing home for children with intellectual disabilities and complex needs to live and thrive." He gave Olivia a smile, that to me didn't seem genuine and only reddened his face.

Alison set down the pen, and we all stepped forward, following the man into the learning living room space.

To the left I could see through to another large room set up with more chairs and small tables, but this one was arranged more for serving and assisting with meals, with brightly coloured plastic dishes, mugs and sippy cups set out on each of the tables.

"What else does the residential services provide?" Olivia asked, before turning to observe the aide and the child over at the other end of the room.

"The organization offers several day programs, foster homes, collaborative care, and clinical services that give people the ability to reach their full potential and live a happy and fulfilling life. They provide clinical support services to all our clients," he said, his pace slowing as we reached the other side of the large room.

"How do you know what services each *client* needs?" I asked. I wasn't supposed to really talk or ask questions, but I was curious since his words sounded more like a sales pitch.

"They collaborate with one of our clinicians to determine the best approach forward. The ongoing collaboration allows them to monitor progress, reassess treatment, and build on prior successes," he said, as he continued to lead towards the other areas of the home.

I raised my eyebrows but said nothing. I didn't want to be rude, however, it all sounded a little too clinical and not the least bit loving and homey as he had originally stated.

He must have registered my disapproval because he said, "They really love the kids here—the staff. They never give up or back down from any challenges." His expression was either one of concern for the kids or over my dissatisfaction, I wasn't sure. "Everything they do is tailored to help kids with special needs live more rewarding, joyful, and sometimes even independent lives—once they are adults," he added, his dialog shifting back to the sales pitch.

"What services do you provide at this location," Alison asked.

"They have programs and services to assist children with a wide variety of different situations and needs. Residential care, foster care, collaborative care, day programs, and clinical care," he said, as though reciting the brochure. "I can get you more detailed information on the specifics for each child if you wish," he added, directing his words solely at Alison.

"Who pays for all of this?" I said, before I could wrangle my curiosity again.

He turned and looked at me, then cleared his throat. "This particular location has the Celaeno Foundation as its benefactor." He gave me a smug smile, then turned to Olivia. "I'm sure you are familiar with them and their work—you're the one who works at the hospital, yes?"

Olivia glanced my way, and I widened my eyes. *Be careful what you say*, I tried to tell her with my expression.

"I have—yes, heard of them, yes—the great work that they do," Olivia sputtered out.

"We'd love to meet the child I inquired about," Alison said, redirecting the conversation for reasons clear to us, though oblivious to this man—salesman.

"Right this way," he said, quickening his pace. I got the impression he didn't like being here, in this facility, and I wondered if he even liked kids. He hadn't even addressed the woman who had been with the little girl, nor had he even glanced down at the child.

"Carlie," he said, as we approached a woman in the hallway near the entrance to another room. She sat at a clean white tabletop desk that had nothing on it but a laptop. "Please assist these ladies with any questions they may have about the facility. They are also here to see Taylor."

"Of course," Carlie said, glancing up briefly from whatever she was doing on the laptop.

"Excellent." He turned back to us. "Ladies—you are in good hands," he said, before hurriedly striding off back up the hall and out of sight.

Carlie lifted her eyes to stare up the hall in the direction the man had retreated. She let out a breath and looked over at us. "How can I help you?" she said then with a smile, a genuinely sweet smile, as she looked to each of us for our requests.

"Not one of your favorite people, I take it," I said, picking up on her discomfort with the facility's coordinator.

She pressed her lips tight together.

"Don't worry—I didn't like him either," I said, making a face like I'd eaten something bitter.

She let out a small laugh, followed by a heavy breath that I understood as relief. She took in a smooth breath, then said, "Not my favorite—no."

"We've all worked with people like that," Olivia said. "We understand." She nodded and smiled at the woman.

"You can talk freely with us," I added in reassurance.

"How many kids live here?" Alison asked, unzipping her jacket, glancing up and down the hall.

"This location has nine children, most of whom have been here 10+ years with no plans on leaving on any time soon," Carlie said.

"How does someone get into this group home—what is the process?" Olivia asked.

"Usually a referral comes from CAS, the Ministry of Community and Social Services, or social workers," she said.

"Who normally pays for it?" I asked, admiring the modern desk she was sitting at.

"Often the disability program in Ottawa pays for their lodging," she said, clacking away on the keyboard of the laptop. "Some things are handled through private donors." She glanced up the way again, as if checking for anyone coming around the corner at the end of the hall.

"What are they provided when they arrive?" Olivia asked.

"Clothes, sometimes. Hygiene supplies. The furniture in their room, often a desk and dresser is provided," she said, "and laundry is done daily." She typed something on the keyboard again. "There's a living room—I'm sure you saw it when you entered. There's a kitchen like a normal home at the far end." She pointed the opposite way down the hall from where she'd been watching. "We have an office that is locked and stores their meds." She pointed at a single door a few feet from where she sat.

"How many people typically work here?" I asked.

"We have a high staff-to-child ratio, to ensure that every child receives constant hands-on supervision. We have six full-time and six part-time. Some part-time staff only come once every two weeks, others four to five days of the week. Most part-timers have other jobs, but they are vital if a full-timer is out sick and must be covered for the needs of the children. Our focus is on providing mental health care within a safe and stable environment," she said, glancing down the hall again.

"What are the different roles/titles of the people who work there?" I tossed out, curious about the other people in the building.

"We have the coordinator—our boss, whom you met, he comes in most days," she said, puffing out a breath. "A system manager and supervisors. And residential counsellors—part and full-time, like me— I'm full-time."

"What do you do?" Alison asked, pulling her trusty notepad from the pouch of her purse. She began feverishly jotting down notes.

"I'm basically a caretaker with a clinical responsibility. I have to follow a plan of care called a BSP—behaviour support plan, that a clinical behaviour specialist has signed off on." She clicked a key on the laptop and then stood up from the desk.

We all watched as she went to the door she'd indicated as the office. She unlocked it, stepped inside out of view, and then a second later exited, locked it, and returned to stand next to the desk. "Printer," she said, waving the papers she had in her hand.

I nodded. "Who stays on the premises?" I asked, more curious than before about the place based on the young woman's anxious behaviour.

"It's kind of like shift work. During the night, we have one staff member while the children are asleep—we alternate. During the day, the rest of us supervise them, creating activities for them, doing our paperwork, and cleaning the house." She pressed her lips tight and drew a breath in through her nose.

"What kind of security is in place?" I turned back to take a quick glance up the hall like she had done. I probably wouldn't have asked so many questions with the coordinator present, but now I felt more comfortable speaking with Carlie without her boss around.

"We have cameras but they're not actually being used at the moment—technical issues." She cut a glance up to what I assumed was a camera over the door to the room, just out of view. "Our staff are very hands-on, and the children need constant supervision." She chewed the corner of her lip. "Would you like to meet Taylor now?" she asked, handing Alison the papers she had printed.

"Yes, that would be great," Alison said, taking the papers she'd been offered.

When I turned in the direction Carlie had moved to go in, the back of my neck tingled, and I froze mid-turn. The skin of my face and arms began to prickle, the sensation like that of static electricity. I'd had the same feeling when I was in Leo's presence, only not exactly. The prickling felt sharper and not like the pop-rocks tickle of sensing him or Purah. I took a cleansing breath in, saying nothing as we were brought up the hall to another open area. Rubbing my arms in hopes of lessening the sensation, I entered the room.

Based on the large almost floor to ceiling windows on the other three walls of the room, the space appeared to have once been a large screened-in porch or more than likely a three-season room, which would follow better the design of the home.

On the far side of the room opposite the entry, there was a wheelchair facing the window. As we approached, I could see there was a small child in it. I watched as Carlie knelt down to one side of the wheelchair. "Hi Taylor," she said in a soft voice, addressing the tiny child. "You have visitors today." She waved for us to come closer, then shifted the wheelchair half a turn away from the window. "Taylor turned 8 years old last month—didn't you, my big boy?" She sat down in the chair next to him.

He was small for his age, I noted, even compared to the twins and their size. Even Hayley was bigger than him. The reason for him being in the wheelchair was obvious, as he was missing most of his legs, and I'd expected that from what Olivia had previously told us. But the grossly over-developed upper part of his body, his ribcage more precisely, was more than evident through the thin fabric of his long-sleeved navy shirt. He smiled up at Carlie.

"Do kids often get visitors or is it normally staff only?" I asked, glancing at Carlie. I rubbed my arms again.

"They can certainly get visitors and they are brought to their families by staff often. They will get phone calls and video calls often with family and friends too—especially this past year with covid," she said. "Come sit." She gestured to the other chairs near the window.

Olivia and Alison took the two chairs next to Carlie, and I took the one opposite the boy.

"Some come from loving families and caregivers who play a crucial role in supporting them, but they come to us needing help, and our role is to help each of them realize their full potential," Carlie began again. "The clinicians can help kids work towards any number of goals, from skill development to eliminating harmful behaviours. Each child receives customized care specifically designed to help them live a better life."

"Does he speak," Olivia asked, taking her gaze off the boy to look at Carlie.

"Hi Taylor. I'm Lynn," I said to him. He turned a shaky head to show me his sweet face. His bright green eyes seemed to recognize that we were there for him, though he made no sound or other movement.

"He is mostly non-verbal and is most often in his mind and content to play on his own. Originally, he came to us for the overnight respite service. It's designed to give families and caregivers support and relief. Everybody needs a break sometimes."

I looked at her and nodded, set my gaze back on Taylor.

"But he started to come more often and eventually he was surrendered and became a member of the residential program. He is part of the high support program for those who need more intensive care. He lives in a world that most just don't understand and seemingly most are not even willing to try. But we do." She reached into a bag hanging off the back of his wheelchair and took out what I recognized as a classic Etch A Sketch toy. "He sometimes communicates using this toy," she clarified for us, placing the toy on the small shelf-like table attached to the front of the wheelchair.

He immediately put both hands on the toy.

"Can you draw for me, Taylor?" I asked the sweet little cherub.

His smile broadened, and he began to turn the two white knobs on the red plastic frame. As he twisted the knobs, the stylus moved across the flat gray screen and through the grey powder under the screen. Solid lines and shapes began to appear as he moved the stylus up and down and side to side.

"You'll know he's done when he claps his hands and rocks side to side," Carlie said, smiling.

"He's really making something," I said, my enthusiasm growing.

"He'll show you—but you have to be quick because he will shake it and the communication will be lost," Carlie explained, followed by a knowing laugh.

Alison and Olivia leaned in, watching along with me as the image took shape.

"He's what they call an autistic savant," Carlie added, checking closer to see what he was drawing. "That's someone who has a mental or learning disability but is extremely gifted in another way, such as performing feats of memory or calculation. Like with Dustin Hoffman's character in the movie *Rainman*."

"Loved that movie," I said, nodding. Then I gasped as the image became even clearer.

"Amazing," Olivia said, snapping a few photos of the image with her phone.

"Wow," I said, in witness of the amazing creation he was making. The design was an extremely detailed image of a floorplan, not of a house, but of an office building layout. The prickling on my skin sharpened suddenly, and I sucked in a breath through my teeth. I peered out the window in front of us, then cut a glance at each of the other windows. I couldn't see anything, anyone, but someone or something was here. I shot a glance at the room's entry just as the facility coordinator entered the room.

Taylor squealed then, the sound piercing as he shook the toy.

Carlie leaned forward to sooth Taylor. "He doesn't like the male residential counselors and only responds to me and the other women on staff. And he feels the same about *him* as we all do." She pointed with her chin in the direction of the approaching coordinator.

"Tell me—does Taylor have any birthmarks?" I asked quickly, as Taylor's screeches switched to softer wailings.

"Yes—pale ones on his upper back. They look like snowflakes."

"Show me," I said, taking a quick look over to the coordinator. He had turned away from the noise, his cellphone up to his ear.

"Olivia—take a picture quick," I said, as Carlie gently lifted the back of Taylor's shirt. Olivia snapped the shot just before the coordinator turned back to head our way again.

"Okay—visiting time is over," Carlie's boss said to us.

"I didn't know there was a time limit," Alison stated, standing up from her chair.

Olivia slid her phone into her purse and snapped it closed.

"Thank you," I said to Taylor, ignoring the boss. "It was a pleasure to meet you."

"Thank you," Alison directed at Carlie.

"You are more than welcome," she said, moving her chair closer to Taylor.

I mouthed a *thank you* to Carlie. She'd given us the inside scoop, alluding to the fact that things here were far from copacetic with the boss. I stood then, and Taylor grabbed my hand. He was surprisingly strong for a little guy, and his tugging prompted me to squat down closer next to him.

His eyes looked to Carlie first, then to me, tilting his head towards to the right side of my face. I leaned in closer to him. "*Lynn*," he whispered into my ear. My mouth dropped open and my eyes widened at the barely audible sound of him speaking my name. Then he mumbled something that sounded like... "*wings*."

Chapter 22

Taylor spoke. Not just any old words, he said my name. No one had mentioned my name while in his presence. How could he know it—let alone say it? Carlie had said he was 'mostly' non-verbal, so it didn't mean he couldn't speak, just that he didn't do it often.

I turned to look Taylor directly in the face. "Yes—I'm Lynn," I said, gazing deep into his bright green eyes. I ignored the nattering of the coordinator behind me, and instead I watched as Taylor's chest rose and dropped from his anxious, labored breathing. "What about *wings?*" I asked him then. Those green eyes of his darted up and to the left, following around as the flustered coordinator came to stand behind Carlie. I patted Taylor's tiny hand, the one that had gripped me so tight, then stood, still gazing down at him.

"Ms. Westlake," the coordinator said, pulling my attention from the boy. He had the sign-in sheet in his hand, and had obviously, by process of elimination, narrowed down which of the names belonged to me.

"Yes," I said, in acknowledgement. I felt Taylor's little hand thread in and around the fingers of my hand closest to him.

"Your visit has clearly upset the child," the annoying man said. "It is best you and the others leave now." He glanced at Alison and Olivia.

I was just about to respond with the fact it had been his presence that had upset Taylor when I noted the expression on Carlie's face. She must have been aware of what I might say, because her eyes were wide, as if conveying a message to be cautious. Taylor was calmer now, except for the strained breathing, so I held my tongue. "He seems fine now—but we need to be heading out anyway," I said, in exchange of what I'd wanted to say. "Thank you again, Carlie—for sharing the wonderful work you are all doing here." I nodded then at Taylor, to let him know I *heard* him too. I didn't understand what he was trying to tell me, but I wanted him to have the knowledge that his words had been heard. I glanced at Carlie again and smiled. She smiled back in relief. I turned then, heading in the direction of the exit and my friends, who were now waiting just outside the archway to the hallway. I couldn't care less what this man had said about our upsetting Taylor. I knew the truth, but I was more concerned about what might happen to Carlie after we left. I'd make sure to have Alison call and check up on her later.

Outside and out of earshot of the facility's coordinator, as we strode to the SUV, I said, "What the hell is going on in that place?"

"The place was starting to give me the heebie-jeebies," Olivia said, shuddering visibly as she slid into the driver's seat of the car.

Alison turned in her seat to look at me in the back seat, giving me a rueful expression. "It took everything I had not to grab that boy and Carlie, and haul the two of them out of there," she said, her words mirroring the regret I was feeling about having to leave them there at the hands of that asshole. "It's a privately funded facility—so there's really not much we can do through regular channels."

"Not that we have something to report other than our feelings about the place and the guy running it," Olivia said. "Would hate to do anything that might risk Carlie her job as well."

I turned and glanced through the back window of the car, staring at the hoity-toity mansion as we drove off, wondering about Taylor, the words not spoken, the fear in Carlie's eyes, and secrets still held within those walls.

"Lynn," Alison said, pulling my attention back as the group home disappeared out of view. "Did you get any of your seer tingles, sensing Taylor?" Her big blue eyes blinked excitedly.

I glanced down at my hands in my lap, remembering the touch of Taylor's tiny hand, his tugging on me, and his words. I glanced back up and saw Olivia looking at me in the rearview mirror, and Alison's inquisitive expression still staring back at me between the front seats. "I'm not sure." I wasn't sure. "I felt something, but I'm not sure it was due to being near the boy." My thoughts switched then to what Taylor had created on that toy. "Olivia, send me the photos—would ya, the ones of the etching he did and those of his birthmarks."

"Uhmm…. can it wait until we get back?" she asked, checking a glance at me in the rearview mirror.

"Yes—sorry," I said. She was driving, I reminded myself. I let my thoughts drift back to the facility, to Carlie and Taylor as we made the journey back to Vicki's house.

What had I sensed? I'd not felt anything when I'd entered the facilities and Taylor had obviously been inside, but the feeling—that strange prickling had only started when I'd turned in the direction to follow Carlie to the room where he had been. Had someone else otherworldly entered the facility? Had they been nearby or outside? The feeling had not been an enjoyable one and I couldn't imagine it had come from being near Taylor, but who knew what it would feel like to be near a halfling—maybe it wouldn't be as clear-cut as identifying an Earthbound, but then I'd only been in the presence of one so far, and Purah who was still a full Pleiadean. The sharp prickling had stopped when the coordinator had come to stand behind Carlie.

"What do you think about the fact that the group home is funded by Thaddeus's organization?" Alison asked. She'd obviously been pondering through her own list of questions about the place and was equally curious as to our take on things. "I mean—isn't he the bad guy? Why would he do that?"

"Watching Taylor, maybe?" Olivia said as we rounded into Vicki's neighborhood. "Watching, waiting to see if others come looking for him?"

"That's a good question," I said, "and a good assumption too." Thaddeus was the bad guy, no doubt about it, so he wouldn't be doing this out of the goodness of his heart. He must have other, more dubious motives. And the possibility he was watching for visitors, others looking to find such a child, was a pretty smart notion on Olivia's part. "You're becoming a clever detective, Ms. White," I directed at Olivia.

"Maybe what I was feeling was one of his followers, watching us from somewhere nearby. I hadn't thought to check for cameras in the room we'd met Taylor in, though Carlie had said they weren't currently working. Maybe they were—or just that one in particular, and why she'd purposely eyeballed the camera over the door to that open area, to let us know we were being watched. And if this is the room Taylor often spent time in, it would make sense to have a camera set up— observe who came to see him." I paused, thinking about Taylor. "I still don't understand how he knew my name."

"Who—the coordinator? What do you mean—he had the sign-in sheet?" Alison stated.

"Not him—Taylor," I said, as we pulled into Vicki's driveway. "He whispered to me my name."

Olivia slammed on the breaks instead of coming to a gentle stop in the driveway. "What?" she questioned, turning to look at me over her shoulder, hands still on the steering wheel.

"Spook?" Alison questioned, gawking back at me now, too.

"I guess I failed to mention that," I said, staring wide-eyed back and forth between the two of them.

"I thought he was non-verbal. Did he say anything else?" Olivia asked, turning fully around, letting go of the wheel finally.

"Mostly—Carlie said," I told her, "mostly non-verbal."

"Did he say more?" Alison asked, in line with Olivia.

I blew out a frustrated breath. I wasn't annoyed with them. I was frustrated that I didn't understand what Taylor had been trying to tell me. "Only one other word." I paused again, hearing the word in my head. "Wings," I said, blowing out another breath of frustration.

Olivia and Alison turned to look at each other, confusion blanketing both their expressions. Then they turned to look back at me.

"Don't ask me—I don't understand it either," I said, perplexed, shifting then to get out of the car.

The others followed, scurrying out of the car, then up the walkway to the front door.

"Can you text me those photos, Liv, when we get inside," I asked, tapping snow off my boots on the front step, before going into the house. "I want to send them to Leo."

"Floorplan—architect," Alison said, "he might be able to tell us more about the drawing." She unzipped her coat but didn't take it off.

"What a strange thing to draw," Olivia said. "Do you think it was a message—the drawing, I mean?" She stopped in the front hall to look at me as I put my jacket on one of the hooks. "Let me send those photos to you before I forget," she added, taking her phone from her purse.

"Your guess is as good as mine—yer the detective now, it seems," I said, grinning at her.

She "*Pffffed*" out a breath. "Right." She laughed then.

"Seriously—you're the one who went with your hunch and found the halfling. That was all you, Olivia," I reminded her, taking her arm and leading her into the kitchen.

"Let's see what Leo has to say," she said in response, grinning back at me, a little glow of pride appearing on her face.

"Hello," Alison called out as we entered the kitchen, though we got nothing but an echo back in reply.

Neither Vicki's nor Eric's cars were in the driveway when we'd pulled in, so I hadn't expected to find them home. Our rental was there, but even Redmond appeared to be out and about. I checked my phone for missed calls or text, just as one came in from him,

> *Grocery shopping with Vicki. On our way back.*
> *Making homemade pizza for dinner.*
> *Did you eat lunch?*

I texted him back,

> *Back at the house now.*
> *Excellent on dinner.*
> *Lunch no—not yet.*

"Are you guys hungry?" I asked then. "Redmond just texted saying he's on his way back from doing groceries with Vicki. Asked if we'd eaten lunch." I was starving. Before addressing the needs of my stomach, I sent the photos off to Leo, with a quick summary of where we'd been and where photos had come from.

I glanced up to see Olivia checking her phone. "I have a few things I have to get done for work—need to meet with Mac this afternoon. I'll grab something at home before heading to her place," she said, sliding her phone back into her purse.

"Ken is over at Don's today," Alison said, "so I have to get home and make lunch for Kevin today."

"I'll drop you off on my way home," Olivia said, jingling her keys.

"Say hi to Mac and all for me," I said, following them back to the front door.

I stepped out into the chilly afternoon air, watching as they ventured back to the SUV. "If I hear anything back from Leo, I'll let you know," I called out.

"Okay, cool," Alison called back, as she slid into the passenger seat of Olivia's car.

Olivia gave me a thumbs up before getting in and shutting the driver's side door.

I waved to them from the front step as they pulled out of the driveway. When they were out of view, I turned and headed back into the house, then stopped as a frosty breeze hit the side of my face. Turning back, I panned the area, searching up and down the street. I rubbed my arms this time because of the cold and not the prickling sensation I'd felt at the group home. A shiver ran up my spine then, reminiscent of something... *foreboding*.

Back inside, I checked my phone to find a text response had come in from Leo, though all he'd written was, *Call me*.

The phone rang only once before Leo picked up. "Lynn," he said, "can you come over here?"

"Why—what's up?" I asked, a bit floored by the directness.

"The sketch," he said then, "I recognize the floorplan. It's the Celaeno building."

"Are you kidding me?" I blurted out.

"I worked on that project—I know the layout, at least part of it. The left right side of the floorplan in the sketch is unfamiliar—must have been constructed after my involvement. But I think it must be the greenhouse you mentioned your friends had seen."

"How could that be?" I questioned. "Why would the boy sketch the Celaeno building—how would he even know how to?"

There was a long pause, then Leo said, "Maybe he's been there."

At his words, a rush of prickling icy frost ran the length of my spine, causing my body to shiver compulsively.

"Lynn?" Leo's voice came, breaching through the sudden shudder of my neck muscles.

"Yes," I breathed out, my inhalations heavy as I steadied myself. Another cold tremor ran down and through my limbs. "I think you're right." Pulling in a calmer breath, I said, "When Redmond gets back, we'll come over. I'll text you when we are on our way. Good?"

I heard him exhale his own heavy breath. "Yes… good."

"Talk in a bit," I said, ending the call.

I heard voices coming from outside and then a loud bang just before the front door swung open.

Through the door came Vicki and Redmond, both carrying several cloth shopping bags full of groceries. "Can you get the door," Vicki said, rushing past me into the kitchen.

"Got it," I said, shutting the door behind them. Redmond brushed by me, giving me a quick peck on the cheek as he followed through after Vicki.

"Is this all to make pizza later?" I asked, peering into each of the bags as they removed items and placed them on the counter and center island.

"Some," Redmond said, "But mostly supplies for the next few days." He placed fresh veggies, cheese, and deli meat on the counter near the fridge.

"Are you good with leftover pasta for lunch," Vicki asked, then she said, "Silly question." She grinned, handing me the leftover pasta casserole dish, making room for the new groceries.

While they put away the supplies of food, I divided the remaining pasta up into three dishes, then I began the assembly line of reheating the food up in the microwave. As the microwave door opened and closed, the kitchen filled with the scent of melty cheese and garlic. "Mmmmm," I let out, placing a spoon in each bowl once they were ready. "Lunch is served." I waved my hands over the dishes like a magician, as if I'd conjured the meal myself.

"Perfect," Vicki said, "groceries are done."

"What a team you guys make," I said with a chuckle. But they were both very efficient in most everything they did, especially with food.

Over lunch, I explained to them what had happened on our trip to the group home. "Leo wants you and me to come over," I directed at Redmond, getting up to rinse out my bowl.

"Oh, let me move the SUV," Vicki said, "so you guys can get your car out." She got up and handed me her bowl to rinse and then headed for the front door.

When the front door shut, I said, "I think Thaddeus had ahold of this boy before he went to live at the group home—tested on him more than likely." I shuddered at the thought. "I think he was the foster person Carlie told us about—the one who had surrendered him when he'd been diagnosed as autistic."

"It would explain his knowing the layout of the building," Redmond said, shaking his head, clearly unnerved by the idea of the child having been in Thaddeus's clutches.

"But how could he know to tell me—to show us that floorplan?" I gave my own head a shake.

"Okay—you are good to go," Vicki said, returning to the kitchen.

"Thanks Vicki—and thanks for lunch too," I said, grinning at her appreciatively.

"You're easy to feed—plus you did all the heating up," she said, with a laugh. She patted Redmond's shoulder. "And you're making homemade pizza for dinner, so I really don't have any cooking duties today. Nice." She nodded, glancing back and forth at Redmond and me. "Okay, kids—I have work to get done this afternoon. Let me know how it goes over at The Haven." She gave me a chin nod, then patted Redmond's shoulder again as she exited the kitchen.

I smirked at Redmond. "Nice," I agreed. Then I snatched my phone off the table and texted Leo that we were on our way.

When we arrived at The Haven, Leo was already waiting with the main door wide open to usher us in. "Come sit," Leo said, leading the way to the sofa area.

"Let me at least take their coats," Max said, rushing in from down the hall and over to the seating area to retrieve them from us.

I handed him my light jacket, then sat on the couch as before. "Thank you," I said, pleased to see him again.

He nodded and gave me a gracious smile. "Redmond," Max said then, waiting as my husband turned over this coat.

"Sorry—yes, here—thank you," Redmond said, handing him his bomber jacket. Then he lowered to sit next to me.

Max gave Leo an exasperated look that reminded me of a disappointed parent whose child had just been rude to their guests. He turned away then to go hang up our coats.

"Formalities," Leo said, glancing quickly over his shoulder at Max, then back at us as he sat down in his usual spot in the chair opposite.

I raised my eyebrows then tightened my lips at Leo's dismissive comment over his friend's civility.

Leo must have caught my expression, because he turned back again to Max and said, "Thank you, Max. That was most kind of you."

Max nodded at Leo, his face stern. Then he shifted his gaze to Redmond and me and gave us a grin and a quick wave before heading back down the hall that he'd previously come from.

Leo turned back again, realigning himself in his seat. "The photos you sent me," he began, "the sketch is of the Celaeno building as I mentioned—the detail is impeccable."

"It was remarkable to watch—I barely believed what he was creating, as I'd witnessed the image unfold." I gave my head a couple shakes to emphasize the overwhelmed. "He must have been in the building—he had to have been," I added, my eyebrows pinching.

"Most definitely," Leo said. "And I believe as you do, Lynn, that the boy must have been one of Thaddeus's test subjects."

"The group home is funded by Thaddeus's organization," Redmond said. I'd filled him in on the drive over here, on what Alison, Olivia and I had learned.

Leo gave a nod. "But that is not public knowledge, I take it."

"No—but the facility's coordinator shared that with us, like it was some badge of honor." I'd wanted to punch that guy in his smug red face.

"The other photos—the ones of the child's back," Leo said, "clearly indicate he's one of the halflings. Were you able to sense the boy—using your gift?"

I hated not knowing the answer to that "I don't know," I said, pausing. "I felt something… I just don't know if it had anything to do with Taylor."

"What do you mean—I thought you could distinguish between different castes?" Leo asked, his frustration matching mine.

"I can—I do," I began, "I just wasn't sure what or who I was sensing. The feeling was different—like with you—the sensation, but it was sharper, sort of an unpleasant static electricity feeling." It was hard to explain. "Usually when an angel is near, I feel it—them, even before I see them. I hadn't felt Taylor when I entered the facility—but he'd been there, in the back room where we'd gone to meet him. The sensation I felt only happened when we went to head in his direction—so either that's how things work with halflings, or… maybe there was another Seraphim in the vicinity, I can't be sure." I ran a hand down my arm at the memory of the uncomfortable sensation. "I was with Taylor already when the feeling heightened in intensity, then it went away while I was still with him." I frowned, staring across at Leo. "Was one of your people there—one of The Guards? Did you send someone to follow us—watch us?"

"No—I would have told you if I had sent help," Leo stated. He glanced down at the floor, rubbing a hand across the back of his neck.

"What?" Redmond asked, leaning forward in his seat. "What aren't you telling us?"

"Nothing—no," Leo said, glancing up. "You said the group home is funded by Thaddeus. I'm thinking he must have lookouts stationed there—nearby."

Olivia had brought up the same idea, and I'd agreed with her theory. "I think so too," I said, nodding slowly, pondering how the sensation had abruptly disappeared as if whoever had been watching had suddenly left the area.

Leo sat up straight in his chair. "What I don't understand is why this boy is no longer one of Thaddeus's test subjects—it is beyond me.

Don't get me wrong—I'm grateful." He put up his hands, palms out as if in surrender.

"Autism," I said, neatly.

Leo frowned. "What?"

"Taylor is autistic," I said. "The residential counsellors told us he'd been given back to Children's Services—that the foster parent couldn't handle the extra care. In other words, Thaddeus had found him defective and more trouble than he was worth." I blew out a breath, disgusted. "What a saint."

"I'd expect nothing else from him," Leo stated, leaning forward in his chair, clasping his hands together. "I'd like to get back into the Celaeno building—check out that new section."

"Mac suspects there's a lower level," I said. "She felt it actually—in her feet."

Leo's eyebrows raised in surprise. "Can't be," Leo said, "not unless… it's under the new section." His eyebrows pinched then, and he glanced down to the floor again, this time rubbing a hand over his jaw.

"There has to be something under the greenhouse," Redmond said, "something they don't want anyone to know about."

"The woman who had given Olivia and Mac the tour denied it—but Olivia sensed her heart race when Mac had asked about the lower level—I told you about that." I glanced at Redmond. "She was clearly lying," I added.

"Amahle—that's her name, the female who gave your friends the tour," Leo said, the muscles in his jaw tightening.

He'd used the word *female* instead of woman, I noticed. "And?" I questioned.

"She's Earthbound—one of Thaddeus's crew," he said. "One of two female followers that were sent down with the twelve males. The other female we have yet to locate."

"Okay," I said, "but I don't know how that knowledge helps us."

"She's his current second in command—it used to be Marcus, but he's heading up the New York City facility now."

I just stared at him. I still didn't understand what or how this information helped us or not. And who the hell was Marcus?

"We—I need to get in that facility," he said. "Now is the best time to do it—while Thaddeus is in New York. Amahle will have her hands full—running things without him. We have to act now," he said, standing up from the chair.

"We?" I questioned, staring up at him.

"If there is a chance that he's holding other halflings or even our Earthbound brethren, I have to get in there—get them out." Leo glanced at Redmond, then back at me. "If my brethren are in there— you'll be able to sense them."

The back of my neck tingled then, enforced by the sudden compulsion to rush over to the building. I drew in a long, cleansing draw of air, holding it as I turned my face to look at my husband. "I can't just sit around—doing nothing—I have to do something," I said, letting my words out with the held breath.

Redmond shot a silent glance at Leo, then focused his gaze back on me. "Well then… I'm going with you."

Chapter 23

Between the three of us, we'd hatched a mostly doable plan to get into the Celaeno building, into the greenhouse, and if all went well, we'd hopefully get down into the lower-level area. The idea was for us to pose as city sewer workers, with me as the inspector on the case, the story being that we had a report of a sewage issue—possible break and leak that could cause toxic damage to the buildings and water in the vicinity.

For proof, Leo had created fake documents for the report that stated it was urgent we check the lower-level plumbing in all buildings in the area. Along with the fake paperwork, Leo made us fake IDs with false names and photos of each of us in our full disguises. We'd all dressed in dark blue city worker coveralls, with the city's water and sewage logos to match on the front pockets, as well as on our hardhats. Since the disguises were created for men basically the size of Leo, my coveralls had to be hemmed using staples and the cuffs of the sleeves rolled up. Leo donned a full beard and mustache, while Redmond concealed his identity using a goatee, and a long blond mullet-style wig under his hardhat. I'd chosen a wig to wear as well, a short dark brown one, and I'd added a pair of dark-framed glasses to wear. There were no work boots my size obviously, so I opted for just wearing my Doc Martins as they could pass as steel-toed boots. Besides, no one was going to be looking at my feet. To add to our disguises, Leo had affixed the same city water and sewer logo to the outside walls of an all-white panel work van, that had conveniently been fitted with tools and equipment suitable for all kinds of maintenance work, should anyone get a look inside. Everything looked totally legit, I have to say.

We parked the van at the main entrance to the Celaeno building, and since Mac and Olivia had gone over the basics about the building and its protocols for entry, we knew we'd have to be let in. And because they wouldn't have been expecting us like they had been with Olivia and Mac, I flashed my city inspector ID badge to the cameras at the front entrance.

"Do you feel anything—sense anything, I mean," Leo asked, watching as the enormous steel door swung open.

"Yes," I said, leading the way in. I did. I felt something as soon as we'd pulled up. The strength of the tingling gave me the sense that, other than Leo, there was at least one other Seraphim nearby.

Redmond and Leo followed behind me, carrying a menagerie of equipment boxes and tools with them, along with expressions of urgency set on their faces.

At the front desk, I directed my urgency to the smaller of the two security guards, a skinny little college-age guy whose name tag read *Trevor*, and who was doing his best to appear important. Obviously, the bigger of the two guards was there as mainly the muscle and based on the fact the blazer he wore as part of his security uniform was about to burst at the seams, it was apparent he spent most of his free time at the gym. I handed the less impressive security guard the paperwork, and said, "We have a water main and sewer breach that runs directly under this building—we're here to assess the damage and repairs needed."

The security guard examined the work order. There was a number on the form that he could call. The number went to The Haven, to Max we'd been informed, where he took care of the receiving end of calls and added to the legitimacy of the ruse.

"You don't look like a maintenance worker," security guard Trevor said, glancing from me to my over six-foot-tall coworkers behind me.

"They're the brawn—I'm the brains. I'm sure you know what that's like." I shot a side-eye to his big security guard partner next to him, who was busily playing some game on his phone.

"Do I," he said, puffing out a breath coupled with an eye roll. "Where did you say the issue was?" He pulled out a big binder about 20x20 inches in size, flipping open the front cover. "We have these laminated floorplans for each level." He flipped the pages to show the top-level layout, which at quick glance showed two boardrooms clearly indicated, and a larger open space adjacent, though that area had no label to indicate what it was for.

"What is that space?" I asked, pointing to the open area next to the boardrooms on the laminated page.

"It's the private residence of the big boss. He's in new York City at the moment," the security guard shared.

"Show me the main floor again," I requested. We knew who that big boss was, and we also knew he was out of town.

He flipped the pages back to the front. "Here," he said, tapping a finger on the page. But there was no greenhouse shown.

My brows pinched. "The new addition?" I questioned, slicing a quick glance at Redmond and Leo.

"Oh—here. It's the greenhouse," helpful Trevor said, flipping to the next page.

"That's where we need to go," I stated, shifting, and heading for the nearest door, the one Olivia and Mac had instructed we needed to go through. We'd already known the greenhouse was where we needed to go, it being the only section built after Leo's involvement with the original construction design.

"Wait!" the security guard ordered, darting around the tall desk to halt us in our tracks.

The tension in my body grew, and I took a sharp breath. "This is an emergency," I stated again, my expression serious.

"You have to leave your phones," he said then, placing a padded black bag on the shelf-top of the desk.

I let out the breath I'd been holding, realizing I had forgotten all about that part of the entry procedure we'd been told about. "Not a problem," I said, drawing out my *company* phone from my coverall's back pocket. Leo and Redmond followed suit. Leo had provided us with fake phones, fake in the sense that they were untraceable, and the only contacts and information on them were that of the bogus water and sewer department.

The security guard placed them all in the bag and into a small cubby before locking it. Then he handed me the key to the cubby, that hung off a long lanyard which he indicated I was to hang around my neck. Before we could go, he handed us all visitor badges to clip to our coveralls. "I'll have to take you," he said, turning and leading us the way to a completely different door for us to go through.

Apparently, for us there would be no tight confined space for sterilization, nor would we be crossing through the all-white lobby and elevator doors that my friends had indicated they had done. Instead, he took us through a security door that led to a long hall, which took us straight to the entrance outside the greenhouse and was clearly not the way Olivia and Mac had gone. The security guard used a white swipe card to take us through from the main part of the first floor, and now he used a green swipe card for the entrance to the greenhouse, which was the same method of passage my friends had indicated their guide had used.

Before entering, I shot a glance up the hall to where I saw an unmarked elevator door. I guessed it was the one Mac had previously asked about on their trip through the building. "Where does that go?" I inquired, already knowing what they'd been told.

"Private elevator—only used by the boss man," Trevor said in response, turning back and opening the way into the humidity filled greenhouse. "Whatever you do—don't touch anything." He pointed a finger to each row of plants, then meandered up the middle isle. "Some of these are seriously deadly—poisonous." He grimaced. He kept his hands pulled in tight to his chest as he walked.

Putting on my work gloves, I glanced at Redmond.

"I'll wait here," he said, giving Leo a nod before granting me a reassuring smile and a wink. He put on his work gloves and remained at the entrance with the toolboxes, while Leo and I proceeded further in, pretending to be checking the watering and drainage system along the sides of the greenhouse.

Near a row of blooming flowers that I couldn't identify, not that I knew anything about exotic plants, came a large white butterfly flittering into view. It was followed by several tinier white butterflies that reminded me of the teeny pale-coloured butterflies that darted in and around the seagrape trees back home. *"Hi, Mom,"* I whispered to the large one in the group. How odd it was to see butterflies in winter, I mused. Turning to the end of the row, I spotted the door, the one that Mac and Olivia had been told led to a system that had was added to accommodate the additional watering needs. Getting Leo's attention, I waved him over. Redmond, seeing us at the far door, rolled the equipment boxes and tools over to where we both now stood. Then I called for the security guard to come over, adding, "We need to get in here."

"That's just a stairwell," Trevor stated, making no move to open things up for us.

"We're going to need to get in there," Leo said, directing the statement at me, while putting on his own gloves. "That's where the primary system is—for these plants." Leo shot a look at the security guard, one full of intensity.

"Trevor," I commanded, "You have to get us in there—or this building and its water main is going to be in serious trouble."

"I don't have the card key for that—I'll have to go get it. Wait here," he said, turning and rushing for the exit out of the greenhouse.

"Water main?" Redmond questioned with a chuckle.

I shrugged. "It worked, didn't it?" I smirked.

Leo pulled a pen from the breast-pocket of his coveralls. "I'm going to use this to get us into the space without that security guard coming in with us."

"A pen?" I asked, frowning.

Leo glanced over his shoulder as if checking for the security guard. "It's a stink pen," he said, like I knew what that was.

I shook my head.

"It gives off a fake—yet very unpleasant odor when you click the end. And it will help deter the guard from entering the room without a gasmask." He gave us a devilish grin.

"Niiiice," Redmond said, the prankster in him showing appreciation.

I pressed my lips together, quelling a laugh. I glanced up then at the glass roof and then the far walls. "No cameras," I indicated, then pulled my own gadget from the inner pocket of my coveralls.

Leo gawked at me but said nothing.

"What?" I asked, shrugging, glancing down at the iPod Touch in my gloved hand. I'd had Vicki charge it up for me the night before. It was an outdated version, one her son had used, that Vicki had kept for listening to music for when she worked out. "I might not be all high tech like you there 007, but this old school device comes with a camera and video option—I'll have you know." I wiggled my eyebrows up and down, then proceeded to videotape the plants for future reference and for Derek to research later. Done with capturing the different varieties of plant life, I slid the thing back into my inner pocket, just as the security guard returned.

Trevor presented a black key card this time and swiped it through the scanner next to the door. When the door popped open, he rushed through it to lead us in and then down the stairs.

At the bottom of the stairwell was a steel door with a small window set in it, though I couldn't see anything through it. I watched then as Leo placed his right index finger against the glass, pressing the tip of his fingernail against it. Not having had the opportunity to use his stink pen at the upper door, Leo withdrew another device, one I already knew was a fake toxins tester he'd rigged to check for potential chemical gases.

When he pressed the small button on the side of the unit, a tweeting sound blared like that of an EMF reader used for sensing ghosts like what you'd see on one of those ghost hunter TV shows. "This is it—we have to get in there," Leo said, giving the security guard a repeat of his intense stare.

"We're really not supposed to be down here—and we're definitely not allowed to go in there," he stated, nervously, pointing a finger at the door. "Strict orders from the boss lady."

Sharp painful sparks bit across my neck, the tingling prickle I'd felt when we'd arrived intensifying now needling my skin. "Look—if we don't get in there, you'll have bigger problems than upsetting your bosses," I said, urgency rushing into my voice as I fought the impulse to rub the back of my neck. "If we don't address the issue—those plants could be impacted—and not just by a water main break, they could be contaminated by raw sewage." I shot a quick glance at Leo and saw he had the stink pen in his hand. "I think your boss would be more pissed off—if you let those research plants be compromised or destroyed."

"Just open the door and I'll be able to tell how bad the issue is," Leo said, positioning himself closer to the door, his words sounding as though it were a simple decision for the young guy to make. Redmond and I both stepped back from the door.

The security guard blew out an unsteady breath. "This job pays shit anyway," he said then, swiping the black card through the door's sensor.

At the sound of the door's release, Leo pulled it open only a few inches, letting the stink spray go. Then he slammed the door shut, shoving the security guard back. "Stand back—we've got a serious gas leak in here." Trevor got a hit of the gas and gagged, then covered his nose and mouth with his hand. "Stay out here," Leo said, reaching for the tool bag Redmond had been carrying. He yanked three gas masks from the bag, handing Redmond and me each one, indicating for us to put them on. And we did. Then he turned to the security guard. "Swipe the card again—then stand back," he said, before pulling on his mask. When Trevor swiped the card this time, Leo pulled the door open just enough for us to get inside, again letting the spray of the stink pen go before yanking the door shut behind us.

Inside the closed room, I glanced back at the door. The window in the door had one-way glass, showing now that you could only see through it from the inside. That must have been what Leo had been checking for with pressing his finger to it, I surmised as I removed my mask.

In the middle of the room there were two folding privacy partitions that extended out from the side walls, meeting in the middle blocking the back section. Immediately to the left were glass cabinets with smaller plant samples and rows of bottles in assorted sizes, all containing various liquids. On a shelf beneath the samples was a clinical-style desk set up with office paraphernalia like pens, tape, and a stapler, along with a dish of paper clips. Lined up next to those were thick notebooks with what appeared to be different years written on the spines. The first date being 2001 with a notebook for each year leading up to 2010. There was one open on the desk with a red ribbon bookmark running down the center. I pulled out the notebook marked 2001 and flipped it open to see pages filled with writing in a language I'd never seen. It was not quite a language, it resembled something more like a code, similar symbols repeating every so often. I pulled out the one marked 2010 and found the same strange writing. Returning the books to their places, I then turned my attention to the book open on the desk, only to find more of the same bizarre writings. When Leo stepped up next to me, I said, "I need to get these to Derek and Vicki."

"You can't take them. They can't know we looked at anything — other than fixing the reported issue," he said, glancing down at the book. He shook his head as if to indicate he didn't understand the language, either.

"Where is the sewer line?" I heard Redmond ask from behind me.

"In that space in the corner, behind that tall metal panel," Leo said, leaving to go help Redmond.

Lucky for us, there was an actual sewer line down here. It had been outlined in Taylor's drawing, and though we could have gotten to the main line through the utility area on the far side of the building, which wouldn't have served our actual needs. Leo and Redmond, following the plan, needed to do some fake repairs, giving the impression something had been done. They also needed to mark the area with a service tag containing the date, a fake signature, along with the same phone number as on the workorder we'd given the security guard. In the meantime, what I needed... were these books. *"I have a way to take them with me — at least parts of them,"* I said under my breath, taking out the iPhone Touch again. Focusing back on the open book, I flipped through starting from the beginning, video taking each page up to where the writings ended at the red ribbon bookmark. I flipped through to the next pages, checking to see that there were no further notes made. I'd learned my lesson with my mother's journal and knew better now not to presume that other writings were not further in.

Sliding the iPhone back into the inner pocket of my coveralls, I panned the rest of the room. I noted that the rolling barriers had been pushed back. I gasped then when I realized this was not exactly a research lab for plants as I'd expected. In fact, this wasn't for plants at all. There were two areas set up on one side with tables and all the bells and whistles like surgery stations, and to the far right there was another table, this one metal and from all the forensic tv shows I'd seen, I was confident it was designed for performing autopsies. My vision blurred then and my hearing muted...

... I'm standing in the oversized hospital room again, the one I had thought was a testing area. There's a small child on a surgery table this time with no other people in the room. An IV bag hangs on a pole next to the table. Beside it is a cart like before, with various medical implements atop a large tray. An antiseptic odor blankets the surrounding area. Glancing at the child again, I see that it's... Taylor. He lets out a tiny cry and then moans as I step closer. The metallic tang of stainless-steel hits my tastebuds then is swiftly altered by the odor of blood wafting up from the stained sheet covering him. I'm not dreaming, I know I am awake. I hear my name being called. It's Leo's voice, but I can't move or tear my gaze away from Taylor. This is a daymare I recognize as Redmond's voice breaks me...

... out of this state. My vision cleared, and I found myself staring at white butterflies... pinned to several display boards. My stomach rolled at the sight. I knew butterflies had a short lifespan and that people sometimes used them for artwork, but these butterflies, with the way the pins had been set in their tiny bodies, looked as though they had been *stabbed*.

"Lynn," Redmond's voice came again. "Are you okay? We have to go."

"Yes," I managed to get out, turning away from the butterflies and back towards the exit out of the room.

"Put your mask back on," Leo instructed, before we exited the room.

Through my thought haze, I saw Trevor was still there waiting as Leo pushed open the door.

"All done," Leo said, through his gas mask. "But it's best not to go in for 24 hours until the fumes dissipate." Leo gave another little shot of the stink gas before closing the door.

"Not a chance," security guard Trevor said, ending with a gag.

"It should be fine by this time tomorrow," Leo added, when he removed his gas mask.

Without a word, I returned my mask to the tool bag and then followed the others as we were led up and out of the stairwell. As we went back through the greenhouse, and then through the long hall to the main entrance, I trailed behind the others as my brain flickered between the reality of my surroundings and that of the images from my daymare. At the desk, I faintly recalled hearing the security guard ask me for the key lanyard hanging around my neck. Someone, Redmond likely, took it off me. I heard Leo's voice then, speaking to the security guard as he was handed back the phones. He said something along the lines of, "If anyone has any questions… have them call our supervisor—his contact info is on your copy of the workorder."

The next thing I noted along with not comprehending how, was that we were back in the van.

"Lynn," Redmond said, his deep voice pulling me from my daze. "You're so quiet—what's wrong?"

"I…," I started to say, forcing the word out past my brain fog as I glanced up at him, "… don't know."

Chapter 24

Central Park, Wednesday, December 29th, New York City

Gabriel strolled along the tree-lined path at the north end towards the heart of the park, instead of appearing directly at the destination he'd requested for the others to meet. In the summer, this was a very popular destination for people-watching, relaxing, and for admiring the architecture and scenery, although it was seasonally quiet now in late December. As Gabriel descended the stairs from the Bethesda Terrace, he could already see his brethren gathering. Even Shamsiel had come at his request.

Michael, Vretil, Uriel, and Raphael stood closest to one of the park's most beloved works of art, the Bethesda Fountain. Shamsiel paced back and forth in front of them. The artwork was also known as the Angel of the Waters, and it was why Gabriel had picked this location. The fountain, being the central feature on the lower level of the terrace, was intended as a gathering space for park visitors after all. It was one of the few formal landscapes providing a contrast to the more natural design of the rest of the park.

Coming to a stop in front of this host of angels, Gabriel tilted his head back to stare up at the bronze statue. The eight-foot-tall sculpture depicted a female winged angel touching down upon the tip of the fountain, and where normally in warmer weather, waterspouts cascaded into the upper basin and down into the surrounding pool, today in the dead of winter, it was currently dormant of any flowing water.

"New York City?" Michael queried, clearly wondering about the location for their meeting.

Gabriel clasped his hands behind his back. "He's here, apparently."

"Who?" Raphael asked, shifting the back of his overcoat to sit on the outer edge of the fountain's basin.

"Thaddeus," Gabriel said, panning the faces of his brethren. "Nice to see you, my friend," he directed at Shamsiel, before anyone could comment. "I should have included you sooner."

Shamsiel nodded. "Darius has been anxious during Lynn's visit to Ottawa," he stated. "You know how he gets."

"So, Thaddeus is here then," Vretil commented. "Why should we care?" He gave a slight upward tilt to his chin as if bored.

"Isn't it better he's not in Ottawa while Lynn is there?" Uriel stated, brushing snow away from the fountain's edge to sit next to Raphael. "Not that he would know she was there—or anywhere else, for that matter."

Gabriel glanced towards the southern shore of the lake, then turned to admire the grand staircases with their granite steps and landings that led to the upper level of the terrace. Turning back, he said, "No—but when he finds out there were *unwanted* people in his building today while he was away—without his permission, he might not be too thrilled." Gabriel rocked back and forth on his heels.

"What people? Not your... don't tell me...," Michael tried to say, his mouth gaping as recognition seeped in.

"Yes—Lynn," Gabriel said, "But she wasn't alone." He blew a frustrated breath out through his nose.

Raphael stood, bumping Uriel's shoulder in the process. "What's the big deal? Olivia and Mac were already there," he stated. "Nothing happened." He patted Uriel's shoulder and then shrugged.

"Well...," Gabriel started to say.

But Vretil cut in, "Who went with Lynn? Please tell me it wasn't my Charge." He rubbed a hand over his jaw.

"No—none of your Charges went," Gabriel stated. "Leo and Redmond went with her." He spread his feet in a firmer stance.

"Leo—why him?" Uriel questioned, fiddling with the top button of his navy peacoat.

"Before you say any more—hear me out," Gabriel said, raising his hands in surrender. He went on to explain how things had unfolded at the group home, how the young boy, Taylor, had drawn the layout of the Celaeno building, including the addition of the greenhouse and its lower level. "The only way this halfling could have known about the layout of the building and its addition—is if he had been there. The detail was impeccable."

"You're sure he's one of the offspring?" Michael questioned, his dark eyebrows pinching together.

"Yes—Olivia took photos of his back. The marks are there." Gabriel confirmed, adjusting the lapels of his long wool camel-coloured coat.

Uriel stood then, too. "Was Lynn able to sense the boy—the halfling?" he asked, stepping around to the side of Raphael.

Gabriel shook his head. "She's not sure." He glanced down at the snowy ground.

"Either she did—or she didn't, which is it?" Shamsiel questioned, speaking up then.

Glancing up, Gabriel scowled at Shamsiel's boldness. He'd obviously come straight from being down South with Darius, as he had no winter coat like the others and wore only a long-sleeved cotton pullover and jeans. Sucking in a breath, he said, "She believes there was another Earthbound nearby—watching, and she couldn't be sure if she was sensing them or the boy—or a combination of the two. She said the feeling intensified, but then dissipated while she was still with the halfling. They also found out that the group home is being funded by Thaddeus's organization, and why Lynn believes there was someone watching." He paused. "The strangest thing happened though, just before they left." Gabriel paused again, this time turning a quick glance to the statue, and its bronze feathers. "The boy spoke... her name."

"Why is that strange?" Vretil asked, taking a step towards Gabriel.

Gabriel raised his eyebrows. "Well, besides the fact that her name was never mentioned in his presence, the boy is autistic, and mostly non-verbal. I'd say that's exceptionally strange." Gabriel rocked on his heels again, sliding his hands into the pockets of his coat.

Vretil shook his head, then ran a hand through his long hair. "What does that mean—do halflings have otherworldly abilities too?"

"Your guess is as good as mine," Gabriel said, taking his hands from his pockets to cross his arms over his chest.

"What about Lynn and the other two going into the Celaeno building," Michael redirected. "Why did they feel the need to go in?"

Gabriel relaxed his arms down at his sides. "Leo suggested it. Said he needed to get into the building to find out what was under this additional structure. He'd been part of the original build—and wasn't familiar with the add-on." Gabriel looked at Uriel. "Mac swears she felt something—something that indicated there was a lower level."

Michael sat down on the edge of the fountain, his bomber jacket open and his hands in his pockets. "Why bring Lynn and Redmond?" he asked, questioning and motioning with his hands still in the pockets.

"Because she can sense the Earthbound," Shamsiel said, answering for Gabriel. He shot a sideways glance at Gabriel as if for confirmation.

"So, what happened—at the building?" Michael asked. "There has to be a reason you wanted to update us. It can't be just about the boy speaking Lynn's name." Michael leaned back slightly, casually crossing his legs at the ankles.

Gabriel panned the faces of his brethren again. "I brought you here for two reasons. First…," he said, continuing on to describe the means and method of the caper undertaken by Leo, and his partners in crime. "They got in and out safely, with footage of the greenhouse and the lab below. Lynn has a video of writings she found in several notebooks in the lab as well. Derek will be working with your Charge, Michael, to decipher them. Lynn believes the boy was held in that lab—or at least one like it." He returned his hands to his pockets.

"Those notes could help us figure out what he's been doing—with this testing," Vretil said. "I hate we can't easily locate his previous test subjects—but maybe we could with these notebooks."

"But there's more, isn't there?" Raphael stated, glancing from Gabriel to the faces of the others.

"Isn't there always?" Shamsiel said, shooting Gabriel another clever look.

"You know...," Gabriel began, "... I update you all—out of courtesy. I'm not required to do so." Gabriel crossed his arms again over his chest, letting his gaze return upward to the beautiful angel statue.

Shamsiel came to stand next to Gabriel, but Gabriel kept his face turned to the sculpture. "You know I worry," Shamsiel said, placing a hand on Gabriel's shoulder. "I worry about all our Charges, and now I worry for these Earthbound. And... I worry we won't find a way to stop what Thaddeus is doing."

Gabriel turned to look at Shamsiel, then at the others.

"We all worry, Gabriel," Michael added.

"There are more details—and I'll tell you everything," Gabriel said. "As I told you already, this halfling boy knew Lynn's name—spoke her name. And we don't know why—or how." He paused. "Well, it wasn't the only thing he said... he spoke a second word." Gabriel cleared his throat as they all stared back at him. "He said... *wings*."

Chapter 25

The Merope Facility, December 29th, 8 p.m., New York City

Thaddeus smiled, recounting the enjoyable day he'd had with performing tests on his new subject. It had gone much smoother and calmer than with the testing on that cripple, Taylor. Despite the boy's disability, he was exceptionally strong for his size and had been quite combative, and though he had relished fighting with the invalid to the point of causing him to scream and thrash, this new patient had been weak and submissive, making his tasks of probing and analysis go quicker.

To treat himself for a job well done, Thaddeus had visited his favorite bakery. Though instead of getting the usual mini icebox cake made with homemade chocolate wafers layered with freshly whipped sweet cream, like he did each morning when in the big city, he'd splurged and gotten himself the large version of the cake meant to serve 6 to 10 people. He'd gotten the large to suit his need for playing his video games all night and the sugar being the perfect means to keep him going. He'd shared a meal with his Head of Merope, Marcus, early in the evening at some restaurant, one that Marcus had recommended, and that Thaddeus had already forgotten the name of. Apparently, he'd had to book it 6 months in advance, *whatever*. Marcus had made the reservation for a meeting with some real estate broker he was banging. He couldn't understand or stomach the idea of such an act with a human, watching maybe, but engaging in—not a chance. He'd made Marcus ditch the date and take him for the meal instead. The food had been okay—not memorable clearly, so he'd been elated to have the cake waiting for him as a finisher. He could have offered Marcus to come up and have some dessert, but he didn't like to share. Besides, it gave Marcus time to go *finish* his meeting.

Only an hour into his all-night gaming session, a blue light began flashing on the speaker atop his bedside table, indicating a call was coming in for him. Thaddeus paused the game in time to hear the soft-spoken male voice of the personal attendant app linked to his phone say, "Call from Amahle."

Thaddeus huffed out a breath. He wasn't in the mood to speak to her, but chose to answer, anyway. "*Attendant*, answer call." He stared at the paused game on the TV, hoping this was going to be a quick call. "Amahle."

"Good evening, sir," she said, respectfully, obviously hopeful of softening what she had to say next.

"What is it?"

"It seems we had an incident at the building today."

"What kind of *incident*?" He tossed the game controller on the bed next to him and fell back on the pillows.

"There was an issue with the water main. On the whole block. Workmen had to come into the building."

"Why did they have to come in?" He glanced at the speaker.

"It involved the sewage lines—and the water lines under the greenhouse."

"The greenhouse!" he hollered, sitting up in the bed. "Was there any damage to my plants?"

"No, but…," she began.

"But what?" he asked, frowning.

"They needed to go to the lower level—into the lab. There was a gas leak," she shot out.

"In my lab—how do you know—did you see the leak?" he asked, furious, ready to blow a gasket or break something.

"No—but the security guard on duty was there—he could smell the leak, said it was wretched."

"Where were you?" he questioned, still glaring at the small speaker on the bedside table.

"I—I was feeding Brutus, playing the music he likes as you instructed," she said in defense. "They told the security guard that it was best not to go in for 24 hours until the fumes dissipated, but I went in and checked. It's all clear and there was no damage to the lab or the greenhouse."

Thaddeus appreciated she was tending to Brutus, but this gas leak, he wasn't buying it. "Send me the video footage."

"Yes—right away. But there are no cameras in the lab—just outside it," she said, as if reminding him.

Like he needed reminding, he'd made sure there were no cameras inside the lab. "Send what you have."

Thaddeus grabbed the wireless keyboard from the shelf on the nightstand, and with a few keystrokes he brought up the logon screen to the facility's internet on his TV's display. Logging into the secure network, he maneuvered to the shared drive, waiting for Amahle to drop in the files.

The first file to drop was labeled 'front desk' but he skipped that, going to the last of four when it rendered this one labeled 'lower level'. Clicking the file, the footage opened in the default video player.

The angle of the camera was set facing the open stairwell, so he could only see the security guard and the city workers descending the stairs. When the participants got closer to the lab's door, they went out of view of the camera. "Useless," he said to the TV. He didn't bother looking at the other files, as his concern was for the lab.

He switched the screen back to his game and picked up the controller, only to find he had logged himself out of the session. He typed in his username, 3astard5on, which was leetspeak—a gamer term, for *bastard son,* but then he didn't bother to put in his password, and instead, threw the controller back on the bed again.

The news of someone being in his private lab unsettled him and now he didn't feel much like playing, which was so not like him. Besides his experiments, gaming was one of the few things he enjoyed doing. For a while, his favorite game had been *Postal*, back when he'd first discovered gaming on PC computers. Later, he'd gotten the version with the full Xbox 360 controller support. Since then, he's moved on to other console games such as *Limbo*, deemed one of the scariest video games. The game was designed to discomfort you while navigating a series of gruesome-death-instilling platforming puzzles. The game-world itself exists in a surreal ether realm with shadowy, black-and-white monsters lurking in the fringes of a dreamlike plane of existence. The game had spoken to Thaddeus, for both the feel of the game and its direct correlation to the title, and for things unanswered, like *Where are we? Who are we?*

Thaddeus glanced around the space and scowled. He had small personal residences at each of his facilities, but his Ottawa condo was the finest. This location, like the rest, didn't have a private chef like in Ottawa, as he wasn't here often enough to employ one, nor did he have all his favorite video games either. One of his current favorites, a single player game and another one of the most violent video games of all times, of course, was *God of War III*, the remastered version for PlayStation. He'd also gotten the *God of War III Ultimate Edition* and *Ultimate Trilogy Edition* that included the original soundtrack as downloadable content. It's considered contemporary classical music, which is Brutus's favorite. It is brooding, rhythmic, and percussive, and delivers on its promise of a loud, wrathful bundle of tunes you can kill gods to. The packaging was fantastic, as it came in a Pandora's Box with a false bottom containing several collector items. The theme of the game was right up Thaddeus's alley, too. The player controls the protagonist, the former God of War, after his betrayal at the hands of his father, Zeus, reigniting the Great War. You battle monsters, gods, and Titans in a search of Pandora, without whom you can't open Pandora's Box, defeat Zeus, and end the reign of the Olympian gods. He had recently tried *Dead by Daylight*, which is a multiplayer online game, but since he was prone to violence through temper tantrums when he played that type, he'd opted to go back to the single player games.

He made a mental note to get copies of his favorite games for each of his residences.

"I miss Brutus," he said aloud. He was bored. Marcus had a condo off-site, so he wouldn't be coming back to the building. "*Attendant*, call Amahle," he said then, letting out a long-drawn-out sigh of air.

"Yes, sir," came the voice of his second in command.

"I'm coming back tonight—make sure Brutus is back on his stand when I get there," he informed her. Then before she could respond he said, "*Attendant*, end call."

Several hours later, when Thaddeus arrived at the Celaeno facility, he went directly down to his lab. But he found nothing missing or disturbed. Nothing to worry about, he thought to himself as he got on the private elevator next to the greenhouse entrance.

Back in his condo, he went straight to his walk-in closet to find Brutus happily waiting for his return.

"Hello, my handsome friend. Did you miss me—I missed you," he said, pressing his index finger to the tank. Brutus bumped his head in greeting against the tank where Thaddeus's finger was pressed. "I wish I could bring you with me when I travel, but you wouldn't enjoy flying." Thaddeus shook his head.

"*Attendant*, call Marcus," he said then, leaving the closet to bring up his secure network on the TV screen again.

"Yes, Thaddeus," Marcus said, when he finally picked up. He sounded out of breath.

"I need you to review some video footage—see if you recognize anyone in it." Thaddeus clicked on the file marked 'front desk'.

"What's the footage?"

Thaddeus heard shushing noises through the speaker. "City workers fixing a gas leak at the Celaeno facility. The footage showed three workers, two males and a female." Thaddeus paused the video recording when he heard Marcus blow out a breath. "What?"

"I don't make a point of documenting every human I come in contact with," Marcus said. "But I'll look when I get a chance."

"Good—there in the shared folder marked 'water and sewage'," he said.

Marcus ended the call.

Must have been *busy* with his real estate broker, Thaddeus considered.

"Call from Amahle," the attendant's voice announced through the hidden overhead speaker, followed by the chiming sound of a call coming in.

"*Attendant,* answer call," he said. "Yes?"

"I have something you're going to find interesting—but I'm not sure you are going to like it."

"What now?" he asked, glancing around the condo, his elation at being home now deflated.

"I just found out from Lyndon, that our little Taylor had visitors."

"Where is Lyndon?" Thaddeus turned to look through the closet and out its window.

"He's just arriving at the building now."

"Let security know to send him up." Thaddeus stalked to the kitchen area of the condo.

"On it," she said, before ending the call.

Thaddeus tore off the black wrappings from the top of a *10 Thousand BC* bottle of exotic water, then popped the top like it was wine. At $14 per 750ml, it wasn't the most expensive water in the world, but it was a highly sophisticated, stylish and a world-class brand, so it was up there. He'd liked it mainly because it was sourced so far from human contamination and pollutants off the coast of Canada that it took a three-day trip to reach the glacier where it was obtained.

A few minutes later, there was a one-tap knock at his condo door.

"Come in," he commanded, downing the last sip of the pricey water.

When Lyndon came through the doorway, he shut the door behind him, then stood quietly waiting for the order to speak. The Earthbound Seraph had longish dull black hair in need of a cut, and dark eyes that showed signs he needed rest, and would have been considered handsome to the humans, Thaddeus thought, if it weren't for the sulfur burn scar disfiguring half of his jaw. He wore a long faded black raincoat, dark jeans, and a similar shade of shirt. His boots were salt stained, and the bottom of his pants were damp.

Thaddeus cringed at the sight. "What information do you have for me?" Thaddeus asked, setting the empty bottle on a small counter next to the fridge. He had tasked Lyndon with keeping an eye on the group home he funded, the one he'd surrendered the child to, with the idea of monitoring anyone coming and going who chose to meet with the halfling. It had been 3 years since Thaddeus had completed his testing on this subject, but this was the first time since the boy had become a permanent resident of the group home that anyone had shown interest in seeing him.

"The kid had visitors. Three women," Lyndon said, stopping to take in the condo's interior, following the walls and furniture around the open space back to Thaddeus.

"Tell me," Thaddeus barked out, impatient. Lyndon had always been an exceptional tracker and had a steel trap memory for faces and places, but Thaddeus' nerves were on a razor's edge with regard to these *visitors* to his facility and now the group home.

Lyndon nodded. "I got a copy of the sign-in sheet from the coordinator," he said, then went on to define what he saw take place, the interactions with Taylor, and then describe each of the humans and their credentials.

"That first one sounds like the same woman who came here with her coworker for a tour a few days ago," Thaddeus acknowledged. He had seen the video footage of their visit, but neither of the other women Lyndon had described met the likeness of the second woman who'd been there for the tour. "The woman with the short blond hair, what was she doing there?"

"Helping the second one, I'm guessing—it's her job to place children in foster homes." Lyndon rubbed the back of his neck.

"What about this third woman, what was her affiliation?"

"I'm not sure—all it had on the sign-in sheet was *colleague* next to her name." Lyndon glanced at the TV screen where Thaddeus had paused the footage of the city workers at the front desk. "Hey, that woman could be her sister, though," he said, pointing at the screen. "If she had long blond hair."

Chapter 26

Yesterday, when we'd returned to The Haven after our caper, I'd done my best to explain to Redmond and Leo about what had happened to me. It was Leo's speculation that what I'd experienced must have been due to a trigger from seeing the surgery and autopsy tables. He'd stated that my *sensorium*, as he had called it, that part of my brain or my brain itself, is viewed as the seat of sensation, the sensory apparatus of my being, my body, when coupled with the wellspring of emotions I'd been carrying concerning Taylor, had created a sort of shutdown, a nightmare of images — or daymare rather, of what it may have been like for him being in that room, being tested on, being tortured even.

Back at Vicki's, I'd retreated to the bedroom to have a rest. Redmond had brought me a plate of the homemade pizza that he'd whipped up for dinner, but I hadn't had much of an appetite. I'd given him the iPod and requested that he transfer the videos I'd recorded to Derek and Vicki. I'd also requested that he not mention what had happened to me. My reasoning on the topic was that they didn't need to worry about me, and what they really needed was the update about what we'd found.

Normally I would have wanted to talk to everyone about what had happened, but I was feeling exceptionally logy after the long day that had started with the strange sensations and the uneasiness of being watched at the group home, Taylor speaking to me, and then the adventure and daymare incident at the Celaeno facility. I wasn't up for rehashing the images and discomfort of what I'd suffered in this messed-up brain of mine. So instead, while Redmond went and brought the gang up to speed, I'd remedied my wounds with a video chat with my daughters. Their stories and enthusiasm in relaying their adventures had somewhat helped in altering my mood and calming my nervous system.

When I'd come out of the bedroom to hand off the phone to Redmond for his goodnights, Vicki had informed me that she and my girlfriends wanted to have a shopping day and lunch together tomorrow. I'd reluctantly agreed, figuring that the malaise and exhaustion from my day would be gone by morning. And I'd be able to endure the shopping part of the day, knowing there would be the reward of a delicious lunch afterwards. Redmond had overheard Vicki talking to me about the plans the girls had made, so he'd cheerfully told me he'd be hanging with the guys over at Don's again.

I'd returned to the bedroom after saying goodnight to Vicki and Eric. Redmond had come to bed shortly after that, and he had given me the details of how things had gone over while speaking with everyone. He'd told me that Derek had confirmed receipt of the video of the notebook, and that he would contact Vicki for the translations needed for working to decode the pages. Alison had told Redmond that she'd documented everything, all of what we'd seen, right down to the butterflies pinned to the board. I had said little to him in response, though I was grateful Redmond had taken the lead to convey the details. He'd known how difficult it had been for me at that lab, and that the images I'd seen in my head had shaken me. He hadn't pushed for me to make conversation, and in place of talk he'd quickly gotten ready for bed, and like those rare nights when I'd been unsettled by something and had trouble falling asleep, he had wrapped me in his arms until I dosed.

Thankfully, I hadn't had any nightmares or dreams last night, or at least none that I remembered, but I was still feeling sluggish this morning, even after my coffee.

"I'm off to Don's," Redmond said, leaning down to kiss me on the cheek. "Ready for your day with the girls?"

I turned my head slightly, giving a side-eye look to Vicki who was sitting in the chair across from me sipping her tea. "Shopping— yaaahhhhhh," I said with a grin, the yah part of the comment trailing off to a sigh.

Vicki laughed, knowing how much I did NOT adore shopping, but she did know how much I loved being with my friends. "We'll be feeding her after—she'll make it through to lunch, I'm sure," Vicki said with a wave of her hand as Redmond shrugged into his coat to leave.

"Food is always an excellent motivator for her—smart," he said back to Vicki, as he left to go down the hall. "Have a great day, ladies," he called from the front door before it shut.

Vicki grinned at me over the rim of her teacup. "We'll take it easy on you. Mac said we're just doing the Bayshore Shopping Center, and that she got us a lunch reservation at Napoli Café, which is in Stittsville as you know, so we'll need to have time to get out there by then."

"Bayshore," I blurted, straightening in my chair, "that mall has three levels."

"Yes, well, none of us have done much in-person shopping since the pandemic, and we have specific shops we want to visit, though we won't be going through the department stores on the ends," she said. "Not unless Mac has something specific, she's searching for."

"Really?" I questioned, slumping again in my chair, and taking the last sip of my coffee. I didn't much care for shopping, but the Bayshore Shopping Center had been one of my favorite malls to visit when I was a teen, not because of the shops but because they had a candy store called Laura Secord that made the best fudge and butterscotch suckers I've ever had. For years, my Aunt Kay worked at The Bay, now reclaimed as the Hudson's Bay, one of the two department stores at either end of the mall, and I had always loved going with my Mom to visit her. Christmas presents from her always came in one of the gift boxes from the store even if she hadn't purchased the gift there, since she had access to an endless supply. At least the place would bring back fond memories, I mused, *and* Laura Secord was still in business there from what I remembered. I'd be sure to get suckers for Hayley and Ryley, and some for myself.

Olivia was driving Mac and Alison to the mall, and they had asked Vicki and me to meet them there at the outdoor entrance to *HomeSense*, the home décor store and Mac's target for shopping. Mac wasn't interested really in shopping for clothes, instead she had her sights set on further decorating her now much bigger home.

Olivia, on the other hand, wanted a few new items to add to her wardrobe for work. She still dressed professionally, though with a little less office feel to her work outfits. She used to shop at the stuffier more formal stores for work clothes, but she's taken a less stiff approach to her fashion in the past few years and does most of her shopping at places like Banana Republic now, swapping her skirts and jackets for a more relaxed bohemian style, since working alongside Mac.

For Alison, her target shop was the Mac makeup store, and had stated that she'd run out of her lipstick and only had a short *nub* of it left in the tube. I had to admit, I was curious to find out what the name for her lipstick was, because it was the perfect colour for her and was only a slightly different shade than her natural lips.

Vicki had said she didn't need anything, though she was gung-ho to check out Laura Secord with me.

When I'd checked the mall map online before leaving, I'd been ecstatic to find that it showed that all our store destinations were on the first floor, even the candy shop. So, I could tolerate a little browsing if it meant no traversing the three levels to check out all the shops.

We did the home decor stuff first for Mac, and with a little searching, she managed to find a few cute throw pillows for her new couch for in the main living room. Her new puppy, Fergus, had chewed the old ones, so she'd had the perfect excuse to get new ones. "These ones are nicer anyway," Mac said, in no real need of an excuse to shop, as we exited from the store through its mall entrance.

Even though the candy store was in view, our next destination was Banana Republic for Olivia to get some new tops. Mac took the lead on that to help find what Olivia needed to get, while Vicki, Alison, and I went together over to the makeup store.

"It should have been Mac going to the Mac makeup store," I joked, as we split off at the end of the pass-through to the main part of the mall.

"I love Mac," Mac tossed out with a chuckle, as they went left down the hall.

Turning right, we went past Laura Secord, and then American Eagle clothing store, to where we found the tiny cosmetics store.

We were barely in the store before a 20something girl in all black clothing and too much makeup, began suggesting that she had *just what I was looking for*. I ignored her, as did Vicki, as we followed Alison as she beelined it to the wrack of lipsticks.

Alison picked up a display tube, checking the colour. Then she returned it to its holder and snatched up two boxes of untouched product below it.

Before following her up to the cash, I checked the bottom of the tube she'd just looked at. The name on the lipstick was, of course, *LOVE U BACK*. I smiled, staring at the tube of lipstick. The colour was a muted nude with pink undertones and a matt finish. I'd always imagined it was called something like *Angel Blush* or something along those lines, but now I knew it was all about *love*, and even more suited to her.

The next objective on our shopping list was suckers. Not just any old suckers, these were the fabulous, can't-get-them-anywhere-else, but at Laura Secord, butterscotch suckers. "I'll take two — no, three bags of those suckers," I told the saleswoman behind the candy counter. "Oh, and a piece of your chocolate fudge." I licked my lips.

"A piece of fudge for me too, please," Vicki said, giving me an elbow nudge in my side. "Here's a cool fact…," Vicki said, taking the wrapped chocolate square from the cashier to put in her purse. "Laura Secord is a Canadian heroine of the War of 1812. Did you know that?"

I shook my head. I'd assumed Laura Secord was the name of the candy maker.

"Well…," Vicki said, moving away from the counter to make room for the next customer. "… she walked 20 miles out of American-occupied territory in to warn the British forces about an impending American attack. She's been frequently honoured in Canada, but she has no relation to the candy company, though it was named after her on the 100th anniversary of her walk, because the owners felt she was a symbol of courage, devotion, and loyalty."

"Go Laura," I said, appreciating the fudge and the suckers even more. I turned then to see Alison had her hands on a French Mint Chocolate Bar for purchase. When I turned the other way down the hall in the direction Mac and Olivia had gone, I spotted the two of them already on their way back. Olivia waved her shopping bags in the air in triumph and Mac gave us the thumbs up indicating their success. And as I had wished for, we were done with the shopping part of our day and were free to head back to the cars and on with the restaurant part of our day.

"Well done, troops," I said to the shopping warriors, holding up the bag containing my own purchase.

Goods in hand, I turned to stroll back down the way we'd originally come. I was two steps down the pass-through hallway to the mall's entrance to the home décor store, when a tingling ran the length of my arms to prickle vibrantly at my wrists, and I stopped. My first instinct was that I was sensing one of Thaddeus's men. Perhaps the one who had been watching us at the group home. Tilting my head back, I glanced way up to the gallery of the 3rd floor. *Nothing*. Returning to stare straight ahead again, I took another step, but the tingling got stronger. Shifting just my eyes, I peered up the nearest escalator that fed people up to the landing on the 2nd floor. *Nothing again*. I turned my head fully and searched the far side of the open area to where the other escalators brought people *down* to the first floor. The floorplan designers had arranged things that way, making it so people had to walk past the shops if they wanted to go up again after coming down. There were stairs near the down escalator, so if you had the energy, you could always go up that way. When I turned back to the *up* escalator, the sensation strengthened as though this *someone* was coming within reach. I panned the faces of the people passing me on my left and right. Vicki called out my name then and I veered my vision briefly in her direction. Glancing forward again, my eyes locked on a model-tall woman coming my way.

As she approached, I could see that her pale skin was flawless. She had large almond-shaped eyes, an elegant nose, and picture-perfect full lips, and her exceptional facial symmetry reminded me of Jennifer Garner from her Alias TV show days, though this woman had much darker hair that fell in waves of jet black to her waistline. The intensity of the sensation grew tenfold as the woman reached me, close enough that she could reach out and grab me... except all the woman did was glance down at me with her amber coloured eyes, and *smile*. Then she continued on her way without so much as a glance back. She hadn't realized what or who I was. But I knew she was one of them. "*Earthbound*," I said, under my breath. When I mouthed the word to my girlfriends, they all turned and stared after the woman.

"She didn't do anything. Like she didn't know," Vicki stated, her head cranked to the side watching as the woman walked away.

"How could she?" Mac questioned, hugging the big shopping bag with her two new cushions in it.

Alison reached out and touched my arm. "Her kind can't sense other celestials, let alone someone like you," she said.

"You have to tell Leo," Olivia stated, hoisting her shopping bag up on one shoulder.

I nodded slowly at my friends, suddenly drained of any energy I had mustered earlier.

Back into the car, I sent Leo a quick text stating that I needed to talk to him about a woman I'd seen at the mall. The rest of the story I felt was better done face to face, so I requested that we meet up later to discuss.

On the drive to the restaurant, I lost myself in my thoughts, speculating about who this woman could be. I knew what she was, but not *who* she was. Was she one of Thaddeus's followers, or was she one of the original Earthbound, I wondered? I couldn't tell. What I did know was that she was stunning, 12 out of 10 on the gorgeous scale, and other than Purah, who was captivatingly beautiful, the only other Earthbound Seraphim I'd seen, were Leo and Thaddeus, the latter being only on video. The males were also exceptionally gorgeous. Mac had described Amahle, the Earthbound female working with Thaddeus, as spectacular when it came to both her looks and her clothing. All these Earthbound it seemed, were striking in appearance, and now I understood better why Leo felt disguises were necessary. If you had a need to interact with the public, it would be difficult to hide that level of beauty, go unnoticed or even stay under the radar from humans, let alone Thaddeus's crew.

"Here!" Vicki announced, pulling me from my musing. "You were quiet on the drive."

"I know—sorry. I couldn't stop thinking about that woman—the Earthbound," I said, shifting to get out of the SUV.

"Can't blame you," she said, exiting out her side of the car. "Bet you're hungry." She smirked at me.

But I wasn't. I was more exhausted than anything, and it didn't matter, because I was more than thrilled to be out of that mall and entering a place I genuinely loved. "Aaahhh, Napoli's Café, how I have missed you." I grinned, following Vicki to the front door where the rest of our crew now stood.

Inside, Mac gave the name for our reservation and then the hostess sat us at a six-top near the window.

When the server came over to the table, he said, "Nice to see you ladies again—it's been a while."

We all agreed, nodding. It had been, for me anyway, years, in fact.

"We're going to get some of the shared appetizers," Mac said, giving him a short list of the menu, *Calamari, Bruschetta,* and *Zucchini Fritti.*

"I'll have the zuppa of the day," I told the waiter, after everyone else had given their orders.

"You feeling, okay?" Mac asked when the waiter left to fill our orders.

"Just not that hungry, I guess," I said, giving her my scrunched-up-whatever face.

She raised her eyebrows as if suspicious. "Oookaay," she said, but let it go.

The others just stared at me, surprised.

Normally I would have been getting a big plate of pasta, along with eating most of the appetizers, but for whatever reason, I wasn't all that hungry. I think my brain had too much weird stuff in it to sort through to realize and inform my tastebuds and stomach that I *should* be hungry.

When the appetizers arrived, they smelled amazing, yet still my hunger remained buried. As the others chatted, I gazed out the window, hoping my brain would rest, though I couldn't keep the images of the lab, of Taylor, and of that striking Seraph female from the mall, at bay.

"Lynn, tell us what it was like to be undercover," Alison asked excitedly, pulling my brain back to those at the table.

"It must have been fun—kind of, eh?" Mac said, grinning and nibbling on pieces of bruschetta.

"Fun…," I pondered. "… I guess it started out that way, but then things got serious when we had to get into the lower level."

Mac's grin dropped.

"What do you mean?" Alison said. "Redmond told us it was fairly easy—you got in, then you got out with what you needed—the videos." Eyes wide, she dipped a piece of calamari into the marinara sauce.

"Ya, we did…," I started to say, as images crowded my mind, "… but I think that was where they tested on Taylor."

"You can't know that for sure," Vicki said, reaching for some of the zucchini.

"I do—I saw it," I said, probably a little too harshly.

Mac shot a glance at Olivia, and I saw Olivia do the two-finger tap on her neck.

"Is my blood pressure rising?" I asked Olivia, raising my eyebrows.

Olivia nodded.

"Don't worry—I'm fine. But I need to tell you what really happened—what happened to me, that is." For the next 20 minutes, as the others picked at the appetizers, I dove into a play-by-play about what had happened once I saw the surgery and autopsy tables in the lower level lab. Then I told them about the *dream* I'd had about the hospital with the sick kids, and the dead child face-down on the metal table. I mentioned that medical staff in the back room, although I left out the part about the man hanging from the ceiling in that room, as it still confused me and didn't seem relevant to the images of the children being tested on.

The server arrived then, dropping off everyone's meals. Once he left, I said, "Taylor was with Thaddeus for 5 years prior to going to that group home. I believe he was tested on during all that time."

"It's no wonder he doesn't like the male attendance—or any male, for that matter," Olivia reminded, her face horrified as if picturing the images I had just described.

"Did you ever call Carlie at the group home," I directed at Alison. "To make sure everything was okay after we left?" I pushed my now cold half-eaten soup to the side.

"Yes—she's fine. Taylor was fine too." Alison gave me a reassuring smile that reached her eyes.

I relaxed a bit after hearing that. "What were those papers she handed you—I forgot to ask," I said to her.

"They were his medical records. Wasn't much, though it outlined his condition—the enlarged ribcage and a few other things." She didn't smile this time.

I looked at Vicki then to see she was checking her phone. When she glanced up and saw me staring, she said. "I'm waiting for a text from Derek. He's working on those pages from the video Redmond sent us."

I gave her a couple slow nods, then returned my focus back to Alison.

"Wait," Alison said, flipping through her notes. She had pulled out her notepad to document things when I had started to recall what had happened at the lab. "The dream... your daymare... and the lab... it's the same."

I frowned at her, puzzled. "Alison, what was the same?"

Chapter 27

Home of Derek (Shortcut) Jones, December 30th, South Carolina

Derek was ecstatic over the idea of having a new puzzle of sorts to decipher, and these writings were the perfect distraction from what he'd considered being in *dullsville* right now in his life. Having sold his business and being basically retired, it had been ages since he'd had a challenge or riddle like this to solve. Vicki had provided him with the accompanying alphabets for each of the languages she had discerned from within the lines of writing. Now all he had to do was figure out what the key to the code was.

For the next several hours, he sat in his office/music room, reviewing different codes that he'd used in the past. Some he had created himself and several others that he had broken, meaning he'd been able to solve them. When that brought no resolution, he went on to research an extensive list of additional codes, their history and uses. After his lengthy examination, he found that none were exactly like this one, though a few were comparable in their structure.

A text chimed on his phone and Derek brought up the paired 'Your Phone' app on his computer. The message was from Luc,

> *Busy? Just checking to see if you want to get on a video chat with Darius and me.*

Derek texted back,

I could use the break from all my code breaking.

A few clicks later and Derek was staring at the faces of his buddies on one of his two split screen monitors. "Hey—what's up," he said to their grinning faces.

"Darius is feeling his usual angst with Lynn and Redmond away," Luc said, leaning an elbow on the armrest of his couch. "So, we thought you might be able to distract him—us, with what you've found so far with the pages from Lynn's video."

"Ya—what he said," Darius added, restless in his seat.

From what Derek could see on the monitor, it looked like Darius was sitting at his kitchen table. The small peninsula behind him had his vitamins and protein powders stacked up on it. His posture was much like that of a second grader sitting attentively at his desk, waiting to raise his hand with a question.

"Well…," he said, pausing a second to see if Darius would actually raise his hand to ask a question. "… codes similar to this format are often made up of hierograms, sacred symbols, emblems, and pictographs, along with actual letters and numbers. And I found that most of the pages Lynn videotaped were filled with various alchemy symbols."

"Alchemy?" Darius questioned, without raising his hand.

"The formal definition is referred to as *medieval chemical science and speculative philosophy aiming to achieve transmutation.* Like figuring out how to change base metals into gold, discovering a universal cure for disease, or the means of eternizing life. It's the process of taking something ordinary and turning it into something extraordinary, usually in a way that can't be easily explained."

"Okay, I think I follow," Darius said.

"Do the symbols make any sense to you?" Luc asked.

"I know what the symbols mean, and I think I understand what was being recorded. Some symbols refer to the seven planetary metals. Lead—Saturn, tin—Jupiter, iron—Mars, gold—Sun, copper—Venus, mercury, well Mercury, and silver—Moon. There are also symbols for solvents and compounds being used like black sulfur, rock salt, oil, wax, and even urine. Most of the pages are about testing and experiments from what I can interpret."

"Oh, man," Darius said, as if trying not to imagine why urine was used.

Derek shook his head. "There are symbols for the processes, equipment and units of measure, as well, like hour, ounce, pound, night and so on."

Luc rubbed a hand over his shaved head. "Were there any other symbols or were the rest just letters?" he asked.

"There were a few more alchemical symbols, the Aristotelian elements; air, fire, water, and earth. There was lots of focus on what is known as the Three Primes; mercury, salt, and sulfur," Derek informed them. "Whoever wrote this, is clearly not analphabetic and definitely a polyglot, to compose something like this as their normal note taking."

"Come again? What's that supposed to mean?" Luc asked, passing a hand around the back of his neck.

"I'm just saying the person who wrote this knows a lot about language and codes—it wouldn't be easy to write out." Derek flipped through some of his own note taking. "I looked over some familiar codes," he began again. "*Atbash*, for example, which is just the alphabet backwards. A would equal Z, simple. *Binary*—you're both familiar with, being computer guys."

Luc and Darius both nodded

"I reviewed the *Caesar Cipher*, the one Julius Caesar invented to use when sending letters, so if messengers were robbed, the robber couldn't read the letters. And it's probably one of the simplest codes ever. You just shift the alphabet by three letters, so A would be X and so on. *The Rot Cipher* is similar.

"If you say so," Darius said, his face full of skepticism, though still no hand raising.

"This writing… this is much like a *Combination Cipher* and a *Columnar Cipher* put together. If you are not familiar, a Combination Cipher uses two or more codes. And this one is using languages instead of codes. But like a Columnar Cipher, which is a type of transposition cipher, you need the key word and the order in the alphabet. There are also places in the writings where a septenary relation is used." Derek shuffled his papers, putting what he'd deciphered and translated on the top of the pile.

"What?" Darius asked, this time raising his hand, his index finger pointing up in question.

"Sorry." Derek chuckled. "Septenary—things relating to the number seven or group of seven, set of seven. A cycle of seven years. The number seven. The seven stars of Pleiades." He gave a lazy shrug. "Oh, and the numbers written in the code—the ones I originally thought were years, they're not. It's military time. 2400, 1400, etc." He held up a printed copy of one of the pages for Luc and Darius to see.

"It just looks like continuous lines of characters and symbols, to me" Luc said, leaning forward and squinting at his computer screen.

"Ya, I thought the same at first glance, but I've determined they are actual words, and each new word starts and ends with a character from the modern English alphabet. Each sentence ends with the circle dot symbol normally used as a solar symbol representing the sun or an alchemical symbol for gold, but in this case, it's used as a period to end a sentence. The code is set up as follows; *English* letter start and end, second letter in sequence is *Sanskrit*, third letter is *Sumerian*, and the fourth is *Enochian*. That last language, I'd originally given Vicki the alphabet for her translations way back."

"Were you able to decipher much? You know—actual sentences and paragraphs, and such?" Luc asked, sitting up and then leaning in again.

Derek rubbed the side of his jaw, his nails making a scratching sound against a week's growth worth of facial hair. "This last page, I used to help me figure out what the previous pages said. The page is like the results page, the summary if you will, of what was done and recorded during the testing or experimenting phase."

"And?" Luc moved his laptop to the coffee table, then rested his elbows on his knees, facing the screen.

"Some stuff is clear, while other pieces confound me," Derek said, tilting his head.

"Welcome to the club," Darius said, giving his head a couple quick shakes.

"I've made other notes that I can send you," Derek said. "Some of the writings are pretty grewsome. It's mainly about testing on the offspring from what I can interpret. That kid, Taylor, is mentioned, his birdlike expended upper torso being a focus for some reason. And there is some stuff about testing on other Earthbound. Surgery on their backs, cutting off appendages and things like that." He paused. "There is also mention of searching for a grown offspring in the rainforest. Mentions changes after puberty for those with normal development, and about fully functional appendages emerge sometime, once into adulthood."

"What the hell does that mean?" Darius asked grimacing. "Like if they were paralyzed, their arms and legs only start working when they reach adulthood? What the…?"

Derek shook his head several times. "Says few make it past the age of 10. Those who make it into adulthood require help to understand the magnitude of their differences compared to full humans."

"This is seriously messed up," Luc said. "Have you told Lynn about what you found, yet?"

"No," Derek said, blowing out a heavy breath. "I was trying to finish it before handing it off to her. From the personal observations recorded — I'm pretty sure that it's this Thaddeus guy who wrote these pages. Let me read this part to you,

> The human females able to go full term often die during childbirth if the child is malformed in the womb and the female cannot receive a cesarean section to remove the halfling. I know of very few Earthbound females who have given birth. Those I have been informed of have had little to no issues in giving birth and their offspring are rarely malformed, all appendages intact. Those I have had first-hand accounts with did not survive the testing performed. Their only use to me is as specimens.
>
> I continue to search for more offspring. I need to figure out how it is possible they were even conceived. Is it the male or the female that provides the essential component for their survival? I will continue my testing and continue to rid the earth of these boat minions.

"Boat minions?" Darius shot out, his expression twisting in confusion.

Derek huffed. "Ya, there's more like those — that make little sense." He turned his attention to his last notes. "Like here,

Unknown if swing will function if a boat minion grows to adulthood.

"Clearly—that part is off," Luc said, stating the obvious. "Not unless he's talking about those little yellow cartoon guys on a boat becoming adults." Luc tightened his mouth, as if suppressing a laugh.

Derek scratched his jaw again. "Right? I had another part that was odd,

Awaiting samples from fast iron.

But I later realized that *fast iron* was an anagram for rainforest, making it, *awaiting samples from rainforest.* So evidently there are more anagrams in this bastard of a code that I need to figure out."

"Looks like it," Luc said. "You'll have to double-check everything, I'm guessing." Luc leaned back into his couch.

"This last part I found interesting," Derek said, tapping the paper in front of him. "Leo told Lynn that the Earthbound were fast healing, but here it talks about testing using the Three Primes, and that sulfur had varying effects on them. Some screamed in pain, some passed out, the effects seeming to be different for each test subject. The notes mention that Thaddeus accidentally burnt his hand, and then later that he tested the sulfur influence on someone named Lyndon and how it had burned half of his face, though it resulted in a different kind of burn and severity of scarring."

"Sulfur can do that?" Darius questioned. "I know it produces a blue flame and sulfur dioxide gas—which is a common pollutant, but can it burn skin?"

"I was surprised too," Derek said. "Sulfur dioxide in the atmosphere comes mostly from fossil-fuel power plants and is one of the primary causes of acid rain—and that can burn. The gas is also a lung irritant. But burning skin on its own—like that, I've never heard of, or it having any of the effects recorded here." Derek turned over the last page of his notes. "The last comments were about Thaddeus going to Merope in New York City to see a new test subject," Derek added. "But that's where the entry ends."

"I think you should send it to Lynn—even if it isn't finished," Darius suggested.

"That's my thinking too," Derek agreed. "I'll send her what I have—better than making her wait. She knows I'll solve the rest." Derek grinned.

Luc turned his attention to typing something on his keyboard.

"Luc?" Darius prompted.

There was a lengthy pause as both Darius and Derek watched and waited as Luc finished whatever he appeared to be working on or searching for on his computer.

"I'm sending my notes to Lynn," Luc said, returning his focus to the camera. "Maybe this sulfur thing is unique to the Earthbound," Luc said then, bringing them back a few steps. "Did you know...," He paused again, "... that sulfur is also known as *brimstone*? It means 'burning stone'."

Darius tipped his head to one side like a confused dog would do. Derek said nothing and only continued to watch as Luc typed something again on his keyboard. They both understood Luc had more coming.

"And in the Hebrew and Christian bibles," Luc started again, "the term 'Fire and brimstone' references that of divine punishment and purification... and the fate of the unfaithful."

Chapter 28

The home of Vicki and Eric, December 31st, Ottawa

When Redmond and Eric had gotten back yesterday from their day with the rest of the guys, I'd shared with both what I'd experienced at the mall, about the woman who had walked by me, the one that I knew without a doubt was one of the Earthbound. After, I'd sent Leo a text letting him know about the incident, though I'd not heard back from him yet. I hadn't really expected a response right away, however I was curious to find out what he knew of this woman, if anything.

As it had been in the afternoon and then last night, my mind was still reeling this morning over what Alison had said about the similarities she'd noted from in my dream and in the real lab. She'd explained she could see things in her mind as I described what I had seen, and that when she had recorded the details, she had discovered there were several overlaps. Like with the items I'd described in the trays atop the rolling side tables, and the tables themselves that had been alongside the beds in my dream and then again beside the surgery setups in the lab. The autopsy table too was the same she'd said, as were the tools next to it, all identical. But the comparison that had gotten to me the most, the one that had pulled the air from my lungs and shaken me to my core, had been when she mentioned the back room. I'd shared that in my dream I'd seen an open door to a back room where two medical personnel had been, and she had said it was the same door that was at the back of the lab. I'd questioned that part as I hadn't recalled seeing any door. She'd further clarified that Redmond had described the layout of the place for them on that video chat update they'd had, and it was why it had caught her attention when I'd mentioned it regarding my dream. I still hadn't told them about the man who had been strung up by the chains attached to the ceiling, because it had felt so out of place and unrelated to Thaddeus's testing on the offspring. I didn't understand it, why it had been a part of my dream, nor did I recall ever having seen this man before. I didn't want to think about it, about him, about the painful sounds and images my memory conjured up, especially the anguished expression on his face. If the relevancy made itself known, I would then tell them about that part of the dream. For now, I pushed down the memory to keep my focus on the halflings.

Before packing my suitcase last night, I'd read Luc's email and reviewed what Derek had sent, the attachment containing his first stab at deciphering the writings I'd recorded. The contents, cryptic and disturbing, did little to settle the unease that had taken me over after hearing Alison's little comparison list. In fact, its details only confirmed the horrific things I believed had gone on in that lab. Redmond had reviewed the translations with me. Then I'd told him about Alison and the list of similarities she'd noted. And as I had expected, after forwarding the email from Derek to my girlfriends, Redmond and I weren't the only ones filled with uneasiness.

"Lyyyyynn," Mac's voice called from down the hall to the bedroom.

"Heeere," I called back to her, through the open door. Redmond had already left to take our luggage out to the SUV for Vicki to take Eric, Redmond, and me to the airport for our 7a.m. take-off time. I was just doing a double-check in the bedroom to make sure we had left nothing behind.

Mac rounded the open door, an exaggerated pout on her face. "Too short," she said, pushing her bottom lip out further. She was still wearing what looked like her pajamas.

"I know," I sighed out, "it always is." I pushed out a complementary pouty lip.

"Why so early?" She frowned, barely suppressing a yawn.

"Long round trip for Eric—we're lucky he likes to fly," I told her. "If he schedules it right, he can be back in time to have a late lunch with Vicki." I smiled.

Changing her pout to a tiny grin, she said, "I made you something." She held out a tiny white box. "It's a handsel." When I looked at her, confused, she said, "It's a token of good luck and good wishes for the beginning of the new year. And for when entering a new situation or enterprise. I made one for each of us—the girls." She raised her eyebrows, aware that all of us were entering a new enterprise with us helping Leo.

I slid the top of the tiny box to find what looked like a ceramic disk the size of a quarter. Lifting it out, I saw it had the relief image of a stylized butterfly on it.

"Change—the butterfly signifies change," she reminded.

"Thank you—I love the sentiment. What a year, eh?" My shoulders drooped in line with the weary memories of it.

"Don't get me started," Mac said, spinning to go back down the hall. "Let's send it out to the universe that 2022 is going take a turn for the better—for all of us."

"Here-here," I sing-songed out, following her down the hall out to the front foyer.

At the front door, I found Redmond standing with all our friends who lined up to say their goodbyes, and I noted Mac wasn't the only one still in her pjs. Both Alison and Olivia had on some form of lounging clothes, as did all the spouses. "Sorry for the early departure," I said, "You can all go back to bed now." I faked a yawn.

"We're up now," Olivia said, brushing her messy bangs back off her forehead. She gave me a playful grin. "Not sure I'll make it to midnight tonight, though. Although, I want to witness this past year leaving and the new one coming in—you know." She laughed, then pulled me in for a hug.

I went down the line with each of my friends and their spouses, getting my hugs while the hugging was good.

Mike was next. "We'll see you soon—don't worry," he said, giving me a reassuring smile.

Then was Alison, whose big blue eyes were all teary while her cheeks bunched in a smile at the same time "Text when you land—and let us know when you get home," she instructed, squeezing me a bit harder before letting me go.

Ken gave me a hug and rock next. "Better things are coming for all of us in 2022," he said, before moving on to give a hug and shoulder-pat to Redmond.

"We'll all come South—to see you guys for the next visit," Don said, squeezing me quick then releasing me from his bearhug grip.

"Sounds good," I said, when I could breathe again.

Last was Mac. "Too short," she said again, making a show of pushing out her lower lip. She hugged me quick then stepped back, swiping away a stray tear.

"The twins are counting on all of you to come visit," Redmond added. "They miss you guys—almost as much as we do." He gave Don a final hug, followed by a firm, manly slap on the back.

Everyone filed out the front door then, jumping into their respective vehicles. And as each pulled away, Redmond and I waved. Then we got in the SUV with Vicki and Eric and headed off to the airport.

At close to 10:30a.m., when we landed back in Florida, I turned off the airplane mode on my cell phone, allowing it to get reacquainted with the local network. Seconds later, a bell chimed, indicating I had a phone message. I checked the call log to find it had been Leo who'd called, and I clicked my voicemail to listen. *"Call me when you can,"* was all Leo's message had said.

I waited until after our goodbyes with Eric, and we were on the road to call him back. But first I sent a quick text to the Ottawa crew, letting them know we landed and that we missed them already. Then, as we drove out of the charter area of the small airport, I hit dial on Leo's number.

"Hey, Lynn," Leo said, picking up my call.

"Hi, sorry for not calling you back right sooner—we just landed back in Florida."

"Not a problem," he said.

I put the phone on speaker as we drove, so Redmond could listen in on the exchange. "Were just driving to the house now—I have you on speaker," I said, setting the phone in the hands-free cradle in the dash.

"Redmond—Good morning," Leo said. His voice sounding as though he were smiling.

"Good morning," Redmond said, smiling in response to Leo's cheery voice. "What's the latest?"

"Not much actually, other than wanting to catch you up on the details about that woman Lynn saw—sensed, at the shopping mall.

"Ya—about that. What's the deal—do you know who she is?" I shot a glance at Redmond, raising my eyebrows. He gave me a quick grin, then turned his focus back on the road.

"I know exactly who she is," he said.

"Well—who is she? Friend or foe?" I looked at Redmond again, widening my eyes.

"With the description you sent me, I knew it had to be Jules— Julianna," he said, then paused. "Just texted you a photo."

My phone chimed in receipt of his text. Checking the image, I said, "That's her—though her hair is longer now."

"I was just surprised she was here—in Ottawa. Last time I had talked with her, she was in Brazil. She's the contact we told you about. Her son is one of the few halflings we know about—of the ones still alive, that is."

"Yes—I remember. Well, clearly she's there now," I said. "I saw her—felt her, big-time." I nodded, even though he couldn't see me. "And again, the feeling had differed from when sensing you—yet still similar." I shook my head at the absurdity of my statement. She had felt like the others, like with Purah and Leo, and *not* uncomfortable like with whomever had been watching us at the group home. I'd speculated if the variation in the type of sensation or discomfort had any association to which group they were part of, the first Earthbound or the smaller group that included Thaddeus. I had described the differences to Alison for her records to keep track of the variants, and the who's who of it.

"I texted her," Leo said, "but instead of responding via text, she sent me a secure email." There was a pause and then the sound of a keyboard clacking. "Her emails stated her son planned to attend the University of Ottawa, and in conjunction she'd been offered a job to teach Environmental Geoscience at the same university as part of the Science department. She wrote that after her son's time in Brazil, he had been extremely interested to learn more about Food and Nutrition Sciences—and they have an excellent program there. So, when presented with the job opportunity at the same university her son wanted to attend, she felt she couldn't pass it up. They had just arrived the day you saw her. She was shopping for winter clothes for both she and her son."

"I see…," I said, not sure what to say or what I was feeling about this information, as it felt a little too casual considering who and what she was.

"It might be good for her to be nearby—help with the Thaddeus situation, maybe. She knows what we've been doing here—The Guards, I mean, so she felt comfortable about moving here. But she doesn't know about you—not really. She knows *of* you—just not exactly who you are, or that you've been involved of late. But I'll bring her up to speed."

"Speaking of being involved," I cut in. "I wanted to send you Derek's draft for the translation of the writings, but I don't have an email for you."

"Oh, use the one on the business card I gave you—it feeds into my secure account," he said. "How did he make out?"

I gave him a quick summary of what Derek had sent, then said, "I'll forward it to you once I'm home."

"Perfect." Leo sounded like he was smiling again. Before ending the call, he said, "I'll have someone keep an eye on Taylor. Max and Julian suggested Lane, their daughter. Since you said Taylor isn't fond of having males around him. Understandably so, knowing what we know now," he added, followed up by the sound of him blowing out a breath.

"That'll work," I agreed. "Talk soon."

"I look forward to it. Later, Lynn—Redmond," he said, before ending the call.

Redmond reached over and patted my hand. "Almost home," he said, knowing that over and above all this crazy new stuff, the thing I was most anxious about, was seeing our girls.

As we pulled into the driveway to the beach house, I could already see Summer and Snow lumbering down the front steps to greet us. Close behind them were Hayley and Ryley, followed by Redmond's parents. We got out of the car then, and Redmond went to open the passenger door to retrieve our bags.

"Hiiii," Ryley called as she hit the last step. Hayley was already running over to us when Redmond shut and locked the car door.

Enzo and Nainseadh waved as they descended the steps, their exhausted smiles a good indication we'd arrived home just in time. After several rounds of hugs and kisses from our excited children, we made our way into the house.

"Let your dad and I get unpacked and then you can tell us all the news," I said to energy-filled twins.

In the bedroom, I texted the Ottawa gang again, making sure they knew we had made it home safe. Redmond sent out a text to Lily and Darius following our unpacking, letting them know we were home and that we needed to coordinate a time to leave for Miami and the festivities at the Fairchild Gardens.

We spent the rest of the day with as much normalcy as we could manage, all the while letting Redmond's parents relax on their last day here with us. Though, Nainseadh insisted on making us an early dinner before we had to head to Miami, a traditional Irish meal especially for New Year's Eve and one of Redmond's childhood favorites. Corn beef and cabbage, along with potatoes, carrots, and onions. It wasn't my favorite, but since it was in the tradition for a new year filled with luck and abundance, I was all for it.

Chapter 29

When Redmond finally heard back from Darius, he'd written that they were up to speed on all the latest celestial events. And that they had already organized the vehicle seating arrangements with Redmond's parents for the long, two-hour trek down to Miami.

The girls were to ride with Darius and Lily, while Redmond's parents went with us. This way it gave Nainseadh and Enzo a well-needed break and some adult-only time, allowing for the girls to talk non-stop with Lily and Darius instead for the long drive. Then for the ride home, we'd switch the twins to being with us. As per their grandparents, the two had been up since the crack of dawn and hadn't stopped their energy train once. And now with us heading down for the spectacular New Year's Eve Night Garden event at Fairchild, coupled with the anticipation of fireworks and possibly being up past midnight, we predicted the girls would crash hard after and it would be a quiet sleep-filled drive home.

At the park's entrance, the four of us met up with Lily and Darius and the twins, all ready with our digital tickets out for scanning.

"Okay, ladies," Lily said, getting Ryley's and Haley's attention. "I'm going to be your guide for tonight's event." She'd texted us on the ride down, letting us know she had downloaded the phone app made for tonight's event, *The Night Garden Fairy Quest*, such that she could use it with the girls. The event tonight was interactive with the app, the backstory being how every year, the Fairy Queen uses her magic to bring the garden to life. The garden is said to contain all sorts of magical creatures, like Archimedes the talking tree and, of course, *Fairies*.

"Tell me what happened to the fairy sisters of the Night Garden?" Lily asked.

"They were trapped in stone statues," Hayley exclaimed, brimming with excitement, and bouncing up and down.

"And what are we here to do?" Lily prompted.

"Help free them," Ryley said, practically dancing on the spot.

"Right!" Lily said, holding her phone up in the air. "You see this? It's my *Fairyscope* for the Fairy Quest, and it's filled with my magic." She had the app open, its screen shining with shades of purple, teal, and magenta that matched the rainbow-colour theme of the surrounding light installation on all the plants, trees, and walkways. "We use this to free the fairies trapped inside. Once we free each of them, we will get the next clue to help find the others."

"Then what?" I asked, feeling excited for not just the girls. I would have loved this as a kid.

Lily laughed. "Free them all, and you'll be rewarded with a key to find their hidden treasure," she said to the girls. Then she grinned at me.

"Good luck!" Nainseadh said, with a little excitement of her own.

"The Night Garden is only open at night, and because it is an outdoor area immersed in nature… what?" Darius said, looking to the girls for a response.

"It can get dark in some areas," Hayley replied. "And we have to stay on the pathways." She grinned smugly at her sister.

"And?" Darius asked. Clearly, they had gone over some rules on the drive down.

"No climbing any walls, trees… no destroying any plants or pathways," Ryley said, making a face as if trying to remember more.

"No touching any audio visual components, or disrupting other guests," Lily finished for them. "Got it?"

"Got it!" the girls called out in unison.

"Got it," I said, grinning back at Lily.

She got smiles and thumbs-up from Redmond and his parents.

Each taking one of Darius's hands, the girls went ahead through the gate with him and Lily. They were followed by Redmond and his father.

Nainseadh came to my side, sliding a hand through and around the crook of my arm, and together we proceeded through to the most gorgeous garden I'd ever seen at night. What I had only seen during the day was brought to life with stunning illumination and magnificent special effects. It was something one must truly see to believe. It was truly an enchanted activity, I thought to myself, as we continued through and along the pathway suggested.

After weaving through the displays of lights and foliage, all while solving the fairy quest, we came to a stop next to an area displaying 10-foot tall dandelion lights. Across from them were picnic tables set up close to several food trucks. A delicious aroma from the Mexican food truck wafted our way, and my stomach growled.

Over the last couple days, I hadn't really eaten much, hadn't felt hungry, which wasn't like me, and other than a few potatoes and carrots from dinner, I'd eaten practically nothing all day. I had figured that the lack of hunger was just my brain too occupied by what we'd discovered, along with the additional information that had followed. My nerves had calmed as we strolled through the garden paths and now my appetite was returning, it seemed.

"The girls are hungry after their fairy quest," Redmond said, approaching the long picnic table I'd plunked myself on. I glanced over to the food truck to see his parents next to it, reviewing the menu board. "They want to split a Quesadilla. I'm going to get some Carnitas street tacos—do you want anything? They have Pollo Asado," he added, as I turned my head back to look up at him.

"Sounds good," I told him, my stomach letting out an audible rumble. "And some guacamole and chips." I gave him a toothy grin. "We'll share those."

He smiled and nodded, then went off to get the food. I watched as Redmond's parents came up to where I sat, each with a cinnamon sugar coated Churro in their hands.

"Just a little treat," Enzo said, taking a seat across from me. Nainseadh giggled, sliding in next to him.

"Yer allowed—you'll need the energy," I told them. "The night's not over yet."

I turned then to see Hayley and Ryley laughing and playing with Lily and Darius near the purple and fuchsia lit trees. Lily waved at me, and I gave her the peace-sign back. Redmond returned then with food, and the twins raced over to the table, climbing up on the bench on the other side of their dad.

"I need some of that," Darius said, as he lumbered up behind the girls.

"Let's go feed you," Lily responded, giving me a wink before leading her giant to the feast.

"Oh-my-gawd-that-smells-good," I said, taking in a long, drawn out sniff. Then I grabbed up a chip, dipped it into the guacamole and shoved it into my mouth. "Mmmmm delishuush," I said, my mouth full of the chip'n guac-goodness.

Redmond laughed. "Good to see your appetite is back," he said, giving my back a little rub.

Then I felt *her*.

"Mum, mum! Look, it's a fairy warrior," Ryley hollered, pointing a finger over to the purple and fuchsia trees they had been standing at.

"Can we go over, Mum—Daaaa?" Hayley asked, standing up in her seat at the table. "Please, Mum—pleeeeeeeease."

I cut a sharp look at Redmond. "It's Purah," I told him, turning my focus back again as the Steward stepped back slightly into the nighttime shadow of the trees.

"Where?" he asked, searching the area the girls were pointing to.

"She's veiled. Can you calm them down? I'll be right back," I said, rushing up from the table to head over to the trees. I'd known right away it was her, because of the distinctive pop-rock tingling sensation traveling over the surface of my skin.

I walked several paces past the heavily muscled titan further into the darkness of the trees, leaving my back to her. "Come further into the shadows," I insisted, waving for her to come over. Silently, she took a few brisk strides my way, coming around to stand in front of me.

She wore the same warrior body armor: white leather and metal fashioned around her arms, legs, and torso, and the same shiny silver headpiece. It really was something from out of this world, with its long tusk and horn-like protrusions arching out from the front, top, sides, and back of it. "Daughter of Gabriel," she began.

But I cut her off. "The girls can see you," I said, through a clenched jaw, wrenching my head back to look up at her face.

"They can—how?" she questioned, her pupils dilating into the back-lit glow of the shattered iceberg blue of her eyes.

"Think about who their parents are," I said, pointing at myself. "And who their grandfather is." I widened my eyes, surprised at her blatant ignorance.

"Oh my gosh—I didn't know they could do that." She dropped her chin to her chest, and that thick white braided hair of hers slid over her armored shoulder. The multi-coloured lights beaming in from the surrounding garden reflected off both the beautiful smooth dark skin of her face and the white opal rainbow flecks of the horns in her helmet.

"Well, you know now—so please be careful." I put my hands on my hips like I did when the girls pushed my buttons. "What are you doing here?" I shifted my gaze to stare at that sickle-shaped battle-axe weapon she held like a staff.

Lifting her head, she said, "Thaddeus knows someone was in his lab. Tell me it wasn't you."

"It was me," I confessed, though it wasn't a crime, not really.

"How could you put yourself at risk like that? If he figures out who was there—that it was you?" She paused, pulling in a breath. "Thaddeus knows of your gifts, your *abilities*. What if he figures out where you are?" She stomped her staff.

"He's not going to find me. I have protection—Archangel, remember?" I stated, my hand still on my hips. "And I can sense him if he gets close—if any of them do. So don't worry." I took a step to the side, walking in a tight circle. "How could he ever put a name to whoever was in his building? We wore disguises, used fake names. Besides, why would he think it was me specifically? It's too random." I stopped in front of her, looking up and dropping my hands. "City workers come into his building—and you assume his first instinct is to think it's me?" I questioned. "That's a stretch. There is no way to trace things back to me, Leo made sure of it."

"Leo—you know about him?"

"Yes, I do now. I was helping him get evidence on what Thaddeus has been doing." I tilted my head to the side. "How do you know I was there?" I asked, placing my hand back on my hips. "I thought you weren't allowed to come down to Earth."

She dropped her chin again, lowering her gaze to the weapon in her hand, twisting the staff as if searching for an explanation.

"What happened to all that *risk* you mentioned about your venturing to Earth, against authority?" I pursued further.

Glancing to me, she said, "I'm the last of us on the 7th star... it gets lonely on Celaeno... and well... I get bored, so I go down—every so often to check... to see what he's up to."

"And?"

She shot a glance over her shoulder, then turned back and leaned down to me. "I overheard him talking to Lyndon," she said, as though whispering yet still using a normal range of voice.

"How?" I shook my head and shrugged.

She tightened her lips like a schoolgirl holding back a secret. "I was in his condo—in Ottawa—veiled. He can't sense me." She shook her head in tiny back-and-forth movements.

"Right." I nodded, dropping my hands again.

"I know you went to see Taylor, too." She pursed her lips again.

"How do you know that? Were you there watching?" My eyebrows pinched, but I already knew the answer. The sensation had not been her signature one, it had been someone else.

She did a side-to-side with her eyes, then said, "Lyndon keeps an eye on things there—he saw you, well, the three of you. He doesn't know who you are. But...."

"But what?"

"Lyndon saw the footage from the day you were at the Celaeno building. He told Thaddeus that one of the women who had visited the group home and the female city worker in the video... that they could be sisters."

"And obviously, that got Thaddeus's attention," I said, finishing the narrative for her. "Again, he still doesn't know it's me—just some woman, possibly two women, who look alike. No foul play here. And we did nothing other than visit with Taylor and do our *jobs* as water and sewer workers." I did air quotes for the word job. "We didn't take anything from the lab—and we didn't disturb anything. Same with at the group home. We just talked to Taylor's aid and watched him draw. Nothing else—except, we took photos—but that's it," I explained. "Oh—and I think we found the writings you mentioned—in the lab. I got video of them." Her immense body swayed at the mention of the writings, though she said nothing in response to what I'd just explained to her.

Suddenly there was a crackling and spray of fireworks overhead, pulling my attention back and over to the opening in the trees. When I turned back... Purah was gone.

I hurried then back over to where Redmond was standing with the girls and the rest of the crew. At my approach, he extended an arm, wrapping it around my shoulders. We all stood staring up at the sky as a heartsome roar of triumph sounded from the spectators as the main fireworks went off in witnessed of the year 2021 leaving and the new year 2022 entering.

Chapter 30

Despite the unforeseen and unwelcome excitement from Purah's appearance during the New Year's Eve festivities, both the girls had needed to be carried to the car and were fast asleep before we had even buckled them in. And they hadn't been the only ones who were tired.

Once we were home and we'd tucked the girls in bed, I'd done a quick recap for Redmond on my conversation with the Steward. Purah's visit and chat had seriously topped off this week's bizarre escapades, and it had ruthlessly stolen whatever energy I'd had left in my reserves. I managed to brush my teeth and wash my face, but when my head hit the cool pillow, I was out like a light.

I glance to the window to see that the moon is shining through the drawn blinds into the bedroom. It's more than moonlight, I realize as it pulls me from the bed. Out in the living room, through the wall of windows, I see a moonbow spreading across the sky, its rainbow glow deflecting in the water droplets of a soft rain coming down near the far side of the beach. I step closer to the windows, witnessing as the night's sky shimmering in an auroral blanket of deep empyreal blue.

Passing through the open sliding door, I venture out onto the back deck. Lightening flickers in the distance, illuminating the lofty night sky. At the deck's edge, I lean over the railing and peer down at the back lawn. On the ground, a wide scattering of feathers, white, black, and varying shades of grey, blow in spirals across the grass.

In the middle of the yard, lit by the moonlight, is a large gathering of light coloured sticks and various foliage, the center lined with grass, feathers, and other soft material like the nest of an eagle. Curled up within it is the tiny body of a young child resting on their side.

The child's back is to me, but even at this height I can see dark marks mottling the upper portion near the shoulder blades. From under the child emerges a slow creeping stain of something dark, spreading around the pale nesting material. A rotten-egg odor of sulfur intermingled with the rusted iron scent of blood wafts up to me on a gust of wind. Bile rises in my throat and my stomach rolls just as lightening crashes overhead. In its radiance, Purah is revealed.

She is kneeling on the ground next to the nest, leaning over the child. She is without her customary armor and instead she is clothed in a long primitive old-fashioned nightdress fashioned of lightweight cloth like raw muslin. Lightening cracks again, revealing that she is crying. For an instant her tears reflect off her beautiful ebony skin in the now swiftly obscuring moonlight.

A spindrift from the ocean explodes, its violent wind closing the distance to blow Purah's hair loose from its braid, twisting it viciously around her face. The strength of the wind's gale billows her nightgown out from her form and feathers whirl like cyclones in a rage all around her. An electric thunderstorm of lightning splinters the sky, emptying a cloudburst torrent of rain.

I wipe the dampness from my face, pushing back my hair. Lightening shatters through the sky again. In its flash of light, Purah lifts her head up to look at me. Another crash of lightening hits and my eyes widen to see a massive spread of wings burst free from the back of Purah's nightgown. Snow white like her hair, the feathers shine bright, though the ends of them are tipped in an inky black. In safe haven, using the span of her wings, Purah covers the child, protecting them from the onslaught of the storm. Lightening lights up the sky and a roar of thunder booms... and my eyes burst open.

The heartbeat of pumping blood filling my ear canal blocked out any other sounds. I turned my head swiftly to the side against the softness of my pillow to see the clock on my bedside table. It showed it was just past 3 o'clock in the morning. I turned fully on my side to look out the bedroom window. The bedroom window blinds were up, not drawn as they had been in the dream. There were no other sounds, the night was quiet. No storm thundering or brewing off in the distance.

As my pulse began to slow, the soft sleepy breaths of Redmond slumbering next to me replaced the deafness of the pumping pulse in my ears. *"It was just another dream,"* I whispered.

I'd read somewhere, once-upon-a-time-ago, that dreaming of angels with wings meant protection, love, and courage, symbolizing that a greater force was watching over you, directing you, sheltering you, or trying to show you something significant which is hidden. Dreaming of angels is supposed to be a good thing and the most powerful sign that good luck will follow your life.

Luc had mentioned that Seraphim were said to have twelve wings and were known as the *flying elements of the sun*. His email had mentioned sulfur as well, and how it was also known as brimstone, that the term *Fire and brimstone* referred to *divine punishment and purification* and related to something about *the fate of the unfaithful*, whatever that means.

The bed shifted when Redmond turned on his side, his heavy arm coming around my middle to pull me close. I let out a soft sigh, feeling safer in his embrace. Working to steady my breathing even more, I drew in a long, calm breath. I repeated it several more times, but my heart continued to pound in my chest. Was it fear I was feeling? You're tougher than some cryptic dream, I told myself. But what if... what if Thaddeus finds me, what if they figure out where I live, where my family lives? Maybe Leo was right, maybe we did need protection, or at a minimum, we needed to learn how to protect ourselves. A shiver ran the length of my spine then, despite the warmth of Redmond's body against me. Fixing my gaze upon the soft streams of moonlight spilling in through the window, I watched as a large white butterfly landed on the sill.

Like the lifespan of a butterfly, this night too was ephemeral.

"Good night, Mom," I whispered, lowering my eyelids.

* * *

The music medley alarm on Redmond's phone startled me out of a remarkably deep sleep and my head shot up off the pillow. "Noooo," I whined, letting my head fall back onto the soft pillow. I flipped the covers over my head.

"Sorry, Babe. It's morning—need to get ready to take my parents to the airport." He shifted off the bed, and then I could hear his footfalls as he strolled away in the direction of our bathroom.

Letting out a defiant grunt, I flipped the covers back away from my face. Turning my head to look out the window, a rush of nightmarish memories flooded my brain from last night's dream. I closed my eyes, but the images from the nightmare played like a black and white movie on the inside of my lids. "*It was just a dream,*" I said under my breath, sitting up and dangling my legs over the edge of the bed as I continued to stare out the window.

"What do you want for breakfast," Redmond called from behind me.

I turned to see him exit the bedroom, and I let out an exasperated sigh.

Dressed and somewhat calmer, I met Redmond in the kitchen as the girls filtered in from their bedrooms. I took a quick peek through the glass patio doors and spotted Enzo and Nainseadh sitting out on the deck, enjoying the morning sun, and sipping their coffees. As I turned back, Redmond handed me a fresh cup of coffee in a mug that had the word, *eh?* written on the side, the one that Mac had sent me a few years back as part of an *I miss Canada* care-package she'd put together for me.

"Hungry?" he asked, shifting back to the big pan of scrambled eggs he was cooking.

"This is good—perfect," I said, tapping a finger on the coffee cup.

Glancing up at me, his eyebrows furrowed. He knew it wasn't like me to turn down food, but he said nothing in response as if letting it go.

I gave him a tight smile before heading out to the deck to join his parents.

"Good morning," Nainseadh said, as I slid the patio door closed behind me. "How did you sleep?"

I blew out a breath. "Okay. You?" I responded, padding my way over to the deck's railing. I glanced over to see the lawn below. Green grass. No feathers.

"Like a log," she said. "The girls really wore me out this week." She laughed.

I turned back, offering her an appreciative smile.

"Wore us both out," Enzo added, slapping his hand on his thigh.

Nainseadh's smile dropped. "Are you okay, dear? You look a little worn yourself."

I forced a weary smile. "I just wish you could stay longer." It wasn't a lie. I loved having them around, and the girls adored their grandparents.

"We would stay longer, but I have commitments with the ladies auxiliary, volunteering at the hospital," she said. "But we'll plan another visit soon—or maybe you can all come up to see us." She sat forward in her seat.

"Need to get back to my weekly card game," Enzo stated, giving his wife a soft elbow jab.

"And out of my hair," she added, elbowing him back and giving me an eye-roll.

"How are you guys going to spend New Year's day?" Enzo asked then, resting his coffee cup on his knee.

I leaned my lower back against the railing. "We normally order takeout—Chinese food typically, because everyone is usually too lazy to cook at this point." I laughed since we hadn't really done much cooking this past week with being away. "Darius and Lily are coming over, I think too."

"That will be nice—that Darius is a good eater," she said, her eyes crinkling with her smile.

I glanced over her head through the wall of glass windows to see Hayle and Ryley sitting at the table, chowing down on their breakfast. "Looks like breakfast is ready," I said, moving from the railing to the patio door.

After getting a good breakfast into everyone, well—everyone except me, it was time for Redmond to take his parents to catch their flight home. There were several rounds of hugs and kisses from each of us before they finally climbed into Redmond's truck to head out.

"Remind me to tell you about the dream I had last night," I said, pushing up on my toes to kiss him through the open truck window.

"Will do," he said with a wink, as the truck pulled away.

"Bye Nanaaaa. Bye Poppyyyy," the girls called, waving as the truck backed out of the drive.

Their grandparents waved back through the open windows. "Love you," I heard Nainseadh say before her passenger side window rolled up.

I crossed my arms over my chest, watching as the truck rolled up our street and then turned left to go onto the main road.

"Mum," Hayley said, getting my attention. "Can we go sit out on the deck?"

"I can't see why not," I said, making my way back with them to the entrance through the carport. "Take Summer and Snow out there with you—they'll enjoy sunning themselves," I added, opening the entrance. The girls took off at a mad dash through the open door and up the stairs.

As I trudged up the stairs, I could hear the dogs scampering across the floor, along with the pitter-patter of smaller feet towards the patio door. When I reached the top of the stairs, there was the swoosh of the sliding glass door opening and then closing shut. I sauntered through the kitchen over to the wall of windows and peered out.

The girls were now cuddled tight together under a blanket in the center of the couch, with Summer and Snow squished in on either side of them. When I slid open the patio door, I caught the sound of their tiny voices speaking just as a fluttering cluster of white butterflies scampered on the air near them on the couch. Ryley extended her hand, pointing and saying something to the butterfly, though I couldn't make out her words. Hayley spoke then, her words a jumble of something I couldn't quite comprehend. "What are you two saying?" I asked.

"Nothing," Hayley said, glancing my way with a sweet grin.

"Ahhh, secret twin language," I said, realizing then and nodding.

Ryley held her arm still as a lone butterfly landed on her outstretched limb. None of them moved, not even the dogs. I watched as they did, mesmerized as the angelic white wings of the butterfly slowly opened and closed as though mimicking breathing.

"*Hi, Gramma,*" Hayley whispered then, leaning in a tiny bit closer to where the butterfly rested on her sister's arm.

A swell of emotion took me over, watching as the two of them gently leaned in whispering to the butterfly.

"I'll be back in a few," I said, turning away to hide my tears, heading back into the house. "*That was the sweetest thing,*" I whispered to myself as I ventured back down to the lower level to tidy up and pack away the temporary bedroom setup. "Normalcy—normalcy," I voiced to the universe, realizing I was an emotional shipwreck, and that the last thing the girls needed was to witness my jumbled emotions.

After stripping the sheets from the portable bed, I rolled it into the storage closet, shut the door, and then turned back to survey the space. Back to normal, I thought, leaning back against the closet door, and letting out an exhausted breath.

A subtle tingling ran the length of my right arm, and then my left. Pushing away from the closet door, I darted over to the door that led out to the carport. Yanking it open, I was met with a gust of ocean air. Stepping out into the coolness of the carport, I shot a glance left and then right. *Nothing*. Leaving the door open, I dashed across to the back yard to see if Purah was once again on the lawn, but my instincts told me it wasn't her as the tingling wasn't the same. At the edge of the lawn under the deck, I found nothing, no one. I turned back and sprinted through the carport towards the driveway. Glancing up the street both ways, I still saw nothing, yet the sensation of exhilarating tingles continued to run up and down my skin. Back through the carport I went into the house. I shut the door and locked it, shooting a nervous glance up the stairs. Then I heard the door at the top of the stairs open.

"Mum," came Hayley's voice.

"Yes," I said, blowing out the breath I'd been holding.

"Can we watch a movie?" She asked.

"Please," Ryley added, obviously standing at the top of the stairs with her sister.

"Sure," I said, attempting to keep my voice calm as I headed back up the stairs. I pulled in a few more cleansing breaths before I reached the top. The sensation was still with me, bristling now along the back of my neck and down my spine.

"Your dad saved *Brave* to the favorites list for you," I reminded them. It was one of their favorite animated movies, and it was one of mine too. "You know how to get it started."

As they and their doggie companions scurried off to the living room to start the movie, I began going from room to room, making sure all the windows were latched. After checking the front door, I went into the master bedroom to double-check that the patio door that led from the bedroom still had the deadbolt turned. Finding it locked, I went back across the room and down the short hall to the en suite bathroom in need of splashing some cold water on my face.

In the bathroom as I rinsed water over my face, an uneasiness swelled in my body. I wobbled as anxiety twisted in my gut. Had one of Thaddeus's people found us, found where we lived, I speculated? Was this what I was feeling, one of them watching us? I leaned my hands against the bathroom counter staring at myself in the mirror as water dripped off my chin. I looked like crap. At the sound of tiny footsteps, I turned to see Hayley and Ryley standing in the bathroom's doorway. "Did you find the movie?" I asked, grabbing up the towel hanging next to the sink to dry my face.

"There's someone flying over the deck," Ryley said, before shooting her sister the side-eye.

"Is it one of those guys flying a paraglider—the ones with the paramotor on his back?" I asked, but I couldn't hear the propeller noise that readily accompanied them.

"No," Ryley said, shaking her head.

Hayley turned her upper body back and forth in a quiet *no*.

I put my hands on my hips. "Or is it one of those kite surfers?" I suggested. We get some pretty blustery winds off the beach at this time of year and the kite surfers loved it. Though the dogs hated them and always bark, but... they weren't barking, I realized. The tingling sensation in my body changed then, shimmying like an electrical current across my back and up the center of my spine. But it wasn't painful, in fact, it was energizing.

"Do you girls feel anything?" I asked, kneeling in front of them, taking each of them by the hand.

Ryley nodded, giving me a tight-lipped smile.

"It's the man," Hayley said. Then the two of them began tugging me using both of their little hands. They pulled me along past the dogs who were lying on the bedroom floor, then through the bedroom door and across the living room to the patios doors, eager to show me the person flying over the deck.

This was a joke, it had to be, and I speculated it could only be one of those recreational kite flyers that often caught the wind and flew past or sometimes even over the seagrape trees on our property. At the open patio door, I stepped out through and on to the deck.

There hovering about 3 feet above the rail of the deck… was the flying man. He was wearing black jeans and a black long-sleeved pullover shirt and black combat boots. When he lowered himself and let his boots touch the deck, I could see he hadn't been using a paramotor or a kite. He, in fact, had… *wings*.

Not some fake contraption strapped to his back like the kite-flyers or paragliders, and there was no parachute, just wings, big-white-full-feathered-spectacular-enormous-grey-tipped wings.

"Leo," I said, more as a question, because the man looked so much like him. So much so, they could have been twins, if it weren't for the fact Leo's hair was a sandy blond and this man had dark chestnut colour hair. And Leo's eyes were light blue, where this man's eyes were so dark, they were almost black. Their features were identical though, right down to the prominent clef in his chin.

"I'm Hayden—but you can call me, *Den*," the winged man said.

I couldn't find my voice, though my mouth gaped open. All I could do was stand there staring at him.

"Our names are alike," Hayley said, catching my attention, still holding my hand as she swung her arm back and forth. Then she dropped my hand and stepped forward. "I'm Hayley."

I grabbed her shoulder and she halted, while Ryley snatched her sister's hand with her free one.

A chime sounded then from my phone in my back pocket. Keeping my eyes on the man—Seraph, Hayden—*Den*, I yanked my phone from my pocket. Taking a quick glance down, I saw the text was from Derek. I looked back up to see the man hadn't moved, although he had rested his hip against the rail sporting a somewhat nonthreatening stance. Glancing down at the text again, I groaned at the message,

> *The writings, I got parts of it wrong. It's not 'swings' and 'boat minions', it's UNKNOWN IF WINGS WILL FUNCTION IF ABOMINATION GROWS TO ADULTHOOD.*

"Ya think?" I breathed out sarcastically, shifting my attention back to our visitor. I gave the winged celestial a cynical grin before drawing in a deep breath through my nose. And then, though I didn't need to, I craned my head back and yelled, "Gabriel—is there something you failed to tell me?"

Chapter 31

Angels, despite their faction, tended to be big and tall, though most did not act in a manner that gave you the impression they were showing off their considerable size or power, like most humans of similar build tended to do. Den obviously knew he was big, though he showed no intention of making us feel small. He'd even brought his wings in, folding them in behind his enormous body, though they still protruded up above his broad shoulders. In Gabriel's case, with being around those in the knowing, he did the same, however he did like you to feel his size as it related to his protection of you. The twins loved how big both he and their dad were, and that Gabriel provided a similar sense of protection to that of their dad. And it was clear the girls felt no danger or intimidation from our newest visitor. Though until I got some answers, I wasn't going to let him get any closer.

I heard Redmond's truck pull into the carport and then the slam of its heavy door shut. "We're out on the deck," I called out to him. Then I directed the girls around behind me, backing them up and in through the open door into the house. "Stay inside," I told the girls, keeping the patio door half open. "Can you come up here—fast," I yelled to Redmond again, stressing the urgency, raising my voice even louder.

"On my way," Redmond called back.

Seconds later, through the partially open patio door, I heard the door to the stairwell to the lower level open, and I shot a panicked expression in Redmond's direction as he came through it. Turning back, I saw that Den still hadn't moved from where he rested against the railing.

Just As Redmond pushed open the patio door further to pass through to where I stood, Gabriel took that exact moment to appear next to Den on the deck. The two nodded at each other as if they were old friends. But considering what they had been keeping from me once again, they probably were.

"What the hell?" Redmond asked, sliding the patio door shut behind him.

"My words exactly," I said, glaring at Gabriel. But before I could say another word, loud beating noises and a sweeping wind filled the air over my head. Tipping my head back, I stared up at the sky.

Then, as Den had done earlier, *Leo* lowered himself to the deck with a swift downstroke of his massive, grey-tipped white wings. He was dressed in similar dark clothing to Den.

"Ooookaaay," I shouted, putting my hands on my hips as Leo moved to stand next to his almost twin. "You guys better tell me everything—and don't leave anything out this time."

"Perhaps you should have someone watch the girls while we talk," Gabriel suggested.

"Probably a good idea," Redmond agreed. "I'll call Darius—his Guardian danger-detector is more than likely screaming off the chart anyway." He pulled his cell phone from the pocket of his jeans.

As Redmond texted Darius, I continued to squint accusingly at the three giants standing in front of us. I shook my head, one hand on my hip, the other now pointing a stern finger at them like I was their parent catching them all up to no good. It was beyond me now to muster any calm words. I returned my hand back to my hip. I was just so furious that it took all I had not to scream at them over, yet another blatant betrayal of crucial facts kept from me.

"He and Lily are on their way over," Redmond said, sliding his phone back in his pocket. "I'll bring the girls down to the carport to wait for them." He kissed my cheek. "Don't start the interrogation without me."

Dropping my hands from my hips, I turned and watched through the window as Redmond gathered the girls to take them downstairs. I couldn't hear what he was saying to them, but the twins seemed excited at the prospect of spending time with Lily and Darius. They waved to me just before heading down the stairs to the lower level. Redmond blew me a kiss and was gone.

"We have a new problem," Leo said then, folding in his wings behind his body as Den had done.

"Don't say a thing—any of you." I blew out a breath and went to sit on the couch. I was beyond exhausted now. "I don't want to have to repeat any of this for Redmond. Got it?"

They all gave silent nods.

Several minutes later, the thunder of Darius' Dodge Charger rumbled faster than usual into the driveway. The squeals of the girls greeting their favorite pixie and giant were swiftly followed by the sound of car doors opening and shutting. Then the car roared out of the drive and away from the house.

A moment later, Redmond reemerged from the house, out onto the deck. "What I miss?" he asked, coming to sit next to me on the couch.

"I'd ask you to sit, but…," I said, eyeing Leo's and Den's folded wings.

"Right," Gabriel said then, raising his hands and doing a spin motion with them, his index fingers twirling in the air.

At that, both Leo and Den turned, allowing the backs of their wings to face us. Then slowly, seamlessly, the enormous, feathered appendages collapsed in on themselves, receding into their shoulder blades. Den reached back over his shoulders, tugging, and bunching his shirt up near his neck. On his back were two grey marks, similar in design to large snowflakes about a palm's width in diameter. Leo did the same with his shirt, displaying liked markings, though the design was unique, like how snowflakes are.

"The wings were *wow*—but that's…," Redmond said, "seriously wow!"

I had to agree. It was spectacular, but I was still pissed at being left out of this flying feathered loop.

Gabriel stepped forward as if to say something, but I held up a hand to halt him. "Leo, you go first," I instructed, glowering at Gabriel. I was fully aware I was dealing with a powerful Archangel and two flying Earthbound Seraphim, but at this stage of the angel game, I needed to be the one commanding and controlling the exchange of information. "You said we have a new problem?" I looked at Leo.

"Yes," Leo replied, pausing as if waiting for me to permit him to go on. When I said nothing further, he continued. "I feel I should explain... more—about... the Seraphim, more precisely where my brothers and I came from." He drew an invisible line back and forth, using his hand to indicate Den and himself. "The seven of us—The Guards," he clarified further.

"By all means—fill us in," I said, making no attempt to hold back my impatience.

Moving away from the railing, Leo came and sat down, taking the patio chair next to where I sat. Leaning forward, he rested his elbows on his thighs, then steepled his fingers together. "I have told you of Thanael and Anael," he began.

"Yes," I confirmed. "The two who remained up North."

He nodded. "Well, they have been paired the longest, and because of it, they were given rings."

"Like being married?" I frowned at the leisurely pace of information being given.

"No. These are rings of creation—used to create living things, new species needed to help balance Earth's ecosystem."

"Okay—that seems logical." I shrugged. But what did I know?

"On the day Thaddeus sent Anael and the others to Earth, she had been using the rings and for whatever reason, she had hidden them in the folds of her clothing—why, she hadn't known at the time, but she was thankful she had." Leo glanced at Den, then back to me. "The remaining Seraphim on the other stars had been horrified that Thaddeus's action had not been dealt with by a higher power, but as you know once the 70 generations were up, he and his followers were cast down by the Stewards."

I gave a slow nod of my head, reaching to the side for Redmond's hand. He'd been silent since the *wows*. He squeezed my hand, though my focus remained on Leo.

Leo's chest rose and dropped with a heavy breath and sigh. "Our brethren and sistren were not built for the challenges presented once they were trapped on Earth. To aid them, Anael and Thanael used the rings. There had never been a need to create ones such as us — like my brothers — warriors, as there has never been a threat of war amongst the Seraphim."

"They created you?" I blurted, sitting up in my seat.

He nodded. "We were originally created to help the rest of the Earthbound survive after being sent down, but in more recent years we've been called upon to watch over Thaddeus, to discover more about his plans, who he is targeting, like these halflings for his testing. When we were called back up North and informed of his current location, all but Kris, relocated to Ottawa. Kris chose to remain in New York City to monitor the facility there, knowing that Thaddeus frequented it often."

"How?" I asked, the one word covering the multitude of questions swirling in my brain.

"How — what?" Leo questioned, leaning back into the chair.

Starting with a simple question, I asked, "How did you get your names?"

Leo smiled, as though grateful for the simple question. "They were given to us by Anael and Thanael. All the original Earthbound — including The Guards, had gone by formal names using *of Haven*, like Leonardo of Haven, until last names became a requirement for us. It was then that we chose our own surnames. My full name is Leonardo Winter."

"Hayden Polar," Den said, snagging our attention. "Please to meet you." He gave us a quick nod and a kind smile.

"Likewise," Redmond said, breaking his silence.

"Tell us about the others, The Guards," I requested, needing to know more about these brothers.

Den came then to stand behind Leo's chair. "Leo — the First Son of Haven," he said, patting Leo's shoulder. "Architect extraordinaire — and then some. He has a photographic memory for anything relating to buildings. He can sense weakness or power in all structures, organic and non."

"Very cool," Redmond said, adding to his previously established appreciation for Leo from our caper in Ottawa.

Leo gave Redmond an appreciative grin.

"Bennet Frost—Ben. Third Son of Haven," Den continued.

"Third?" I questioned, feeling like I'd missed a step.

"Kris is the second, but I'll get to him last," Den shared, letting out a long, drawn out breath. Starting again, he said, "Ben is a Professor of Human Kinetics. His thing is science—more specifically, the study of all living things. He's also the one who trained us to fight. He's a master of movement and martial arts—those that require no strenuous force. Only touch and pressure point combat and reverse weight influence." His hands clenched into fists, then relaxed. "He has expertise in nutrition, athletic enhancement and stamina, along with Thai chi and meditation as well. He can sense strength and weakness in any living thing."

"Those are nice to have," I said, raising my eyebrows.

"Yes—very helpful," Den said, coming around Leo's chair to sit in the one next to him. "Then we have Marquis Malouel—Marq, Forth Son of Haven."

"Interesting name," I commented.

"He's an interesting fellow," Den said, "His last name he borrowed from the Dutch painter Jean Malouel." I knew nothing about famous artists, but I nodded anyway. "Marq is a photographer and gallery owner. He started with art early on, then as the times changed, he moved on to photography and then video—specifically surveillance and security. He still loves art. He has designed all our fake identities over the years, but his specialty is the internet and structure security, including biometrics. He can sense both security and threat to safety, like a vibration that gets stronger as the threat gets closer."

"Two thumbs up for the artist," I said, "I might like him to put in a system here at the house."

"I've been meaning to put in a security system," Redmond said with a grin.

"He would do it in a heartbeat—just ask," Leo said, before tipping his chin to Den to go on.

"Fifth Son of Haven is Zach—Zachery Glacier, our resident firefighter. He's a pyrotechnics and explosives expert. He's a speed reader, has read almost every book written—those worth reading, as he says. He and Kris speak the most languages of the seven of us, comprising the 30 most spoken. He can sense any danger to do with fire, explosives both natural and manmade."

"He is also the second largest of The Guards next to Den," Leo added.

Den gave a tight grin, shifting in his seat. "Nicolas North is next. Nic is the Sixth Son of Haven, and he is an Oncology Nurse at the Queensway Carleton Hospital."

"Really? Wait until Olivia hears about that," I said, smacking my hand on the couch cushion.

"She's going to freak out," Redmond stated, chuckling.

"Why is that?" Leo asked. "Besides the obvious wing thing?"

"She runs the Childbirth Program there—and Mac works with her on the program." I "*pffft*" out a gust of air, holding in a laugh. I couldn't help it, with imagining their faces when I got to tell them about the Angel Nurse named Nic.

"How serendipitous," Den said. "I'm sure they will appreciate this even more. Like Ben, Nic loves science, his specialty being genetics and diseases for all things living, especially humans, his current focus being on *children*." Den smiled, glancing down as if recalling a memory. Looking up at us again, he said, "He has a way with animals and children. He's like the whisperer of the innocent and pure. He has the ability to sense clean health along with illness or distress." His gaze dropped again as he paused. "Then there is me," he said, lifting his chin high. "Seventh Son of Haven." He gave a tiny bow while still seated. "Bodyguard for visiting diplomats—Artist on the side. I have some of my work at Marq's gallery."

"He's an expert in hand to hand and he has taught all The Guards this specialty," Leo said, continuing for him. "But he remains the most proficient, he's the strongest and biggest of us all."

"And I have a degree in criminology, and I speak French," Den added, as though completing the details of a dating profile.

"Bravo," Redmond said, clapping his hands as if witnessing a grand performance. Though I could tell he was very impressed with the descriptions of all The Guards.

"And Kris?" I prompted, smiling at Den approvingly.

He nodded, his lips tightening into a thin line.

"Kris," Leo said, taking over. "Kristopher Snow, Second Son of Haven. Well, he's a chef and owner of a very popular restaurant called SNOW. He is an expert in all things regarding weaponry, especially knives of all kinds, being he has witnessed the evolution of several skillfully crafted. He can identify any weapon in sight or on a person or in the vicinity. Like if someone is carrying or if there are weapons in vehicles—don't ask me how—he just does. He is also an expert in all things food and drink. And...."

"He's an arrogant son of a bitch," Den cut in.

"Yes, he can be a bit self-centered. Has to have the very best in his restaurant, so he travels the world for such things. He's given Julian and Max some amazing recipes. And he's always good to their daughter," Leo added.

"Ya, but he has no interest in chasing down the traitorous Earthbound," Den interjected again.

"Do all Seraphim have wings?" I asked, sensing some tension building, offering them another straightforward question to answer.

"They—we do, yes," Leo said, shooting Den a disheartened look. "And though they are composed of all white, the tip colour of the primary feathers varies. Those from Pleiades are blacked tipped to match the markings on their backs. Ours are in shades of grey, as are our markings," Leo explained, continuing to provide more specifics about their wings. "Each of us has snowflake shaped marks on each shoulder blade representing the spots where our wings emerge. Although the marks are not identical, no two pairs are alike. They measure about 5 inches in diameter depending on the size of the shoulder blades, considering females have smaller builds—but not always, as you have seen with the Steward, Purah. Our wings are connected to our cardiac and respiratory systems. Severing them can kill us as it cuts off our heart and lung function. Our wings allow us to adapt to any atmosphere as well." He paused. "Remember how I told you that the Seraphim couldn't travel like other angels?"

"I remember," I said, blinking, barely digesting the whole wings thing.

"Once a Steward sends a Seraph down to Earth—to the location they request, their wings are used to get them from place to place if needed."

"I see how that could work," Redmond said. "But what if someone sees you?"

"It's only the Earthbound Seraphim who can't veil themselves," Leo clarified. "Hence the disguises."

I nodded, transfixed as he went on.

"Hayden and I flew here within the cover of night, but he was too eager to wait, and he had to come see you." Leo looked back at Den. I glanced over at him and caught him smiling and shrugging. "All Seraphim have wings, it's a fact, but they don't hang off our bodies," Leo went on, opening his hands palms up as if illustrating the obvious. "They lay dormant in the shoulder blades and come out when needed."

"What about Halflings?" I asked.

"Similar to us, they have pale, almost white markings on each shoulder blade. Halflings are weaker than full Seraphim, but they can be stronger than humans."

"And do they have wings?" I brought my hand up to touch the back of my shoulder.

"They do, in fact. Apparently sometime around the equivalent of 20 human years they are given use of those wings. The only major problem being that the halflings more than likely don't know they have wings... until they come out. And there has only been a handful of halflings that even survive to their 20th birthday, that we know of." He paused, shifting in his seat. "No one knows why the 20th year is so important, only that these halflings have the equivalent age in appearance to a human 20-year-old. If they live that long, they are healthier, usually well-built, and often considered exceptionally appealing in appearance. Pre-wings they are strong but come into full strength after the full development of their wings, if they survive."

"Survive?" Redmond questioned, shooting probing glances at each of the Angels.

"Those who survive proper development of their wings will have the full capacity of them, but they lack the instinct of their use. It must be taught. They also do not have the natural ability to fly, so that too must be taught. The biggest challenge is helping them to accept what they are. And getting to those who were not raised with a Seraph parent, the presentation of wings and the pain that accompanies the first release, can be devastating to the body and mind."

"This is the reason you told us about Anael's daughter—the halfling that you're looking for." I stated, grasping the urgency now.

"Well—not fully," Leo said. "Finding Anael's daughter before she reaches her 20th birthday, is something we need to do—yes, but at the time I told you of her, I had yet to explain the full issue, because the concern involved you knowing about our wings. But that is not why we are here now."

"It's about Kris," Den said, blowing out an anxious breath. "We were all summoned yesterday to the North, for Anael to provide us with more details on her daughter." Den glanced at Leo before going on. "All of us arrived, except Kris. We can't locate him, and no one has heard from him." Den ran a hand over the back of his neck.

"Our fear is that Thaddeus has him," Leo stated, sitting forward in his chair again.

Den's chair creaked under his weight. "It's one of ours that's missing—so we understand if helping us is too much to ask," he said.

"It's not too much to ask—of course we'll help," I said, sitting forward on the couch.

"We'll all help where we can," Redmond confirmed.

"There is still the issue of your safety," Gabriel said, his worry directed at me. He'd kept his comments to himself until now. He glanced back and forth between Leo and Den.

"We've decided that it's best that we set up a South Haven—here, in this area, to alternate monitoring you and your family, while remaining watchful over Thaddeus," Leo directed at me. "We've identified a property—secured it this morning. Now we need to make some provisions for setting up shop." He turned his attention to Redmond. "Do you think you could help us coordinate things at this end with us, Redmond? You are more familiar with the area and the services."

"Absolutely," Redmond said. "Darius and I can go check out the place today if you want—get things rolling." He stood as if he was ready to go.

"I'll need more information to pass on to my friends, in order to help locate Kris," I said, standing then to get a move on things.

"There is something else," Gabriel said, stifling our go-get-em momentum.

"What," I questioned. I half expected that there'd be more, yet I still hoped for *none*.

"When you went to see the halfling at the group home, were you able to sense him?" Gabriel asked, his worried expression showing he already knew the answer.

"No," I said. "I don't think so. I had been more concerned about the fact that I had been sensing another like Leo—an Earthbound, possibly one of Thaddeus's people keeping an eye on visitors. Why?"

"It's the twins." Gabriel's brow furrowed.

"What about them?" I interrogated, the sudden need for them to come home overwhelming me.

Leo stood and put a hand on my shoulder. "You were able to sense us. And the twins were able to sense us too." He glanced over at Den and then Gabriel.

"And they can sense Thaddeus and his followers too. But you'll be here to protect us—taking turns, right?" My gut churned with uneasiness.

"Yes, but there's a greater threat, greater danger—the true danger is that...," Gabriel sputtered, "... the twins can sense halflings—they sensed that little boy at their school."

"How is that a greater danger?" I scrutinized, shaking my head.

Gabriel drew in a breath. "If Thaddeus finds out... what they can do... he won't need you."

Thaddeus shut off his video game, hearing only the hum of his TV as he perused the numerous biographies on his bookshelf. He'd had enough distraction from his game and was now in need of inspiration. "*Life*, by Keith Richards," he said aloud, reading the spines of the books. *"Dreams from My Father*—Barack Obama," he continued down the line of books. *"On the Road*—Jack Kerouac, *A Moveable Feast*—Hemingway, *The Andy Warhol Diaries, The Autobiography of Malcolm X,* and *De Profundis and Other Prison Writings,* by Oscar Wilde."

There were no women writers on his shelf. He didn't care for reading about the lives of females.

But his favorite biographies were the ones written by or about the wickedest men in history. "Pol Pot—*Anatomy of a Nightmare*—one of my favorites," he said, caressing the spine of the hardcover book. He'd always hoped for a biography on John Charles Cutler, the senior surgeon and acting chief of the venereal disease program in the U.S. Public Health Service, who was found later after his death to have been involved in some extremely controversial and unethical medical experiments regarding syphilis. Thaddeus had only read articles on the man—but had found him fascinating all the same.

"Ah here—this one," he said, sliding a well-worn hardcover book from between two others on the shelf. "Albert Fish *In His Own Words*—*The Shocking Confessions of the Child Killing Cannibal.* Just what I need to aid in my relaxation."

Thaddeus rested back on his bed, fluffing two of the pillows behind his head. Opening the book and cracking the spine, he let out a contented sigh.

"Call from Marcus," the soft-spoken voice of the attendant announced, followed by chiming indicating a call coming in.

Thaddeus slammed the book shut. *"Attendant,* answer call," he barked out. "Marcus—what?"

"You asked me to look at that video footage of the city workers—the ones who fixed the gas leak," he said.

"Yes—and?" Thaddeus said, beyond irritated.

"Well, I enlarged the images." Marcus made a sound as though he were clearing his throat.

"Spit it out, Marcus—what did you find?"

"The woman—I'm pretty sure she's the one I saw in New York City—speaking to the Watcher, though she had long dark blonde hair then."

Thaddeus sat up in bed. "I'll call you back," he said. "*Attendant, end call.*" Without bothering to dress, Thaddeus grabbed the sheet of paper off the counter, the one Lyndon had provided him, then he rode his personal elevator down to the lower level private lab.

In the lab, he did a thorough pass and examination covering every area in the lab like he had done when he'd first returned from New York, checking that nothing had been disturbed. After finding everything in its place, he went to the exit door. Before shutting off the lights, he turned back to look at his desk. It was then he noticed that the last page of his journal had been flipped. He always, always, left it open to the last page.

"What was the name again?" Thaddeus said out loud. "Mizz...?" He held up the photocopy of the sign-in sheet for the group home. "... *Westlake.*"

The Guard Trilogy Extended Series

Book 4 - The Haven
More to come…

Learn more about author N. L. Westaway at
www.NLWestaway.com.

Milton Keynes UK
Ingram Content Group UK Ltd.
UKHW040626041223
433598UK00026B/153/J